The Quick
And
The Dead

A Novel of "The 'Nam"
by Robert Vaughan

A DELL/JAMES A. BRYANS BOOK

This book is dedicated to my sons, Joe and Tom, who are, at this writing, schoolboy athletes. Once, while I was in the 'Nam, I saw a young man with a battlefield wound, who, but a few short months before, had heard the cheers of a hometown football crowd. I cried that such young men should be subjected to the failures of old men's policies, and I pray that my children, and other fathers' children, will one day be spared the folly of war.

Published by
Dell Publishing Co., Inc.
1 Dag Hammarskjold Plaza
New York, New York 10017

Dell TM 681510, Dell Publishing Co., Inc.

ISBN: 0-440-07203-4

Printed in the United States of America
First printing—October 1984

FIRST BODY COUNT

Andy Culpepper got up and worked out the kinks. It was his first patrol and he'd been lying behind a mound of vegetation called a berm all night. The fire-fight itself had been over almost as soon as it began and the surviving Viet Cong had fled through the jungle.

"Peterson, Culpepper, count the dinks. We need a body count," called out Scottie, the corporal in charge of the patrol.

Andy went with Peterson, and they counted the bodies. There were fourteen of them. After the count, they started through them, stripping them of weapons, papers, money and watches.

"Look 'em over real close before you touch 'em. Sometimes they're booby-trapped," said Peterson, "But I don't think they had a chance to get to these guys."

Andy saved the one he knew he'd killed for last. He rolled him over and looked at him. He didn't look any older than Andy, though it was hard to tell, for his face was ashen-gray. There was no light in his eyes at all.

He was wearing a T-shirt, and, smiling up from the front of the T-shirt was the face of Mickey Mouse. That bothered Andy Culpepper a great deal. He had thought he was shooting at a nameless, faceless, God-less Communist. Instead, he'd killed someone his own age who was wearing a Mickey Mouse shirt . . .

CHAPTER ONE

NOVEMBER 22, 1963

Jacob Steele Culpepper stood at the front window of the little airport terminal at Manhattan, Kansas, and watched as a young girl, about eighteen he would guess, arrived at the passenger unloading zone. She had been brought by three boys. They all got out of the old car with a boisterous slamming of doors and horseplay, and the boys vied for the honor of carrying her baggage. The girl stood by, aloof to their shenanigans, accepting their homage as if it were her due. She was a slender blonde who was very pretty and sure of herself. She flirted outrageously with the boys who had accompanied her, and she found ways to move her body to accent her sexuality.

The man who had been watching the girl stood just over six feet tall. He had a strong chin, salt and pepper hair and gray eyes. He was wearing the uniform of a United States Army Major, but even had he not been in uniform one might have guessed he was a soldier. Perhaps it was the erect way he stood at the window, as if on parade. Or perhaps it was an attitude, sensed more than seen, that here was a man who was accustomed to giving orders, and having those orders followed.

Whatever quality made Jacob Steele Culpepper look like

a soldier came to him honestly. He was a graduate of the United States Military Academy at West Point, and he was the son, grandson, and great-grandson of Academy graduates.

The only deviation from an otherwise impeccable record of Culpepper service to the United States Army had been by Jacob's great-grandfather, General Ambrose Culpepper. General Ambrose Culpepper resigned his commission to join the Confederacy. He was a hero at the battle of Shiloh, and today his statue stands among the many others which mount silent and eternal vigil over the battlefield where armies fought and died so many years ago. Jacob's grandfather, Creighton Culpepper, fought as a Second Lieutenant against Geronimo, and rose to command a Division during the First World War.

A more recent hero among the Culpepper line was Jake's own father. Lieutenant General Ian Perry Culpepper, called "Iron Pants" by everyone, fought well in World War II, but it was in Korea that he made a name for himself. Iron Pants Culpepper held the line during those bleak, early days of the Chinese incursion into the Korean War. For two weeks, General Culpepper's Corps stood off assault after assault by forces which vastly outnumbered them. His heroic stand allowed the entire American army to readjust its lines in time to keep from being kicked into the sea. For that, Iron Pants Culpepper received the Medal of Honor.

"General Culpepper was an inspiration to his men," General MacArthur wrote in his citation. *"He moved from one end of his line to the other, adjusting his defenses to gain the maximum effective use of his firepower. He was often exposed to enemy fire, and on one occasion his jeep was caught behind enemy lines, making it necessary for General Culpepper, his aide, and his driver to engage in hand-to-hand combat in order to make good their escape."*

Major Culpepper didn't have a flashy name like "Iron Pants." His friends simply called him Jake. When Iron

Pants was making a name for himself as a Corps Commander, Jake was still in West Point. Jake did manage to get to Korea before the war ended, but he never had the opportunity to do anything heroic. He served as a Second Lieutenant in the line and was no different from the thousands of other soldiers who served honorably, if not heroically, in that war.

Iron Pants was retired now and living in Hampton, Virginia, close enough to Fort Monroe to still exercise some influence on the Army. It was Iron Pants who, in what he considered to be a good career move for his son, got Jake his orders for Vietnam.

"Boy, you need to get a Vietnam tour on your form 66," Iron Pants had told Jake. "I realize it isn't much of a war, but right now it's the only war we've got. Anyway, with you and Virgie bustin' up, you got nothing to stay in the States for, do you?"

"No," Jake said, thinking of his ex-wife. "I guess not."

"Then listen to me," Iron Pants said. "I've never steered you wrong yet."

Jake's mother had died when Jake was twelve, and he had been raised by his father, a stern disciplinarian who had always treated Jake more like a soldier than a son. One might say that Jake had been on active duty from the age of twelve. That fact, and the love/hate relationship he had with his father, had done much to shape Jake's personality.

"Passengers for Frontier Airlines flight to Kansas City should board the plane now," came a voice over a loudspeaker.

Jake crossed the macadam parking area, climbed the portable stairs, then showed his boarding pass to the stewardess at the door. She looked at him with a smile which let him know she had noticed that he was a good-looking man, but when she saw that he wasn't receptive to her flirtatious signal, she moved aside to let him pass through.

The airplane was a DC-3. This particular craft was a vintage model built in 1935, when Jake was only seven years old, but the thought of flying in such an old aircraft didn't particularly bother Jake. The DC-3 had long since proven its dependability, and the flight to Kansas City, even in this plane, would take no more than an hour. At Kansas City, Jake would change to a jet for the longer flight to San Francisco.

Jake found an empty seat and took off his jacket. He folded it neatly and put it on the overhead rack, then started to sit down, but a young woman moved quickly to slip into it before he could. It was the girl he'd been watching at the terminal.

"I beg your pardon, Miss, but I . . ."

The girl looked up at him and smiled sweetly. "I do hope you don't mind," she said. "I absolutely have to ride over the wing or I get deathly airsick."

Jake looked toward the rear of the plane and saw another empty seat. He sighed and reached for his jacket.

"No problem," he said. "Enjoy your flight."

"Thank you," the young girl said. "You don't know how much I appreciate this."

Jake moved to the rear of the plane, then sat in his new seat and stared through the window at the starboard engine. It coughed, sputtered, and belched clouds of smoke before the propeller became a spinning blur. The plane taxied slowly out to the end of the runway, turned into the wind, then started on its take-off run. A few moments later they lifted into the air, and Jake looked down on the stream of cars as they passed over the highway which ran by the airport. Not until that very moment did he feel that his tour at Fort Riley was officially over.

"Jake, you can't be serious," Virgie had said when they arrived on the post two years earlier. "You don't really mean to say we have to stay in this . . . this, God-forsaken place, do you?''

"Maybe the post is a little isolated," Jake agreed. "But it is a good career assignment."

"A little isolated? We'd have to go to the North Pole to be more isolated!''

Jake was a newly promoted Major on his first field-grade officer assignment, and he was very much looking forward to it. He and his family had just returned from a tour of duty in Germany. Jake had driven Virgie and the two boys, then thirteen and eleven, to Ft. Riley from Columbus, Georgia. Virgie's parents lived in Columbus, and Jake had taken his leave there while they waited for the car to arrive from Germany.

The car was a brand-new Mercedes Jake had bought just before they left Germany. He was very proud of that car. He would never have been able to buy one like it in the States because it was too expensive. By buying it in Germany, however, he had saved nearly forty percent on its purchase price. Virgie complained about the car, saying it was far too ostentatious for her tastes. Despite Virgie's complaints, she had no reservations against taking the car as part of the divorce settlement. She gained custody of the kids, too, and took possession of all the furniture, china, crystal and silver. She also got the passbook savings account, the savings bonds, and one hundred and twenty dollars-a-month for child support.

"Major, you may as well face it," Jake's lawyer told him. "The only thing you are going to get out of this marriage is you."

". . . .*extreme mental and physical cruelty,*" the divorce decree read, "*to the point of danger to life and limb of the complainant.*"

That charge hurt Jake. He had never hit Virgie, nor had he ever threatened to do so. The thought of violence against a woman was totally foreign to his personality. Virgie knew this, and she admitted that she knew it, but, other than adultery, this was the only available grounds for divorce.

"If you want to confess to adultery, I'll change the grounds," she said.

"No, I won't confess to adultery. I've not committed adultery."

"Oh come now, Jake. Do you expect me to believe that you were totally faithful to me while you were in Korea?"

"Yes."

"I don't believe that."

"I'm sorry. It's true."

"How do you know I was faithful to you?"

"Were you?"

"Do you really want to know?" Virgie asked.

"No, I suppose not."

"It doesn't make any difference now, anyway, does it? We're getting a divorce."

"I don't want a divorce."

"Jake, we've been through all this," Virgie said. "I don't care whether you want a divorce or not. I want it, and I am my own person. Don't you understand? I feel stifled by you. I have to live my own life, I have to do my own thing."

"What about doing a wife and mother thing? You are a mother, you know. No divorce paper is going to change that."

"That's my problem, it isn't yours."

"It might be a problem for the boys."

"I'll deal with it, somehow."

"Maybe the boys could live with me."

"Oh, that's a good idea," Virgie said sarcastically. "You're going to Vietnam. What will you do with them?"

"When my mother died, I lived with my father in the Philippines. I can work out something."

"Yes, and raise two more Prussian militarists, just like you?"

"Whatever I do with them, I would do it because I wanted them around me. To you they are a burden."

"Listen, don't worry about Mike and Andy, okay? You'll see them often enough to be super-dad. Then you can go back and play army, and jump through your apex when your Commanding Officer calls." Virgie brushed back her red hair angrily, ground out her cigarette, then lit another one almost immediately.

"Virgie, would there be any chance for us if I resigned my commission?"

"You could never do that. You love the army too much."

"Yes, I do love the army," Jake admitted. "Do you hate it that much?"

"I loathe and despise the army. Therefore, I cannot help but loathe and despise you." Virgie brushed her hair back again, and it glistened in the light of the table lamp. Jake felt a pain in his heart. Ironically, she had never looked more beautiful to him than she did at this very moment. He had never wanted her more than he wanted her right now.

"This isn't fair, Virgie. You knew I was a career officer when you married me. I'm a fourth-generation Academy graduate."

"Oh, how could I forget the generals Culpepper, or dear old West Point? Hold out your hand and I'll kiss your Academy ring. In the meantime, you and the army can kiss my ass. I've had it with the Officers' Wives' clubs, I've had it with the Colonel's receptions, and I've had it with the I.G. inspections. You may be the fourth-generation Culpepper to graduate from the academy, but I promise you, there will be no fifth-generation graduates in the Culpepper family. I want out, and I'm taking Mike and Andy with me."

"Sir?"

The stewardess touched Jake lightly on the shoulder, bringing him back to the present. He looked around at her.

"Yes?"

"Sir, we'll be landing in Kansas City in just a few moments. "Would you please fasten your seat belt?"

"Will they serve lunch on the plane?" Jake asked the clerk at the TWA ticket desk.

"No, I'm sorry. Your flight doesn't leave here until one-thirty."

"All right, thank you," Jake said. He slipped the ticket folder into his inside jacket pocket, then walked across the lobby to the cafeteria. He got a hamburger, fries, and a carton of milk, but when he looked around for a table, there wasn't one available.

"Fine," he mumbled, disgustedly. "That's just fine."

"Yoohoo! Over here! Come and sit with me."

Jake looked toward the voice and saw a young woman waving him over. She was sitting alone at a table for two. At first he was confused as to why she would call him over, then he recognized her as the same young woman he had watched arrive with her entourage—the one who had taken his seat on the plane. He smiled at her, and started toward her.

"Since you were gracious enough to let me sit over the wing, the least I can do is share my table with you," the girl said. Jake found himself looking into the biggest brown eyes he had ever seen. Her hair was blonde, though it was so bright a blonde that he was sure it wasn't her natural color. It was teased and swept up in a style made popular by Jackie Kennedy.

"I didn't exactly let you have the seat," Jake said as he sat down. "You took it."

The girl laughed. "Perhaps I did at that. My name is Kristin O'Neil," she said, sticking out her hand. "Do you have a name other than Culpepper?" she asked, reading his name tag. "Or are you going to be dreary and tell me it's Sergeant, or Captain, or General or something like that?"

"My friends call me Jake. And since you are sharing a table with me, I would say you qualify as a friend."

"Where are you going, Jake? To some far-off romantic place?"

"I don't know how romantic it is," Jake replied. "It is far off. I'm going to Vietnam by way of the University of California, at Dunlap."

"I know—you're taking a Vietnamese language course there," Kristin said.

"Yes," Jake replied. "As a matter of fact I am. How did you know?"

"I'm a student there," Kristin said. "In fact, I was one of the more vocal students in trying to prevent the course from being taught."

"You didn't want your school to teach Vietnamese? Why? What have you got against the language?"

"I have nothing against the language," Kristin said. "I just didn't want the Department of Defense on our campus, that's all. I don't think the military and the civil school systems should mix."

"But they are already mixed. The ROTC provides the military with a significant number of officers."

"Did you come from the ROTC?"

"No, I came from the Military Academy at West Point."

"Oh, that's quite an honor, isn't it?"

"I guess it depends on your perspective. My wife, that is my ex-wife, thought West Point was a millstone around my neck. I think she considered it and the military the other woman in my life."

"Are you terribly—what is the term the ROTC guys use—gung-ho?"

"I try not to be overbearing about it," Jake said.

"So, after your course at Cal Dunlap, it's off to Vietnam?"

"Yes."

"Didn't they just murder their President there a couple of weeks ago? I wouldn't be in such a hurry to get there if

I were you. I wouldn't want to be in a country where the people shoot Presidents for sport."

"Hardly a sport," Jake said. "There was a popular uprising of the people. Perhaps it is difficult for Americans to understand a coup, but sometimes a coup is absolutely the only way to get rid of a repressive government."

"Are you saying Diem led a repressive government?"

"I think the facts bear that out."

"Then why have we been supporting him?"

"What?"

"We have been supporting Diem for some time, haven't we?"

"Yes, against the Communists."

"I see. Repression is all right as long as it is not communist repression. Is that it?"

Jake smiled. "Miss O'Neil, are you taking a great delight in baiting me?"

"Not particularly," Kristin said, laughing. "It's just that you happen to be sitting at my table, and you also happen to represent the military-industrial complex. It seems a shame to pass up an opportunity to interrogate you."

"Is this an interrogation, or an inquisition?" Jake asked.

"A few simple inquiries from a citizen who is concerned over the direction our government is taking in Vietnam."

"We are taking the only position we can take. We are defending democracy."

"As in Diem's brand of democracy?" Kristin challenged.

Jake sighed in defeat. "It's obvious we aren't ever going to agree on this. The truth is, I'm a military man and I just go where they send me."

"I've just completed a course in twentieth century history, and I believe that was the defense used by the Nazi war criminals in Nuremburg, wasn't it?"

"My God, you're being a little tough on me, aren't you?"

"I'm afraid we are going to wind up fighting a very

dirty little war over there," Kristin said. "I don't think the average American has any idea what we are letting ourselves in for."

"That's a little heavy for your type, isn't it?"

"My type? What do you mean?"

"I saw you when you arrived at the airport in Manhattan," Jake said. "You were surrounded by beaus, and . . ."

Kristin laughed richly. "Surrounded by beaus? My God, Jake, no one talks like that!"

Jake blushed a little. "Well, you get my meaning, don't you? You are a young college girl, a very pretty college girl, and you shouldn't be worrying about such things as foreign policy and military tactics."

"I see. I should just worry about proms and dates and that sort of thing, is that it?"

"Sort of."

"Tell me, Jake, when you were in West Point, did you worry about proms and dates and so forth?"

"No, of course not. But it was different with me."

"Because you are a man?"

Jake smiled. "I guess that does sound a little prejudiced, doesn't it? I'm sorry."

"That's all right," Kristin said. "Even Dr. Mainwaring says I come on too strong some times."

"Dr. Mainwaring?"

"He's a professor at school, and he's a brilliant man. He is also a pacifist, who believes that we are gradually getting in deeper and deeper in Vietnam."

"Well, I don't want you and Dr. Mainwaring to worry about it. The American involvement goes only as far as being advisors. Believe me, it will never go beyond that. We aren't going to let this thing turn into a war."

"I wish I could believe that," Kristin said.

"Jake!" a man's voice called, and Jake looked up to see an officer he knew from Fort Riley, coming across the cafeteria toward him. Jake smiled.

"Now here's a guy you ought to talk to. He can give

you an argument. He's so far to the right he thinks the John Birch Society is a leftist organization. Carl, how's it going? What are you doing here? I thought you were on leave.''

"I'm coming back early to save a few days," Carl said. "I'm catching the two o'clock flight back to Manhattan. Listen, have you heard the news?''

"What news?''

"About Kennedy.''

"No," Jake said. He smiled. Carl made no bones of his dislike for President Kennedy, and was always coming up with jokes about him, most of them off-color.

"Jeez, I can't believe you haven't heard.''

"All right, tell me. But remember, there is a lady present, so watch your language.''

"You really haven't heard, have you? Jake, some nut in Dallas just shot the President. He's dead, Jake. Who would've thought that could happen here?''

CHAPTER TWO

Jake looked through the window of the Pan Am 707 jetliner. The flight from San Francisco to Saigon had taken twenty-two hours and he was tired.

Outside the airplane the sky was the dark, crystaline blue which could only be found at 35,000 feet or higher. Far below the airplane a layer of thick clouds lay like a great ocean of cream, fluffy and whipped into swirls and peaks. The cloud layer was so dense that it covered the ocean. Jake stared at the clouds, but he was thinking of Kristin O'Neil.

Jake had seen a great deal of Kristin during his three month course at Cal Dunlap. He had been attracted to her from the first, but she seemed so much younger that he felt awkward about it. Also, he had never been able to develop the comfortable ease with sexual matters that others seemed to have. Even Virgie, his own wife, had been more sexually open than Jake. It was no wonder that someone as young and uninhibited as Kristin would be amused by Jake's prudishness.

Jake regretted his prudish ways. He wished he could loosen up, but his inhibitions were deeply ingrained by an incident from his youth. It was an incident Jake wished he could forget, but he knew that was impossible. It came back to haunt him time and time again.

*　　*　　*

It happened in the summer of 1940. He could remember the year well, because it was the first summer after his mother had died.

Jake was thirteen, and he lived with his father at Fort Stotsenburg in the Philippines. Jake's father was a Regimental Commander in General MacArthur's Command, and they lived in the Regimental Commandant's quarters, a large, old house with screened porches and breezeways to compensate for the stifling summer heat. Colonel Culpepper was authorized a housekeeper, and he hired Emma Cruz, the twenty-two-year-old daughter of the Filipino Post Sergeant Major. Emma Cruz had Spanish and Oriental blood, and the combination made her an exceptionally pretty girl. Though Jake was seven years her junior, he was coming of an age where fantasies began to develop, and one of his strongest fantasies had to do with the beautiful young Emma Cruz.

Jake once overheard some of his father's officers making ribald jokes about her. They said some things that Jake didn't quite understand, though he had an idea of the intent. The officers laughed and rubbed themselves between the legs. One of them wondered aloud if Iron Pants was "getting any off the Filipino girl."

"If he's not cuttin' her, someone should be," another said. "She's too juicy a piece to just waste."

"Are you volunteering for the job?" another asked, and they all laughed again.

Jake was embarrassed by their words. He was embarrassed for his father and for Emma, and he hoped neither of them ever heard such talk. Jake continued with his own fantasies about Emma, and though they were laced with as much eroticism as a thirteen-year-old boy could project, they were also ennobled by his genuine, secret love for her.

One Saturday night during the summer of 1940, Jake went to bed at around ten o'clock. The oppressive summer heat caused him to roll about restlessly on the sweat-dampened sheets. Finally, after perhaps an hour of tossing, he decided to slip out to the front porch and make his bed in the swing.

There had been a Regimental party at the Officer's Club that night, and his father had attended. There was no one in the house except Jake and Emma. Jake thought of Emma as he lay in the swing, and to the tune of taps, played in a distant sallyport, he finally drifted off to sleep. He was awakened a while later by his father's voice.

"No," he heard his father say. "Don't go to bed yet. Stay a while and keep me company." Jake got out of the swing and looked through the screen door. His father was in his dress whites, though the jacket was unbuttoned, and his tie was askew. Emma was in her sleeping gown, a gown designed more for cool sleeping than for modesty.

"Keep you company, sir?" Emma said. "You mean you want to talk?"

"No," Colonel Culpepper said. "Not exactly."

"Then I don't understand. What do you want?"

Colonel Culpepper reached out and touched her neck, then let his hand slide down to rest on her breasts.

"I think you know," he said.

"Colonel Culpepper, no, sir. Please, don't," Emma said. She pushed his hand away, then covered her breasts with her arm.

"Don't fight me, Emma. You want me as much as I want you," Colonel Culpepper said. "I know it. I can feel it."

"Please, Colonel, such a thing wouldn't be proper. I could never do such a thing. You don't want to make me do something that is wrong, do you?"

"It's not wrong, Emma. You are a full grown woman now. Surely you know how a man can be made to suffer. Don't you know that I lie awake in my bed every night, just thinking about you? Don't you know it drives me mad to be around you and want you as badly as I do?"

"Would you prefer that I leave?"

Leave? Jake thought. Why would Emma want to leave? The thought of her leaving frightened him, and he almost rushed inside to plead with her to stay. But the strange expression on his father's face frightened him even more, and he instinctively knew that if he went inside now, his father would be very cross with him. He stayed on the porch and listened.

"Don't you like it here?" Iron Pants asked.

"Yes, of course I do. But I won't stay here if my staying causes you to suffer so."

"There is a way to ease my suffering," Iron Pants suggested. He reached out to grab Emma's hips, and began bunching the material of her nightgown up in his hands. Her long, shapely legs were gradually being exposed, inch by tantalizing inch.

"Please, don't do this. Don't make me betray my honor in this way," Emma said. Her voice was barely more than a faint whisper.

Jake pressed his face against the window screen and looked in. The screen pressed little squares into his forehead, but he didn't move. He wasn't sure what was going on, but he could perceive the fright in Emma's voice, and that frightened him. Nevertheless, he felt compelled to stay here, to watch and listen.

Emma pulled herself away from Colonel Culpepper, and Jake thought his father was going to chase her. Instead, he walked over to the bar and poured himself a drink.

"I'm going to have you, Emma," he said matter-of-factly. "I'm going to have you tonight."

"Colonel, please don't do this thing. You don't really want to do this, you know you don't."

Colonel Culpepper drained the glass, then wiped the back of his hand across his mouth.

"I'm afraid I do want to do it," he said.

"Please, sir, why don't you just go on to bed? We'll forget all about this, and tomorrow it will be as if it had never happened."

"I'm sorry, Emma, but it isn't that easy," Colonel Culpepper said.

Colonel Culpepper walked back over to her and stood there looking down at her.

Run away, Jake thought. Just run away, don't let him come back to stand near you. But Emma remained motionless. She returned Colonel Culpepper's look, and Jake thought he saw her tremble a little. Still, she didn't move away.

"Oh, Colonel, don't you know I have my own girlish dreams of love and romance? But you are an American colonel, and I am the daughter of a Filipino Sergeant. I know there can never be marriage between us. And without marriage, any love we might share would be wrong, no matter how much we might want it."

"Then I was right," Iron Pants said. "You do want me."

"No," Emma said. "Not this way."

"Take it, Emma. Let us take what we can."

Emma closed her eyes and leaned her head into Colonel Culpepper's chest for a moment. "Oh," she said. "If only I could."

"You can."

"No!" Emma said. Then, as if summoning some inner strength, she pulled away.

"No," she said. "No, I can't do this. I won't do this!"

"And I, miss, won't be denied," Colonel Culpepper said. "Not now. No, by God. Not now."

"I won't make it easy for you," Emma said.

"You won't make it easy for me?" Iron Pants said loudly. "Emma, it hasn't been easy for me from the moment you arrived. Don't you realize the torture you have put me through? Don't you know what you have been doing to me? I can come into a room moments after you have left and I can still smell you there. I can feel you there. I've wanted you from the moment I first saw you, and now, by God, I'm going to have you."

"Please don't do anything foolish. Jake is sleeping."

At the mention of his name, Jake felt a pang of guilt, but he didn't leave his vantage point.

"Telling me that isn't going to stop me. Either you take off your gown willingly, or I'm going to take it off for you."

Emma didn't move. Iron Pants looked at her with a pained expression on his face.

"No," Emma said quietly. "Please, don't."

"It's too late," Iron Pants said in a guttural, choking tone. He reached down and grabbed the hem of her gown, then pulled it up and over her head. He tossed it carelessly behind him.

Jake stayed glued to the door screen, mesmerized by the sight. He'd never seen Emma naked before. He'd never seen any woman naked except for a picture one of his friends had shown him in the secrecy of a dark garage.

Frightened, yet unable to leave, he stared at her, at the dark triangle of hair, the softness of her belly, and at her breasts, with nipples drawn tight by their sudden exposure.

"Get on the sofa," Iron Pants said. His voice was deep and charged with emotion.

Emma moved to the sofa, mechanically, unprotestingly.

Jake watched his father remove his own clothes then. A moment later, Jake's father was standing there with his engorged penis thrusting toward Emma, who had not made a move or a sound since she lay on the sofa. Colonel Culpepper moved down over her then, and thrust into her.

The two naked bodies met on the sofa. Jake's father kissed Emma's lips, face, neck, shoulders, and even her breasts. To Jake's amazement, Emma seemed to return them. They thrashed about savagely, and yet, the fury was intermixed with an unexpected and strange tenderness.

Was Emma experiencing pleasure or pain? Was the fire and ice Jake watched part of a game, or was Emma truly being victimized?

Jake watched, fascinated, erotically aroused, and yet,

because of his uncertainty as to Emma's actual reaction to it, terrified for her. The sofa rocked with the power of Iron Pants' thrusts, and finally Jake heard his father gasp.

Iron Pants stood up then and looked down at her. His penis shone wetly as he walked away from the sofa. He took another long drink from the bottle.

Emma stayed on the couch. She lay motionless for a long time, and Jake was afraid that his father had hurt her badly.

Iron Pants pulled on his clothes and took another drink before he spoke to Emma, whose breathing was just now returning to normal.

"Emma, I'm sorry," he finally said. "I couldn't help myself. You've got to understand that. I couldn't help myself."

"I'll leave tomorrow," Emma said.

"No, please," Iron Pants said quickly. "Please, don't leave. I promise you, Emma. Nothing like this will ever happen again. Please don't leave. Stay with us. I need you. Jake needs you. You are safe with me, Emma. I give you my word of honor. You are safe with me. But, you must say nothing. You must never speak of this to anyone."

"I . . . I'll say nothing, this time," Emma said. "But if you ever try this again, I'll tell my father, and then you, or he, or I, or all three of us, will be dead."

"Fair enough," Iron Pants said. He started for the door and Jake, so engrossed in watching the drama unfold, almost didn't move from the front porch before his father left. The boy jumped over the railing and crouched in the hydrangea bush until his father was gone.

Jake stayed there for a few moments, then he climbed silently back onto the porch. He looked in through the screen and saw Emma still lying on the couch. He pushed through the door and walked over to her, looking down at her. Her eyes were tightly shut. Tear tracks ran down her face, and her chest shook in silent sobs. Jake trembled in anger and hate for his father, for anyone who would do this. He put his hand out, hesitantly at first, then with full commitment, and rested it on her forehead.

Emma opened her eyes and saw him. With a sob, she reached for him and pulled his head against her naked breasts. "Oh, Jake," she cried.

"I hate him," Jake said. "I hate him, hate him, hate him." Tears of anger and shame slid down his face. Emma took Jake back to his bedroom then and put him to bed, bathing his forehead with a cool cloth. She had been so concerned over him that she didn't cover her nakedness, and Jake closed his eyes tightly to avoid looking at her.

Emma didn't mention it the next day as she served Jake breakfast before church, and Jake couldn't look her in the face. When Jake went outside, Sergeant Hollings, Iron Pants' driver, was standing by the car. Iron Pants was sitting in the back seat, reading the paper, acting as if absolutely nothing had happened the night before.

"Good morning, Master Culpepper," Sergeant Hollings said, smiling broadly.

Jake looked at his father. How could his father just sit there after what he had done last night?

"I'll ride up front with you, Sergeant," Jake said.

"Certainly, if you wish," Sergeant Hollings said.

"I would prefer that you ride back here with me," Iron Pants said.

"No," Jake said resolutely.

"Have it your own way," Iron Pants said, going back to his paper. Jake was disappointed. He had hoped that his father would insist, so he could defy him openly.

Pointedly, Jake slipped into the front seat with Sergeant Hollings.

Later, at Church, Jake sat in the Commander's pew, thinking of all his sins. He had gazed upon his naked father, that was the sin of Ham. He hated his father. That was another sin. And if the sins of the fathers are visited upon the sons, then Jake had his father's sin to atone for as well. Jake closed his eyes and waited to be struck down by an angry God. When the bolt of lightning didn't appear, Jake took it as a sign that God was allied with him in his hatred for his father. It was a hatred he would always carry with him.

"Coffee or tea with your lunch, Major?" the stewardess asked with a practiced smile, bending over his seat.

"Coffee," Jake said.

She set his lunch tray before him, then added a cup of coffee. As Jake started his lunch, he thought of his dinner last night. He had shared it with Kristin O'Neil.

It had been nearly three weeks before he called her the first time. He was surprised when she accepted his invitation to dinner, and even more surprised by the enthusiasm with which she accepted. Evidently the age difference did not seem as significant to her.

After that first outing they were together frequently, though Jake always managed to keep their relationship in its proper perspective. That all changed on the night before Jake left, however. On that night Kristin moved into Jake's world with such authority that he couldn't dismiss her.

"Did you hear from Virgie?" Kristin had asked. Kristin was sitting on the sofa in the living room of Jake's apartment. She was wearing blue jeans and a man's blue cambray shirt, pulled and tied just beneath her breasts to bare her midriff. She kicked off her shoes and pulled her legs up under her, then took a sip from a glass of red wine. The wine caught a beam of light from some hidden source and the burgundy glowed brilliantly as if it contained some secret, inner flame.

"Yeah," Jake said. "I heard from her."

Jake was in a tiny kitchen which was really part of the living room of his efficiency apartment. He had a couple of small steaks in the oven, and was busily slicing fresh mushrooms for a salad.

"What did she say? Will she bring the boys out to see you off?"

"No. I offered to pay their way. I even tempted her with the idea of her taking the boys to Disneyland at my expense, but she wouldn't do it."

"I'm sorry, Jake. I know you wanted to see them one more time."

"I don't know," Jake said. "Maybe it's just as well this way. It's awfully hard to see them for a few minutes knowing you are going to leave them. And I don't mean just Vietnam. I don't fool myself, Kristin. Virgie is going to keep a very, very, tight control on them. I doubt if I will get to see them more than two or three times between now and the time they are grown."

"I know what you mean about it being hard to see someone for a short while only to lose them," Kristin said. "I feel that way about us."

Jake looked up in surprise.

"You feel that way about us? What do you mean?"

Kristin put the drink down and walked over to the counter which separated the kitchen from the living room. She leaned across the counter and kissed Jake. It was a very light kiss, no more than a brush of her lips against his, but Jake felt a tingling sensation like a tiny charge of electricity.

"I mean I don't like losing you," Kristin said. "Did you think you could just move in and out of my life? It's not that easy, Jake. I'm going to miss you terribly."

"You got used to having a father-figure around, did you?" Jake said, trying to make a joke of it. Jake looked every bit of his thirty-five years. His hair was brindled, and years of outdoor duty had put squint lines around his eyes. Kristin, on the other hand looked much younger than her years, and even younger dressed as she was tonight. One of the first times they went out together, someone mistook Kristin for Jake's daughter. Kristin had laughed about it, but it had embarrassed Jake.

"You aren't my father, Jake," Kristin said. She moved around the counter to stand in front of him, so close to him that he could feel the heat of her body. "I wouldn't be having these urges if you were my father."

"What sort of urges are you talking about?" Jake asked. His tongue felt thick, and he was extremely aware of her nearness, and the musk of her sexuality.

"Oh, just your ordinary, run of the mill, horny as hell, hot-to-trot urges," Kristin said, running the tips of her fingers lightly around Jake's ear lobes.

"Kristin, you don't know what you're saying," Jake said, taking a step back from her.

"Oh, yes, I do. I know exactly what I'm saying. I'm not a little girl, Jake. I'm a woman."

"You shouldn't tease like this," Jake said.

Kristin smiled seductively at him, then began unbuttoning her shirt, slowly and deliberately, until it would have come all the way open had it not been for the fact that it was tied just beneath her breasts.

"I'm not teasing," she said. "I'm deadly serious."

Kristin untied the knot, then let the shirt hang open. Her breasts were bare beneath the shirt. One side of the shirt slipped a little, and the nipple of that breast winked at Jake.

"I . . . uh. . . .the steaks," Jake mumbled. "They'll burn."

"Better the steaks than me. I'm burning up," Kristin said. She reached for him and pulled him to her, mashing her bare breasts against his chest.

"My God, girl, do you know what you are doing to me?"

"I hope so," Kristin said. She kissed him, hungrily.

"I'm not used to such . . . such honesty in a woman," Jake said, not wanting to use the word 'aggressiveness.'

"Oh? Tell me, Jake, do you think I'm too bold in making the first move?" Kristin asked between kisses.

"No, it's not that," Jake said. "It's just that I thought I would make the first move."

"You're such a gentleman I'm afraid you would never do anything if I didn't take matters . . . in hand," Kristin said. As she said the words "in hand," she reached down and boldly put her hand on that part of Jake which was now reacting most strongly to her seductive charm.

Things were going fast for Jake. He was from an earlier, more inhibited generation, unused to freedom that came with the sexual revolution of the sixties. Despite Jake's unfamiliarity with such aggressive action, he discovered that he liked it, and he had no difficulty in catching up to Kristin's level of arousal. A moment later it was Jake who led them into his bedroom. They made love and it was the most torrid, intensely erotic sex Jake had ever experienced. After that they had their steaks without even bothering to dress. Then they made love again.

Kristin was quite an inventive partner, and she made love almost as if it were a game, a wonderful game, but just a game. Not since the very early days of his marriage to Virgie, had Jake demonstrated such stamina or recuperative powers.

The next day, Kristin went to the airport with him and stayed in the gate lounge with him until his flight was called. She kissed him goodbye in the middle of all the other couples who were kissing goodbye, and suddenly she didn't seem too young for him anymore.

But that was twenty-two hours ago, and the stewardesses had just collected the custom declaration cards preparatory to landing in Saigon. Jake was now in Vietnamese air space.

Three rows in front of Jake on the same airplane, was a young woman whose tall, dark beauty had already caught the attention of everyone on board. Like Jake, she was coming to Vietnam for the first time. Unlike Jake, she was not coming on military orders, but for her own, private reason.

Melinda Lanier was much more than just a beautiful brunette with dark blue eyes and regal features. She was a rightful claimant to the title of princess, because her father was King of a tiny European principality. The very existence of her father's picture-postcard kingdom was entirely dependent upon tourism, and the continued good graces of the French government. The royal bloodline, however, was authentic, and it stretched unbroken for several hundred years.

Until Melinda was eighteen she had been next in line for succession to the throne. That was because no male heirs had been born. Then, when Melinda was sixteen her mother died and her father remarried, this time to a beautiful American film star from a wealthy Philadelphia family. The blonde film star was known for her cool but sultry beauty, and the fairy tale marriage made world-wide headlines. It also eventually produced the prince her father had always wanted. When the prince was born, it moved Melinda into the background. She was no longer interesting copy to the press because she was no longer the successor to the crown.

Melinda and her father's new wife did not get along very well. In order to keep peace in the family, the King sent Melinda to the United States for schooling.

While Melinda was in America she lived a life dedicated to the pursuit of pleasure. She drank hard, she attended as many parties as she could manage, and she moved in the shadowy circles of the underworld. She started keeping regular company with an underworld gambler who had a criminal record. She married him, despite an urgent plea from her father not to do so. That marriage, predictably, ended in divorce. After that Melinda got involved with a married man, had an abortion, and wound up in a messy divorce as the "other woman."

The newspapers and gossip magazines had a field day

with Melinda, and the resultant scandal was the greatest ever to occur in her father's small kingdom. Melinda's conduct caused her father to take the extreme and almost unheard-of action of *expuger de l'arbre genealogique*, expulsion from the family tree.

Melinda thus found herself disowned and penniless. She was an anachronism, a princess in a world grown too old for fairy tales. But she had four assets. She was beautiful, she was of royal blood, albeit disenfranchised, and she had wits and courage. She also knew Henri Marquand.

CHAPTER THREE

Henri Marquand was a Frenchman who had been born in Vietnam. His father and his grandfather had also been born in Vietnam. That made Henri, technically, a third-generation native Vietnamese, but he considered himself first, last, and always, French.

Henri's wealth qualified him for membership in a select group of wealthy Frenchmen who had formed a social group known as the Francindochine Culture Societé. The Societé met often in a private club behind high walls in Saigon. They claimed to be an organization founded to promote the welfare and social well-being of the French-Vietnamese, and French nationals living in Vietnam. Often this welfare and social well-being was promoted by providing expensive and exotic diversions for the club members. The Societé carried on gambling, international intrigue, and financial manipulations on a grand scale. The most sought-after, and the most available commodities provided by the Societé however, were the pleasures of the flesh.

Henri was the social director of the club, and he took it as his special mission to outdo all who had held this position before him, in regard to the procurement of girls. It wasn't enough that his women were pretty. They also had to be cultured, and they had to possess some other trait of unique desirability.

Henri set out to attain the unattainable, but only for

those members who were willing to pay extra for the privilege. Therefore it was not unusual to see an internationally famous actress, or the daughter of one of the wealthiest and most influential families in the world, turn up as one of Henri's "special" guests. Women whose faces graced the *Societé* pages and covers of magazines the world over, were often seen in residence at the club.

It was to become one of the girls of this club, that Melinda came to Vietnam.

Cao Ngyuen Mot sat behind the wheel of Marquand's Mercedes at Ton Son Nhut airport. The airport which had once been so beautifully landscaped in order to provide a fitting welcome to air travelers to the "Pearl of the Orient" was now primarily a military base. Instead of graceful terminals and lounges, there was an endless line of buildings and warehouses, all bearing the prefabricated and lusterless stamp of the military.

The roar of military, commercial and civilian aircraft of all nations beat at Mot's eardrums. A group of Air Vietnam stewardess wiggled past the Mercedes, all wearing traditional Vietnamese costumes, the *ao-dai*. The costumes the girls wore were all the same color, as they were dressed in the uniform of Air Vietnam. They wore skyblue butterflies in white silk trousers with flowing overblouses and shirts. They fluttered long, false eyelashes at Mot, though they couldn't see him behind the shaded windows of the Mercedes.

From his position in the car, Mot would be able to see the Pan Am airliner when it arrived. He would go into the terminal and have Melinda Lanier paged, then he would take her to Marquand's rubber plantation just north of Saigon.

Mot worked for Marquand, as had his father before him. Mot's father was killed by the Viet Minh during the French Indo-China war. Marquand had kept Mot's mother on the payroll, however. Mot had been born on Marquand's plantation, and he had been schooled in a private school Marquand operated for his employees.

Mot appreciated the fact that Marquand had provided a private school, because Mot learned a great deal there. He learned to speak French and English and developed a taste for Western literature and an appreciation for Western music. He studied religion and philosophy, and there, in the school, he developed a thirst for freedom and independence.

"True independence," Mot's teacher had said, "cannot be bestowed. True independence, by the very definition of the word, must be taken."

Mot's teacher was a man named Ling Sanh Phat. Phat was an older man who had studied in Paris, and had lived for a couple of years in New York. While in New York he had been unable to get a job commensurate with his education, so he worked for the New York City Street Department. For a while he had worked with another Vietnamese, a baker who had learned his trade from Escoffier but who was also unable to get a job in his profession, and thus was forced to work on the New York streets. That man's name was Tong Van So, though he later changed it to Ho Chi Minh.

"Do you understand what I am saying?" Phat asked Mot one day after classes were over. "If we want our independence, we must take it."

"But we have taken our independence," Mot said. "The French no longer control our country."

"The French have left, that is true," Phat explained. "But they have been replaced by puppets, and the strings of those puppets are being pulled by the Americans. Do not fool yourself, Mot, into thinking we are free to do as we wish. We may do only so much as the Americans allow us to do. That is why I am fighting the Americans, and their puppets."

"You?" Mot had gasped. "You are Viet Cong?"

"No," Phat replied. "The term Viet Cong is a slanderous epithet which comes from the Americans and their puppets. We are members of the National Liberation Front, and we are freedom fighters. I have watched you very carefully, Mot. You could be one of us. We need young men who are unafraid to ask questions. We need young men who are fired with idealism. If we are ever to have true independence, it will be because young men such as yourself have taken it for us."

Mot refused to join the NLF when Phat made his first attempt to recruit him. He refused on the next several attempts as well. But when Diem was assassinated, Mot was finally convinced that the Vietnamese people were not in control of their own destiny. That was when he decided to join.

Today, Mot was fulfilling his first mission. He had come to Tan Son Nhut to pick up Melinda Lanier for Marquand, but that had merely given him the cover he needed to breach the inner security lines of the air base. He had used that opportunity to plant a bomb just outside an American officers' mess. It would explode at 12:30, just when the mess was full of diners.

"Jake! Jake, over here!"

Jake was following the line of passengers who were deplaning from the 707, and he looked over in the direction of the voice to see his old friend Lieutenant Colonel David Purcell. Purcell was standing behind a white-and-black striped barricade, waving at Jake. There was an American M.P. and a Vietnamese soldier with the letters Q.C. on his helmet liner, who stood guard just in front of the barricade. Purcell tapped the American M.P. on the shoulder and pointed to Jake, then said something. The M.P. nodded, then walked over to Jake, who, like all the other passengers, was in civilian clothes.

"You are Major Culpepper, sir?"

"Yes."

The M.P. saluted, then stepped back. "Sir, Colonel

Purcell has made arrangements with customs. You may go with him."

"Thank you," Jake said, and he broke the line and walked over to Purcell, who was now smiling broadly and extending his hand.

"Welcome, my good man," Purcell said. "Welcome to the land of sliding doors and slant-eyed whores."

"Jeez," Jake said. "Is it always this hot? I can barely get my breath."

"It's straight up noon," Purcell said. "What do you expect?"

"You mean it gets better in the evening?"

Purcell laughed. "No, but the mosquitoes come out then, and they bother you so much that you don't worry about the heat. Have you eaten lunch?"

"No."

"Well, come on, there's a good officers' club very near here. We can grab something to eat, then we'll go down to the Rex Hotel."

"What's at the Rex Hotel?"

"Your boss," Purcell said. "What's new from the States? How did operation Desert Strike go?"

"Smooth as a whistle from what I heard. I wasn't part of it, of course. I was in school."

"Well, don't worry, you'll make up for it here. Vietnam is just like Swift Strike One, Two and Three, only without Sergeant Phillips' distillery."

Both men laughed as they recalled the field exercises they had shared, and the enterprising sergeant who had found and utilized a still in the North Carolina mountains.

They walked across the sun-baked ground to the officers' club, then they pushed open the screen door and stepped inside. There were two large floor fans pushing a breeze across the dining room so that it was a little more bearable than it had been outside.

"Ah," Purcell said, pointing to a table near an open

window. "A table by a window. That's a nice surprise. Let's grab it."

They took no more than three or four steps toward it when the world seemed to explode. There was a deafening roar and a searing flash of light. Jake was hurled across the floor and slammed against one of the upright fans, then buried beneath falling debris.

Jake pulled himself to an upright position and tried to look around the dining room, but the smoke and soot hung heavily, obscuring his vision and burning his lungs with cordite. His ears were still ringing from the sharpness of the explosion, so that he was only barely aware of the cries and moans of the injured and trapped. Jake felt of himself gingerly, and discovered to his relief that he wasn't hurt.

Purcell had not been as lucky, though, and Jake drew in his breath sharply when he saw the colonel's grotesquely twisted body near him. Just two weeks before Colonel David Purcell was due to go back to the States he was killed in the blast of Mot's bomb.

Mot's mission had been successful. The bomb had gone off as planned, and the American officers' dining hall had been destroyed. Many men were killed.

Mot joined with the others in the crowd for a few minutes, and when he saw the carnage he had created, he got sick. A Vietnamese soldier who saw Mot throwing up teased him.

"It is good you are a Saigon cowboy and not a soldier," he said. "We have no place in the Army for mamma's boys who throw up at the sight of a little blood."

Mot didn't answer him, but walked rather weakly back to the car. He sat there for a few moments, trying to convince himself that what he had done was right. He was fighting for freedom, and in the entire history of the world, no nation ever won their freedom without bloodshed. He did what he had to do.

Mot started the car and turned the air conditioner on

full, then put his face in front of the vent, letting cold air blow on him. He was still there when a beautiful European woman tapped on the window. Mot let the window down.

"One of the officials told me this is the car of Henri Marquand," the girl said, speaking in French.

"Yes," Mot said, answering in the same language.

"I am Melinda." The girl gave no other name as if she realized that was all the name she would need. "Why did you not meet me?"

"I'm sorry," Mot said. "There was a bomb, some people were killed." Mot pointed to the American officers' mess hall. There were several military ambulances parked there, and one helicopter, with its blades spinning and its lights flashing. There was also a rather substantial crowd of people who had no purpose, other than to satisfy their morbid curiosity.

"Oh, how awful," Melinda said. "Does this sort of thing happen often here?"

"We are at war," Mot said. "This was an act of war."

"Let's go, please. I've no wish to stay around. There might be another bomb."

Melinda stood beside the car, and Mot realized that she was waiting for him to open the door for her. He got out and opened the door.

"Have you luggage?"

"Yes, but I can't pick it up until tomorrow. It must go through customs."

"I hope you have nothing valuable in your luggage. The customs inspectors will steal it," Mot said.

Mot put the car in gear, then drove away from Ton Son Nhut. He got on Highway 13 and started north to the Marquand Plantation.

Melinda sat in the back seat of the Mercedes and peered through the window at the teeming filth and squalor around her. Mot watched her in the mirror.

She was an exceptionally beautiful girl for an Occidental, Mot thought. Her features were not squared off like most

western girls, and her skin was smooth without any trace
of facial hair. Facial hair was another trait of Occidental
women that Mot didn't like.

Of course, this girl would have to be beautiful, because
she was going to be one of Marquand's whores.

Suddenly Mot felt a great hatred for the girl. Who was
she to have the right to ride so elegantly in the back of a
chauffeured limousine? She was nothing but a whore, after
all. Any man who had her price could have her. He could
have her if he had her price.

Mot felt a quickening of his pulse, and a slight pressure
in the front of his pants. He studied her again. Did he want
her? He smiled as he recalled a statement he had once
heard Marquand make.

"I wouldn't kick her out of bed," Marquand had said,
speaking of another girl.

Yes, Mot thought. He wouldn't kick this girl out of bed.

"Driver," the girl spoke. Again, she spoke in French,
and her voice was soft and husky, just the kind of voice
such a girl should have, Mot thought.

"Yes?"

"Why are there so many things in the road?" She
asked. "Every five hundred meters or so, there are barrels
and barbed wire stretched out in the road. It seems to me
as if that would make traveling very difficult."

"It does," Mot said. "That is why they are there."

"I don't understand."

"Suppose I were the one who planted the bomb at Ton
Son Nhut," Mot said. "Suppose I had driven to the base
in this car, and I threw a bomb at the American mess hall.
If there were no barriers in the street, I would have a
headstart and I would surely escape. But with these barriers,
I can't go too fast, because I have to stop and weave
around them."

"Oh," the girl said. "Yes, I can see why they would
want to do something like that. Are you really a terrorist?"

Mot looked quickly in the mirror at the girl. She had

surprised him by her question but he saw that she was smiling. He smiled back at her.

"Are you really a princess?" he asked.

"Why do you ask that?"

"Marquand says you are a princess. Are you?"

"If he says so, then it must be true."

"Why are you here?" Mot asked. "Why are you in Viet Nam?"

"Why are you here?"

"I was born here."

"Some of us are not so lucky as to be able to remain in the place of our birth."

Mot reached the first police checkpoint then, and he stopped and rolled down the window. A Vietnamese policeman leaned through the window of the car. He looked at Mot, then he looked at the girl in back.

"Who is the round eye?" he asked in Vietnamese.

"Ask her yourself."

"Does she speak Vietnamese?"

"We have been speaking in French. She speaks no Vietnamese."

The policeman laughed ribaldly. "You mean she can't understand anything I say?"

"Not if you say it in Vietnamese."

The policeman looked at Melinda. "Hey, baby, I would like a good time tonight. Can you show me a good time?"

Melinda looked at him, then she looked through the window, totally ignoring him.

"You can come to the bunker with me. I will share you with my friends. When we finish, you'll be very sore."

Melinda made no indication that she heard him.

"Why is the girl with you? Is she the whore of your master?"

"She is my sister," Mot said.

"Your sister? Don't give me that. She is a roundeye."

"She is my sister in Christ," Mot said, noticing that the policeman was wearing a cross.

The policeman looked at Mot with a strange expression. Finally he sighed. "I do not appreciate your games," he said.

"Then do your job and allow me to do mine. Don't question me about who I have in the car."

"You have papers proving you are no deserter?" the policeman asked.

"Yes," Mot said, pulling out the deferment papers Marquand had purchased for him at great cost.

"Then you are free to go. Only next time, leave your friend, your sister in Christ," he added with a sneer, "with me."

"So," Melinda said as they drove away from the roadblock. "I am your sister in Christ, am I?" This time she spoke in perfect Vietnamese, and she laughed.

"I didn't know you could speak our language," he said.

"I speak it." She leaned forward and put her hand on Mot's shoulder. He felt the pressure of her fingers, and wondered how they could be cool and hot at the same time. "And you have made a friend this day. You didn't realize I spoke Vietnamese, you could have joined with the policeman in ridiculing me. I am as he said, you know. I have come to be a whore for Marquand."

"We are all whores," Mot said, thinking of the bomb he had planted. "In one way or another."

CHAPTER FOUR

General Barclay had a suite of rooms in the Rex Hotel. The rooms served as his personal quarters as well as his office. A small air conditioner cooled his quarters, but the office had to rely on overhead fans. They clattered and clanked as they spun, doing little to dispel the heat which seemed to hang over everything like an oppressive blanket. Jake was in General Barclay's office, sitting in a wicker chair while a U.S. Army doctor dressed the cuts on his forehead and cheek.

Jake had hung around the scene of the bomb blast for several minutes after the explosion, helping with the rescue operation. Finally, when the last seriously injured soldier had been pulled from the wreckage and all the dead had been lined up in a neat row, an Army sergeant took Jake to the Rex Hotel. There, he met his new commander, and his wounds, though minor, were looked at for the first time.

General Barclay had been on the phone when Jake arrived, and now he hung up the phone and started toward Jake. Jake started to get up, even though the doctor was bathing his wounds with peroxide.

"No, no," General Barclay said, waving at him. "You sit still and let the doc get you taken care of. It's a hell of a welcome to Saigon, I must say."

Barclay stuck his hand out and Jake took it. He had

served with General Barclay before and had known him for many years before that, because General Barclay and Jake's father had served together. "How are you, Jake? How's old Iron Pants?"

"He's fine, sir," Jake said. "I spoke to him on the phone shortly before I left. He sends his regards to you."

A captain came into the room.

"General? We need to release Colonel Purcell's body for shipment back to the States."

"Yeah, go ahead, Smitty," General Barclay said. Barclay took a cigarette from a package, tamped it on his lighter, then lit it. "Poor bastard," he murmured through puffs. "He was really looking forward to your arrival so he could go back. None of us figured it would be like this."

"Are bombings common over here?" Jake asked.

"More common than I'd like to admit," Barclay said. "That's the bitch of this war. The other guys don't want to come out and fight. They'd rather knife you in the back than meet you on an honorable field of battle."

"Are we calling it a war?" Jake asked. "I thought it was a police action."

"That's no longer an operative term," Barclay said. "We tried to use that word in Korea, remember?"

"Yes, sir," Jake said. "Well, I sure hope this thing doesn't grow into something like Korea."

"Don't worry, it'll never get that far. The VC know better than to meet us face to face. So, if they won't play in our ball park, we'll play in theirs. We've got a few surprises for them, and that's where you come in."

"Surprises? What sort of surprises?"

"How's his head, doc?" Barclay asked. "Will he ever play the piano again?"

"As good as he ever could," the doctor said. He put a couple of adhesive bandages in place, then closed up his bag.

"Jake, come on back here, will you? I have a few things I'd like to show you."

Jake followed the General across the room, and down a hall to a door. The door had a sign barring entry to all unauthorized personnel. The General unlocked the door and they stepped inside. It was hot and stuffy, and the General flipped on a light.

"We don't keep it cool in here, because no one is in here that much. But this is the heart of Phoenix."

"Phoenix?"

General Barclay opened up a map of Vietnam. The map was marked with red and black markers at towns and villages.

"Everywhere you see a red marker, we are looking for Phoenix targets. Black shows the targets already hit."

"I don't understand, General. What is a Phoenix target?"

General Barclay laughed. "You want to hear the official explanation?"

"Try me."

"Phoenix is a project aimed at identifying and excising the VC political infrastructure. It is run by the South Vietnamese, but under the direction of the CIA. It is to neutralize the VC's political control, and divest the guerrillas of the support of the people."

"What the hell does that mean?" Jake asked.

General Barclay took one last puff from his cigarette, then ground it out in a jar-lid which served as an ashtray.

"It means," he said, as he exhaled the last puff, "that we go into a village and find out who is, and who isn't VC. The ones who are VC, we terminate."

"Terminate?"

"Kill."

"What? Arrest, or what?"

"No arrest," General Barclay said. "Kill. We send an execution squad in and we kill the son-of-a-bitch. And his family."

"And his family?"

"Yeah," Barclay said. "First of all, if he is VC, then you know damn well his family is too. Shit, Jake, Dave Purcell was killed today, along with several other good men. It wouldn't surprise me a bit if the bomb hadn't been planted by some twelve-year-old girl."

"It was a pretty big bomb for a twelve-year-old girl, sir."

"Well, you get my point, don't you? We have caught little girls dropping grenades down in the gas tanks of our jeeps. They pull the pin, and tape the handles down. They drop the grenade in the gas tank, the gas eats away the glue on the tape, the spoon pops off and. . . . boom. Little girls, little boys, old men and women, they are all the same. Hell, don't go feeling sorry for the guy's family. This is a war, Jake, but it is different from any war any American has ever fought before. Have you ever seen an ant war?"

"An ant war, sir?"

"Yeah, you know, when one colony of ants attacks another colony. Like red ants against black ants."

"I don't recall whether I have or not."

"Well I've seen 'em," General Barclay said. "And not only in nature, but once on a National Geographic film. My God, Jake, you should have seen it. The film was shot through a microscope so everything was greatly enlarged. It was so awesome and so total in its destruction that it was beautiful. Every ant, I mean every goddam one of 'em, was involved. It was total war, for God's sake. Husbands and wives and all the children were fighting. Well, let me tell you something. This war is like that. It's the American ants against the Vietnamese ants, and believe you me, everyone of the Vietnamese ants is a warrior ant."

"I thought the war was between Vietnamese."

General Barclay cleared his throat. "Well, yes, it is. I was just making an analogy. Now, Jake, I'm putting you in sector D here, just north of Saigon. You will be the principal American advisor to all Vietnamese troops there, and you will supervise Operation Phoenix.''

''You want me to supervise Phoenix? I thought the CIA and the Vietnamese were supposed to do that.''

''Yeah, they do, and they will handle most of it. But there is a problem with the Phoenix operation, and we haven't learned how to deal with it yet.''

''What is the problem?''

''The dinks we kill are fingered by the other dinks. We haven't learned anyway to separate the good information from the bad. You know, in theory, if a guy got pissed off at his neighbor, all he'd have to do is finger him as a VC, and we'd do his dirty work.''

''How are you handling it now?'' Jake asked.

''That's just it. We aren't handling it now. If we get a finger, we hit him. We may be offing a few good guys, but statistically, we've got to be getting more bad guys than good. Anyway, that's where you come in.''

''How?''

''Once the finger is made, there won't be a hit until you okay it.''

''General, how can you ask me to accept a responsibility like that?'' Jake asked.

''How can I ask you to accept the responsibility? Because you are a soldier, Jake. Killing is part of your job.''

''Yes, in combat, but . . .''

''Goddammit, Jake, I'm trying to make you realize that this *is* combat. I told you. You have to forget about the old rules. You have to forget about the old morals. The concept of war has changed, and we have to change with it.''

''I'm not sure I like the change.''

''None of us do,'' General Barclay said. ''But when you consider the alternative, which is total atomic warfare, then the choice becomes easy.''

Jake sighed. ''I hope I have something to go on when I make these life or death decisions.''

"You will," General Barclay said. "You'll have Father Sachs."

"Father Sachs? A priest? What does he have to do with it?"

"Quite a bit," General Barclay said, smiling. "Just wait; you'll see."

The town of Phu Cuong sits on a bend in the Saigon River, about fifteen miles north of the city. Phu Cuong supplies fish to the markets of all nearby hamlets, and the fishmongers of the hamlets come to town every day to buy. They walk along the bank of the river and poke through the catch, which, when laid out, stretches for almost a quarter of a mile.

To the occasional visitor the smell is very strong, but of course, the Phu Cuong resident isn't aware of it. To him the fish market is an exciting place. It is the center of great activity. In addition to the customers and vendors there are also the passengers of the bus line and the ferry service, both of which use the market as a terminal.

There are also many portable sidewalk cafes which are marvels of logistic ingenuity. Their owners, men and women alike, assemble the cafes every morning and disassemble them every night. They carry them about in two large boxes suspended on their shoulders as they shuffle down the street. In one box, packed neatly, with every item exactly fitted into place like a ball within a ball, there are tables and chairs, and even the box, which becomes part of the counter. In the other box are utensils, spices, and other paraphernalia to stock the restaurant, and of course, the box itself, to complete the counter. Within moments the sidewalk cafe can take on the appearance of a permanent fixture. There were at least a dozen of them set up in the village square. To one side of the square, there was an outdoor altar, and at the foot of the altar stood a Western man in priestly garb. He would have commanded some attention even had he not been in vestments, for he was six feet four inches tall and that made him stand head and shoulders above all the Vietnamese who were around him. His hair was as black as theirs, but his eyes were blue and his face was very white, and that also set him apart.

He made the Sign of the Cross, then turned to the dozen or so who were present for his Mass.

"Benedicat vos omnipotens Deus, Pater et Filius, et Spiritus Sanctus. Amen."

With the final blessing, the Vietnamese crossed themselves and left the outdoor church. Father Klaus Sachs stepped up to the altar and began retrieving the Chalice, Paten, Purificator and Corporal. He recalled the words of Pope Pius XI: "It is not only ordained priests, but the entire body of Christians who form a holy priesthood to offer spiritual sacrifices to God in the Mass."

He also knew that anyone who took the Sacraments in good faith, believing them to be administered by a priest, derived the same degree of spiritual blessing from them, even if the man who administered the sacraments was an impostor.

Such as he was.

Though Klaus Sachs had completed seminary, he had never taken the vows of priesthood. He told the Bishop it was because he didn't feel worthy, but what he really meant was that he didn't feel strong enough. He could not face the idea of a lifetime of abstinence and saintly behaviour, so he left Holy Mother Church, not only abandoning the priesthood, but abandoning Christianity as well.

For the first few years, Klaus seemed intent upon making up for lost time. He atoned for those years of piety and study, by experiencing all the sins he had previously and so studiously sought to avoid. After a while that began to pale and he sinned when he sinned, but not in the same manner of obligation with which he started his secular life.

Klaus applied for a job with the U.S. Government, ending up as an agent for the CIA, and, because with them, all secrets are known, the fact that he had studied

for the priesthood came to light. Thus, when the CIA field
station put Klaus to work, the cover they selected for him
was that of a priest.

"Father, hear my confession?"

Klaus turned toward the speaker, and recognized Mr.
Dom, one of his Vietnamese operatives.

"Of course, my son," Klaus said. They moved around
behind the altar, and Klaus made the Sign of the Cross,
then inclined his ear to hear. By that action, all others,
Catholic and non-Catholic alike, knew they were to give
them privacy for confession.

"In the village of Phat Chat," Mr. Dom said. "There is
a Captain Sanh. He is an officer in the Popular Forces, but
I know he is a VC."

"How do you know this?" Klaus asked.

"I have checked it with many sources," Mr. Dom
replied. "He is a high ranking officer in the VC, and he is
a terrorist. It was he who planted a bomb in a theater last
month. Many were killed."

"Yes, I remember the incident," Klaus said. "Mr.
Dom, you know that if what you are saying is true,
extreme sanction will be taken against Captain Sanh."

"He must be killed," Mr. Dom said. "Many innocents
have lost their lives because of him."

"And his family?"

"Yes, them too," Mr. Dom replied. "All must be
killed. All of them."

"I must have verification from another source," Klaus
said. "From someone who doesn't know you. If I get that
verification, I will recommend the sanction."

"I can kill them myself."

"No," Klaus said quickly. "Not until we have authorization. I will see Colonel Purcell tonight."

As Jake rode in the jeep from the Rex Hotel to his
BOQ, he looked out at the festering boil which was Saigon's
inner city. Saigon's population had increased almost ten-

fold in twenty-three years. The newly arrived people moved into one-room hovels with relatives who already lived in the city, or built little shanties onto existing structures, pushing out into the already crowded lanes and alleyways. Streets which were once broad enough to allow a double stream of cars had been turned into narrow, twisting labyrinths, barely wide enough to allow a walking man passage.

The alleys were dark, even at high noon, because the overhang blots out the sun. There were holes and passages leading from one alley to another, and people scurried about like moles through tunnels, sometimes going for months at a time without ever seeing the light of day.

The driver of the jeep turned through a gate and they were suddenly inside a small compound. The compound was surrounded by a high concrete fence, and Jake saw rows of concertina wire and embedded, broken glass, at the top of the wall. There was a guard on the gate, and he saw guard towers at each corner. There was one long cinderblock building in the center of the compound. It was a two-story building, which looked very much like the bachelor officers' quarters in the States. To the left of the long building, was a much smaller building. The bottom half of the walls of the smaller building were made of wood, the top half was screenwire.

"Damn, it's like a prison," Jake said.

"Yes, sir, I guess it is at that," the Sergeant said. "But this here prison is to keep the bad guys out."

Jake saw a Vietnamese driving a Lambretta. He was allowed through the gate without question.

"How do we know who the bad guys are?" Jake asked, pointing at the Vietnamese.

"Well, sir, they's one real easy way to tell," the Sergeant said. "Iffen they shoot at you, they're bad guys."

"That's a comforting thought," Jake said.

The Sergeant stopped the jeep in front of the building.

"Your stuff was already brought over here, Major. If

you'd like to go into the O-club and have a drink, I'll find out which room is yours 'n get your key for you."

"Thanks," Jake said. "If there was ever a day when I needed a drink, this is the day.".

The O-club was in the smaller building, and Jake stepped inside and looked around. A red leather bar curved around the corner. The wall behind the bar was solid, and it was decorated with artifacts of the war: the tail rotor of a helicopter, bent and twisted out of shape; a VC flag; a Chinese AK-47 rifle, and an unrecognizable piece of leathery material, bearing the legend, "Ho Chi Minh's Penis."

There were several bowls of freshly popped popcorn on the bar, and Jake sat near one and got a handful. It wasn't until that moment that he realized he hadn't eaten all day long, his lunch having been spoiled by the terrorist bomb.

A smiling Vietnamese bartender took Jake's order, adroitly mixed a martini, then retired to the other end of the bar. There were a couple of officers sitting at a table across the room, and another quietly strumming a guitar at the opposite end. Jake didn't know any of them, and for the moment was disinclined to meet anyone. He kept to himself, speaking only to thank the Sergeant when he got the key to his room and to thank the bartender when his glass was refilled.

After four martinis Jake began to feel their effect, and he was trying to decide whether he wanted a sandwich from the club, or a meal from the mess, when a priest sat beside him.

"Padre," Jake said.

"Hello, Jake."

Jake looked at the priest in surprise. How did he know him? Jake wasn't Catholic, and he had never seen this man before in his life. Then, he remembered General Barclay's words about a Father someone. Jake thought real hard, then he managed to bring up the name, even through the fog of his martini-relaxed mind.

"Father Sachs, I believe?" Jake said.

Klaus smiled. "That's very good," He said. "I see you've been briefed." Klaus spoke with a German accent.

"Not thoroughly."

"Thoroughly enough to remember my name," Klaus said. "I take it, you were also told of the Phoenix program."

"Yes," Jake said. Now the fog began to drift away, and the pleasant relaxation he had been building was gone.

"That is good, also. I want you to approve a sanction."

"When?"

"Tonight," Klaus said. "Right now."

"But, you can't expect me to sit here and give approval just like that?" Jake said. "I don't know who it is, or anything about him. I have to have some time to . . ."

"Major, there is no time," Klaus explained. "The war was going on before you arrived in this country, and it will be going on after you leave. It doesn't stop and give new men time to get adjusted. You have to come here ready to go."

"I realize that, but nevertheless—"

"Look, don't worry about it," Klaus said. "It's my job to check them out, and believe me, I do that rather thoroughly. I won't come to you for authorization unless I'm convinced it's needed. Besides, it's better that you don't know who it is. This keeps you from dwelling on it. All I need is your approval for the sanction; I don't need your approval for the target."

"And if I don't give my approval?"

"We'll do it anyway. I have other lines of authority."

"Then why even come to me?"

Klaus smiled. "In truth? I think so the credit of the operation is spread around."

"Are you serious when you say I can't stop the operation, even if I wanted to?"

"You can delay it by maybe fifteen minutes," Klaus said.

Jake turned away from Klaus and picked up his drink.

"Then never come to me again," he said. "You have my blanket approval."

Klaus smiled again. "We are going to get along well."

Back in Dunlap, California, it was raining. Kristin O'Neil was listening to Joan Baez records and writing a letter to Jake.

Kristin had not been able to put her relationship with Jake in its proper perspective. The first time she saw him, she had found him attractive in a Prussian-like way. She thought to entertain herself with a little harmless flirtation. The idea of getting such a man to show some interest in her intrigued her.

She wanted to take some of the starch out of his backbone.

It didn't work quite that way, however. Rather than being put off by his quaint code of honor, she found it admirable. There was a gentleness about him too, which, when contrasted with his crisp military exterior, made him all the more vulnerable.

She had wanted them to make love, not only because she found him physically attractive, but also because she felt it would be a delicious irony. For a while she was afraid that they would make love only if she initiated the action. Then, when Jake managed to overcome all the demons and barriers which seemed to be in the way, and they did make love, it was more wonderful than anything Kristin had ever experienced.

Among some of her friends there was a joke. "Let Jason search for the Golden Fleece," they said. "I'm looking for the Big-O, the ultimate orgasm."

Kristin had found the Big-O. It had been a mind-blowing, soul-shattering, ass-tingling experience which was beyond her powers of expression. In fact, it had been frightening in its intensity, and she was almost glad to see Jake leave, for fear she would lose control of her own life.

Kristin considered herself on the cutting edge of social change. She was committed to civil rights action for

Negroes, a sane nuclear policy, and a standard of independence for women. And yet, had things continued as they were going, she could have abandoned everything she thought she believed in, just to be with Jake. She could be quite happy ironing his shirts and darning his socks and raising his children. She could see herself as a pioneer wife with him, living off the land in some remote hill country, willingly acquiescing to his male dominance.

But of course, that was not to be, because Jake was in Vietnam, and she was in California. Thank goodness for that, she thought. She had caught herself in time, and she would not be abandoning all she stood for. In fact, as she was telling Jake in the letter, she was going to a civil rights rally on this very night. Martin Luther King was giving a talk at the auditorium, and Kristin was a member of the committee who had made the arrangements for him to come.

> *I don't know how you feel about Dr. King, but I think he is one of the greatest human beings since Gandhi. Indeed, if Gandhi had died earlier, I would truly believe Dr. King to be a reincarnation of Gandhi. Oh, I can see your face now, Jake Culpepper. You probably have that silly-assed smile, and you are shaking your head and you are teasing me because of my intensity.*
>
> *But Jake, I need my intensity. It is the only evidence I have that I am alive. You are a beautiful man, Jake, not only physically, but inside as well. I respect your sense of honor and your dedication to duty. I wish you could respect my intensity.*
>
> *I read in the papers that there was a bomb blast at a mess hall at the airfield in Saigon. I know it is foolish to worry about everything that happens over there, and that the chances that you were involved are probably very slim. But I did read the casualty list with a degree of*

*apprehension. Take care of yourself, mister. Brief
though our interlude was, it was, to quote you,
'intense', and thus, important.*

Kristin signed the letter and put it into an envelope. She
had just finished addressing it when there was a knock on
the door.

"Kristin, it's me, Larry."

"The door's open, Larry. Come on in," Kristin called,
licking the flap and sealing the letter.

Larry Cantrell came into Kristin's apartment and looked
around. Larry was about five-ten. He moved with the
muscular grace of a jungle-cat, and thought he was in
street clothes, one could see the strength and power which
made him an honorable mention All-American football
player in his sophomore year. Even standing still, he
looked fast.

Larry was a Negro, and now his cinnamon colored face
and black hair glistened with diamonds of water from the
rain.

"Dr. King is here," Larry said, smiling broadly.

"He is? Where? Oh, Larry, can I meet him?"

"He's getting some rest now. He drove down from San
Francisco, and of course, he just arrived in San Francisco
this morning. He's been in fifteen cities this week."

"I'd say he does need a rest," Kristin said.

"But don't worry. One of his staff promised that everyone on the reception committee would get to meet him."

"Oh! Isn't that exciting?" Kristin squealed, and,
spontaneously, she hugged Larry. Larry stiffened quickly
and stepped back away from her.

"What is it?" Kristin asked. "What's wrong?"

"Nothing's wrong, girl. I just don't want some white
cop to come by and see me raping you, that's all."

Kristin laughed. "Raping me? Don't be ridiculous. I put
my arms around you, that's all. And I did it, not you."

"White cops don't always stop to figure things like that out," Larry said.

"Then we have to change that, don't we?" Kristin said, seriously.

Larry looked at Kristin, then he laughed.

"That's right, Goldilocks. Me 'n you is goin' to change the world."

The Reverend Dr. Martin Luther King's voice filled the auditorium with its resonance. It had the sing-song melodic quality which was common to southern Negro preachers, and yet, in Dr. King, this quality was carried to the highest state of the art. From King's lips the words took wing, and in every heart in the auditorium there was a response to his clarion call.

After the speech, Kristin hurried to the room in the Student Center where the reception was to be held. She showed her pass to the policeman on duty in front of the building, then crossed the lobby and started down the hall. The hall was crowded, but she had expected that. She wasn't going to be put off by the crowd. She was going to see Dr. King if she had to get down on her hands and knees and crawl under their legs.

It took Kristin several moments of skillful maneuvering, but finally she found herself in the meeting room. She stood on tiptoe, and she saw him on the other side of the room. Someone was talking to him, and he was looking at them with those deep, dark eyes which carried so much of his power.

"Hey, girl!" someone said angrily, as Kristin pushed closer to Dr. King. "What do you think you doin? Ain't no white girl got any business in here anyway."

The speaker was a young Negro girl, and her eyes reflected the years of anger and resentment which had built up in her.

"I . . . I'm sorry," Kristin said. "I just wanted to get closer to Dr. King."

"You ain't got no right," the girl said. "Why don't you go look up George Wallace. I'm sure he's makin' a speech somewhere."

"I'm sorry," Kristin said again. Hurt and embarrassed, Kristin turned and started to leave.

"Hold on, Kristin," Larry's voice called across the room. "Hold on, girl, you're not leaving. You're going to meet Dr. King."

"Please," another voice called. "Let the girl through."

Kristin felt her heart stop for a moment, because the last voice was the voice of King himself.

Larry pushed his way through the crowd, then reached out and took Kristin's hand in his own. He pulled her with him, until a moment later she was standing in front of Dr. King.

Kristin felt a fluttering in her stomach, and perspiration under her breasts. Dr. King reached out to shake her hand.

"Bring the other young lady to me," Dr. King said.

A moment later the young black woman who had spoken harshly to Kristin was standing there with them. She was looking sheepishly down at the floor.

"What is your name, my dear?" King asked Kristin.

"Kristin O'Neil."

"And yours?" he asked the black girl.

"Nicole Coleman."

Dr. King took Nicole's hand and Kristin's hand, and put them together, holding them together with his own hand.

"Nicole, behold your sister, Kristin," he said. "Kristin, behold your sister, Nicole. You are sisters in the sight of God, and what God has joined together, let no work of man put asunder."

Kristin looked at Nicole, then she smiled, and both women embraced. The others in the room cheered, and Kristin never felt a warmer, more loving feeling in her life than she did at that very moment.

*   *   *

Larry brought Kristin a Coke and handed it to her, then sat on the sofa beside her. It was nearly midnight, and Dr. King and his party had long since left. So had most of the others, and now there were no more than half a dozen who remained. Kristin was the only white person.

"I'm going this summer," Larry said.

"You're crazy, man," one of the others said. "Anyone who would go down into redneck country just to get a sandwich at some white man's lunch counter is crazy. They got people down there will break your head without thinkin' twice about it."

"You heard Dr. King, same as I did," Larry said.

"Yeah, I heard him. I heard him talkin' about non-violence. And that's the part I like."

"You didn't hear him at all," Larry scoffed. "He said we have to be prepared to accept the consequences of changing unjust laws. We aren't to be violent, but we must be prepared to accept the violence which comes to us."

"And you are ready to do that?"

"Yes," Larry said. "And so should all of us. Unless we want our grandchildren to be sitting around a lounge talking about this very same subject."

"Hey, listen, man. You think our grandparents could'a been sittin' aroun' like we are now? They couldn't even get in school, let alone a university. I say things are moving along all right, and we should just let it be."

"You think our brothers and sisters in Mississippi could sit around a college lounge like this?" Larry asked.

"That's their problem."

"No, man, it's our problem. And all of us have to work on it, not just Dr. King."

"I don't know, Larry. You could get yourself killed down there," Kristin said.

Larry looked at Kristin.

"When I say it is our problem, I mean it's yours, too," he said. "Black and white, we are in this together. That is, if you mean what you say about wanting change."

"That's not fair, Larry," Kristin said, her eyes misting over quickly. "You know that I mean what I say."

"Then how about going with me?"

"What?"

"Go with me," Larry said. "Go to Mississippi with me."

"Larry," one of the others said. "If you think it's dangerous for you down there alone, you get caught somewhere with a white girl. They'll lynch you for sure."

"There is that risk," Larry said, looking coolly at Kristin. "How about it, Kristin? Are you more than talk?"

"What . . . exactly, did you have in mind?"

"I thought we could get another couple, and the four of us would drive through Mississippi. We would start at the north end of the state and drive all the way down to the Gulf coast. We would drink from white water fountains, eat in white restaurants, and camp in white picnic areas. What do you say?"

"Who would go with us?" Kristin asked.

"I don't know. We'll find somebody."

"Jimmy and I will go," Nicole spoke up.

"What? Wait a minute, baby, you ain't talkin' for me," Jimmy said.

"Then I'll find someone who is man enough to take your place," Nicole said, and the others laughed.

"What about it, Jimmy?" Larry asked. "Are you going with us?"

Jimmy ran his hand through his hair and sighed, then he threw his head back and laughed.

"Sheeeiit," he said. "I might as well let some cracker take a shot at my black ass. Defensive linebackers been after it for four years now, and they ain't got it yet."

"You're sure you want me to go?" Kristin asked. "I'll just be more danger for everyone."

"You're my sister aren't you?" Nicole asked.

"Yes," Kristin answered with a smile.

Nicole took Kristin's hand. "Then you're goin' with us."

CHAPTER FIVE

Major General Barclay rode comfortably in the deeply cushioned backseat of the big air-conditioned Buick staff car. The car was highly shined and red flags bearing two white stars fluttered importantly from the two front fenders. General Barclay was shielded from the heat and the stares of the curious Vietnamese by the darkly tinted glass, and though he could see them, they couldn't see him.

The car picked its way through the sputtering cyclos, the darting taxis, and the brightly painted busses with all the authority due its high-ranking occupant. General Barclay found the busses particularly interesting. They were so crowded that many people found it necessary to dangle out the windows or ride on the back bumper, hanging on to whatever they could grab. The tops of the busses were heavily laden with the personal belongings of the passengers: boxes, baskets, bicycles, sewing machines, chickens tied together by their legs, and goats lying calmly, unsurprised by anything that was going on around them. Occasionally one of the passengers would climb to the top of the bus, pick through the luggage until he found what he was looking for, then return to his spot with the others.

General Barclay was visiting Henri Marquand because Marquand had his finger on the pulse of Vietnamese life. General Barclay had the theory that most of the information the U.S. Army received was colored by the vested interests of the parties who provided the information. If the Vietnamese Army wanted a certain area to be pacified, they said that it was. If, for some reason they wished to maintain a heavy military presence in a certain area, they just told the U.S. that the area was heavily infested with VC.

Henri Marquand had no vested interests, other than his own survival. General Barclay believed that any information he received from Marquand would be valid information.

That was the expressed purpose for Barclay's frequent visits to Marquand's country estate. The real reason was somewhat more earthy. Marquand was able to provide General Barclay with lovely, clean and discreet young women. Barclay had learned of Marquand's unique service from the man he had relieved, Major General Phillip Pinnell.

"After all," Pinnell said. "It's not like we are some rear-rank, buck-assed privates. We can't just go down to Plantation Row or 100 P Alley and pick us out a good-looking young whore. My God, can you imagine what the stateside papers would do with something like that? And yet, we have needs just like other men. That's why this Marquand thing is so perfect. Besides, Marquand is a good man to know. He can cut through all the phoney bullshit that we have to put up with from the ARVN commanders."

Barclay had taken Pinnell's advice, and in the eight months he had been in the country, he had visited Marquand at least twice a month. Now, he heard that Marquand had a new girl, a real European princess. That, Barclay wanted to see.

General Barclay's suite of rooms at the Rex Hotel were actually quite nice. But compared with the estate of Henri Marquand, he might as well have been living in a barracks with the enlisted men. Marquand's estate was as beautiful as anything Barclay had ever seen anywhere. Exquisitely tended gardens, cool splashing fountains, and well-fed, beautiful people created a new world. Barclay was affected the same way every time he visited.

The car came to a stop beneath the portico.

"Wait in the car," Barclay said to his driver. "I'll be a couple of hours."

"Yes, sir, take your time, sir," the driver answered.

"I intend to take as much time as I deem necessary," Barclay snapped back, a bit irritated by the driver's insolence.

"Monsieur Marquand is by the pool, General," a Vietnamese houseboy said.

Barclay thanked him and walked around to the pool. There were half a dozen beautiful, bikini-clad blondes in and around the pool.

"Ah, General Barclay, what a pleasant surprise this is. Welcome," Marquand said.

Marquand was wearing a pair of white swimming trunks and they showed off his deep tan to perfection. Marquand was a connoisseur of fine food, and his every meal was a gourmet's delight, but he had managed to maintain a trim figure despite all that. He was, in addition to being exceptionally wealthy, very handsome, and that added to the long list of qualifications to make him a successful playboy.

"I thought we could talk about some of the village pacification programs we have recently instituted," General Barclay said. "I want to see what you've heard."

"Certainly, certainly we can," Marquand said. "But later, eh? I have a new young lady I would like you to meet."

"The, uh . . ." Barclay coughed. "The Princess?" he asked.

Marquand smiled broadly. "Ah, mon General, I see you have heard of her."

"Yes," Barclay said.

"Would you like to meet her now?"

"Yes, I think I would." Barclay said. His tongue thickened so that it was difficult for him to talk.

Marquand turned to a white-jacketed servant who stood near him, and spoke in rapid Vietnamese. Barclay heard the name Melinda.

"I think you will appreciate her," Marquand said. "In the meantime, a gin and tonic, perhaps?"

Barclay accepted the cool drink, and was half finished when Melinda came out to them. She smiled at Marquand, then greeted Barclay by extending her hand, palm down.

Barclay took a short gasp. He had never seen anyone quite as beautiful as this creature before him. She had long, dark hair, and deep blue eyes beneath delicately arched eyebrows. Her cheekbones were high and her skin was absolutely perfect. Her lips were full and sensual. The girl was smiling, as enigmatically as the Mona Lisa.

"How are you?" Barclay asked.

The smile broadened.

"Isn't that for you to decide, General?" she asked.

Melinda's English was perfect, but there was just the suggestion of a French accent, a subtle softening of the words which tended to caress the language. And still there was that smile, a beautiful twinkling of the eye that made it appear as if she were drawing intense pleasure from the situation.

"For me to decide?"

"Yes, isn't that why you sent for me. Don't you wish to make love, General?" Melinda asked.

Barclay tried to answer, but he found that he was quite unable to speak.

Melinda laughed, a lilting, musical laugh, and she took his hand in hers, then led him from the pool to a nearby bedroom.

"This is what you wanted, isn't it?" she asked, her huge, dark eyes pools of false innocence.

"Yes," Barclay said, finally finding his voice.

Melinda put her arms around Barclay's neck and pulled him to her.

From the first moment of Melinda's kiss, Barclay became disassociated from reality. All thought and feeling were blotted out, with the exception of the white heat of the kiss and the spreading fire of his sexual arousal. He was never aware of actually removing his clothes, nor could he remember precisely how or when Melinda removed hers. But he found himself in bed with her, feeling her wonderfully smooth skin, her soft curves and firm breasts. Her expert yet passionate lovemaking beckoned him to the ultimate explosion. It wasn't until several moments later that Barclay realized that it was all over, and that his system had been subjected to such a heavy charge of sex that all other senses had been redirected to cope with it.

Barclay lay in bed until reality returned, then he looked at the beautiful creature who was lying beside him. Her head was propped up on an elbow and her hair hung down across her shoulder, not hiding her breast, but draping it to make it even more sensual.

Barclay reached for her, but Melinda moved back, deftly avoiding his grasp.

"Uh-uh, lover," she said. "I like to leave my men hungry for more."

Melinda got out of bed, slipped a silk robe over her nudity, kissed Barclay lightly on his forehead, then left the room.

A few minutes later Barclay was standing beside the swimming pool with Marquand, holding a fresh drink.

"What do you think of her?" Marquand asked.

"Monsieur Marquand, I must have her again," Barclay said, his voice almost pleading in its urgency.

Marquand smiled. "And, so you shall, General, so you shall," he said. "Now, tell me about the bridge at An Than."

"The bridge at An Than?"

"Yes, aren't you dedicating it today? I would have thought you would be there for its opening."

"No, Major Culpepper is the senior American advisor in the area," General Barclay said. "Besides, he has been working with the Vietnamese for six months now. I'm sure they'd rather have him there than someone from MACV."

*   *   *

The people of Cao Lanh had turned out to attend the grand opening of a new bridge built for them by United States Army Engineers.

The old bridge had been of wood and rope, and it allowed foot traffic, bicycles and carts to cross the small river which separated the highway from the village. No vehicles could use the old bridge, though there was another bridge about ten miles downriver which vehicles could use, and a dirt road which ran back to the village. Because of that, the village wasn't completely isolated, and the small wood and rope bridge served very well to allow foot traffic across. It had served its purpose without problem, until the last rainy season, when a flood destroyed the bridge.

The Vietnamese government requested the U.S. Corps of Engineers to build another bridge, and the Vietnamese government drew up the plans. The villagers were pleased to get a new bridge, but they didn't realize that the bridge replacing the one they lost would be a big steel and concrete bridge capable of allowing five-ton trucks to cross. That meant that their village, which had been spared the military traffic, and, consequently, any of the fighting, could become embroiled in the war. The villagers were not pleased about that at all.

"So, Major Culpepper," Colonel Nghya said, smiling, and looking at the flag-draped bridge. "It is a wonderful thing we have done for the poor people of Cao Lanh, is it not? This shows the concern the Vietnamese Government has for its people."

"Yes," Jake said. "But Colonel, I overheard some of the villagers talking. They are not pleased with this bridge. They wanted a small one, like the one that was lost in the flood."

"Ah, they are peasants, unable to think of the future of

their village," Colonel Nghya said. "Pay no attention to them."

"But weren't you just saying that this bridge proves your government's concern for the villagers?"

"Of course, and this only supports my point. You have been here for one-half of your tour, Major. You should realize by now that our country is divided into two classes of people. There are those of us who, by the results of our own initiative, are the leaders, and the others, who by their sloth and laziness, are the followers. Obviously, to such people, abstract thoughts of the future are not possible. These people don't really know what they want. It is up to us to tell them."

"So much for the principles of democratic reform," Jake said sarcastically.

Colonel Nghya, who was already smoking, lit another cigarette from the butt of his old one, then flipped the old one away. Half a dozen children ran to the discarded cigarette butt, fought over it, and one of them emerged victorious, happily taking the few remaining puffs as he ran away.

"Please, do not misunderstand," Jake's Vietnamese counterpart told him. "We are for democratic reform, but first I think we must create a stable enough society to accept democracy. Don't you agree?"

"I'm not sure that I do agree," Jake said. "It seems to me that such a policy of waiting for a stable society is merely an excuse to delay democratic reforms. Isn't that what President Diem said? Wasn't he merely waiting for a stable society?"

"President Diem was making no progress with the war," Colonel Nghya said. "He was so busy consolidating power for himself and other members of his family that there was none left over for anyone else."

"The military, you mean?"

"Yes. After all, if stability and democracy are going to come to Vietnam, it is going to have to come as a result of a working partnership between the military and the government.''

"With no regard to the wishes of the people," Jake said.

Colonel Nghya removed the cigarette from his mouth by using his ring finger and little finger, and he held it out in an almost effeminate way. He smiled at Jake.

"You think to trap me, do you? Well, I'm sorry, Major, but I won't fall into your trap. Perhaps we don't always take into account the wishes of our people, but I assure you, we do take into consideration their best interests. Ah, I see the band is formed. They are about to play the national anthems of our two countries. This is quite a moment, Major. Visible evidence, through this beautiful bridge, that the policies of our governments coincide, even though you and I may have our own differences of opinion.''

The band was from the Vietnamese Army, and they were dressed in starched khaki uniforms with gleaming silver helmet liners and white Sam Browne belts. At the signal from their director they raised their instruments, each one gleaming so that the bridge and the village was reflected in the bells and tubings of the brass pieces.

The first notes of *The Star-Spangled Banner* began, and despite Jake's uneasiness over participating in what he felt was an affront to the villagers, he still felt the same sense of thrill that he always did at hearing the national anthem played.

With an amazing sense of ironic coincidence, the first explosions on the bridge went off just as the anthem reached the part of 'bombs bursting in air'. At the first thump most people just looked toward the bridge in surprise. But the first was followed by a series of explosions, and the entire bridge went up in smoke. The villagers screamed and the dignitaries who were standing ready to cut the ribbons dove for cover, along with the soldiers and the members of the band.

Jake watched from the reviewing stand. He was far

enough from the explosions not to be in any personal danger from flying debris, but close enough to watch with morbid fascination as the bridge slowly crumpled, then fell into the water to become a useless pile of twisted metal and broken concrete.

The smoke was still hanging in the air when a soldier reported to Colonel Nghya. The soldier spoke in Vietnamese, but Jake, by virtue of his Vietnamese language class and his six months in Vietnam, understood him.

"Colonel, did he say they have the sappers trapped?"

"Yes," Colonel Nghya answered. "We had patrols all around here, anticipating something like this."

"You mean you knew the bridge was going to be blown?"

"We received some letters threatening to do so," Nghya said. He smiled. "Now it seems as if our VC friends have been—what is the quaint English saying? Hoisted by their own petard? Come, would you like to go with us?"

"Yes," Jake said.

Jake followed Colonel Nghya to a nearby jeep, and seconds later they were roaring down the road with a roostertail of dust flying behind them. Less than a mile from the edge of the village they saw an armored personnel carrier and another jeep. Three dozen Vietnamese soldiers were standing in a semi-circle around four young Vietnamese men. None of the young men were armed, nor did any of them have on an armband or anything else which would suggest that they were VC. One of the four had been shot and he was being supported by two of the others. His stomach was bright red with blood, and as Jake looked at him, he realized that the young man was going to die quickly if he didn't get medical attention soon.

"Colonel, that man needs a medic," Jake said.

"That man is one of the ones who just blew up our bridge," Colonel Nghya answered. "He will be attended to when he answers the questions we have for him."

"You can't deny him medical attention," Jake said.

"Major, I remind you that your duty as a military advisor does not extend to questions of my domestic policy. And even if it did, you have advisory status only, not command status."

"Nevertheless, I do not intend to stand by and be a party to this. Either you get that man medical attention right now, or I shall return to Saigon at once, and speak to General Barclay. I'm sure General Barclay will wish to speak to your General."

Colonel Nghya sighed.

"Very well, Major. If it will make you feel any better, I will attend to his wounds," Nghya paused for a moment. "And then I will have him executed."

Colonel Nghya called to one of his officers, and a couple of men took the wounded man over to one of the jeeps. The wounded man was laid down, and a couple of men bent over him to start to administer to his wounds.

"Thank you, Colonel," Jake started. "I think you will find that . . ."

Jake's comment was suddenly interrupted by an explosion, and he looked over toward the jeep where the wounded man had been taken. There was still a puff of smoke at the jeep, but where the wounded man had been there was now nothing but a pile of bloody rags. The wounded man had managed to set off a grenade just as the medics bent over to help him. He'd killed himself and the two Vietnamese medics.

"Oh, my God," Jake said.

Colonel Nghya laughed, and Jake looked at him, shocked that anyone could laugh at such a moment.

"Oh, Major, don't look at me with such shock on your face," Colonel Nghya said. "The blood of those men is on your hands. You are the one who insisted that I provide him with medical treatment. Maybe now you have learned a valuable lesson in the way we conduct our war."

Jake held onto the windshield of the jeep and fought against the urge to be sick.

* * *

Three days later, General Barclay stopped by to see Jake at his field headquarters. Jake was surprised by the General's visit, and he stood quickly to welcome him.

"Sit down, sit down, Jake," Barclay said. "I'll only be a few minutes. I have something for you."

General Barclay opened a manila envelope he was carrying and brought out a paper and a box.

"Jake, you have been on more than a dozen operations now, and you have been in combat situations every time. I'm told that you have always handled yourself in a way to make the U.S. Army proud. You were also involved in the capture of the VC sappers at the Cao Lanh bridge the other day."

"There was nothing to that, sir. The ARVN's already had them by the time Colonel Nghya and I got there."

"Did they?" General Barclay asked. He chuckled. "Well, maybe that's why Nghya did it. Maybe he's trying to make his own action look a bit more heroic."

"What are you talking about, sir?"

"Nghya has put himself in for a rather high-ranking Vietnamese medal for his part in capturing the VC the other day. And he has recommended that we give you the Bronze Star."

Jake chuckled. "Neither of us deserve anything, General."

"Well, now I'm not so sure about that," Barclay said. "You have performed every duty I've assigned you in a forthright manner, and, whether or not this little episode deserves a Bronze Star or not, I'm sure that you do. So, I'm giving you one."

"Not with the "V" device, I hope. Because if so, I won't accept it. I won't be a hypocrite."

General Barclay laughed. "I rather thought Iron Pants' son would say something like thing like that," he said. "So, you'll be pleased to know that the Bronze Star is being awarded for performance of duty, and not for valor."

Jake smiled and reached for the paper. "In that case, I'll accept."

"Good, good. And perhaps you'll accept this as well, Colonel." General Barclay pulled out another sheet of paper and handed it to Jake.

"Colonel?"

"Your orders came this morning. You made Lieutenant Colonel, Jake. Congratulations."

Jake smiled broadly and took the paper which had his promotion orders.

"I, uh, took the liberty of bringing you a set of silver leaves," General Barclay said, stepping up to Jake and taking the gold oak leaf from his collar. General Barclay put the new leaf in place. "This is the same set of leaves your father put on my collar ten years ago. There, that looks much nicer, don't you think?"

Jake stepped over to a mirror and admired his image, turning so that the silver leaf of his new rank was prominent.

"Yes, sir," he said. "I must confess to a certain appreciation of it myself."

"Jake, about the incident at the bridge the other day. I've already spoken with Colonel Nghya's superiors. You were right, absolutely right, to insist upon medical treatment for the wounded VC. Hell, the fact that he set off the grenade doesn't mean anything. He would have done it sooner or later anyway, and perhaps with a greater loss of life."

"I keep trying to tell myself that, General," Jake said.

"Well, it's true. Oh, by the way, I also spoke with Colonel Nghya's superior about one of the prisoners, a man named Mot. I had him freed."

"*You* had him freed? Why did you do that, sir?"

"Monsieur Henri Marquand made a personal request on Mot's behalf. Mot is a good man, Jake. Hell, he's no communist. He works for Marquand, and has worked for him from the time he was born. In fact, Mot's father was an employee of Marquand, and he was killed fighting against the Viet Minh on the side of the French.''

"But he was with the others, General," Jake said.

"Marquand explained that. Mot had just gone to see the bridge dedication. When the VC blew it up, he got scared and ran. He was just picked up in the sweep by accident. Listen, if I have learned one thing in this country, it is to recognize our friends. Now you take Marquand. He was born and raised in this country, and so was his father and grandfather. He speaks Vietnamese like a native, because he is a native. And yet, he is also one of us, if you get my meaning.'' General Barclay put his finger to his skin and then to his eye. "He's a white man, Jake, and he and his family have had to shoulder the 'white man's burden' for a long, long while. I often visit Marquand, and I always come away from those visits refreshed. I tell you, Jake, you've got to find someone in this country in whom you can have complete confidence.''

"Maybe so," Jake said. He ran his hand through his hair and sighed. "General, the truth is, I don't know who or what to believe anymore. This . . . this Phoenix business, for instance. I feel that I should tell you how I am handling it.''

"I know how you are handling it," General Barclay interrupted. "I haven't said anything about it, because, well, goddammit, Jake, to tell the truth, I passed it off to Purcell and then to you because I didn't want to deal with it myself. I figure that kind of business is better left in the hands of the CIA anyway. They are trying to involve the Army, perhaps to spread some of the responsibility around. But I just wash my hands of it.''

"Like Pilate, General?" Jake asked.

"Yeah," General Barclay said. "Like Pilate." Barclay smiled. "Ah, what the hell, Jake. I've only got four months left in this place, and you have less than six. This time next year all this will be behind us forever, and we'll be sitting in an O-club somewhere in the States telling drunken war tales. What do you say?''

"General, I say that day can't come soon enough for me,'' Jake answered.

The brakes of the Vietnamese Army truck squealed as it stopped at the gate to the Marquand plantation.

"Get out here,'' the lieutenant called.

Mot, who was riding in back of the truck hopped down without a word.

"Next time we catch you, your whoremaster will not be able to free you,'' the lieutenant said. ''I know you are Cong.''

Mot looked at the lieutenant, but he still didn't speak.

"Come. If we stay longer I'll shoot him, and then I'll be in trouble,'' the lieutenant said.

The driver, who had learned to drive a vehicle only in the past few weeks, let out the clutch and drove away at high speed.

Mot started up the long road to the main buildings. He had been stupid to get caught. He hadn't been involved in the destruction of the bridge, but he had known the bridge was going to be destroyed and he went to see it. He thought he would learn how to do it in case he ever had to blow one himself.

The government had suspected that the bridge would be destroyed, however, and troops were deployed in such a way as to catch Mot and the others as they ran. Had it not been for Marquand's intervention, Mot would probably be dead now. The others were.

"Mot?'' a voice called, and Mot looked off the road to see Marquand. Marquand was on horseback, and he leaned over to pat the animal's neck. Marquand was wearing tan riding breeches and a lime green shirt. He was also wearing a holster and pistol. ''Were you injured?''

"No,'' Mot said.

"You did a foolish thing, you know.''

"I only meant to watch the dedication," Mot said. "Invitations were issued."

"Yes," Marquand said. He continued to pat the horse's neck. "I know you are with the NLF, Mot." He sighed. "I rather hoped that none of the plantation people would get involved. I hoped we were all one big, happy family."

"I am Vietnamese," Mot said.

"As am I."

"Then you can understand why I must get involved. Unless your sympathies are with the Americans."

"My sympathies are with myself," Marquand answered. "I have no room for politics. My concern over your involvement is not with politics, but with your safety. I will do what I can for you, Mot, when I can. I will keep your secret, and when my intervention is helpful and does not place me at risk, I will intercede on your behalf. But I tell you now. My concern is for myself. I intend to keep all doors open, and that includes the Saigon government and the Americans."

"I understand," Mot said.

"Go to your mother now. She is worried about you."

"Yes," Mot said. "Thank you."

The plantation consisted of the main house, then several smaller houses. The larger of the smaller houses were actually quite comfortable, and in the nicest of them all lived Mot's mother, Cao Ngyuen Le.

Le welcomed her son with an anxious kiss, then happily drew water for him to take a bath. For the two days he was held captive, she feared she would lose him as she had lost her husband so many years ago.

Le was nearly forty-five, but one would have guessed she was much, much younger. She had high cheekbones, and her dark eyes sparkled like black diamonds, framed by eyelashes as beautiful as the most delicate lace. Her skin was smooth and golden, and her movements were as graceful as palm fronds stirred by a breeze.

For a short while after her husband was killed she had

been the mistress of Henri Marquand. She had terminated that relationship when she learned that mistress was all she would ever be. Marquand had no intention of marrying her. She broke off the relationship because she was Catholic and very serious about her religion. She could not continue to live with him in adultery without placing her soul in mortal jeopardy.

Sometimes Le wished she had left things as they were, whether it was a sin or not, because it had been an extremely pleasant arrangement. Had she not broken it off she might well be living in the main house now. And yet, she knew that Marquand had never really loved her. He had enjoyed her company, and he had enjoyed sharing his bed with her, but he had never really loved her.

For her part, Le had been proud of the fact that the man who was called ''the Whoremaster of the Orient'' had been able to find satisfaction with her. He had his choice of the world's most beautiful woman, and yet he had chosen her.

Sometimes Le recalled the moments of passion, and she would imagine herself in bed with Marquand. She allowed him to make love to her in her mind. She drifted sensually along with her erotic thoughts, losing herself in sexual fantasy. Then she would feel very guilty, and she would say her rosary and pray for forgiveness.

She confessed her lust to Father Sachs.

''It isn't just Henri Marquand,'' she confided to Father Sachs. ''I must confess to the sin of lustful thoughts. I consider myself to be a young woman, still. It is difficult to be without a man, and sometimes my hunger is so great I would debase myself with any man.''

Le had made that confession to Father Sachs just yesterday, and as he left, it seemed to her that he held her hand much longer and a bit tighter than necessary. The expression in his eyes as he told her goodbye had also been somewhat discomfiting.

But all that was behind her now. Now her concern was with the safety of her son. Marquand had secured his release from the authorities this time. Le knew that if he was arrested again, there would be nothing anyone could do.

CHAPTER SIX

"Hey, what do you say we get somethin' to eat at that little store up there?" Larry asked.

Larry was driving the old Plymouth stationwagon that he, Kristin, Jimmy and Nicole had bought in Memphis, and they were on Highway 21 in Neshoba County, Mississippi. For the last six weeks they had been a part of the Mississippi Summer Project, a civil rights drive to register black voters throughout the state.

Their summer had not been easy. They had been subjected to high-pressure fire hoses, dogs and truncheons. They had been cursed, spat upon, and pelted with rocks, bottles, rotten fruit, and even excrement. However, they were still alive, and that was more than could be said for three of their co-workers: Andy Goodman, Mike Schwerner and James Chaney. Officially, the three young men were listed as missing, but there was little doubt in the minds of any of the civil rights workers who had come to Mississippi as to what had happened to them. Kristin prayed that they were still alive, but she had an uneasy feeling that their worst fears were true.

"You want to stop at that place? Man, if we are gonna integrate somethin', I don't want to get my head busted over some redneck store like that," Jimmy said.

"I'm not thinking integration," Larry said. "I'm thinking eating. We'll stop down here and let Kristin go buy some stuff. You know, bologna, bread, mayonnaise. . . ."

"Maybe a pickle," Jimmy said. "Man, wouldn't a big ol' dill pickle be good about now?"

Larry stopped the car and turned off the engine. They were near a heavily wooded area, and they could hear the breeze stirring the leaves of the trees. Frogs croaked from the cypress knees, and, from somewhere deep in the forest, a working woodpecker drummed loudly, its efforts amplified by the resonance of the swamp.

"Listen to that, doesn't it sound peaceful?" Larry said.

"Peaceful? Man, I bet that place is just crawlin' with snakes. Rattlesnakes, cottonmouths, pythons," Jimmy said.

"There are no pythons indigenous to North America," Kristin said.

"Yeah? Well, it's just like these redneck bastards to import some," Jimmy said. He opened the back door and it squeaked and groaned. Larry laughed. "And now the sound of the twentieth century intrudes upon the scene."

"Twentieth century?" Jimmy said. "Man, who you tryin' to kid? Are you tryin' to tell me this here is a twentieth century car? This is a nineteenth century car if there ever was one. This car is some old ugly shit, man. You have to go a long way to find a car older or uglier than this one."

"It's only ten years old," Larry defended. "This is a '54 model."

"I think you got that confused, man. I think this is a '24."

Larry laughed. "I don't think they even made station wagons in '24."

Kristin got out a paper and a pencil.

"Okay, bologna, bread, mayonnaise, milk—anything else?"

"My dill pickle, girl. Don't forget my dill pickle."

Kristin smiled and wrote it down. "And a jar of dill pickles."

"Kristin, can you carry all that back here?" Nicole asked.

"Yes," Kristin said.

"I'll get the quilt out and spread out a place for us to eat," Nicole said. "Look, there's a nice patch of grass in the shade of that tree, right over there. We can have a picnic lunch."

"Ain't that sweet?" Jimmy said. "All day singin' 'n dinner on the ground, just like our brothers 'n sisters at a camp meetin'."

"A camp meeting might not hurt you," Nicole said.

Larry had stopped the car about two hundred yards from a small country store, and Kristin walked along the edge of the blacktop road toward the store. It was early August, and it was hot, but the trees were tall enough so that Kristin was able to walk in the shade. The weeds and grass were full of dust, and as she walked through them, little puffs rose from her feet. Grasshoppers and other insects fluttered before her, and occasionally a cockleburr would stick to her and she would have to stop and pick it off.

Kristin thought of the summer she had just spent. There had been some wonderful, exciting highlights. They had registered hundreds, perhaps thousands of new voters. Old Negroes in their sixties and seventies, who had never had the privilege of casting a vote in their lifetime, would be able to vote in this year's election. Kristin felt very good about that.

But there had been some bad times, too. There were several incidents where hecklers gathered and the mood grew ugly.

The police were there during those times, and the civil rights workers were told that the police were there to protect them from the angry citizens of the state. Kristin wondered, however, why the police stood in solemn, helmeted lines, facing the workers, instead of the crowd of hecklers who had gathered nearby. She wondered, also, why, when the citizens began shooting BB-guns at the civil rights workers, the police made no attempt to stop it. And when the police did go into action it seemed as if the person on the receiving end of the policeman's billyclub was always a civil rights worker.

Kristin was almost to the little store. It was of unpainted wood, with a sagging wooden porch out front. Some of the boards of the porch were rotted out, and Kristin believed that many of the boards on the wall were in just as bad a condition, though they were covered with large, sheet-tin signs.

"IF YOUR SNUFF IS TOO STRONG, IT'S WRONG. USE TUBE ROSE."

"R.C. COLA. BEST, BY TASTE TEST."

There were two gas pumps in front of the store. They were round, with glass cylinders at the top. There was a hand pump to the side, and gas was dispensed by pumping the handle back and forth until the glass was filled. The glass container was graduated to mark ten gallons. The amount of gas sold was determined by the graduation in the glass cylinder.

An old black pickup truck was parked to one side of the store. The body of the truck was rusting, and one of the doors was wired shut. Tire marks behind it, however, showed that it was a working truck, and not merely an abandoned vehicle like the car on the opposite side of the store. The wheels, hood and engine were all gone from the car, and weeds grew up through the place where the engine should have been. A rusting license-plate on the front bumper of the car said "Alabama, Heart of Dixie". The plate was dated 1956.

The door to the store opened just as Kristin reached the front drive. A man came out, drinking an orange drink. He was dressed in coveralls and a St. Louis Cardinals baseball cap. His face was wrinkled, though from age or the hardness of his life, Kristin couldn't tell. He looked right at her but Kristin wasn't sure he even saw her. He got into the old pickup truck, started it with a whining grind of starter and engine, and then drove away with the rattling nearly drowning out the crunching sound of the tires on the gravel.

It was hot in the store, though a tall stand-up fan roared near the counter. It was pointed toward the grocery clerk, a heavy-set woman in a bright print dress. The woman was sitting on a stool, reading a *True Confessions* magazine.

The store smelled of animal feed and soap. The floor was of uncovered wood and looked just like the porch. Kristin walked back to the meat counter and peered through the glass. The clerk saw her, then came back to her.

"Heavens, dear, I didn't even hear you drive up. Can I help you with somethin'?"

"I'd like two pounds of sliced bologna," Kristin said.

The woman began cutting the meat from a large roll.

"D'ja hear 'bout them three bodies they just found over to the dam?" She asked, as she carved thick slices with a big butcher knife.

"No," Kristin said. "No, I haven't heard anything about it."

"They was freedom riders, down from N'Yawk. Two of 'em was, anyway. The third one was a colored boy from Meridian."

"Goodman, Schwerner and Chaney," Kristin gasped.

"Yeah, that's who it was. I 'member the name Goodman anyway. That's a joosh name, ain't it?"

"I . . . I don't know," Kristin said. She felt sick and she put her hand on the edge of the counter. Until this moment Kristin had always held on to the irrational hope that they would be found alive and well, that Andy Goodman would show up somewhere, smiling at her, anxious to swap stories about their Mississippi experiences.

"Well, it's a shame," the woman said. She tore off a long roll of brown butcher's paper, and wrapped the meat carefully, then taped it down. "I mean, I don't want Yankees comin' down here agitatin' our colored folk, any more'n anyone else. But I sure don't want to see any of 'em kilt. The press up north got enough bad to say 'bout Mississippi as it is, without addin' on to it by some damnfool killin's. The truth is, those young men prob'ly had good hearts, 'n prob'ly thought they was doin' good. But they just didn't stop to think of the trouble they was causin' for ever'one. Now they are off down here dead, 'n their mamas is gonna be cryin' for 'em back home. Their mamas prob'ly shouldn't'a let 'em come in the first place. Anythin' else I can get for you, chile?''

The woman handed the brown package across the meat counter to Kristin, then she saw that Kristin was crying.

''What is it? Why are you cryin' like that?'' The woman gasped. ''Good Lord, don' tell me you are one o' them civil rights workers? Did you know them boys?''

Kristin nodded. ''I knew them. I knew one of them quite well.''

''Oh dear,'' the woman said. The woman looked through the dirty front window of the little store. ''Are you here with coloreds?''

''Yes,'' Kristin said.

The woman's eyes grew wide with fear. ''Chile, I'm here all alone,'' she said. ''I ain't never caused nobody any trouble, 'n I swear to you, I didn't know nothin' 'bout those boys 'till I heard about them findin' the bodies this mawnin.' Please, don't let the coloreds with you hurt me.''

The woman's frightened reaction so surprised Kristin that she quit crying, and she looked directly at her.

''Why are you so frightened?'' she asked. ''What do you expect to happen?''

''Please,'' the woman said. ''You don't have to pay nothin' for the bologna. It's yours. Just, don't let 'em hurt me.''

''Don't worry,'' Kristin said. ''They aren't even with me. We are parked down the road. And I have every intention of paying for my purchases.''

Kristin finished buying her list, then left the store,

puzzled and a little angered by the woman's irrational reaction. Then, as she walked back toward the car, she thought again of the three young men whose bodies had just turned up this morning.

Kristin remembered the three young men from the training program they had all attended at Western College for Women, at Oxford, Ohio.

"Some of you will be arrested, some of you will be beaten, and some of you may lose your lives," James Foreman had told them. Foreman was an experienced civil rights worker, and he was there to tell the new recruits what they would face when they went to Mississippi to help register voters.

Kristin, Larry, Jimmy and Nicole had attended the training session, along with 700 others. Schwerner, Goodman and Chaney had been among them.

Kristin never got to know Schwerner and Chaney very well, but she remembered Andrew Goodman. He was a slim, clean-cut, dark-headed young man, who believed intensely in the cause. Kristin remembered that he was once selected to play the role of a jeering antagonist, and he played the role well, believing the realism would help the others. Afterward, he was upset and told Kristin, "Even though I didn't believe a thing I shouted, I was almost caught up in the emotion of it. I touched the animal part of human nature, Kristin, and I found out that we all have it. It's frightening, and I didn't like it. I didn't like it one bit."

Kristin didn't see Andy again after the training session ended, though they did make a tentative date to meet after the summer's work was completed.

"I tell you what I think we should do," Jimmy said, his words interrupting Kristin's musing. Kristin had told the others the news of the three bodies, as soon as she returned, and they had discussed it for a while, until finally they fell silent, each lost in their own thoughts.

"What should we do?" Larry asked.

Jimmy took a large bite from his sandwich. His face was set in an expression of fierce anger, and he chewed thoughtfully for a moment. "I think we should get the hell out of this redneck state, get us a bunch of brothers, then start back through Mississippi, kickin' ever' white ass we find."

"Including Kristin's white ass?" Nicole asked.

"No, of course not," Jimmy said. "But ever' other white ass."

"Jimmy, in case you didn't notice, two of the bodies they found this morning were white," Larry said.

"Goddammit!" Jimmy shouted, and he threw his sandwich away angrily. "Goddammit, goddammit, goddammit!"

"Whooee," a strange voice suddenly said. "Now I'd say that's one pissed-off nigger. What you so pissed off about, nigger?"

Kristin gasped, and looked around. There were at least half a dozen white men coming toward them, and every one of them was armed.

"What do you want?" Nicole asked.

"What do we want? What do we want?" One of the men taunted. He spat out a stream of tobacco and looked toward one of the other men. "You hear this here girl, Harley Mack? She's wantin' to know what we want."

The one called Harley Mack was younger than the others. He was in his mid-to-late twenties, while the others appeared to be in their thirties and forties. All were dressed in khaki pants and khaki shirts, and all were wearing badges.

"Well, now, I tell you what I might want," Harley Mack said. He rubbed the front of his pants. "I might be wantin' a little poontang."

One of the other men laughed. "Harley Mack, would that be 'coon-poon-tang'?"

All the men laughed at that one.

"Why don't you just go on away and leave us alone?" Kristin said. "We weren't bothering anyone."

"Well, now, we can't just let you go," the first spokes-man said. He spat another stream of tobacco. "You see, the truth is, we all been made deputies when they formed a posse to find them dead civil rights workers, 'n now we is swore to uphold the law. I reckon that means we gotta take you in."

"Take us in for what?" Larry asked. "What law have we broken?"

"Well, sir, for one thing, you are trespassin' on private property."

"We just stopped along the road to eat," Larry said.

"Well, now, that may be true. But you see, you done crossed over that ditch there. The ditch is the boundary of the road easement. On this side of the ditch you are on private property. Fac' is, you are on my cousin's property."

"What we gonna do with 'em, L.B.?"

L.B. spit his quid out, then he scratched his cheek.

"Well, I tell you, what with all the excitement of findin' them other bodies 'n all, I think they would just get in the way if we took 'em to the jailhouse."

Kristin began to feel a little easier. Maybe they were going to let them go.

"We could take 'em to the old smokehouse over there," Harley Mack said, pointing. "It ain't used no more."

"Yeah, we could do that," L.B. said.

"What about their car, L.B.? All the Feds around here, if they see the car they'll start askin' questions."

"I could torch it," Harley Mack suggested. He giggled. "I'm gettin' pretty good at that. The other one went up pretty good."

"You!" Kristin said. "You burned Andy's car."

"Harley Mack, you gotta big mouth, you know that?" L.B. said angrily. "Don't listen to him, girl, he didn' do nothin' of the kind."

"Shit, let's jus' kill 'em 'n dump 'em in the swamp," one of the others said. He smiled, a yellow-toothed, ugly smile. "We gots to feed our alligator garfish a nigger ever now'n then, just to keep 'em happy."

"No," L.B. said. "Let's take 'em to the smokehouse while I figure out what to do with 'em."

"What about the car?"

"Leave it. There's so many sightseers 'n all now, it'll be a couple of days afore anyone gets suspicious over it."

"Let's go, niggers," Harley Mack said.

Kristin and the others were led through the swamp for about half a mile. They had to walk through water and mud, and fight the branches which slapped against them.

Nicole was shaking in fear, and Kristin looked at her.

"Snakes," Nicole said under her breath. "I'm scared of snakes."

"Don't let them know," Kristin said. "Whatever you do, don't let them know."

"Hey, you, white nigger bitch. I didn't say you could talk. Did I tell you you could talk?"

Mercifully, they reached the smokehouse several minutes later. Harley Mack opened the door and motioned with his shotgun that they should all go inside.

Just as Nicole started through the door, Harley Mack stopped her with the barrel of his gun.

"Not you," he said. He smiled, wickedly. "I'm gonna change my luck with you."

"Whooee, listen to Harley Mack," one of the others said. "I believe he's got a hard-on for that nigger girl."

"You don' want the white girl, Harley Mack?"

"Naw," Harley Mack said. "Besides, she prob'ly been screwed so many times by niggers that she ain' no different from a nigger girl anyhow. So I might as well get me a real nigger as a half-assed one."

Harley reached for the front of Nicole's shirt and he jerked down, so that the buttons popped off. Nicole's shirt hung open, and her white bra contrasted sharply against her dark skin.

"No!" Kristin screamed, starting toward Harley Mack. "Leave my sister alone!"

Kristin just reached Harley Mack, when she saw a quick, angry, movement from the corner of her eye. There was a sharp pain on the back of her head, then everything went black.

Like a cork, surfacing from deep within a pool, Kristin floated back to consciousness. She opened her eyes and realized that she was lying down, with her head on Nicole's lap. Nicole was rubbing her forehead gently, with long, cool fingers.

Kristin looked into Nicole's face, and saw that it was puffed and bruised. One eye was nearly swollen shut.

"Nicole, oh no, they . . ." Kristin tried to sit up, but a wave of dizziness and nausea overtook her, and she fell back down.

"Shush," Nicole said, holding her finger over her lips. "Everything is going to be okay now."

"Okay, now pull," Kristin heard Larry say, and she looked over to see Larry and Jimmy pulling on one end of a long board. The other end was jammed against a crack in the wall.

Jimmy and Larry pulled and strained, but nothing happened.

"Hold it, hold it," Jimmy said. "If we pull any more, man, we're gonna break this board, 'n we ain't gonna make a dint in the wall."

"They wrapped a chain around the door and locked it," Nicole explained.

They heard thunder in the distance, then, a few moments later the rain began.

"Well, if it rains hard enough, maybe we won't have to worry about them comin' back and settin' fire to the place," Larry said.

"Fire? You mean they are going to burn us up in here?" Kristin asked in a frightened voice.

"No," Larry said. "We'll find some way out before that happens."

It grew dark, and the rain continued to fall. It banged against the walls, and dripped into puddles on the ground. It blew in sheets across the swamp, and drummed into the trees. The steady rhythm of the rain was punctuated now and then with great, jagged streaks of lightning and sharp reports of thunder, snapping shrilly at first, then rolling through the valleys, picking up the resonance of the hollows, and cascading like a pounding surf out of the hills with a deep-throated roar.

"Hold me, honey," Nicole whimpered to Jimmy. "Please hold me."

"It's okay, baby. It's okay," Jimmy soothed, and as the last light faded, Kristin could see Jimmy cradling Nicole's bruised body in his arms.

Kristin was jealous then. She was jealous of the love Jimmy and Nicole had for each other, and the comfort they could take from each other under circumstances such as these. A few moments later, she heard sounds which indicated just how far the comforting was going, then a brilliant flash of lightning verified her suspicions. They were caught in the act of making love, held in the light like dancers under a strobe, and Kristin's jealousy fell away, to be replaced by a feeling of happiness for Nicole. Kristin was glad Nicole had this moment of joy.

"Kristin," Larry's voice said then, and she could hear the emotion and hunger in it as he spoke.

"Yes?" Kristin heard the hunger echoed in her own voice, and she knew then that she wanted what Nicole had. "Yes," she said again, without waiting to be asked.

Larry came to her in the dark, and as she felt his hands move across her body, she gave herself over to him, determined to share with him whatever comfort and joy there might be left in their lives.

*   *   *

"Wake up," Larry hissed.

Kristin opened her eyes.

"Hey, everybody, wake up," Larry said again.

There was just enough light to be able to see, and Kristin realized it must be early morning.

"Look," Larry said pointing to the corner of the building. "There was so much rain last night, that it washed away some of the floor. I think we can get out that way."

"Yeah, man," Jimmy said excitedly. "We can pry up some of those boards and crawl under."

Jimmy and Larry took the board they had been working with the night before, and within a few minutes, they had pried away several planks from the floor. After that, it was a simple matter of getting muddy, but they managed to crawl under the base of the smokehouse and then they were free.

"All right!" Jimmy said happily, and Kristin and Nicole laughed in relief.

"Hold it," Larry said, holding up his hand. "Quiet!"

They grew quiet and listened, and they heard what Larry heard. Some men were coming toward them.

"Quick, over there," Larry said, and the four of them found shelter behind a nearby clump of trees. They hid behind the cypress knees and looked back toward the building they had just vacated.

"When L.B. finds out we did this, he's gonna be mean," someone said. "He's gonna be hard to handle."

"Yeah? Well what's the sumbitch gonna do, go to the sheriff? If he does, I'm gonna tell ever'thin' I know about those three bodies they just dug outta the dam yesterday, 'n they ain't no one gonna come out smellin' good."

There were two men who came into the clearing then, and Kristin recognized one of them as Harley Mack. They were carrying shotguns and a can.

"Hey, niggers, you still asleep in there?" Harley Mack called. He giggled, then began splashing the contents of the can on the walls.

"Gasoline," Larry hissed.

"Lis'sen, I didn' leave any blankets or anything in there to keep you warm. So I'm gonna make up for that now. I'm gonna warm you up good."

"Harley Mack, I don't know. . ." the other man whimpered.

"Listen, if I'd a known you were gonna be so candy-assed, I'd a left you home," Harley Mack said. "Now gimme the goddamn matches."

Harley Mack took a match, lit it, then tossed it toward the gasoline-soaked wall. The old building burst into instant flame.

"Come on, Harley Mack, let's get out of here."

"Yeah, okay," Harley Mack said. "Let the FBI check this place out. They won't find nothing but a pile of ashes."

Kristin and the others were quiet until they could no longer hear the two men. Then Kristin shivered.

"If we hadn't gotten out when we did, we would still be in there," she said.

"Yeah, well, we did get out," Larry said. "Now, I don't know about the rest of you, but I'm for getting the hell out of this state, as well."

"Larry?" Jimmy said.

"Yeah?"

"Listen, those two motherfuckers think we dead, right?"

"Yeah."

"That means they ain't gonna be on the lookout for us. What say we follow 'em, 'n as soon as we get the chance, we . . ."

"We what?"

"Kill the motherfuckers."

Larry looked at Jimmy for a long time, then he sighed. "No."

"No? No? Why do you say no? They raped my woman, man. They raped my woman and they made monkeys outta you 'n me. And if we hadn't escaped, we'd be bar-b-que, right now. And you don't want to do anything about it?''

"Yeah, man. I want to wring their scrawny-assed red necks," Larry said. "But I believe what I'm down here for, don't you understand? I believe in the man, King. And if I come down here 'n kill a couple of these white bigots, then I've just gone against everything King stands for and everything I believe in. No, man, I'm not going to kill anyone, unless its in self-defense."

"This is self-defense, man. The motherfuckers tried to kill us."

"They tried, but they didn't succeed."

"Larry's right, Jimmy," Nicole said. "Baby, don't you think I would like to see them pay for what they did? But if we are going to win this war, we've got to win it Larry's way. Come on, let's go, huh?"

Jimmy let out a sigh of disgust.

"Yeah," he finally said. "All right. You win. We'll try it your way for a while longer. But if your way don't work, I'm gonna try it my way. And if I have to kill a few of these redneck motherfuckers, then I'm gonna do it."

CHAPTER SEVEN

Jake returned the salutes of the Vietnamese gate guards as he left the headquarters compound of Sector A, then he turned south on Highway 20, headed for Saigon. Highway 20 was a relatively well-secured road, but nevertheless, MACV didn't approve of one American jeep travelling alone.

"You should always travel in convoy," the director of security at MACV told Jake. "That way you have mutual protection in case of an ambush."

Jake didn't agree with that idea. Jake figured that an ambush was much less likely if there was just one jeep. Why would the VC make the effort for one American soldier?

At the little village of Dinh Quan, a Vietnamese policeman held up his hand to stop Jake. This was nothing unusual. All Vietnamese officers above the rank of major felt they had the right of way, and traffic was frequently stopped to let the colonels and generals pass ceremoniously by.

Jake looked around and discovered that he had stopped right in the middle of a busy market area. There were several dozen vendors selling from small stalls or from quilts spread out on the ground. Piles of goods, much of it black-market, stood on proud display, and hundreds of shoppers picked through the wares. Jake could hear them bickering over prices, and he smiled at their commerce.

Several children ran up to Jake's jeep as soon as he stopped, and they laughed and shouted at him.

"Well, what a fine looking bunch of young men and women you are," Jake said, speaking to them in their own language.

The children were delighted that he could speak to them, and even more gathered around. Jake saw an old woman selling sticks of fresh pineapple, and he bought one for himself, then directed that the remainder be divided among the children.

A two-and-a-half ton Army truck stopped at the intersection in front of him, and five young men jumped down. They all looked to be in their late teens. None were in uniform, and Jake wondered about it, because nearly everyone that age was in some kind of uniform, even if it was the Home Guard.

The five young men looked around at the crowd which had gathered, but none of them said anything.

There was something else unusual about them, and as Jake looked at them he realized what it was. The expressions on their faces were more serene than anything he had ever seen. They were almost beatific. He put his hand on the top of the windshield and half raised from his seat to look at them.

A jeep came from the same direction as the truck and it stopped at the back of the truck. The jeep was mounting a .50 caliber machine gun. A soldier in the jeep actuated the bolt of the machine gun, then pointed it toward the five young men.

"Hey, wait a minute, what's . . ." Jake started to shout, but his shout was interrupted by the sound of the gun. It didn't pop like a small gun, it roared in earth-shaking, stomach-jarring explosions.

The five young men began to fly apart. Arms and legs were literally cut away. One of them was completely cut in half. The top of his body toppled over backward, and the bottom half stood for a moment gushing blood, then fell forward.

Then the gun stopped, and the relative silence of bickering Vietnamese again filled the air. Only the children watched; the vendors and the buyers in the market place seemed oblivious to the killings, and the commerce went on.

"Di Wi," Jake shouted at a nearby Vietnamese Army captain. *Di Wi* was the word for captain. "Di Wi, what's all this about?"

"Never mind, Captain, I will explain everything to the Colonel," a familiar voice said.

Jake looked toward the sound of the voice and saw Klaus Sachs coming toward him. Sachs was dressed in his vestments.

"My God, no," Jake said, sitting back down in his jeep. "Don't tell me this was . . ."

"A Phoenix operation," Sachs said. "If you would wait for a moment, please." Sachs walked over to the mangled bodies and made the Sign of the Cross above them.

"Memento etiam, Domine, famulorum qui nos praecesserunt cum signo fidei et dormiunt in somno pacis.

Ipsis, Domine, et omnibus in Christo quiescentibus, locum refrigerii, lucis et pacis, ut indulgeas, deprecamur. Per eumdem Christum Dominum nostrum. Amen."

"How can you do that, you hypocritical bastard?" Jake asked angrily, when Sachs returned to the jeep. "How can you walk around, wearing the cloak of a priest, then saying a blessing over the people you murder?"

"Colonel, we are in the same boat, you and I," Sachs said. "We are merely following the orders of our government. You are a born American, I was born in Germany, but I am a naturalized citizen. I think our love for our country is equal. Do you not think we should be here, helping these people to find democracy?" Sachs said the word with equal emphasis on each syllable.

"Yes, I think we have the right to be here."

"Then we should do our duty without question," Sachs said. "You ask how I can wear the garments of a priest? To the faithful, to those who believe I am a priest, I am a priest. I have brought spiritual comfort to many in my time here, and I will not apologize for that. I just prayed over these men. I don't know if they were Christian or not, but if they were, I wanted to do this for them. Anyway, what right do you have to question me? These men died under your orders."

"Under my orders? What do you mean?"

"Colonel, do you not remember? You gave your carte-blanche authority to execute anyone we found guilty under the Phoenix program."

"I said I didn't want to be bothered," Jake said.

"Precisely. And because you refused to intervene, these men died."

"Sachs, if it is the last thing I do, I am going to get this Phoenix program stopped," Jake said angrily. The truck which had been blocking the intersection now moved out of the way, and soldiers began tossing the bodies, and pieces of bodies into the back of the truck. Jake started the engine of his jeep.

"I hope you do get it terminated, Colonel," Sachs said sincerely. "I hope to God you do."

As Jake drove the rest of the way to Saigon, a sea of frustrated rage churned his insides. Everywhere he turned, he encountered lies, fraud, greed, cowardice and stupidity. He was convinced now that the only way this war was going to be won was if the U.S. fought it. But if the U.S. fought, they would have to make it a total commitment. They couldn't be half-assed about it.

Jake thought of the U.S. Air Force captain who had taken him on a recon flight two weeks ago. It was a two-seat airplane, but a small, Vietnamese soldier had squeezed in behind the rear seat. The Air Force captain explained that because the Americans were technically advisors, every mission they flew had to have a Vietnamese "student" on board. In most cases the Vietnamese students couldn't even fly. They were just along for the ride, and to pay lip service to the rules of engagement which governed the American participation. Thus, even on the recon flight, the Vietnamese had to be aboard.

"Look at the kind of shit we have to fly, Colonel," Captain Shark had said after they came back from the flight. He pointed to the aircraft out on the strip. "B-26s, T-28s. We can't get parts or books, or charts for these damn airplanes, because the Air Force hasn't used any of this equipment since before Korea. Most of our men have trained on jets. If our government wants to fight this war with this shit, then they should call up some maintenance officers and NCO's who were in World War II, and had experience with these birds."

"No," the Captain continued. "No, what they should do is shitcan all this stuff. I lost two friends yesterday. One of 'em was really close. They went down in a B-26. They weren't shot down, Colonel. The goddamn wings fell off the plane. They just came apart in mid-air."

"What about the VNAF? Do they need better equipment?"

"You're kidding, aren't you, Colonel? You might as well give the gooks a bunch of Cessna 150s. All the hell they do with what they have now is sightsee, and a little 150 wouldn't use quite as much fuel. They don't do any fighting, that's for damn sure."

The Captain who had complained so bitterly to Jake about the poor equipment they were saddled with went down the very next day. He tried to pull out of a strafing run, and one wing fell off the plane. He and his "student" were killed instantly.

When Jake reached the outskirts of Saigon, he discovered that there was another student riot going on. He was routed around the main area of disturbance, but despite the re-routing he caught a few whiffs of tear gas, and he could hear the flat thump of gunfire as more gas canisters were shot into the crowds.

Suddenly several students erupted from a nearby alleyway, and they saw Jake's jeep. It was clearly marked with American markings, and that seemed to further incense the crowd.

"Go home, American bastard!" they shouted. They ran up to him and began spitting at him and the jeep.

One of the rioters picked up a rock and smashed Jake's windshield. Jake covered his face with his arm to protect it from flying glass and he stepped on the accelerator, hoping he wouldn't hit anything as he sped away. One of the students grabbed the side of the jeep and tried to hang on, spitting in Jake's face. Finally he let go, and as Jake sped down the street he could see the student bouncing and sliding along the pavement behind his jeep.

Suddenly, with an insight born of frustration and nurtured with fear, Jake was able to equate the plight of the United States with that of the young student who lay hurt and bleeding in the road behind him. The U.S. was being pulled along by events, and now they could neither hang on nor let go.

Jake made Olympic circles on the table in the bar of the Caravelle Hotel. The Caravelle was Saigon's most elegant bar and hotel. For tonight, Jake had taken a room here, rather than going to the BOQ, where he normally stayed when in Saigon.

It was here that the press corps stayed, drank, ate, slept with the beautiful Vietnamese girls who worked the bar, and filed their stories. Jake seldom came here. He was disgusted with the phoniness of the correspondents who stood around in neatly tailored jungle-fatigues, telling lies of their adventures. Often one reporter's lie would end up in another reporter's story.

"Hello, Colonel, may I join you?" a soft, female voice asked.

Jake started to wave her away. She was one of the Vietnamese bar girls. She was an exceptionally beautiful woman, and, like all the Caravelle women, very cultured. But she was a whore, no different, except for her price, from the whores who worked the doorways and corners of '100 P Alley'.

Jake hesitated for a moment.

Why not? Who the hell did he have to be faithful to? Certainly not Virgie. She had returned to Columbus, Georgia, and by now had probably slept with half the men in Fort Benning with a few from Fort Rucker thrown in for good measure.

How about Kristin? No, they didn't have any kind of agreement. Jake was certain Kristin wasn't holding herself pure for him. In fact, she would probably laugh if she even heard the term, "pure".

Jake smiled at the girl, and her hesitant smile deepened. She sat down at his table.

"I have a room here," Jake said.

"You don't want to have a drink first?" the woman asked.

"I'll buy a bottle of champagne," Jake said. "We'll take it up with us."

"Oh," the woman said. "What are we celebrating?"

"Arbor Day," Jake said.

"Arbor Day? I don't understand."

Jake laughed. "Never mind. Come on, let's get the champagne and go up."

A moment later, Jake was standing at the large, tinted window in his room on the seventh floor. From his room he could look out over the Saigon River, and, in the evening sun, the river gleamed like molten gold.

"It's pretty from up here," Jake said. "Where you can't smell it, or see the turds floating in it."

"Why do you talk that way?" the girl said from the bed behind him. "I thought you bought champagne to be happy."

Jake turned toward the bed and saw her lying there, totally nude, waiting for him. She was on her side, and her head was propped up on her elbow. Her other arm was resting on her bare skin, with her hand at her hip. Her fingers seemed to be gracefully inviting him to the center of her charms. Jake smiled at her and walked over to the bed. He began taking off his own clothes.

"Honey, if a man saw something like you waiting in his bed and he wasn't happy, I'd say there was something seriously wrong with him."

The woman laughed, then lay on her back and raised her arms to him.

Jake reached over and turned off the light as he went to her. Without the lamp, there was only the soft, golden light of sunset, and the girl on the bed with him softened in the shadows.

He bent his head to hers, and their lips met. There was an old army adage that whores never kissed, but this one did, and she did it with skill. Her teeth nibbled against his bottom lip, and her tongue teased his.

Jake felt the sensations of pleasure wash over him, and he wondered what private devil, what misguided code of honor had caused him to deny himself all this time.

He looked into the girl's eyes and saw that they were half closed almonds, shielded by lashes of delicate lace, and he wondered that anyone could be as beautiful as she was. He put his face beside hers, and he could feel her breath on his cheek and neck.

Jake felt himself approaching the pinnacle, and he forced himself back, holding onto the delicious agony of the quest. Finally he heard the girl beneath him take several sharp gasps, then he felt her quiver, and her hands gripped his back. She let out a long, genteel sigh, and, when she did, he surrendered himself to the white heat which had been pulling at him for several moments. He felt himself slipping down and through, draining himself of all sensation. For the moment, there was no memory of Captain Shark and the airplane which shed its wings, nor was there an execution in Tan An, nor was there a Phoenix program, nor was there a phony Father Sachs. There was only the connecting flesh and the splash of seminal fluid, and the rush of white heat which blotted out everything.

But only for the moment.

CHAPTER EIGHT

It was six-thirty in the morning. That was awfully early to call anyone, Jake knew, but it also increased the chances of Kristin being home.

Jake was in the San Francisco airport, having just returned to the States from Vietnam. He had a few hours before he was due to catch his flight to Atlanta, so he thought he would call Kristin and talk to her. If she wanted him to delay his flight back east, he was prepared to do that, but, only if she asked.

The phone rang half a dozen times, and he was about to hang up, when it was answered.

"What do you want? Do you know what time it is?"

The answering voice was a man's voice, and it surprised Jake.

"I'm sorry," Jake said. "I was calling Miss O'Neil. I must have the wrong number."

"No, you got the right number, man. But Kristin has crashed."

"Crashed?" Jake gasped. "What? A car wreck? An aircraft accident?"

"No, man, crashed. Like, asleep, man. What are you, crazy?"

"I'm sorry," Jake said. "Listen, tell her that Ja . . . tell her that Colonel Culpepper called. Tell her I just wanted to say hello."

"Colonel Culpepper wanted to say hello. Yeah, man, I'll do that, only next time, don't call in the middle of the night, okay? I mean. . . ."

There was a clumping sound, as if the receiver had been dropped, then Jake heard Kristin's voice on the other end. It was breathless and apologetic.

"Jake? Jake, is that you?"

"Yes," Jake said. "I'm sorry if I disturbed you. I wrote that I would be calling you today. Did you get my letter?"

"Yes, I got it," Kristin said. She laughed nervously. "When you said you would be calling today, I didn't think you meant so early in the morning."

"I gathered that," Jake said. "It does seem to be a bit crowded over there."

"Oh, that was just Larry. He was over for a working session last night, and it was so late, I invited him to stay."

"Look, you don't have to explain anything to me," Jake said, but the tone of voice in which he said it suggested that he felt he *was* owed an explanation.

Kristin sighed.

"You're right," she said. "I don't have to explain anything to you."

"Good," Jake said. "Then we understand each other. I've got to go."

"Jake? Jake, wait a minute," Kristin said. "We don't understand each other, do we? I mean, you don't understand me."

"It's all right, Kristin," Jake said. "Really, it's all right."

"Look, would you like to come over? Larry and I are going to a confrontation seminar today, and I'll be gone until pretty late tonight. But if you could get here before nine, we could visit a little."

"Do you have to go to the seminar?"

"Yes, I told you Larry was over here working last night. This is what we were working on. We're the ones giving the seminar. There's no way I couldn't go. People are coming from all over the country to attend.''

"Yeah," Jake said. "There's no way."

"But maybe I could take a couple of hours off tomorrow."

"A couple of hours tomorrow," Jake said. "No, don't bother. I wouldn't want to put you out any."

"Goddammit, Jake!" Kristin exploded. "What do you expect? You drop back into my life after being gone for a year. I have my own life to live. Besides, we don't have any kind of understanding between us. Where was it said that I would drop everything when you came home?"

"You're right. We don't have any understanding between us."

Kristin sighed again.

"Jake, please come over. I'll leave as soon as I can today."

"No," Jake said. "Listen, Kristin, you're right. I don't have any right coming on like this. I'm sorry. I just thought . . . well, to tell the truth, I don't know what I thought. Anyway, I've got to catch a plane pretty soon. It was no big deal, anyway. I just wanted to say hello, that's all.''

"Jake? Jake, I hate to leave it like this," Kristin said.

"Yes, well, right now there seems to be very little we can do about it. You take care of yourself, you hear?''

"Jake, you'll write, won't you? You know my address, I don't know where you'll be. You will write?''

"Yeah," Jake said, though not very convincingly. "Yeah, I'll write.''

Jake hung up the phone, then walked back over to the ticket counter. He looked up on the TV monitor, and saw that his flight had been cancelled. Ticketed passengers were advised to take a later flight, or make arrangements with another airline.

"Cancelled?" Jake said aloud, though speaking to no one. "Why was it cancelled?"

"Mechanical trouble," a woman's voice said, and Jake

turned to see a tall, leggy, blonde stewardess. He recognized her as one of the stewardesses who had worked his flight across the Pacific. "Looks like we are both stuck here."

"You were going on? That would be a lot of work for you, wouldn't it?" Jake asked.

"I wasn't going to work this flight," The stewardess said. Her name tag identified her as Peggy. "I was just going to deadhead it to Atlanta." Peggy looked at Jake and smiled. "Colonel Culpepper," she said, reading his nametag. "You just got back from Vietnam, didn't you? I saw you on flight seven-one-five."

"Yes."

Peggy looked toward the bar. "Well, Colonel Culpepper. It may be seven a.m. here in San Francisco, but it's four p.m. in Saigon. Do you think that's late enough for us to have a drink?"

Jake smiled. "I'd say so," he said.

Two hours later, Jake lay in bed in a nearby motel room with the sheet pulled up to his waist. His uniform was draped over one chair, and Peggy's stewardess uniform was on another. Peggy came out of the bathroom with a towel wrapped around her head. Her body was still damp from the shower, and still nude. Jake looked with appreciation at the perfection of her build, and he felt a faint reawakening of desire as he recalled their recent lovemaking.

Peggy sat at the dresser and began applying makeup. She put lipstick on with a brush, staying meticulously within the lines of her lips. She began to work on her eyes.

"Were you a model?" Jake asked.

"No. Why do you ask?"

"You do that so skillfully," Jake said. "You might even say professionally."

Peggy smiled.

"I learned in 'Grooming 101'," she said.

"You took a college class in makeup?"

Peggy laughed this time. "Not college, stew school." She turned and looked toward Jake. "Since our flight doesn't leave until nine tonight, what do you say we just skip it and spend the night here? Do you know San Francisco? There are some really neat places to see."

Jake thought of it for a moment, and he almost said yes. After all, he would have stayed on with Kristin had things worked out differently. Things didn't work out with Kristin though, and now he was anxious to get to Columbus, Georgia, and see his kids.

"No," he said. "I think I had better go on."

Peggy walked over and sat down on the edge of the bed. She put her long, cool fingers on Jake's chest.

"I understand. You are anxious to get back to your wife, aren't you?"

"My wife? No," Jake said. "What made you think I was married?"

"I don't know. You have the look of a married man."

"You mean you thought I was married, and yet you went to bed with me anyway?"

"Sure, why not?"

"Wouldn't it matter if I was married?"

"Why should it matter to me if you are married? I'm married."

"What?" Jake gasped. "I didn't know stewardesses could be married."

"If we are already on, and we have seniority we can be," Peggy said. She looked puzzled. "Colonel, do you mean to tell me that if you had known I was married, it would have made a difference to you?"

"I . . . I think so, yes," Jake said.

"Why?" Peggy laughed. "Surely you weren't planning on making an honest woman of me, were you?"

"No, I guess not," Jake said.

"Well, then, you see? There's no harm done, is there?"

"No. There's no harm done," Jake said.

*　　*　　*

Jake took the nine o'clock flight, which actually didn't leave until 10:15. The plane landed in Atlanta at 8:00 a.m. Atlanta time, and Jake caught a flight from Atlanta to Columbus at 11:00. At 12:30 he walked up to the Hertz car rental desk in the Columbus airport, but before he could rent a car, he saw a bright red Mustang on display behind velvet ropes.

The Mustang had been introduced while Jake was in Vietnam, and this was his first view of one. He walked over to look at it.

"You like that car, Colonel? I can put you in it," a man said. The man identified himself as a salesman with the auto dealer who was displaying the car.

"Can you put me in this very car so that I don't have to rent one?" Jake asked.

"I could if you wanted to. Or, you could look around at our selection downtown, while we are setting up the finance for you."

"No finance," Jake said. "I'll pay cash, but I want this one."

The salesman smiled. "Colonel, you just bought yourself a car," he said.

Just a little over an hour later Jake was driving away from the airport in his new car. The car was quick and responsive, and fun to drive, and he felt good about it. He felt so good that, for the time being at least, he wasn't bitter about losing the Mercedes.

"I don't know why cars are so important to you," Kristin had told him once, when he had complained about the Mercedes. "Cars are just transportation, after all. What difference does it make whether it is a new Mercedes, or an old Plymouth?"

"You are wrong," Jake said. "Cars are much more than mere transportation. They are symbols."

"That's the trouble with the world today," Kristin said. "There are too many symbols. There are symbols of racial superiority, symbols of manhood, symbols of wealth, symbols of power. If things could just be as they are without all this symbolism, the world would be in a much better shape.''

Jake smiled as he recalled the conversation. What did this car symbolize, he wondered? Was it a quest to recapture youth?

Jake turned off Reese Road onto Macon Road. He had never been to Virgie's Columbus house, but he did know her address, and he did know Columbus well, from having spent many years stationed at Fort Benning. A short time later, he stopped in front of a small, but neat, brick house. It was about two-thirty in the afternoon, and the house looked quiet. Jake walked up to the door and rang the bell. A moment later it opened, and he saw Virgie.

''Jake! Jake, how good to see you,'' she said. She stepped back from the door. ''Come in.''

Virgie was wearing a green and white striped pullover, and a matching green pleated skirt. Her makeup was impeccable, and her hair was perfectly styled and shining like burnished copper. She looked exceptionally pretty, and Jake wondered if she had done all this for him.

Virgie kissed Jake lightly.

''You are looking good,'' she said. ''Tan and trim. Vietnam must have agreed with you.''

''I wouldn't go so far as to say that,'' Jake said. He looked around the house. ''Where are the boys? Oh, in school, I suppose.''

Virgie laughed. ''Things haven't changed that much since you left. They still don't have school on Saturday.''

''This is Saturday? I'm sorry, I've been enroute for so long that my time is all screwed up. If they aren't in school, where are they?''

''They are spending the day and the night in the country with friends,'' Virgie said. ''They'll be back tomorrow.''

''Oh, well, I suppose I can wait one more day.''

Virgie looked at her watch. ''Jake, I have to show a house at three. Why don't you stay here and rest while you

wait for me. There's sure to be a football game or something on TV."

"They don't play football in April," Jake said.

"Whatever. Wait for me, okay?"

"Yeah, I could use a little nap. What do you mean,
show a house?"

"Oh, didn't I write you? I have my realtor's license
now. I work for Douglas Parker. If I sell this house, I'm
going to make seven hundred and fifty dollars, and that
ain't bad."

"No, I guess not," Jake said. "Well, I wish you good
luck."

Virgie kissed Jake lightly, then hurried away. Jake went
over to the recliner chair and sat down, leaning back. It
was too much like the airplane seats he had spent the last
two days in, so he tried the sofa, but it was an ornate,
Victorian sofa which was hard and uncomfortable. Finally
he gave up and went into Virgie's bedroom.

The bedroom furniture was the same furniture he and
Virgie had shared for many years, and a flood of familiar
sights, smells, and impressions came to him. For an instant he felt an overwhelming sadness for things lost, and
he wished with all his heart that things had turned out
differently.

Jake walked over to the dresser and ran his hand across
the top of it. That was when he saw the sunglasses. They
were Army Aviator glasses, and they were in a leather
case, embossed with gold lettering.

Chief Warrant Officer Jerry Dent
United States Army

What were these glasses doing here? Was Virgie sleeping with Jerry Dent?

Jake hated himself for doing it, but he went into the
bathroom and opened the medicine cabinet door. He looked
among the bottles of makeup and nostrums until he saw

what he was looking for. On the top shelf, put behind a tin of Band Aids, he saw a small brown plastic container. He took the container down and opened it, and saw several rows of tiny pills. A drugstore sticker was on the inside of the lid.

For Mrs. Jake Culpepper
Take one pill per day for birth control.

"Damn!" Jake said. He snapped the lid shut and put it back. He felt a sense of anger, but even more than anger toward Virgie was anger with himself for prying in the first place. He felt anger and shame.

Jake took a shower, then he went into the bedroom and lay down. He was asleep within a very few minutes.

"Well, sleepy head, are you ever going to wake up?"

Jake opened his eyes and saw Virgie sitting on the side of the bed. She was smiling down at him.

"Hi," Jake said. He stretched and ran his hand through his hair. The room was dark, except for a light which splashed in from the hall. "What time is it?"

"About eight," she said. "I would have let you sleep longer, but if we are going to go out and eat, we need to go before everything starts to close. How about letting me buy you a steak to celebrate?"

"My coming home?"

"That too," Virgie said. "But also this afternoon. Jake, I sold the house!"

"You did? That's great," Jake said.

"You bet it is. Listen, hurry and get ready. There's a place nearby, I'm going to go call and reserve us a table."

"All right," Jake said. "I hope I don't need a tie. I don't have any suits with me, and I'd just as soon not wear my uniform."

"A shirt and slacks are okay," Virgie called over her shoulder as she left the room.

Jake had brought his suitcase in earlier, and now he went through it to pull out a fresh change of clothes. The suitcase was next to the dresser, and he noticed that the sunglasses were gone. Evidently, Virgie had considered them incriminating enough that she took them while he was asleep.

The steaks were good and so were the after-dinner drinks. The conversation was mostly about the two boys.

"Mike and Andy have been wonderful," Virgie said. "You would be proud of them, Jake. Mike has grown so tall, and Andy isn't far behind. You'd probably like Andy the best—he plays football—and all the macho things that you would appreciate."

"And Mike?"

"Mike has his music. Mike is . . . well, he's different, Jake."

"Different? In what way is he different?"

"Oh, in a nice way," Virgie said quickly. "He's a very gentle boy. Gentle and shy. He's very sensitive, too. He feels things acutely. He feels for the Negroes, and he feels for the poor. He doesn't approve of war, either, I'm afraid."

"No one does," Jake said. "War is not something one does by choice, but by necessity."

"Well, don't worry, Andy certainly takes up for you in all their discussions."

"Takes up for me? You mean I have to be defended?"

"To a degree, yes," Virgie said. "You are a warrior, after all, and as such, the total antithesis of Mike's idealism."

"My God, Virgie, what does Mike think I am, some sort of monster?"

"No. He's just sensitive, that's all. And he doesn't understand you."

"As long as we are talking sensitivities and misunderstanding here, how do they feel about Jerry Dent?"

Virgie gasped. "What?"

"Jerry Dent. I saw his sunglasses in the bedroom before you moved them. You are sleeping with him, aren't you?"

Virgie blinked her eyes a few times, and tears began to form.

"Jake, you have no right," she said. "You have no right to question my life. We aren't married anymore."

"I'm just concerned about the children, that's all," Jake said. He regretted the statement as soon as he made it.

"That was a cheap shot," Virgie said quietly.

"You're right," Jake agreed. "It was a cheap shot and I apologize." He reached his hand across the table and took Virgie's hand in his. "Listen, I'm sorry," he said. "I really am sorry."

Virgie smiled at him through her tears. "All right," she said. "You are forgiven."

Jake looked at his watch. "Wow, I didn't realize it was this late. I don't know if I'm going to be able to find a room or not."

Virgie laughed. "Are you hinting that I should ask you to stay with me?"

"I don't know, maybe I am."

"Would you like to?"

"Yes," Jake said. "Yes, I would like that very much."

A while later, Jake carried a beer and a Coke into the living room and set the drinks on the coffee table in front of the sofa. Virgie had gone to change clothes, and she came back to sit beside him. She had put on a yellow silk gown which showed off her body very well, even to the two nipples which stood out in bold relief.

"Do you like the couch?" she asked as she sat beside him.

"It isn't very comfortable."

"I bought it at an antique auction. It belonged to the Governor of Alabama in 1880, or something. I don't think it was supposed to be comfortable. I think it was supposed to encourage his guests to make their stays short."

"I'm certain it did its job well," Jake said. He put his

arm around Virgie and his hand fell easily and comfortably to her breast.

"Titty rump, titty rump, titty rump, rump, rump," he said softly. It was the last line of an old joke, and a very inside joke between them. He hadn't said it, or even thought it since their good days together, and he surprised himself saying it now.

Virgie looked up at him, and there were tears in her eyes.

"Oh, Jake. If only things could have been different," she said.

Jake kissed her, and the kiss, like his arm around her, felt familiar and comfortable, and he felt an aching sweetness.

"I've missed some things," Virgie said.

"So have I," Jake admitted.

"Maybe we can make up for some of what we have missed," Virgie suggested. "That is, if you would like to."

"I would like to," Jake said. He kissed her again. "Virgie, I want to go to bed with you. I want to make love to you, and I want to be welcomed home from Vietnam, the way I was welcomed home from Korea."

"Let's go into the bedroom," Virgie suggested.

Jake followed Virgie into the bedroom, and as soon as they stepped through the door, she turned around and kissed him again, this time more demanding than before. Their mouths opened, and tongue pressed against tongue as they hungrily tasted each others lips.

"Jake, wait, let me turn out the lights," Virgie said.

"What for? The kids are gone."

"It'll be nicer. You'll see."

Virgie turned the lights out, then she lit a match and held it to a candle on the bedside table. The flame flickered a bit at first, then straightened into a motionless point of light, perched above the slender white taper.

Virgie turned to look at Jake. "Now," she said softly. "Isn't this better?"

They kissed again, deep and demanding, then separated, but only to take off their clothes. Because she had fewer clothes to remove, Virgie was nude before Jake, and she stood in front of him, waiting anxiously. The tip of her tongue flicked out to wet her lips, and her eyes looked at him hungrily. Her body glistened like gold in the candle light, and the inverted triangle of her pubic hair stood in bold relief against her incredibly smooth skin.

"It will be good to wake with the smell of you in my bed again," Virgie said.

By now Jake was as naked as Virgie, and Virgie put one hand behind his neck and used the other to trace patterns of pleasure across his skin, then down to his most sensitive part.

"I'd like to shake hands with an old friend," she said jokingly, huskily, as she grabbed him. "I haven't had the pleasure in quite a while."

Virgie lay back on her bed and pulled Jake down with her. Jake explored her body with his hands and fingers, feeling the dampness of her arousal and the heat of her desire. She began to whimper and run her hands across his back, begging for the ultimate invasion.

Jake answered her demands, moving into her, thrusting vigorously at her, bouncing against the spring action of the bed.

Tiny whimpers began deep in Virgie's throat and grew louder until they were almost a wail, and Jake, remembering that Virgie had loud, explosive orgasms, covered her mouth with his. She sucked his tongue so far into her throat that it hurt him a little, but the hurt was one of excruciating pleasure. Virgie thrust her hips against him and her bucking action provided the additional stimulus that brought on the beginnings of orgasm. Jake felt the muscles in Virgie's stomach and thighs tighten, then jerk convulsively. The orgasmic pinwheel inside him exploded and he drained himself in satisfying surges into her inviting womb.

Afterward, they walked back into the living room, still nude, and Virgie sat on the sofa while Jake ate a piece of left-over pizza he found in the refrigerator. He looked back at Virgie. There were a couple of spots of dampness on her thigh, evidence of their recent love-making. They glistened in the soft light, and Jake found it very exciting.

"You look cute standing there, eating your curds and whey," Virgie said.

"Do you want some?"

"No." Virgie was silent for a moment, then she spoke again. "Jake, I wish it hadn't happened."

"The divorce?"

"No. The divorce was inevitable. In fact, it should have happened years ago. What I wish is that we hadn't made love."

"You didn't enjoy it?"

"You know damned well I did," Virgie said. "I enjoy having sex, and if I like my partner, I enjoy it even more."

Jake felt a hollowness in the pit of his stomach, and he turned to look at Virgie.

"Let me get this straight. Are you telling me that you have such frequent sex that you even have it with partners you don't like?"

"After the fact, they have sometimes proven to be disagreeable, yes," Virgie said.

"But you like me?"

"Yes."

"And Jerry Dent?"

"Yes," Virgie said quietly.

"Well, if you like me, and you enjoyed the sex, why do you wish it hadn't happened?"

"Because I can't trust you to keep it in its proper perspective," Virgie said.

"What do you mean?"

"I know you, Jake. You are such a straight arrow, you are probably thinking already that we should remarry. You probably think it would be wonderful for the boys."

"I must confess to having given it some thought, yes," Jake said.

"I figured as much. Oh, Jake, don't you understand? I don't want to be married to you, or to anyone. I didn't like myself very much when I was married to you. I didn't like living a lie."

"What lie were you living?"

"The lie of being a dutiful officer's wife. Only your being an officer didn't really have anything to do with it. I would have felt the same way if you had been a business executive, or a farmer. Jake, didn't you know? Are you trying to tell me that you had no idea about the affairs I had?"

"No," Jake said. The hollowness turned to nausea. "I didn't know. Are you saying you had affairs while we were married?"

"Of course I did. If you didn't know, Jake, you were the only one. There was Mario, and Wayne and Garret from the Little Theater Group at Fort Riley. And there was a captain from personnel when we were in Germany. And while you were in Korea . . ."

"No," Jake said in a choked voice. He held up his hand. "No, don't run through the list. I don't want to hear any more."

"Jake I just want everything out front with us from now on. I owe that to you."

Jake was suddenly acutely aware of his nakedness. He started toward the bedroom to get dressed.

"Jake, haven't you anything to say?" Virgie asked.

"Yes," Jake replied. "Consider your debt paid."

CHAPTER NINE

The boat was docked in Cho Lon. It was large, and unpainted, except for the great evil eye which was put there to ward off any wicked spirits which might come to plague it. A gangplank stretched from the boat to the wooden dock, and men and women alike moved up and down the wet boards, bent over under the load of their sacks of rice.

Half a dozen soldiers stood by in varying degrees of attentiveness, watching the proceedings. Ostensibly they were to check for possible deserters or smugglers, but a five hundred piaster note would turn their heads long enough for any illegal transaction to take place.

Mot and his mentor, Ling Sanh Phat, slipped the orange 500P note to the soldier nearest the gangplank, who turned to watch a small skiff on the river as Mot and Phat went inside the boat.

The interior of the boat was dank and unpleasant. It had one large planked deck of damp, smelly wood and it was packed with people.

Whole families had spread blankets on that portion of the deck to which they laid claim as their own. They surrounded themselves with possessions, not only those things they were taking to their destination, but the provisions necessary to sustain them during the week-long voyage. The air was rancid with the smell of dried fish, molding

115

cheese, excrement from frightened dogs and chickens and rotting vegetables.

Mot and Phat found a place for themselves, then settled down to wait for the voyage to begin. Like the others, they had brought their own food. Mot's mother had cooked rice and bits of fish for them, and she had wrapped their lunch securely in palm tree fronds.

Several hours later the boat was rocking its way through the South China Sea. Mot stood up and walked to one of the portholes, picking his way gingerly through the clusters of people who were squatting on the deck, laughing and talking. He looked through the glassless opening and saw the coast, a verdant green shoreline some five miles distant. He watched it for a while, then returned to sit beside Phat. Phat moved over slightly to make room for him.

Mot and Phat were on the boat because it was going to be hijacked just off the coast of Phan Thiet the next morning. Ten skiffs, carrying five men each, would intercept the boat just before dawn. They would force the Captain to put in to shore where the people would be taken off the boat, and the boat would be loaded with weapons and ammunition to take back to the Saigon area.

If everything went as planned, it would be a smooth, bloodless operation. But if fighting broke out, the fifty well-armed men would be able to handle it, especially with Mot and Phat working from the inside.

"The passengers will be disturbed, but, if they make no trouble, they won't be hurt," Phat had explained to Mot, when he transmitted the orders to him. "Anyway, it is for them that we do this thing. Don't forget, we are fighting for the freedom of all Vietnamese."

That had been yesterday, when they were planning the operation. Now, as Mot looked around at the passengers, he recalled the conversation and wondered if what they were doing was right.

"Phat," Mot said, speaking in English to lessen the chances of being understood. "Look around you."

"What?" Phat asked. "Look around me at what? What do you wish me to see?"

"These people," Mot said. "Look at these people. Are we doing the right thing? Do you think these people care whether we are fighting for their freedom or not?"

Phat looked around as directed. "Do you think they do not care?" he replied.

"I don't think half of them even know what country they are in," Mot said. "Or care. And the information they do get are the lies the government wants them to hear."

"Don't worry. Soon they will all know the truth."

"What is the truth to these people? Their truth is the truth of momentary reality. They make a hole in the field, plant rice, spread that field with shit and flood it with water. That's all they really care about. We fight and die for them, yet we are treated as the enemy, as something unclean. It gives one pause for thought, I must say."

"Has your resolve weakened?" Phat asked.

"No, of course not," Mot said. "My resolve is as strong as it has ever been. It is their resolve that I am worried about. Suppose we win freedom for them. You have said yourself, freedom cannot be given. It must be taken. Will these people take their freedom?"

"Yes," Phat said. "With the proper leadership and proper education, the freedom we win will be enjoyed by all of our people."

"And who is to provide that leadership and education?"

"We shall, of course," Phat said. "That is, those of us who survive the battles will provide for them."

"And those of us who die?"

"We will be the inspiration for the others," Phat said.

Mot smiled and put his hand on his teacher's shoulder.

"In that case, I would much rather be a leader than an inspiration," he said.

Mot and Phat grew quiet after that, each of them lost in their own thoughts. The sun which had been streaming in through the portholes and cracks during the afternoon faded away into that peculiar Vietnamese evening which knows no twilight but merely goes from light to dark. Throughout the boat lanterns were lit and conversation grew subdued as shadows gathered around the golden glows of the kerosene lamps. The passengers began eating their evening meal.

Mot took two of the palm-wrapped rice packages and handed one to Phat.

"It's good," Phat said. He smiled. "We have eaten much worse in the field," he said.

"Yes, but once we ate grandly, do you remember?" Mot said. "We attacked the headquarters of the 15th Special Infantry, and the commander had just set an elegant feast."

Phat chuckled. "Ah, yes, I remember that well. Never, in all my travels, have I eaten like the meal we had that day. The government troops know how to eat well."

"And yet, you will remember, such food was only for the officers," Mot said. "The soldiers had rice, such as we are having now."

"Not as good, I would say," Phat said, using his fingers to shove the last bit of rice into his mouth. He licked his lips appreciatively.

After their meal, they lay down in their space, and a short while later, Mot was lulled to sleep by the gentle rocking of the boat and the quiet throb of the engine. Sometime around three in the morning, he was awakened by the frightened voice of a woman and the gentle murmurings of Phat.

Mot sat up and saw that the woman was holding a baby. The baby was naked and dirty, and it's puffy little eyes were swollen shut. The baby's skin looked to be red.

"What is it?" Mot asked. "What is wrong?"

"The baby is sick," Phat answered. "The woman has asked me if I can help."

"Can you?"

"The baby has a fever," Phat said. "Perhaps if we take it on deck and bathe it with cool sea water, we can bring the temperature down."

"Let's try it," Mot suggested.

The stars were spread brightly across the sky and the moon hung like a great silver orb, splashing a shining pathway which stretched from horizon to the shore. The breeze was refreshingly cool after the stuffy hold, and Mot was glad they had come on deck.

Phat got a bucket of cold sea water and began bathing the baby with it. The baby screamed at first, then began whimpering again. After half an hour the whimpers turned to sighs, and Phat stood up, holding the baby in his arms. The baby opened its eyes and looked into Phat's face, and Mot could see that the eyes were clear and healthy-looking in the lantern light.

"Let the Americans build their bridges and roads to win the hearts and minds of the people," Phat said. "We can accomplish the same thing by winning the children."

"And yet, when our people attack the boat at dawn, will we not undo all that you have done here?"

"I think not," Phat said. "I think not."

Mot was awakened again a short while later. When he opened his eyes, Phat put his fingers to his lips to signal quiet.

"It is nearly dawn," Phat said. "We should go on deck now."

Mot followed Phat up the ladder and back out onto the deck. In the east, a thin bar of red broke over the South China Sea. To the west the land was little more than a dark shadow. Then, gradually, like shadows moving within shadows, Mot and Phat saw the approaching boats. They were long and slim, and they moved quickly across the water, propelled not by outboard motors which would have given them away, but rowed by the men on board.

"There they are," Phat said. "Now, we must stop this boat."

Mot and Phat walked back to the stern of the boat. There the pilot stood by the tiller while an old woman, probably his wife, worked at a charcoal stove cooking his breakfast soup. The pilot saw Phat and Mot approaching him.

"You are up early," he said.

"Yes," Phat said. He pulled a pistol and pointed it at the pilot. "I'm afraid it has to do with our job. If you would be so kind as to stop the boat, please?"

"Are you pirates?" the pilot asked.

"We are fighters for the National Liberation Front," Mot said proudly.

The pilot breathed a sigh of relief, then he smiled.

"In that case I am your friend," he said. "I feared you were pirates. What would you have me do?"

"We are going to use your boat for a while," Phat said. "We have some weapons we wish to transport."

"The passengers," the pilot said. "When they see the weapons, they will talk."

"The passengers will be put ashore before the weapons are loaded," Phat said. "Stop the engine, please. Our friends will be aboard momentarily."

The approaching boats touched alongside a few moments later, and forty men boarded, leaving only one man per boat. The boarders moved quickly in bare feet to establish control of the big boat, and less than ten minutes after they boarded, all passengers were disarmed and the pilot was heading for shore.

"Mot," Phat said a few moments later. Mot had been moving through the passengers, assuring them that those who cooperated would not be hurt. Phat had been talking with the assault team leader.

"Yes?"

"I have spoken with Mr. Xuan. We are to go with him when we reach shore. Tonight, we attack Hoa Duc. Are you prepared for combat?"

Mot felt a fluttering in his stomach. He always felt a little frightened at the thought of battle. But though frightening, he also found the prospect thrilling.

"I am ready," he said.

"Are you frightened?"

"Yes," Mot admitted.

Phat smiled broadly. "That is good. That means you are not crazy. I would not want to go into battle with one who is crazy."

After the passengers were taken off and the boat reloaded with weapons, those men who did not stay with the boat followed a trail which led off into the jungle. Mot and Phat went with them, for they would be joining the attack force Xuan had spoken of.

The trail wound at least ten miles along a snake-infested, insect-swarming stream, and finally ended in a small clearing. There were a couple of straw thatch huts in the clearing, over which flew two flags, one the red and blue flag with the yellow star of the NLF, and the other the solid red flag with yellow star of North Vietnam. On the ground in front of the straw hut there was a straw and clay model of the village of Hoa Duc. The model was complete with road and rivers, and every building in the entire village.

"That is our target," Xuan said, pointing to the target. Three companies of government troops are there."

"Any Americans?" Phat asked.

"Only two," Xuan said. "They are advisors, and they stay in this hut. But don't worry. We have two loyal friends in the village who are beautiful young women." He smiled broadly. "They will find a way to immobilize the Americans."

"When do we attack?" Mot asked.

"Tonight," Xuan said. "Captain Tho will brief us this afternoon. He is our friend from the North."

"Will Captain Tho lead us?"

"No," Xuan said. "This will be our operation."

When the briefing was over, Mot spent the afternoon wandering around the clearing, looking at the setup. There were only a couple of huts visible, but there were several tunnel openings all around, and he soon learned that there were entire rooms underground, consisting of billets, ammunition storage and an exceptionally complex communications setup. Though he never saw more than thirty or forty people together at any one time, he soon learned there were well over three hundred here. Such a sight made him feel good. He had never met with more than a handful of sympathizers in the past, and though his determination was strong, he often had the idea that he must be fighting for a losing cause.

Mot ate lunch at about three in the afternoon, then someone gave him a hammock and he found a place in the shade to erect it. He slept all afternoon because he knew he would need to be fresh later.

It was after midnight when Mot and Phat took up a position about one hundred yards from the southern perimeter of the village of Hoa Duc. Mot slapped at the mosquitoes and peered toward the village, which was surrounded by a high barbed wire fence, and dotted with several guard towers.

Mot and Phat were with a little less than one-half of the attacking force. The remainder of the force was crawling around to the northern side of the village. The plan was for the weaker force to hit first, from the south, then when the village defenders were committed to the south, the remaining, stronger part of the attack force, led by Xuan, would hit them from the north. It would take nearly two hours for everyone to get into position, so that meant that Mot had to contend with the mosquitoes for two hours without moving. Mot could contend with the mosquitoes,

but he was worried about what the two-hour wait would do
to his nerves.

Shrill laughter reached Mot's ears, and he gasped in
surprise, wondering who would be so foolish as to compromise their position. Then he realized that it wasn't any of
his men. The laughter came from a government patrol.

Mot and the others drew back into the bushes to watch
as four government soldiers came down the trail. They
were all armed, but they were carrying their rifles upside
down over their shoulders, holding them by the barrel.
One was telling a joke.

Mot saw the leader of his group make a signal, then, a
moment later, he saw four shadows loom quickly from the
jungle and grab the four soldiers. The soldiers had their
throats cut before they even perceived that they were in
danger.

Only the leader of Mot's group had a watch, and he
consulted it often. Finally, Mot saw him raise his hand,
hold it for a moment, then bring it down sharply. At that
exact moment the two mortars they were carrying fired,
and seconds later, a pair of explosions ripped through the
village.

Rifle and machine gun fire began then, ripping through
the limbs and the leaves of the trees. At first, nearly all the
fire was coming from outside the village, but within a
moment the village defenders began returning the fire. The
sharp rattle of small-arms fire kept up a constant barrage,
then Mot heard a whooshing noise, followed by tremendous explosions from somewhere close by.

"They have called in their American artillery," their
leader said. "Come, we can't stay here. We must move
toward the camp!"

Mot and Phat stood up, but at that very moment, an
artillery round landed right in front of them. There was a
blinding explosion and a blast of hot air and stinging dirt
and twigs. Mot was knocked down by the concussion, and
when he stood up a moment later his ears were ringing.

"Phat, that was close," he said. "That shell knocked me down!"

Phat didn't answer, and Mot looked toward him to see why. What he saw made him instantly sick. The whole top of Phat's head had been blown away by the explosion.

"Come, Mot!" the leader shouted at him. "Come, we can't stay here!"

Mot wanted more than anything in the world to throw down his gun and run away.

"Come, toward the village. The American artillery will not shoot at the village!" the leader said.

The leader had rallied all the men now, and they started running toward the village, firing their weapons and shouting defiantly. Mot joined them, not in any mood of heroism, but because he was terrified of the artillery bombardment and was willing to do anything, to go in any direction, to get away from it.

To Mot's surprise, the firing from the village grew sporadic, then broke off altogether. The defenders were fleeing!

Suddenly the firing started anew, but this time from the other side of the village. Now the defenders were trapped in the middle. Within a few minutes most of the defenders were either killed, or had escaped into the jungle. Mot joined his comrades in the village square, then he and the others fired their weapons joyously into the air. They had won!

At daybreak Xuan set up tables in the middle of the village, and all the villagers were required to "pay taxes" to the "Provisional Liberation Government."

"We must hurry," Xuan told the others. "The village will be bombarded, soon."

"But surely, if we leave they won't attack," Mot said. "They would be destroying a village needlessly."

Xuan smiled. "The government will ask the Americans to destroy the village in order to cover their shame for not fighting. The Americans will destroy it because they are frustrated. And the villagers will compare us to the government and the Americans. We attacked in the night, we killed the mayor and the schoolteachers, and we took some taxes. But we didn't destroy their village. They will remember this, and they will support us from now on.''

Mot looked over at the villagers. Some were standing in line to pay their ''taxes,'' and some were standing around the several bodies which had been collected and put in the center square. There were two American bodies among the Vietnamese, and Mot walked over to look down on them.

One of the Americans was a black man. He was a big, strong-looking man, and his short, springy hair was matted with blood from the head wound which had killed him. His eyes were open and unseeing. They were big and brown, the same color as the eyes of all Orientals.

Mot wondered why a black man would fight a white man's war. Who was this man, and why was he over here? Mot had read about blacks in America. He knew that there was hate and distrust between whites and blacks. And yet, this black man had not only fought America's war, he had fought bravely.

Mot heard a whistle blow, and he looked toward the center of the square. Xuan was signalling for all of them to leave, and Mot, with one last glance at the dead black soldier, joined his comrades and they loped off into the jungle.

They were nearly three miles away when the planes came. They watched from the safety of the jungle as the planes bombed and strafed Hoa Duc until it was no more.

CHAPTER TEN

Jake's stateside assignment was as a battalion commander with the 102nd Airborne Division, stationed at Fort Caldwell, Kentucky. It was his first field-grade command assignment, and he took a great deal of pride in the fact that in the first year he was there, his battalion consistently scored highest in the IG and CMMI inspections. He also submitted several recommendations for changes in the Airborne TO&E, based on his experiences in combat situations with similarly sized units in Vietnam.

One of Jake's suggestions was a shocker. He was a battalion commander in an airborne division, the proudest and most elite unit in the army, and yet, Jake recommended that the airborne division be eliminated. He wrote:

> The concept of vertical envelopment upon the field of battle is still a logical one. But, as armor changed the concept of cavalry, similar advances in technology have changed the concept of the airborne.
>
> Instead of vertical envelopment via the parachute, battlefield insertions should be made with the helicopter. Such insertions ensure command and control during every moment of the operation. Final commitment for insertions can be made at the last possible second, and the incidence of minor injury (sprained and bro-

ken limbs, etc.), as well as equipment damage, is much less likely.

The use of parachute insertion should be maintained for special operations consisting of small, highly trained units, but the concept of an entire airborne division is as outmoded as the concept of a horse cavalry.

Jake's report was published in the *Army Times* and the *Army Digest*. The result was a storm of letters of angry response ranging from new young privates who had just received their parachute wings, to retired generals who had helped develop the airborne concept during World War II. Partly because of Jake's report, and partly because he was a fairly recent returnee from Vietnam, Jake was invited to testify before a House Armed Services Committee hearing, to be held on Monday, the 23rd of May, 1966. It was an invitation which Jake couldn't refuse.

Jake's father issued his own invitation, and asked that Jake stop by and see him on his way to Washington. Jake didn't refuse his father's invitation either.

General Culpepper lived in a twelve room, red brick Georgian Colonial home just outside the gates of Fort Monroe, Virginia, overlooking Hampton Roads. The house, which dated from before the Civil War, had been built by Ambrose Culpepper. It was occupied briefly by General Grant during the Peninsular Campaign, but reclaimed by General Culpepper's widow after the war. It remained in the Culpepper family, and the Generals Culpepper had traditionally retired to it after their tours of duty. Iron Pants lived there now, and someday it would be Jake's home.

A private graveyard was enclosed by a stone fence behind the house. Years after the battle of Shiloh, Ambrose Culpepper's remains were brought back from the military cemetery at that battlefield, and reburied alongside his wife's grave. Jake's grandfather, grandmother, and

mother were also buried there. There was a tombstone for
Iron Pants, and Iron Pants tended the site regularly. There
were also two tiny graves, one for a brother who had been
born, and died, before Jake. The other was unmarked, and
the rumor, though unsubstantiated, was that it was the
grave of a still-born Negro child, the result of an indiscretion by Ambrose Culpepper.

Jake left the plane at Patrick Henry airport in Newport
News, and took a taxi to his father's house. As they
stopped for a light on Jefferson Street, a panel truck pulled
up beside them. The truck was covered with painted flowers and peace symbols, and as Jake looked over toward it,
a young girl smiled at him and held her fingers up in a
V-sign. The light changed and the panel truck drove
away.

"D'ya see that shit?" the driver asked. "I bet that little
ol' girl ain't no more'n sixteen, 'n she probably screws
like a mink. That's all they do, you know, all those peace
protestors. They just have sex orgies all the time." The
driver said the word orgy with a hard 'g'. "If I had my
way we'd round up ever'one of those beatnick bastards
and put 'em in jail. What do you think about 'em?"

"I try and not think about them," Jake answered.

"Yeah," the driver agreed. "That's prob'ly the smart-
est thing to do, all right. Here you are, buddy. Hey, that's
quite a house. You know the guy that lives here?"

"Yes," Jake said without elaboration.

Jake paid the driver his fare, then stood on the walk for
a moment after the cab left. He looked toward the house.
It looked quiet inside.

Across the street from the house was a beach and, as it
was late May, the early vacationers were already there. A
little girl squealed and a boy laughed, and Jake looked
over toward them. Then, instead of going up to the house,
he put his garment bag down behind the low brick wall
which ran across the front lawn of his father's house, and
walked across the street and beach to the breakwater wall

which thrust out into the sparkling blue Chesapeake. He stood there for a moment, thinking about his father and dreading the moment of meeting.

Jake had never been close to his father. He had been unable to forgive his father for the transgression he had witnessed against Emma Cruz, and yet he had never told his father that he knew about it. Their relationship after that could only be described as cold, though proper.

Jake's father was reassigned to the States immediately after the summer of his indiscretion, and that reassignment probably saved him from becoming a prisoner of the Japanese. When the Philippines fell, Iron Pants was en-route to Europe, leaving Jake with Jake's grandfather, General Craighton Culpepper, retired. Jake attended a military boarding school during the winters, but he spent Christmases and summer vacations right here in this very house.

When Iron Pants returned from Germany, Jake lived with him, though they never grew any closer.

Jake had not seen his father since returning from Vietnam, though they had spoken over the phone. Iron Pants had never suggested that Jake visit him, nor had he visited Jake. The matter of their emotional estrangement was simply not mentioned, as if it didn't even exist. Then Iron Pants asked Jake to visit him on his way to Washington, and Jake was so surprised by the request that he agreed to it before he could fashion an excuse as to why he couldn't. Jake turned his eyes away from the impressive edifice that was his father's home and looked down the beach. To the south was the resort area, and, though it was early in the season, the beach was already peopled.

Pier One, an expensive and popular restaurant, perched on the end of a long pier jutting far out into the water. Across the street from Pier One was an amusement park with a roller coaster, fun houses, and assorted other diversions. The roller coaster was in operation, but instead of the screams and squeals of delight, only one person, a young boy of about twelve, was riding it. He sat white-knuckled and tight-lipped in the front seat as the cars clacked hollowly through the twists and turns of the track.

Jake was at the extreme north end of the resort strip, so that the only thing across the street from him was a small refreshment stand where a very large, garishly blonde and heavily made-up woman listened to a baseball game.

It looks like Bob Gibson has really got his stuff working now, fans, that's the third strikeout in a row, the radio was blaring. The woman was reading a racing form as she listened to the game.

Jake walked over to the refreshment stand. His mouth felt dry, and he thought he would have a soft drink before he reported to his father.

Jake smiled. "Reported" was a good word for it. He had always regarded his father as more of a Commanding Officer than a parent.

The blonde looked up from her racing form. A cigarette was dangling from her lips and there was an ash formation on the end, almost a half-inch long.

"I'd like a Coke, please," Jake said.

"Twenty-six cents, sport," the blonde said without making a move for the cooler.

Jake put a quarter and a penny on the counter, and the woman put it in the cash register.

"You'd be surprised at the punks who grab a Coke 'n run," she said. She pulled a Coke from a chest full of ice water and put it on the counter. Ice still clung to the side of the can, and the top was beaded wet.

Jake returned to the seawall and stood there to drink his Coke while he looked out over the bay. Finally, when the drink was finished, he bent the can double, tossed it in a nearby trash can, and walked back to his father's house. He had to face him sooner or later.

The front door was locked and Jake had no key, so he rang the bell. A moment later, the door opened, and a woman stood there. She looked to be in her forties and had probably been very pretty when she was much younger, though there was a tiredness to her looks now. Her hair was gray, though enough brown remained to indicate what the color had been. Her name was Maggie Humes, and she had been Iron Pants' housekeeper for the last ten years.

"Hello, Maggie," Jake said.

"Jake," Maggie said, and she hugged him. "Please, come in. Did you drive? I didn't hear a car."

"No," Jake said. "I took a taxi from the airport. He laid his garment bag across a chair. "Where's Dad?"

"He's out back, by the pool," Maggie said. "Go on through. Would you like a beer?"

"No, thank you," Jake said. "I just had a Coke."

"I'll take your things to your room," Maggie said, picking up the garment bag.

"I can get it later," Jake said.

"No, I'll do it," Maggie said, and she was two steps up the stairs before he could protest further.

Jake walked through the house, through the old dining room and parlor, and through the new kitchen and den which had been built on, then through the sliding glass doors which led to the flagstone patio out back. HIs father was sitting in a lawn chair under an umbrella, looking out over the pool, so that his back was to the house. Jake walked over and sat down in the chair beside him.

"Well, you seem to have kicked up quite a bit of controversy with your dump-the-airborne idea," Iron Pants said.

"I guess I have at that," Jake answered. It was typical of his father to greet him in the middle of a conversation, as if they had been talking all along with no separation.

Iron Pants chuckled. "You know, I had a similar experience myself. I was only a captain then, and my paper didn't receive as much publicity as your idea did, but I advocated the abolition of the cavalry at a time when it was considered almost sacrilegious to even suggest such a thing."

"Did you catch a lot of flak?" Jake asked.

"Quite a bit, as a matter of fact," Iron Pants said. "But I survived it, and so will you. You are absolutely right, you know. The airborne is obsolete. Hell, it was obsolete from the very beginning. The Germans got away with an air-drop in Holland because no one had ever heard of such a thing. But from that very first drop until today, there has never been an unqualifiedly successful combat drop. It's been a morale builder in peacetime, but nothing more than a dangerous toy during wartime. That's why the 102nd is going to change from Airborne, to Airmobile."

"I haven't heard anything like that," Jake said.

"The decision has been made, it just hasn't been announced," Iron Pants said.

Maggie came out to the pool then.

"It's nearly dinnertime," she said. "Would you two like a sandwich out here, by the pool?"

"That would be nice," Iron Pants said. He held his hand out for Maggie, and she came over to stand beside him. "Did you tell Jake?" he asked.

"I thought you might want to."

"Tell me what?" Jake asked.

"Maggie and I are married," Iron Pants said.

Jake looked at Maggie's face, at the intense pride and joy in her eyes, and he felt good for her. He smiled. "Well, congratulations to the both of you," he said. "When did it happen? Why didn't you tell me about it?"

"It happened about a month ago," Maggie said.

"And we didn't tell you because we didn't want to make a big thing of it," Iron Pants said. "Hell, the truth is, I should have married this woman a long time ago. She's been wonderful to me, Jake. I honestly don't believe I could have gotten along without her."

"I'll, uh, get the sandwiches," Maggie said, embarrassed by Iron Pants' words.

"I approve," Jake said, after Maggie left.

"Oh, so you approve," Iron Pants said. "Well praise

the Lord, I have finally done something which meets with your approval,'' he added sarcastically.

"What? What do you mean?" Jake asked.

"Jake, it cannot have escaped your attention that our relationship has not been what one would call warm and loving," Iron Pants said.

"I suppose not," Jake said. He stared at the pool, at the ripples of water coming from the spot above the circulating hose. "I never thought of you as a man who wanted or could accept a warm and loving relationship."

"Could you have given it?" Iron Pants asked.

"I don't know," Jake admitted. "I've always given you respect."

"Respect I could get from a buck private in the rear-assed rank," Iron Pants said. "From my son, I always hoped for more."

"You've never said anything," Jake said. "You've never indicated that."

"That you are my son, and I love you?" Iron Pants said.

The words sounded strange coming from his father's lips, and Jake would have hardly been more shocked had his father suddenly slapped him.

"Sentiment doesn't come easy to me," Iron Pants said. "It never has. Unfortunately, that's a trait I seem to have passed on to you. I can understand that in you. What I can't understand is how you can be so inflexible, how you can find me guilty with a little boy's perception, and continue to punish me with a grown man's conviction."

"What are you talking about?" Jake asked.

"Jake, do you think I don't know you have been playing judge and jury on me all these years?" Iron Pants said. "You think I don't know how you have condemned me for what happened between Emma and me? Goddammit, I thought you would mellow after a while, but it's been over twenty-five years and you're as self-righteous about it now as you ever were."

"How long have you known that I knew?" Jake asked.

"Hell, Emma told me about it the very next day," Iron Pants said. "She said you had watched us that night, and you were quite upset by it."

"You must admit that when a son sees his father commit rape, it can have a traumatizing effect," Jake said.

"Rape? Is that what you call it?" Iron Pants asked.

"Yes," Jake said.

"It wasn't rape."

"If it wasn't rape, I'd like you to explain to me what it was."

"Jake, I hate to admit this, but I don't think I could ever explain it to you. Not now, not in a hundred years."

"Good," Jake said. "That means you won't even try."

Iron Pants sighed.

"Yes," he said. "That means I won't even try. Listen, I'm sorry I brought it all up. I want to talk to you about the hearings. What are you going to say?"

"I guess it depends on what they ask me," Jake said.

"They are going to ask you to give an appraisal of our efforts in Vietnam."

"They're not going to like what I tell them," Jake said.

"What are you going to tell them?"

"The truth."

"You may also learn that the 102nd is going over there, very shortly."

"You mean I'm going back to 'Nam?"

"You've been back less than eighteen months. You could probably get a six-month deferment, then return on some staff job. Or, you could stay with the 102nd, and command a battalion in combat. Which will it be?"

"I guess I'll stay with the division," Jake said.

Iron Pants smiled. "I rather thought you would," he said. "We may have our differences of opinion, Jake, but on that one thing we are alike. Battle is in our blood, and we had no more say so on that than we had on the color of our eyes. If there was a way to examine it under an electron microscope I think we would find that the blood grandfather Ambrose shed at Shiloh is identical to the blood that is in my veins and yours. It is the blood of a warrior.''

"It's a family curse,'' Jake suggested.

"A curse? Why do you say such a thing?''

"Dad, have you measured the public sentiment, lately? Being a soldier is not the most popular profession right now.''

"Ah, don't worry about it,'' Iron Pants said. "When the people realize what we are doing, when they understand that it is important that we save Vietnam, they'll come around.''

"But we aren't going to save Vietnam,'' Jake said.

Iron Pants frowned.

"What do you mean?'' He asked. "What kind of talk is that?''

"You asked me what I was going to tell the committee, and I said I was going to tell them the truth. The truth is that the way we are conducting this war now is going to lead us down the road to disaster.''

"You'd better be a little more specific,'' Iron Pants said. "If not, they'll throw you out on your ass before you can say half a dozen words.''

"Can you accept specifics?''

"Try me.''

"You still have contacts at the highest level—let me ask you. Is this Administration, is our country, willing to wage all-out war to prevent a communist takeover in Vietnam?''

"Our policy has been to avoid all-out war.''

"Then you would say that we aren't willing to turn the entire country, north and south, into a parking lot.'' Jake said.

"No, of course not. But we will provide the South Vietnamese with the wherewithal to defend themselves, and we will maintain an American presence there for as long as necessary.''

"And how long is that? Forty years? Fifty? Don't forget,

in one form or the other, this war has been going on since
1940. It has become a way of life for the Vietnamese. And
in all revolutionary wars, the most inspired fighters are
always the have-nots. In this case that means the VC.
When we chose up sides, it's too bad we didn't choose the
VC. If I had one division of VC, and I could equip them
the way we have equipped the ARVN, I could take the
whole country inside a year. Instead, we send our young
men over to die for a cause that is as lost as great grandfather Ambrose's Confederacy. We are pissing away American lives in a self-defeating policy of stupidity.''

"You'd better explain that,'' Iron Pants said.

"Dad, I saw young American flyers lose their lives in
planes that were already obsolete when you were in Korea.
I saw American soldiers cut to pieces by mortar fire when
they knew where the VC were, but couldn't return fire
because of the rules of engagement which governed them.
In the sector where I was an advisor, I saw South Vietnamese
colonels who wouldn't make a pimple on a corporal's ass
in our army, and I saw second lieutenants who were over
fifty years old and should have been Generals, but they
were from the wrong family, or province, or religion.
Now, if that's how the war is going to be fought, I'm
telling you now that the only thing we are going to get out
of it is a damaged international reputation, and half a
dozen new strains of venereal diseases.''

Iron Pants threw back his head and laughed out loud.

"By damn, boy, you tell 'em,'' he said, slapping his
leg. "You tell that bunch of stuffed-shirts in Congress just
what you told me. Maybe they'll listen to you and get off
their dead asses and get something done.''

"You mean you agree with me?'' Jake asked in surprise.

"Hell yes, I agree with you,'' Iron Pants said. "Listen,
we've received a few privately submitted reports of our
own. Don't think you aren't the first one to make such an
observation. The only problem is, can we make our government understand the situation here? Hell, I've talked to

President Johnson about this, half a dozen times. I told him it was about time to shit or get off the pot, and I think he understands. But he's walking a pretty thin line right now, trying to win the hearts and minds of everyone in the world.''

Jake laughed. ''Did I tell you what General Abrams said about the hearts and minds?''

''No.''

''Well, you know how he is always chewing on a cigar,'' Jake said. Jake put his hands up to his lips and imitated pulling a cigar out of his mouth. He spat, as if spitting out pieces of the cigar. ''Boy, grab 'em by the balls, and it stands to reason their hearts and minds'll come along.''

Iron Pants laughed appreciatively at the story.

''Abe's a good man,'' he said. ''But of course, with the same name as my father, he could hardly be otherwise, could he?''

Maggie brought bacon, lettuce and tomato sandwiches out to the poolside then, and the three of them ate and talked, and Jake realized that he and his father had communicated more on this afternoon than at anytime he could ever recall.

There was a small TV in Jake's room, and when he went to bed that night he watched the eleven o'clock news.

''Thousands of servicemen, marching in the 17th Annual Armed Forces Day Parade along Fifth Avenue in New York, were halted today by anti-war demonstrators,'' the announcer said. ''The demonstrators broke through the police barricades and rushed toward the marching troops, shouting for the U.S. to get out of Vietnam. Many were carrying flowers, and they threw blossoms at the soldiers. Fifty, including eighteen women, were arrested.''

The picture on the screen was of pushing, shoving crowds, typical of the demonstrations scenes which were becoming more and more prominent on television news

reports. There were signs saying, "Stop the War in Vietnam"
and "Peace now!" Then, Jake gasped and sat bolt upright
in bed as he saw a woman being put into a van.

It was Kristin O'Neil!

CHAPTER ELEVEN

Jake sat in an anteroom of the Senate Office Building while he waited to be called as a witness before the Senate Committee on Third World Development. He had already testified before a special Department of Defense committee on the reorganization of an airborne division into an airmobile division. Before that committee, Jake had advocated the formation of a military unit which would depend upon helicopters instead of parachutes for vertical envelopment, and he was pleased to learn that others had shared his view to such an extent that, as his father had told him, the division to which he was assigned was being so reorganized.

But an appearance before a reorganization committee was not the only thing which had brought him to Washington. He was also appearing before the select committee of Senator J. Maynard Carter, senior Senator from Oregon.

Senator Carter's committee was actually mandated to explore methods of increasing American influence among the third world nations, but Senator Carter was using his committee to look into the Vietnam War. His justification was that the war was diverting American foreign interests to Southeast Asia at the expense of the other third world countries.

Senator Carter was a man with political aspirations higher than the U.S. Senate. His White House ambitions, as well as a personality profile of the Senator, were featured in the latest *Time* Magazine, and Jake looked down at the cover to see the Senator's face looking back at him.

The Senator was young, and he looked even younger than his years. He had a heavy shock of wavy, blond hair which was so long that it would have earned him an instant Deliquent Report had he been on active duty in the Army. His power base was with the liberals and the young dissenters of America. He hadn't come so far as to advocate a withdrawal from Vietnam, but he was solidly against any request by the Department of Defense to allow them more freedom of action. The dissenters, who believed that more freedom of action for the military meant a widening of the war, therefore flocked to Senator Carter's side in placing limits on the involvement. Senator Carter's insistance upon strict military limitations not only hamstringed the military, but seriously undercut the efforts of his fellow Democrat, President Johnson, to find a solution to the war. Senator Carter was extremely critical of President Johnson, had made several speeches at peace rallies, and had even marched with them, in order to, as *Time* quoted him saying, "open a meaningful dialogue between members of the government, and those who have legitimate questions on the conduct of this war."

"Colonel Culpepper, you have just been summoned by the committee, sir," a committee messenger said to Jake. Jake set the Magazine aside, then followed the messenger into the committee room. There was a long table in front of the room, and at its center sat Senator Carter, looking just as if he had stepped there from the cover of *Time*.

Jake was sworn in as a witness, and all eyes and cameras turned toward him. He sat ramrod straight in his chair with his ribbons making a splash of brilliant color across the chest of his tropical worsted tans.

"Colonel Culpepper, how many human lives have you taken?" Senator Carter asked for his opening question.

"What?" Jake asked, surprised by the question.

"It's a simple enough question," Senator Carter said. "How many lives have you taken?"

"Senator, I object to that question," Jake replied.

"This isn't a court of law," Senator Carter said. "You do not have the right to object to the question. You do have the right to refuse to answer, if you wish to stand by the Fifth. Do you feel that answering this question will incriminate you in any way?"

"No, sir, I do not," Jake said.

"Then I will ask you again, Colonel. How many human lives have you taken?"

"I don't know," Jake answered.

"But you have taken lives?"

"I'm a professional soldier, Senator, and I have been in several fire fights. I fought in the Korean War, and I have already had one tour of duty in Vietnam. I've just learned that I will be returning there shortly."

"To take more lives?"

"To perform my duty, Senator."

"And what do you perceive your duty to be, Colonel?" Senator Carter asked as he ran his hand through his hair.

"Senator, my duty is whatever you tell me it is."

"What *I* tell you it is?"

"You are part of the policy-making body of this country, Senator."

"Policy-making, Colonel, not war-making," the Senator replied.

"I would like to remind you, sir, that war is the product of policy. In fact, it is considered to be the result of a failed diplomacy. You make the diplomacy. When you fail, people like me clean up your mess."

There was a ripple of laughter from the gallery.

"That's just the point I'm trying to make, Colonel. Despite the wishes of the military to broaden this problem, we are *not* at war now," Senator Carter said. "Our diplomacy goes on."

"Nevertheless, our diplomacy has failed, Senator. We should be at war," Jake said.

"Let me get this straight. Are you advocating that we declare war?"

"Yes, sir, that is what I am saying. That is, if we intend to win there."

"But we don't intend to win there," Senator Carter said.

"Then, if you will excuse me, Senator, what in the hell are we doing over there?"

The gallery laughed.

"We are trying to apply diplomatic leverage, Colonel. A subtle nuance that you, and others in the military, don't seem to understand. Our only purpose there is to prevent the Communists from winning."

"What is the goal of the Communists?" Jake asked.

"Colonel, I will ask the questions," Senator Carter said petulantly.

"Mr. Chairman?" one of the other Senators said. It was the first time anyone on the committee, other than Senator Carter, had spoken.

"Chair recognizes Senator Boxley from California."

"Senator, I think the Colonel had a valid question, and I think it should be raised. What is the goal of the Communists in Vietnam?"

"Very well, Colonel Culpepper," Senator Carter said. "Since you raise the question, sir, I shall ask you. Have you some insight as to the goal of the opposing forces in Vietnam?"

"Yes, sir," Jake said. "The answer is obvious, Senator. The goal of the Communists in Vietnam is to win their war, and if you ask me, our convoluted policy is going to help them do just that."

"Would you care to explain that, colonel?"

"Senator, if the Communists consider this conflict a war, and their goal is to win it, while we don't consider it a war and have no intention of winning, the outcome is inevitable. The Communists will win."

"Are you saying that the military, which we are asked to support with ever-increasing amounts of money, is going to lose in Viet Nam?"

"No sir," Jake said. "The military is not going to lose this war. You are. The coin won't stand on its edge, Senator. If we don't win, we lose."

The gallery was packed with supporters and protestors of the war, and the supporters cheered and applauded, while the protestors jeered and booed.

"Colonel, you seem to have presented a picture of U.S. foreign policy painting itself into a corner," Senator Boxley suggested.

Senator Boxley, the junior Senator from California, was as conservative as Senator Carter was liberal. Boxley had been a supporter of Senator Joe McCarthy and, even though McCarthy and his brand of anti-communisim had been discredited, Senator Boxley still got a lot of support from his tough stand against communists. He had argued from the floor of the Senate that the U.S. should get out of the U.N., or, barring that, should at least suspend all monetary support for the organization, until they came around to "our way of thinking."

"An apt analogy, Senator," Jake said, and this time everyone, supporters and protestors alike, laughed, and cheered.

"And you, I suppose, have a solution?" Senator Carter asked.

"A solution? No sir," Jake said. "I don't have a solution. I have answers."

"You have answers? Isn't that the same thing as a solution?" Senator Carter asked.

"No, sir," Jake said. "It isn't the same thing at all."

Senator Carter sighed and ran his hand through his wavy hair again. "Very well, Colonel Culpepper. Suppose you give this committee the benefit of your military wisdom, and provide us with those mysterious answers.''

"Yes sir," Jake said. "The answers are simple, Senator. They have been voiced by every solider, marine, airman and sailor who has ever served in Vietnam. We should drive it or park it.''

"I beg your pardon?"

"I mean, Senator, those of you who do establish our foreign policy must make a decision. If the safety of our country depends upon our fighting in Vietnam, then let us fight to win.''

The hawks in the gallery cheered so long and so lustily that the chairman had to gavel them into quiet.

"Please continue, Colonel Culpepper," Senator Boxley said. "I like the way you are talking. In your opinion, sir, given all the support you need, the military can win in Vietnam?"

"Oh, yes," Jake said. "But we are going to have to be willing to pay the price.''

"What is that price?" Senator Boxley said.

"Senator, at the conclusion of World War II, my father was on a review board which questioned Japanese veterans of the jungle fighting. The Japanese soldiers were asked who, in their opinion, were the most fearsome junglefighters in the world. They answered, Americans. Well, that seemed a little strange, since the jungle is not an environment common to Americans, so they were asked to explain. Their answer was that Americans were the fiercest jungle fighters, because when they fought they took away the jungle. Now, we can win in Vietnam, but in order to do it, we are going to have to turn that place into a supermarket parking lot. It is going to require an all-out, unrestricted operation. Do we want to do that?''

"What is the alternative to that?" Senator Boxley asked.

"There is no alternative.''

The gallery reacted once again to Jake's words, booing or cheering as they interpreted their meaning.

"You are wrong, Colonel," Senator Carter said. "The solution is to keep this conflict limited, to deny the Communists their goal with the minimum force."

"Senator, you haven't given us a solution, you have given us a mathematical equation."

"A mathematical equation? I don't understand."

"The policy we are now following will not achieve its goal in Vietnam. What it will do is ensure the death and wounding of X number of Americans each month. The equation is, X is the number of casualties per month, Z is the total number of casualties we are willing to absorb before we withdraw or turn Vietnam into a parking lot. Given the numbers for X and Z, we can then find Y, which is the length of time we are going to stay in Vietnam. The way things are set up now, Senator, the job of the military is to supply you with bodycount, both our own and the enemy, until, in your judgment, the total Z is satisfied."

"Colonel, you make it sound like we are operating a slaughter mill," Senator Carter said.

"We are," Jake said. "Unless you change your policy now. If it is your decision that Vietnam is not worth going to war over, then we should cut our losses now, and get out as quickly as we can," Jake said.

Once again, the peace demonstrators erupted into cheers, only to be gaveled down by Senator Carter, irritated that Jake had undercut him with the people he considered his own constituency.

Finally, Jake was dismissed by the committee, but the Senator from California asked Jake if he would come to his office to speak with him.

"Colonel, I like the way you handled yourself in there," the Congressman said.

"Thank you," Jake said.

"You showed a clear grasp of the situation, one which I wish all of my colleagues shared. You realize, of course, that we won't be able to go into Vietnam and turn it into a supermarket parking lot.''

"Of course," Jake said.

"And, as you indicated, that leaves only one solution," the Congressman said.

"Withdrawal," Jake said.

"Yes, I'm afraid so."

Jake smiled. "I thought you were considered a hawk."

"I'm a pragmatist, like yourself," Senator Boxley said. "And like Richard Nixon. Nixon realizes that we can't go over there and kick ass and take names, so he has developed a plan of withdrawal which will get us out of Vietnam with an honorable peace."

"Nixon? What does he have to do with it? He's just a former Vice-President."

"Nixon will be the Republican candidate for President next year, and he'll win," Senator Boxley said. He smiled proudly. "I've been appointed to his campaign committee. And I'd like to have you working on our team as well."

"Senator, you must realize that it is illegal for an active-duty soldier to participate in any political campaign?"

"Overtly, yes. But you could be of great covert assistance."

Jake felt an uncomfortable tingling in the back of his neck. "I'm not sure I follow you, sir."

"Colonel Culpepper, you are a highly regarded military man, from a family with a strong, military tradition. Your father has the ear of President Johnson, as well as the confidence of the Joint Chiefs of Staff. There are bound to be times when you will come across information which might be of use to our campaign. All you have to do is share it. Believe me, you will be amply rewarded for your patriotic service."

Jake stood up.

"Senator, as a United States Army Officer, I have a security clearance which prohibits me from discussing any classified information with anyone except in line of my duty.''

"Well, yes, of course," Senator Boxley said. "But there are degrees of classification which I am certain that you, as an intelligent, discerning individual, will be able to prioritize. All I am asking is that, in the interest of national security, you share some of your information with us."

"How would that be in the interest of national security?"

"Jake—may I call you Jake? Believe me, getting Richard Nixon elected to the Presidency is in the best interest of national security."

"I'm sorry, Senator, but I wouldn't feel right doing anything like that," Jake said.

Senator Boxley looked at Jake with flat cold eyes for just a second, then a practised smile spread across his face.

"Yes, well, of course I understand. After all, if you were not a man of integrity, we wouldn't be interested in you now, would we, Colonel?" Jake noticed that it was Colonel again, and not Jake. "I appreciate your sense of honor, and I won't ask you to do anything which you feel might compromise it. I do hope, however, that we will have the opportunity to work together, some time." Senator Boxley shook Jake's hand and walked with him to the door. Jake couldn't leave soon enough.

Jake visited his career branch in the Pentagon next. It was there, at branch headquarters, that decisions were made which affected the careers of all professional officers. No officer would think of visiting Washington without calling on his career branch chief. He could use the opportunity to review every piece of paper the army had on file about him. He could read all his old efficiency reports, see the progress of the promotion lists, ascertain where the next command openings would be, apply for advanced schooling and enter his choice of assignments. Jake knew his next assignment—Vietnam. But while here, he could

submit a preference for a Stateside assignment upon his
return.

His career branch chief was Colonel Bill Lambert. He
was a full colonel, and Jake had known him for several
years.

"Oh, by the way, Jake," Colonel Lambert said, after
Jake had reviewed his file. "We got a letter from a young
woman, asking for your address. You haven't gotten someone knocked up, have you?" he teased.

"Who is it from?"

The branch chief laughed again. "Oh, I see. You mean
you might have gotten someone pregnant, it just depends, is
that it?" He reached into another file folder and pulled out
a letter. Jake recognized the neat penmanship immediately.
"It's from . . ." Colonel Lambert started, but Jake
interrupted.

"Kristin O'Neil," Jake said.

"Then you know her?"

"Yes."

"What do you want to do about this letter?"

"Nothing," Jake said. "I'll take care of it, thanks."

"Well, okay, nothing else for you here. The full colonels Board is meeting this summer."

"Yeah, but I'm not in the zone of consideration."

"You are for five percent. Your OERs look good, Jake.
I'd say you've got a shot."

"It would be nice," Jake said.

Colonel Lambert looked at his watch. "Well, what do
you know? The sun is below the yardarm. It's time for a
martini. What do you say? Would you like to toss down a
few?"

Jake looked at his own watch. "Only if you want to
come to the airport lounge with me. I've got to catch a
flight. I'm going to meet my kids in Nassau. They're
going to spend some time with me."

"Really? Well, that'll be nice, you'll enjoy that. I'm

meeting some people at the club, so I can't go to the airport with you, maybe next time you're in town."

"Yeah," Jake said. "I'll see you then."

"Oh, and Jake? Keep your head down over there, okay?"

"My dad just told me the same thing."

"Listen to old Iron Pants. He knows what he's talking about."

CHAPTER TWELVE

Mike ran the Joan Baez tape back, then started it through again. He walked back over to the bed and lay down with his feet propped up against the wall.

"To me it's very simple," he said. "The matter of individual conscience was decided by the Nuremberg war trials. The U.S. Government was not only a party to the trials, we were one of the instigators. We cannot bind others to their conscience while refusing to accept that principle in our own dealings."

Andy was sitting at Mike's desk, and he took a long swig of beer before he answered.

"All right, but look, no one is asking you to gas Jews, right? I mean what are you saying here, Mike? Are you saying Dad is a Nazi?"

"No, I'm not saying Dad is a Nazi, I'm . . ."

There was a knock on the door of the room.

"Boys, are you in there?" Virgie called.

"Yeah, mom," Andy answered. He leaned down and hid the beer in the waste can beneath Mike's desk. "Come on in."

Virgie opened the door and stepped inside. She was dressed to go out.

"I'm going to dinner with a friend," she said. "You two guys better get to bed, you are going to be leaving fairly early tomorrow. Are you packed, Andy?"

"Why do you always ask me if I'm packed?" Andy replied. "Why don't you ask Mike?"

"Because I never have any trouble with Mike," Virgie said.

"She likes me more," Mike teased. " 'Course, that's only natural. I'm her real child. You were abandoned by your real mother. We found you in a shopping cart in Piggly Wiggly."

"Mike, that's a terrible thing to say."

"That's all right, mom, I can take it," Mike said, carrying the joke on. "I've always known."

"But it's not true, whatever gave you the idea that . . . ," Virgie saw both boys smiling then and she stopped in mid-sentence. "Very funny," she said. "I just hope your father appreciates your sense of humor as much as I do."

"We're going to be in Nassau," Mike said. "What's there not to appreciate?"

"Yes, well, try to remember what I said about getting in bed early. I'll see you when I get back."

Virgie kissed both of them and left. Andy reached down and retrieved his beer.

"The way I see it," Andy said, returning to the conversation, "is this. We are in a war. It's our duty to go if we are called."

"You aren't thinking for yourself, Andy," Mike said. "That's our father talking."

"No, I am thinking for myself. I don't have any intention of making the Army my career. But I'm not going to run from it."

"I am."

"What do you mean?"

"I mean I'm not going."

"Even if they call you?"

"Even if they call me."

"What the hell are you going to do?"

"I'll go to Canada."

"Dad's not going to like that."

"No, I don't suppose he will. But that's what I'm going to do, and I wish to hell I could convince you to do it too."

"No," Andy said. Andy drained the rest of his beer, then crushed his can. "Mike?"

"Yes."

"The truth is, I'm going in right away."

"What?"

"I went down to see the recruiter last week. I'm going in next month."

"But . . . I thought you were going to school. You've got a football scholarship to Auburn."

"There's no way I'm going to play the first year, you know that," Andy said. "And probably damn little my sophomore year. This will just be like red-shirting for two years. When I get out of the Army I'll be two years older and more mature. I'll be more ready for school, football, everything. And, I'll have the military behind me. I've been thinking about it a lot, Mike."

"I wish you wouldn't do it," Mike said. He looked at his brother seriously. "Andy, since Mom and Dad got their divorce, we've been a team, haven't we?"

"Yes."

"I mean, we've stuck together through some pretty difficult shit."

"That we have, brother."

Mike sighed. "I can't help out if you do this."

"I know," Andy said. "But it has to come sometime, you know what I mean? We are each going to have to get out on our own."

"I . . . I wouldn't like to think of anything happening to you over there," Mike said.

Andy smiled. "Shit, I wouldn't like to think of it either. Ah, enough of this. Think we'll score in Nassau?"

"Score?" Mike said. He laughed. "That's high school,

Andy. Strictly high school. You are an old graduate now.
You need to think more mature things.''

"Yeah? Well what do you suggest?"

"Think about whether or not we will get our wicks
wet," Mike said.

"Get our wicks wet? I see, that's a lot more mature, is
it?"

"Absolutely," Mike said.

"Yeah, well, I'll show you mature," Andy said. He
took another can of beer from Mike's desk drawer, shook
it up, then pointed it toward Mike as he pulled the tab.
Mike was showered with beer. Mike grabbed one and
started shaking it, but Andy, laughing at him, ran from the
room. He had nearly made it to his own door, when an
open can of beer hit the wall just beside him. It exploded
like a grenade, drenching Andy.

"Now," Mike said, laughing, "*that* is mature."

Jake wanted to rent a car, but Mike and Andy talked
him into renting three motor scooters instead, and they
drove them all over the island, the boys laughing and waving
at girls, and teasing Jake because he looked so out of place
on a motor scooter.

"Hey, dad, you know how to tell a happy motorcyclist?"
Andy shouted.

"How?"

"By the bugs on his teeth," Andy said, laughing uproari-
ously at his own joke.

Andy was the youngest, and easily the most outgoing of
the two. It was Andy who struck up conversations with
strangers, and who would walk up and down the beach,
flexing his muscles for the girls in bikinis, without shame
or self-consciousness.

"I banged my head enough in football to get these
muscles, why shouldn't I be able to show them off?"
Andy answered, when Mike commented on it.

"I think maybe you banged your head one time too often," Mike replied.

Now the three of them were riding their scooters, carrying a bucket of cold chicken, looking for a quiet place on the beach to picnic. Andy raced to the front, stating that he knew "just the place."

"I saw it yesterday when we rode by," he said, as they stopped their scooters under the shade of a drooping banyan tree.

It was a pretty place, with a secluded crescent of beach. The water was a deep blue, going through all the blue-green-purple colors in the spectrum as it passed over reefs while coming in from the sea.

"See, we can eat here in the shade, soak up some rays on the beach, and then hit the water to cool off."

"It's not too shabby," Mike admitted.

They had worn swim suits under their clothes, and now they slipped out of their pants and shirts and went down to the water's edge. Jake went in with his two sons, and they horsed around a bit, then Andy thought he saw a conch, and he and Mike dove through the waves trying to find one while Jake left the water and sat on the sand to watch them.

Mike was two years older than Andy, but Andy was already the bigger of the two. Andy had a thick, muscled neck and broad shoulders, and strong football player's thighs and legs. He had made honorable mention All-Conference in high school the year before, when he was a senior, and had accepted a football scholarship from Auburn University, the same school Mike was attending.

Mike's body was leaner, though he was certainly not weak. Mike was a runner, but he never ran in competition. He did it, he said, because it relaxed him. Jake had never liked all the running in Army PT, and he couldn't understand why anyone would run just to relax, but he was glad that Mike had some physical outlet. Had it not been for his running, Mike would have been the total esthete, content with his music, art, and ideas.

The ideas, Jake learned, were not always compatible with his own.

Both boys came out of the water then, and Andy, who was always hungry, headed for the chicken.

"First dibs," he called, pulling out a large piece. Mike got a piece for himself and for Jake.

"Dad, why are you going back to Vietnam?" Mike asked, sitting down beside Jake.

"Why? Because I have orders, that's why."

"But you don't believe in the war. I saw you on TV when you were before the committee, and I read about it in the paper. You are against the war."

"Mike, I am a professional solider," Jake said. "I don't have a position one way or the other. I do what my duty says must be done."

"Even if it is killing innocent people in an unjust war?"

"What war is just?" Jake replied. He sighed. "I know this war is difficult for people to understand. I admit, I don't understand it. But I understand duty, and I understand honor, and I understand country."

"That's the motto of West Point," Andy said around a piece of chicken.

"As a matter of fact it is," Jake said. He looked at Mike and Andy. "You two are the first male Culpeppers in five generations who chose not to go to West Point."

"I can take art at Auburn," Mike said. "Could you see me as an art major in West Point?"

"Auburn is a fine school, and I am proud of your grades there. But the words duty, honor and country shouldn't just apply to West Point. It could very well be the guiding principle for any citizen."

"It is my guiding principle," Mike said.

"Good. I'm glad you see it that way."

"That's why I burned my draft card," Mike said. "And when I am drafted, I am going to Canada."

Jake looked at Mike in shock. "You don't mean that!"

"Yes, I do mean it," Mike said.

"You could disgrace me that way?" Jake asked.

"I hoped you would understand," Mike said.

"Understand? How the hell could I understand something like that?"

"Honor," Mike said quietly.

"Honor?" Jake spat out angrily. "You'd run to Canada to avoid the draft, and call that honor?"

"Yes," Mike said. "For I consider it dishonorable to fight in a war which is unjust."

"What about you, Andy?" Jake asked. "Do you feel the same way?"

"No," Andy said. "But I respect Mike's right to feel that way."

"What does that mean?" Jake asked disgustedly. "That you might do the same thing as Mike when the time comes, only you don't want to tell me?"

"Dad, Andy has already enlisted in the Army," Mike said.

"What?" Jake asked in a quiet voice. "What are you talking about? I thought you had a football scholarship."

"I do," Andy said. "I already talked to Coach Shug Jordan. The scholarship will still be good two years from now."

"I don't understand. If you are going into the army anyway, why didn't you apply for the Academy?" Jake asked.

"Sheeit," Andy said. "Their football team couldn't beat Vassar."

"There is more to a higher education than football."

"Not to me," Andy said, getting another piece of chicken.

"Then, don't enlist now. Go to Auburn like you planned and take ROTC. That way you could still come into the army as an officer."

"I don't want to be an officer," Andy said.

"What? Why not?"

"I told you, I don't intend to stay in the Army for more'n a couple of years. I just want to get over to 'Nam, bust head, and get it over with."

"Bust head?"

"Yeah, you know, waste a few Congs."

Jake looked at Andy with as much shock as he had looked at Mike, then, the incongruity of having two brothers with such totally different attitudes struck him as humorous and he laughed.

"You two little shits," he said. "I wish I could just cut the two of you down the middle and graft you together again. Damn if one of you isn't a commie and the other one a friggin' nazi."

"Maybe we ought to start a new party," Mike suggested with a laugh. "The Fascist-Socialist-Militarist-John Birch-Love society."

"Yeah," Andy suggested, lying down on the beach with his hands folded behind his head. "The love part, that's what I like. Where the women are concerned, you can make me the Secretary of Lovin'."

"Oh?" Jake teased. "And are you experienced?"

"I've been around," Andy said mysteriously.

"Yeah," Mike laughed. "Suzie Morgan let him cop a feel at the prom this year."

"I'm going to cop a feel of your ass right now, sucker," Andy said, and he started for Mike, who, laughing, ran from him.

Jake watched them running and laughing, in and out of the water. They were at extreme opposites in almost every way, and yet it was obvious that they were very close as brothers. How could that be? Even as he asked the question though, he knew the answer. Wasn't he just like them, in an even more complicated way? After all, he shared many of Mike's questions about this war, and yet, by training and tradition, he publicly allied himself with the position taken by Andy. There, encompassed within one personality, was the polarity exhibited by his two sons. And, truth to tell, he didn't know which was the dominant pole.

CHAPTER THIRTEEN

Kristin walked for a long way down the beach, staying just along the line between wet and dry sand. Shells, large and small, lay on the beach and they caused tiny eddies to form and swirl as the waves rushed in over them, then back out again.

It was dawn and the water had not yet turned blue, but was still a pearl gray in the early morning light. The beach was practically deserted. One old man combed the beach diligently, while his wife, wearing a wide-brimmed straw hat, pointed out things he missed.

In the distance a lone figure stood in a familiar slouch, looking out over the sea. Kristin smiled and hurried toward him. She had been a little worried that he wouldn't be there.

"Dr. Mainwaring, I believe?" Kristin said as she approached him.

Dr. Mainwaring, who was just barely taller than Kristin, turned toward her. He had a receding hairline, bushy eyebrows and penetrating brown eyes. He was not a particularly handsome man in the classical sense, but there was a sensuality about him to which Kristin reacted strongly.

"Ah, my dear, so you did come," Dr. Mainwaring said. "I wasn't sure you would."

"I told you I would be here," Kristin said.

"Yes, so you did. I wasn't sure I could believe you."

"Why not? Have I ever given you cause to doubt me?"

"No," Dr. Mainwaring said. "But then I am the quintessential pessimist, always ready to believe that the worst thing that could happen, probably will. That way, I am always pleasantly surprised when my unhappy expectations do not materialize."

A jet fighter suddenly appeared above them, flying so fast that it was over them silently, like an image in a movie with the sound track out of synch. The airplane had been flying fairly low, but it pulled up over them and climbed out over the ocean, rising like a rocket on twin pillars of fire from its two powerful engines. The noise hit them then, bursting over them like a quick peal of thunder, then receding as rapidly as the plane, so that within a few seconds there was only a whisper of sound and two shining dots in the distance to mark the plane. A plume of jet exhaust hung in the sky over them, curved like the blade of a Turkish warrior's scimitar.

"He's out early," Kristin remarked.

"Yes," Dr. Mainwaring said. "In order to become proficient at killing babies, one must train diligently."

"I wish you wouldn't say that," Kristin said.

"You wish I wouldn't say what?"

"I wish you wouldn't say that everyone in the service is a baby killer."

"It's a good buzz word," Dr. Mainwaring admitted. "It helps to galvanize feelings against them."

"Yes, but there are some people in the service that I care about. Larry is in the army and so is Jimmy."

"They both sold out," Dr. Mainwaring said.

"That isn't fair," Kristin said. "They think you and I, and all the others who were engaged in the civil rights struggle sold out. We abandoned their struggle for this one."

"Are they unable to see that this war threatens not only the civil rights of all Americans, but the very existence of life itself? We haven't abandoned the civil rights movement, we have just expanded it. What I can't understand is how people like Larry and Jimmy can fight in this war. They are fighting to uphold the very things we have been trying to change.''

"They felt they had no choice.''

"Larry had no choice, I know,'' Dr. Mainwaring said. "He was drafted by the Green Bay Packers, I believe, at the same time he was drafted by the U.S. Army. If he ever wants to play for the Packers, he will have to fulfill his government obligation first.''

"Do you blame him for that? Larry stands to make a great deal of money playing professional football. Are you saying he should just walk away from the opportunity?''

"No. I'm saying that a person should set goals in life, then strive to attain those goals.'' Dr. Mainwaring sighed. "Larry has obviously done that. I am just sorry that his goals are so material.''

"You aren't being fair,'' Kristin said. "Larry's whole life has revolved around making it as a football player. It is the only way of expression for people like Larry.''

"I see. And what about people whose entire life is dedicated to the military? There are, you know, families in this nation who are third- and fourth-generation militarists. They attended military boarding schools and academies, as did their parents before them, and their children now. Kristin, there's an entire segiment of our society which is dedicated to war. That is their only means of expression. And yet, to allow them that expression endangers us all. Can't you see that?''

"Jake,'' Kristin said.

"I beg your pardon?''

"Jake,'' Kristin said again. "I know someone just like that. His name is Jake Culpepper and he is a colonel in the army. His father and his grandfather and—who knows how far back—were all generals.''

"And no doubt Jake Culpepper's burning ambition is to become a general just like them?''

"I suppose so," Kristin said. She thought of Jake for a moment. It had been a long time since she'd heard from him. "But, Jerry, I think you are wrong about Jake. He's not dedicated to war. I received a few letters from him when he was in Vietnam. He didn't always approve of what was going on."

"Generals need wars in order to be generals," Jerry Mainwaring said. "If you can't understand that, Kristin, then your friend has not only pulled the wool up over your panties, but down over your eyes as well. He's as responsible for killing babies as LBJ."

"You have no right to talk like that," Kristin said, stung by his remarks.

"Oh? Why not? I thought one of the things we were fighting for was the right for the truth to be heard."

"Yes, but . . ." Kristin started.

"Oh, I see. It depends upon the truth, doesn't it?"

"No," Kristin admitted. "Truth is truth, even when it hurts."

"That's my girl," Jerry said, reaching out and putting his arm around her to pull her close to him. "But some statements are better left unsaid, and I apologize for my indiscretion. I should close my mouth now and let our actions do our talking this afternoon when we go down to the airbase to prevent the planes from leaving."

Kristin shook a little, and Jerry could feel it.

"Are you frightened?"

"A little," Kristin admitted.

Jerry chuckled. "Well, you have a right to be. Lying down on the runway in front of a 707 isn't exactly a cup of tea, you know. Come along, dear. I have a room for us."

"What about Pauline?" Kristin asked.

"Pauline is asleep. She won't wake up until ten or so, and by then I'll be back. What about your friends? Who are you crashing with?"

"A bunch of people who were at the rally last night," Kristin said. "One of them had access to a beach house, and he invited as many as wanted to come. I slept on a couch.''

"That must have been lonesome," Jerry suggested.

"It was the way I wanted it," Kristin said. "There's no way I'm going to get involved in one of these group-gropes. Sometimes I think half the people we meet in these things are in it for the sex.''

"Don't be hard on them, my dear," Jerry said. "They are young people, fired with the zeal of dedicating themselves to a cause. They are thrown together with the opposite sex, and that excitement naturally manifests itself in a desire to share, and to touch. I am not immune to such feelings." Jerry ran his finger lightly around Kristin's ear. "And neither are you, as, witness the little tryst we are about to share.''

"It's different with us," Kristin said. "We aren't stretching our hands out to grab the first warm body we come to. With us there is a spiritual and emotional commitment. It isn't just sexual gratification.''

"Of course not," Jerry said.

The room Jerry had rented for them was in a small motel which featured, "Every room with an ocean view.'' It was painted in a nauseous shade of pink and green, but Kristin closed her eyes to it. After all, she wasn't being asked to live here, just to make love here.

Jerry opened the door and Kristin went inside. The room smelled of Lysol and Kristin could see that it was exceptionally clean even if the color scheme wasn't to her liking.

Jerry began taking off his clothes as soon as the door was shut behind him.

"We'd better hurry," he said. "We've a lot of things to do before the demonstration.''

As Kristin watched Jerry strip out of his clothes, she thought of all the activity of the night before. She had lain on the couch and listened to the writhing, groping bodies on the floor, feeling no desire at all to join them. Now, for just a fleeting instant, she had the same thought. Was their haste to have sex this morning any different from what she observed last night?

But of course it is, she answered herself. After all, she and Jerry shared a commitment to each other.

"You must hurry, my dear," Jerry said again. By now he was totally naked, and turning down the covers of the bed.

A bed, Kristin thought, not the floor. And here they were alone, two lovers sharing with each other, not engaging in group sex. What they were doing now was right. No, not right. It could never be right with Pauline, the innocent wife, sleeping in ignorance, while her husband cavorted with one of his female students. But if it was not right, then at least it had more meaning than a mindless orgy.

Kristin took off her clothes quickly, then slipped into bed beside Jerry. She reached down and began to fondle him until he was ready, then she positioned herself to allow him to come over her. The penetration was easy and familiar, an intimacy she had first shared with Dr. Jerry Mainwaring when she was a student in his first class. She had been surprised, and flattered, when she realized that he, a nationally respected professor, was actually coming on to her, then an eighteen-year-old girl. They had made love the first time on the leather sofa in Dr. Mainwaring's office. Since that time they had made love many times, and, though Pauline knew nothing of their affair, she had come to accept Kristin as a family friend.

Kristin heard Jerry's breath shorten, and his pace quicken, and she knew he was about to climax. It surprised her that it was happening so quickly. She had experienced a few pleasurable strokings, but her own orgasm was nowhere near.

Jerry's body suddenly grew taut, he let out a long, slow sigh, then collapsed across Kristin's body. She lay there beneath him, telling herself that her emotional and spiritual commitment to him was enough to offset any physical dissatisfaction she might experience.

Jake knocked on the door of the Commanding General's office at Travis Air Force Base. Jake was the delay-party departure officer in charge of seeing that all personnel and equipment of the 102nd Airmobile Division met their flight station times. In such capacity, he had to report to the Commanding General daily, to give him an up-to-the-minute briefing on the status of the debarkation.

"Jake," General Tongate said, greeting Jake as he walked in. General Tongate offered Jake a cigar, and when Jake declined, the General took one for himself. "How is the deployment going?"

"Smooth as silk, General," Jake answered, shoving a piece of paper in front of the General. "Twenty-one serials have departed with an average station time of plus seven minutes."

The General looked at the paper as he lit his cigar. He smiled around the puffs of smoke which rose from his action.

"All right," he said. "I'd say this was a prime operation. Jake, you sure I can't talk you into staying here as my transportation officer?"

"I'm sure, General," Jake said.

"Yeah, I was afraid of that." General Tongate shoved the paper Jake had given him to one side, then picked up another paper. "You want a little action, don't you?"

"Not particularly, General. I've had a little action," Jake said. "But if my boys are going into action, then I want to go with them."

"Well, Colonel Culpepper, it may just be that you and your boys are going to get a little action sooner than you anticipated."

"What do you mean, sir?"

"According to this FBI report, we are going to be

visited this afternoon, by upwards of one hundred thousand demonstrators. They are going to hold a 'lie-in'.''

"A lie-in, General? What is that?''

"They are going to lie on the runways to prevent our planes from landing and taking off.''

"Damn,'' Jake said. "That will sure bring things to a screeching halt.''

"It would if we let it happen,'' General Tongate said. "But I don't intend to let it happen.''

"General, how are you going to stop it?''

"I'm just going to stop it, that's all,'' General Tongate said. "I'm the Commanding General of one of the mightiest military installations in the entire world. Do you think I'm just going to sit around on my ass and let one hundred thousand unarmed punks take over? No, by God! It's not going to happen.''

"Do you have a plan to stop it?''

"I'm activating every garrison man at my disposal,'' General Tongate said. "The base security force, the Air Police, the bakers and clerks. I'm ordering every one of them to full alert by noon today. They will fully armed, and they will take up positions all around the base, with orders to allow no unauthorized entry.''

"How many men will that give you?''

"About five thousand.''

"You will still be outnumbered twenty to one,'' Jake said.

"Yes, but my men will be armed.''

"That's just what I'm afraid of,'' Jake said. "General, someone is going to get hurt that way.''

"Well, it won't be any of my men, I can assure you that.''

"No, sir. But it might be the entire Department of Defense.''

General Tongate ran his hand through his shock of white hair and sighed.

"All right," he finally said. "Do you have any ideas?"

"Yes, sir," Jake said. "As a matter of fact, I do have an idea."

It was much more than a mere demonstration. It was a "happening," an event which gathered not only one hundred thousand protestors, but press coverage from the major TV networks, newspapers, and national magazines.

The demonstration was well planned, right down to the establishment of aid stations and command posts. There were field leaders who were equipped with walkie talkie radios, and they radioed reports back to the headquarters, and received instructions from the headquarters as to where to go next to best marshal their efforts.

Kristin was working at the command post which was situated on the back of a flat-bed truck. She had a chair and a table, and she was writing down on a chart the names of the field leaders and their positions, and logging their reports.

"Paul Clary just called in," one of the radio operators said. "He is at the north gate, and he says that the guards are spread pretty thin there."

Kristin plotted the information on her chart, while Jerry Mainwaring leaned over her shoulder.

"Tell Nancy to move as many over to support Paul as she can," Jerry said.

A young man was brought into the aid station then, bleeding from the head. Two others were supporting him.

"What happened?" Jerry yelled down from the back of the truck. "Was he hurt by one of the military?"

"Naw," one of the two young men with the injured man said. "One of our people from way in the back threw a beer bottle."

"Attention, attention, soldiers are loading on one of the airplanes," a voice over the radio said.

"All right, this is it," Jerry Mainwaring replied. "Notify all field leaders to move toward the plane. Get between it and the runway, do you understand. Get between the plane and the runway!''

The message was relayed, and a few minutes later there were shouts and cheers from far in front of the crowd of people. Kristin could see a movement.

''We're in place!'' one of the radio messages called out triumphantly. ''We are in place. This mother's goin' nowhere.''

''All right!'' Jerry said, rubbing his hands gleefully. ''Tell me we can't stop this shit!''

Over the next couple of hours there were two or three other attempts to take off. The soldiers were taken from one plane and put on another, but the protestors managed to react each time, in time to stop the plane before it could even leave the parking area.

Late in the afternoon, Kristin heard sirens, then she saw a general movement of the crowd, until she realized that a couple of jeeps were driving through toward the command post.

''Pigs!'' someone shouted. ''Here come the pigs and baby killers!''

''Let them through,'' Jerry replied. He smiled. ''Let them through. They have probably come to negotiate a surrender!''

Jerry's comment was answered with cheers and laughter, and the crowd parted to let the jeeps approach.

Kristin watched the approaching jeeps with a feeling of victory, savoring her triumph with as much delight as the others. Then, when the first jeep stopped, she gasped. The man riding in the right front seat was Jake Culpepper!

''Who is in charge here?'' Jake asked, when the jeep stopped.

''The people are in charge here, pig,'' one belligerent young man shouted from the crowd. ''Can't you see that? The people are in charge.''

''Then who speaks for the people?'' Jake asked.

''Dr. Mainwaring can speak for us,'' Kristin said.

Jake looked at Kristin, and she saw a look of surprise on his face which must have mirrored her own.

"Is he here?" Jake asked Kristin.

"Yes," Jerry said. "What do you want, General?"

"He is a Colonel," Kristin said quickly. "Colonel Jake Culpepper."

Now it was Jerry's time to be surprised, and he looked at both of them for a moment, then smiled at Jake.

"Well, well, so you are Kristin's Jake," he said. "What can I do for you, Jake?"

"You can tell all these people to go home," Jake said. "It's all over."

"It's all over? What do you mean it's all over? Have you decided not to ship out any more troops?"

"No," Jake said. "I mean we have already shipped out the rest of the division. They left today."

Those of the crowd who were close enough to overhear the conversation laughed and booed.

"How did they leave?" someone shouted. "We haven't let a plane take off from here all afternoon."

"I know," Jake said. "We've been shuttling garrison troops from one plane to another all day as a decoy. The real troops were bussed to Oakland and they took off from there.

"What?" Jerry shouted angrily. He looked up at one of his radio operators. "Sheila, have someone get to a phone. Find out if the troops really left from Oakland."

"How have you been, Jake?" Kristin asked. Despite the fact that they were in the middle of a crowd of one hundred thousand people, the interest of the crowd was now held by the process of checking on Jake's claim, and they were able to talk in relative privacy.

"I've been getting along," Jake said. "And you?"

"Yeah," Kristin said. "I've been getting along too. You never wrote. I even tried to find out your address from the army, but I never heard anything."

"I know. I thought about writing a few times, but I was afraid it would be a waste of time."

"I would like to have heard from you," Kristin said.

"Why? It's fairly obvious that we are going in opposite directions now."

"No, I don't believe that, Jake," Kristin said. "I think we are both going to the same place. We have just taken different routes, that's all."

"Son of a bitch!" Jerry suddenly shouted. "He's right. They all left from Oakland!"

"Goddammit! Let's tear this place apart!" someone shouted, and his shout was echoed by others, but Jerry held up his hands until he finally managed to quiet them.

Jerry looked at Jake and smiled. "So, my friend," he said. "You have won, for today. But we shall see how our battles come out in the future."

"I don't plan to have any more battles with you," Jake said. "My job was to get my division embarked. I did that. My job is now finished."

Jake got back in the jeep, and the driver turned the siren back on and turned the vehicle in a big circle. The crowd pushed menacingly close, and for a moment, Kristin thought they were going to be so angry at having been fooled, that they would rush the jeep and turn it over. She held her breath in fear of just such a thing, but it didn't happen. The jeep completed its turn and started back toward the gates of the base. Kristin watched Jake as the jeep drove away. He stared straight ahead and didn't show the slightest twinge of fear. She had never known anyone she admired more than she did Jake at that moment.

CHAPTER FOURTEEN

Larry shifted his duffle bag higher onto his shoulder and walked from the customs line to the center of the terminal. He was at Da Nang airport, and he was looking around for the counter which said "in-country transportation."

The terminal was full, noisy and hot. There wasn't an empty chair or even an empty spot against the wall. Soldiers either lay or sat around waiting for a flight, and Larry knew from his brief conversation with the transportation clerk that the wait could be as long as a week.

The thought of a week of living out of his duffle bag, fighting the heat and the boredom of waiting, was not a happy one, but it was one Larry prepared himself to face.

"Hey, bro, what's shakin'?" Someone called. Larry turned toward the voice and saw a familiar face. He smiled happily.

"Jimmy? Hey, what are you doin' here?"

"I got a letter from Nicole, sayin' you'd be comin' into Da Nang, so I copped a couple of days to come meet you. Hey, man, you know the dap?"

Jimmy started a series of gestures and moves which passed for a handshake, thought it was more like an intricately choreographed dance. Larry tried to follow it, but he wasn't very successful.

"It's easy to tell you jus' got in country, my man,"

Jimmy said. "You ain't got all the moves down yet. Where you goin'?"

"Ben Hoa," Larry said. "Then to the 102nd Airmobile."

"Yeah? Hey, I'm with the Big Red One at Phy Loi. We won't be that far apart."

Larry looked over at the in-country transportation counter and saw a long line. "That is, if I ever get there. I may stay here the whole time."

"No sweat, bro," Jimmy said. "Most of the Air Force transport dudes are brothers. They'll help us out. That's how I got up here to meet you in the first place. The transportation clerks will always help."

"Yeah?" Larry said. "Why?"

"Why? 'Cause you a brother, man. We got us a brotherhood over here that's bad, man. I mean bad. If we'd'a had this brotherhood in Mississipi we'd'a kicked some white ass." Jimmy reached under his fatigue blouse and pulled out a black, braided cross. "Look here. You see this cross? You get you one of these crosses, and anytime you see a brother's got one on, why, you gotta help 'im, no matter what."

"What is the significance of the cross? Is it religious?"

"Yeah, sort of," Jimmy said. He giggled. "The white officers and NCOs don't like it much, but they kinda scared to ask us to take it off, like it would be against our religion or somethin'."

"Where do you get one?" Larry asked.

"Come on," Jimmy said. "There's a little place just out the gate where you can get all kinds o' shit. You can pick one up there for five hundred P."

"How much is that?"

"Officially? It's about five dollars. But don't go tradin' a dollar for a hundred P. You can do better'n that. Least, you could 'fore all the new guys got in country and started runnin' up the price of ever'thin' from sandals to pussy. Come on, we'll get you a cross, then hit the ville. There's no sense in even tryin' this line for a couple of hours, anyhow.''

"What about my duffle bag?"

"You got anything real valuable in it?"

"Just my issue."

"Fuck it. Leave it here. Anybody steals it, we'll just steal another one," Jimmy giggled.

Larry dropped his dufflebag in a pile with several others, then followed Jimmy out the door. Da Nang consisted of red dirt and green "hooches," as the huts were called. It was hot, dirty, and smelled of open sewage and rotting vegetables and fish.

"Damn, this place stinks," Larry said.

"Yeah, well whatta you expec', man? You're in the asshole of the world." Jimmy took a pass from his billfold. "There. Show 'em this. They never look anyway."

Larry and Jimmy flashed their passes at the Air Base gate, and a few minutes later were walking down Plantation Row, as the string of bars, restaurants, souvenir stands and massage parlors were called.

"Hey, black GI, you wanna changee your luck? I number one fuck, you try me, you see. I like black GI's. Black GI's habba number one cock!''

The girl who uttered the proposition was leaning against the front wall of one of the bars. She was wearing baggy white pants, and a black blouse which was fastened with only one button. Her breasts could be seen through the opening of the blouse, but they were broken down and sagging, like she was. She was dirty and unkempt.

"Listen to her talking about changing out luck," Larry said. "That's what that redneck son of a bitch said that night with Nicole."

"I don't like to think about that night," Jimmy said. "When I think of how easy it is to blow someone away now, I get sick at my stomach because I didn't waste that motherfucker. Anyhow, don't pay any attention to this bitch. She's a pig, man. They won't even let her inside the

place. Here, get your cross in here, then we'll go next
door to Magic Fingers.''

Larry laughed. ''Magic Fingers?''

''Yeah, man, wait'tl you try it.''

Larry picked out a black, braided cross and started to
pay the price the woman ask for it. Jimmy reached out and
grabbed the money angrily.

''Hold on, goddammit!'' He said. ''You the kinda
sonuvabitch runnin' up the cost of pussy. I told you, man,
don't pay the bitch what she asks for.'' Jimmy looked at
the clerk, and held up two fingers. ''Two hundred P,'' he
said. ''Two hundred.''

The woman, who had asked for eight hundred, came
down to seven hundred, and after a little spirited give and
take, sold the cross for the five hundred piastres that
Jimmy had indicated Larry should get it for in the first
place.

Larry put on the cross, then followed Jimmy next door.

The Magic Fingers was entered through a beaded curtain.
To the right as they went in, was a long bar. To the left, a
handful of tables, nearly every table occupied by GI's and
scantily dressed Vietnamese women. Most of the GI's
were black, though there was a scattering of white GI's.
There was a jukebox against the front wall right by the
door, and a Dionne Warwick song fought with the conversation and the laughter.

Two girls met them. Unlike the hag who had proposi-
tioned them out front, these two were very pretty.

''You buy Da Nang tea?'' they asked.

''Yeah,'' Jimmy said. ''We'll buy you some tea.'' He
rubbed himself. ''Then we'll go up to your room and have
a ti-ti bang-bang.'' He giggled.

''Neber hoppen, GI,'' one of the girls replied, matching
his giggle, but she leaned against him in such a way as to
indicate that, once the price was negotiated, it very well
would happen.

The waitress brought beers for Jimmy and Larry, and tiny glasses of a golden liquid for the two girls.

"What is that shit, man?" Larry asked.

"Tea, just like they said," Jimmy answered. "Man, these girls couldn't sit here and drink whiskey all day, they'd be drunk on their ass all the time."

Both girls finished their tea and asked for another one. Jimmy laughed.

"Now the trick is, man, to talk 'em into goin' upstairs with you before they put too many of those things down, 'cause ever'one they drink costs fifty P."

Larry followed Jimmy's lead, and three drinks later they were walking up a narrow flight of stairs to an upper floor. The girl with Larry, who said her name was Lonnie, pushed open a door then turned toward Larry and smiled.

"My room," she said.

Larry went inside. The room was very small, about eight by ten, and dominated by a double bed. The bed had a stained mattress, but no linen. The pillow was a long, hard cylinder. There was a Vietnamese calendar on the wall and the only thing about it Larry could understand was the date; September 15th, 1967.

"Okay," Lonnie said. "You give me money and we make love now."

"I thought you came up here with me because you were in love with me," Larry teased.

"Yes," Lonnie said. "Love you very much."

"Enough to make love free?"

"Neber hoppen."

Larry laughed and handed the girl the money.

"You're okay, Lonnie," he said. "A guy can always know where he stands with you."

Lonnie smiled when he gave her the money, and, quickly, she took off what little she was wearing. She lay back on the bed, and Larry noticed that she had no pubic hair. At first he thought she had shaved herself, then noticed that there was some, though very little. It shocked him a little, and it made him feel as if he were taking advantage of a very young child. It was an uncomfortable feeling.

Jake rode in the jeep at the front of the convoy. Stretched out along Route 14 behind him were ten trucks, all supposedly bearing supplies. In fact, the trucks were empty, and each was being drawn by a volunteer. The entire convoy was a decoy, conceived by Jake, and named Operation John Wayne.

"My idea," Jake said, repeating what he had written in his report, "is to suck the VC into an ambush. If they figure they can hit us hard, and hurt us a lot, at a minimum risk to themselves, they are going to do it."

"That's the way they play the old ballgame," the USARV G-3 said.

"All right, then here's what I want to do. I'll put out word through normal channels that I'm moving supplies along 14 to set up a fire-base at Ban Don. That's close enough to the Cambodian border that they'll be able to move in all their support troops, and they'll figure they can hit us and withdraw back into Cambodia. But I'll have two companies in position to block their retreat back to Cambodia, and, the moment they hit us, we'll counterattack with two more companies brought in by helicopter. There are good landing zones here and here, which we will secure before hand."

"Sounds pretty good," the G-3 agreed. "What are you calling it?"

"How about Operation John Wayne?"

"Operation John Wayne?" The Division AG who was in on the planning, laughed.

"Yeah," Jake answered. "You know how John Wayne always manages to get there in the nick of time? Well, that's what I want the choppers to do."

"I hope they make it," the AG said. "Otherwise the poor son-of-a-bitch you got in charge of the decoy is going to knit barbed wire with his asshole."

"I'm going to be that poor son of a bitch," Jake said.

The G-3 looked up. "I don't think the old man is going to like you being with the convoy."

"I'm going with the convoy," Jake insisted.

Jake got his way, and now, as the convoy moved through the area where he was certain the ambush would take place, the hackles on the back of his neck raised.

"Keep your eyes peeled, Simmons," Jake said. He held his M-16 in his lap and patted it nervously.

"Colonel, if I open my lids any wider, my eyeballs are goin' to fall out," Simmons said. Simmons was SP/5 Edward Simmons, a redheaded boy from Wyoming. "I reckon my ancestors felt like this when they was lookin' for Indians," he added.

"Goodnature Six, this is Three, over," the jeep radio popped. Goodnature Six was Jake's call-sign, Six being the sign for Commanding Officer. Three was Captain Worley, Jake's S-3 officer, and, for purposes of this convoy, the assistant convoy commander. Captain Worley was riding in the last vehicle, a trail jeep.

Jake reached for the mike.

"This is Six, go ahead."

"I just caught sight of someone on the hill behind us. I think we are about to have company."

"John, did you copy?" Jake asked.

John meant John Wayne, and Jake's message was meant for his Executive Officer, who was in command of the counter-ambush forces. They couldn't actually discuss details over the radio, because they knew the VC would be monitoring the transmissions.

"Roger," the XO answered.

Jake held the mike in his lap and started looking up on the hills which were on both sides of the road.

"Any time now," he said to his driver.

Suddenly there was an explosion in the road just ahead of them. It was so close that dirt and rock rained down on them.

"Jesus!" Simmons shouted. "Oh, sweet Jesus! That nearly got us!"

There were other explosions along the line behind them, and Jake twisted around in his seat to see one of the trucks burning. The VC had planted charges in the road along the killing zone, then they set the charges off when the convey was in place. Fortunately, the spacing of the vehicles in the convoy was such that only one truck was hit by the planted charges.

"John, we've been hit!" Jake shouted into the mike.

"Roger, we're on our way," the XO answered.

Jake and Simmons left the jeep and hit the ditch alongside the road. The normal procedure was to speed through the killing zone as quickly as possible, because often the VC would mine the ditches alongside the road as well as the road itself. The convoy couldn't speed through, however, because more than half of it was blocked by the burning truck.

Automatic weapons fire rained down on them from the rocks above, and Jake heard the rounds whistle by as they hit the ground and the vehicles behind them. The bullets pinged and whined, and Jake heard windshields shattering under the attack.

The procedure for abandoning the vehicles was odd numbers to the left, and even numbers to the right. That way they wouldn't be subject to surprise attack from the rear.

Jake returned the fire, spraying a burst toward a group of rocks where he had seen VC.

A rocket-propelled grenade landed in the ditch with them but didn't explode. Simmons picked it up and tried to toss it out.

"No, get down!" Jake shouted, but the shout was too late and the device exploded. Simmons' hand was blown away, and as he spun around, Jake saw a stain of bright red blood on his chest.

Jake went to him quickly, and began applying the compress bandage from the packet on Simmon's belt. At that moment, helicopter gunships came over them and the hills on both sides of the road exploded as the gunships fired salvo after salvo of rockets at the ambushers.

"Listen to that!" Jake said. "Listen, Simmons, we're givin' 'em hell!"

Simmons opened his eyes and looked at Jake. His lips moved but no words came out. His eyes rolled back in his head so that the pupils were completely invisible.

"Shit!" Jake shouted. He pounded his fist on the ground beside Simmons. "Shit, shit, shit, shit!"

There was a great increase in the rate of fire from the hills, and Jake could hear the sound of American M-16s. In fact, there were a lot more M-16s firing than AK-47s.

Jake looked up and saw that American soldiers from the counter-ambush companies were coming down over the crest of the hills, sweeping out in all directions. He realized then that all the fire which had been coming toward the bait column had stopped. He heard shouts and cheers from up and down the ambush line, and, a few moments later, he saw Major Bailey, his XO, coming down the side of the hill toward him. Bailey was moving in a sideways gait, sort of slipping and hopping down the hill. He held his M-16, butt against his hip, barrel pointing up jauntily, like a great white hunter posing for a cigarette commercial photo. He looked down at Jake and smiled.

"We kicked ass, sir!" he said. "We've counted more than seventy dead on the hills, and right now we're chasin' the sons of bitches right into our trap. By god, I doubt that more than half a dozen of the little cocksuckers'll get out of this."

"Did you lose anyone?"

"No, sir, not a man," Major Bailey said. "Not a single man. How about you?"

"My driver was killed," Jake said. Jake looked around and saw his S-3 coming toward him. Captain Worley had been in position at the far end of the line on the opposite side of the road.

"Captain Worley, what are our casualties?" Jake asked.

"Johnson and Clay were in the truck that got hit by the mine," Captain Worley said. "Johnson didn't get much more'n a few cuts, but Clay's got quite a bit of metal in his legs. Other than that, no one hurt, and no one killed."

"I wish that was true," Jake said, pointing to Simmons. Someone had draped a poncho over Simmons head and shoulders, so the wound that had killed him couldn't be seen. He looked like a GI who had just lay down and draped a poncho over himself to keep out the sun.

"That's your driver, isn't it, sir?" Captain Worley asked.

"Yeah."

"I'm sorry."

"Yeah, but, even so, we're going to get a VC body count of three hundred or more," Major Bailey said. "Three hundred of them for one of us. I'm sorry about your man, Colonel, but you have to admit, that's a pretty damned good trade. Division will have to say this was an acceptable loss."

"Yeah," Jake said. "Division will say it is an acceptable loss. But will Marcey?"

"Marcey?"

"Simmons' wife," Jake said.

"This way!" Mot called to the fifteen or so men who remained from his company. Mot, now a veteran of three years fighting, was a sergeant in the Dau Tieng Company. They had been following a trail to the east, to sanctuary on the Cambodian side of the border. But when they crossed a small stream, Mot turned south.

"No, we must get across the border," one of the others said.

"We'll never make it," Mot said. "The Americans will have soldiers there, blocking us off."

"How could they? They don't know where we are going."

"They know everything," Mot said. "Haven't you figured this out yet? We didn't ambush the Americans, they ambushed us!"

Than Ngoc, a Lieutenant in the Army of Liberation, came back to see what the discussion was about.

"What are you doing, Sergeant Mot?" he hissed. "We've got to get across the border."

"No," Mot said. "The Americans will be waiting for us. We've got to work our way south."

"We are going across the border!" Than Ngoc ordered.

Mot pointed his AK-47 at the Lieutenant.

"Lieutenant Ngoc, if you wish to cross the border, go ahead. I am going south here," he said.

"Fool! I will report you to the Central Committee. You will be shot!"

"If you go east, you won't live to talk to the Central Committee," Mot said.

"We shall see about that," Ngoc replied. He looked at the others. "Come with me," he said.

"I choose to stay with Sergeant Mot," one of the others said, and three more agreed with him. The remaining men, about ten, went with the Lieutenant, and they crossed the stream, heading east.

"I will report this mutiny," Ngoc called back angrily.

Mot watched Ngoc and the others as they crossed the stream and started across the rice paddies for the hills beyond.

"Mot, let us go quickly," said one of those who stayed with him.

"Wait," Mot said. He held up his hand. "Let us see if they make it."

Mot and his four companions hid behind the stream bank and watched. Ngoc and his followers moved out onto the rice paddy, running quickly along one of the dikes.

Suddenly two helicopters appeared from behind and

over Mot's head. They were flying fast and low, and they
zipped by overhead, totally unaware of Mot's existence.
They started for Ngoc and his men.

Mot raised up and started firing at the two helicopters.
The others with him joined in, and Mot was rewarded for
his efforts by the sight of black smoke streaming back
from the engine of one of the helicopters.

Both helicopters opened fire on Ngoc and his men, and
Mot saw Ngoc and the others dive off the dike and splash
down into the flooded paddy. Automatic weapons fire
coming from the vegetation across the paddy told Mot that
he was correct in his belief that the Americans would be
waiting in a blocking position. As Mot stared across the
paddy, he saw scores of American soldiers coming out of
the trees, moving toward Ngoc and his men.

The helicopter Mot had hit turned and started down
toward the paddy to make an emergency landing. Mot
fired again at the helicopter, and he saw the front windshield of the ship shatter as his bullets sprayed into it. The
helicopter, which had been coming down in a smooth
descent, suddenly lurched, and fell over on its side. It
crashed hard, then exploded into a great, greasy ball of
flame.

"Son of a bitch!" Mot heard one of the American
infantrymen shout. "Lookit that!"

The remaining helicopter made another pass over Ngoc
and his few remaining men, then the Americans closed
with them. The fighting was short and furious, then it
stopped. Ngoc, and every man who had started across the
rice paddy with him, lay dead.

"Let's go," Mot said quietly. He started down stream,
keeping under the trees so he wouldn't be seen by any
aircraft who might be flying over them.

"Sergeant Mot, you'll be in command now," one of the
others said. "Ngoc was our last officer."

"Yes," Mot said grimly. "I know."

CHAPTER FIFTEEN

Larry Cantrell was assigned to Headquarters and Headquarters Company, 502nd Airmobile Infantry (detached), stationed at Di An.

Di An was a large, flat, ugly camp which consisted of row upon row of eight-man tents with the sides rolled up and the tops covered in dust. Most of the tents had floors of some sort constructed from cargo pallets, or plywood. One of the better floors was in the CP tent to which Larry was directed as soon as he arrived. There, the unique make-up of the 502nd was explained to him. The 502nd was not a full regiment, but it was greater in strength than an ordinary battalion. The 502nd was normally a part of the 101st Airborne, but it was operating as a detached unit, answerable not to Division Headquarters but directly to Headquarters, USARV in Saigon. That gave its commander an autonomous command, unique among combat units of such size.

"The reason we are unique, is because General Westmoreland knows that Colonel Culpepper's got his shit together," said the Sergeant who was doing the explaining.

"Colonel Culpepper?" Larry asked.

"Yeah, Colonel Jacob Steele Culpepper. I served with his ol' man, when his father won the Medal of Honor in Korea, and believe me, the son is just as tough. If you don't believe it, ask the VC. We just kicked some VC ass last week while you were still shacking up in some San Francisco whorehouse.''

The Sergeant who was speaking was Sergeant ''Pappy'' Phillips. He was the Battalion Sergeant-Major. He was a big man who had developed a slight belly-rise in his late forties, but was still powerful enough looking to be intimidating. He spoke with an Ozark mountain twang, despite the fact that he had been out of the hills and in the army for over twenty years now.

''I think I have heard of the Colonel,'' Larry said.

''You mighty damn right you have heard of the Colonel,'' Pappy said. Pappy was looking over Larry's 201 file. ''Hey, Cantrell. Son of a bitch! You're the football player, aren't you?''

''Yes,'' Larry said.

''Goddamn! I saw you on television when Cal Dunlap beat the shit out of Nebraska. Damn, you were good. Boy was that a game!''

''Thanks,'' Larry said.

''What the hell you doin' over here? Why aren't you playing in the NFL? Didn't you get drafted?''

Larry smiled. ''Yeah, that's why I'm here.''

''No, I mean by the pros.''

''I was drafted by the Green Bay Packers,'' Larry said. ''But the U.S. Army had first pick.''

''Yeah, ain't it the shits?'' Pappy said. ''I know where you're comin' from. I pitched a little for the old St. Louis Browns.''

''Really?'' Larry said. ''How long did you play for them?''

''About five years,'' Pappy said. ''I had a pretty good fast ball for a while. Then I lost my arm, and never developed enough stuff to compensate for it. The war come along and I got drafted. I don't think the front office ever missed me. Still, I like to recall the days when I was there. I struck out Joe Dimaggio three times in a row, once.''

"I'd like to have seen that," Larry said.

Pappy looked at Larry, and saw the black braided cord around his neck.

"You into the black power shit, Cantrell?"

"I'm proud of my race," Larry said.

"No reason why you shouldn't be," Pappy said. He pointed to the cord around Larry's neck. "I just noticed your black cross. That is what that is, isn't it?"

"Yes," Larry said. "Is there a regulation against wearing it?" he challenged.

"No, not as long as you wear it under your shirt," Pappy said. He ran his hand across his gray hair. "Look, Cantrell, I think you guys gotta right to be pissed off about a lot of things. Shit, they didn't even let Negroes play in the majors in my day, and that meant keepin' out guys like Satchel Page. But the men who work for me ain't got any color. You wanna wear that thing, you go right ahead. But I don't allow any racial harassment of any kind. I don't let the white boys pick on the black boys, and I don't let the black boys pick on the white boys. You got that?"

"Yes, Sergeant."

"I figure, a man like you, I don't really have to say this to. You set an example by who you are. But remember this: you are an American soldier first, and a black man next."

"Do you give this same lecture to the white soldiers who arrive?" Larry asked.

"You goddamned right I do," Pappy said. "I'll ship one of those redneck bastards outta here so fast your head will swim."

"Sergeant, I served my time in Mississippi," Larry said. "I made the freedom rides and the voter registration marches. I was there when they killed three of my fellow workers and buried them in a dirt dam. I figure that part of my life is behind me now. All I want to do is serve my time over here, get back to the States, and trade this uniform for one supplied by the Green Bay Packers."

Pappy looked at Larry for a moment, then he nodded his head. "Can you drive, Cantrell?"

"Of course."

"I tell you what I'm goin' to do. The ole man needs a new driver. He lost his old one. I'm goin' to assign you to him."

"What happened to his old one? Did he go back to the States?"

"No, he was killed last week," Pappy said. "Like I said, our ole man don't sit around on his ass. He goes where the action is. Now, what do you say? Do you want to drive for him? The one good thing, you are E.D. from all details."

Yeah," Larry said. "I'll drive for him."

"You got it," Pappy said.

Le stood barefoot on the cool tile floor, and looked through her bedroom window at the exquisite garden just outside. Night-blooming flowers, their colors subdued by the darkness, made their presence known by a soft scenting of the air. A nearby palm tree shifted in the breeze and the frond passed across the moon, gathering beams and scattering a flash of silver.

Le felt a heavy wetness in her womb, and the rapturous sensations which had exploded throughout her body at the time of her orgasms lingered with her now in pleasureable tinglings. Above her head the ceiling fan turned swiftly and its broad paddles whispered a cooling breeze to tease her sweat dampened body. Behind her on the bed lay the man whose tender supplications and skillful attentions had brought Le to the ecstasy she most recently enjoyed. He, like Le, was naked. And yet, whenever Le looked at him, even without clothes, he was never truly naked. Even when he wasn't wearing it, Le could see his priestly collar, for the man in Le's bed was Father Klaus Sachs.

"You are very quiet," Klaus said from the shadows of the bed.

"Yes," Le answered. "I know."

"Why are you so quiet?"

Le turned toward him, and her eyes glistened with tears. "In order to satisfy my lusts, I have sacrificed my soul," she said.

Klaus sat up, and a spot of semen on his thigh glistened in the soft light.

"Le, what is your soul?" He asked.

"Why do you, of all people, ask me that? You are a priest. Don't you know what a soul is?"

"Yes, I think I know. The human body is composed of millions and millions of individual cells, each cell capable of sustaining the process of life in a laboratory. This collection of cells forms man, and man's awareness of himself as one person, rather than as a collection of millions of life forms, is a soul. Now, as you are still aware of yourself as one person, then you most certainly have not forfeited your soul."

"But I have sinned," Le said.

"We all sin."

"But my sin is the greatest of all, for I have lain with a priest. I have cause you to break your vow of celibacy."

"Le," Klaus said. He sighed and pinched the bridge of his nose. "Le, the sin is mine, not yours. How can you assume to have the power to accept my sin as your own? Christ accepted the sins of us all when He went to the cross. For you to say you have accepted my sin is for you to usurp powers which aren't yours."

"But," Le started, only to be interrupted by Klaus.

"There are things I wish I could tell you," he said. "There are many things which you don't know, and which you can't know. But believe me, please believe me, when I say that you need not stand before God in shame for what we have done. The sin is mine, and mine alone, and I will bear it."

"I cannot let you bear it alone," Le said. She came to him and embraced him. "I love you too much."

"If you truly love me, then do as I say," Klaus said. "Do not distress yourself for my transgressions."

Le kissed him, and he returned her kiss, and in a moment all her troubling thoughts were put aside by the flood tide of feeling which rushed over her. The fires were renewed, not only in her own body, but in Klaus as well, for she saw at once that he was ready for her again.

Le reclined on the bed, already damp and musky from their earlier session, and she spread her legs to receive her lover again. She felt him thrust deeply into her.

Le gave a gasp of pleasure as she surrendered to the exquisite, silken sensations which overtook her. She took his lips and tongue eagerly and gave herself up to him to receive him deeply into her, joining with him in the rush to the ultimate pleasure.

Then it started, a tiny sensation that began deep inside her, buried in the innermost chamber of her being. It began moving out then, spreading forth in a series of concentric circles like waves emanating from a pebble cast in a pool. The waves began moving with more and more urgency, drawing her up tighter and tighter like the mainspring of a clock until finally in a burst of agony that turned to ecstasy, her body attained the release and satisfaction it had been seeking.

There were two more after that: one nearly as strong, then another not quite as strong but intensely satisfying in its own right. Then, when she felt Klaus reach his own goal, it was as if she was struck by lightning when a new, unexpected orgasm burst over her, sweeping away all that had gone before it and bringing her to a peak of fulfillment so intense that every part of her being from the tips of her toes to the scalp of her head tingled with the kinetic energy of it. She hung precariously balanced upon the precipice for several seconds, and during those rapturous moments her body became so sensitized that she experienced not her own sweet pleasure but could feel, through Klaus, the muscle-jerking release of pent-up energy which was his own orgasm. The waves of pleasure that swept over him moved into her own body so that his climax and hers became one massive burst.

As Le coasted down from the peak, she fell, not like a stone, but floated like a leaf, meeting new eddies of pleasure, rising back up a bit before slipping farther down. Finally she lay beside Klaus, watching the fan whirl above them.

"I had better leave," Klaus said after a while. "I wouldn't want to be here if Mot came home."

"Mot will not be back for one week," Le said.

"Oh?"

"He is visiting friends in the province of Tuy Duc."

"Tuy Duc? Le, I told you not to let him go there again. Tuy Duc is a dangerous place to be."

"I told him you said that," Le said. "But what can I do? Mot is a man now, and he will do as he wishes."

"You . . . you told him I said this?" Klaus asked in a choked voice.

"Yes," Le said.

"Why did you tell him I said it?"

"He wouldn't listen to me. I thought your words would have more weight." Le sighed. "But they did not. He went anyway. I'm sorry. Was I wrong?"

"In a few more hours it will not matter," Klaus said.

"What do you mean?"

"It will not matter," Klaus said again.

Mot lay on the sleeping mat beside the young girl who had proudly given her body to a hero of the revolution last night. He was now a Captain in the Army of Liberation, having attained that rank by surviving. He was regarded as a hero by all he encountered, yet he had done very few heroic things.

Mot looked over at the young girl. He had no idea how old she was, though she didn't look much over seventeen. Her breasts were little more than slight pillows of flesh,

though the nipples were the nipples of a woman. She had
been proud of her ability to please him last night, and now
she slept the peaceful sleep of one who had done her best
to serve the cause.

You think what I do is heroic? Mot thought, as he
looked at the sleeping girl. He reached down and brushed
her long hair away from her face so he could see her. The
battle against mosquitoes and snakes and all sorts of biting
insects is not heroic. The battle against skin diseases and
malaria and dysentery is not heroic. It is not heroic to be
hungry and wet, and to suffer from the heat, and yet, all
these things we must do. It is not even heroic to fight
against the Americans, when you lose the element of
surprise and the American firepower and numbers can
become very deadly. I am not a hero, I am an accident.

The girl moved against Mot, and feeling the pressure of
her body against his made him aware that his bladder was
full. He got up from the mat and walked to the door to
relieve himself. That was when he saw them. So high that
they were practically invisible, a flight of B-52s were
coming toward them. There were nine planes in three
groups of three. The first three banked away sharply, and
he wondered why, then he realized that this village was
very close to the Cambodian border, and the airplanes
would have to turn sharply to keep from overflying the
border.

But why had they come here in the first place? The
second V of three aircraft banked away, and then the
third V.

Suddenly Mot got a sinking sensation in the pit of his
stomach. Those planes were dropping bombs! He couldn't
see anything yet, but he knew it. Within a couple of
minutes, the bombs would come crashing down on the
village!

"Awake!" he shouted. "Everyone awake! Find shelter!
B-52s! We are being bombed by B-52s!"

The young girl with whom he had spent the night was up instantly. Her eyes were wide with fear.

"Bombs!" Mot shouted. "We've got to find shelter!"

"Come!" the girl said, and she darted out the back of the hut, with Mot right behind her. The girl ran toward a tree, then dropped down and disappeared beneath a bush. Mot realized there must be a hole there, and he went with her.

Mot's shouts had awakened a few others, and they in turn shouted at others, so that the village was awake and everyone was running toward some sort of shelter.

By now Mot's fears were realized, because the bombs had fallen far enough so that the whistle of their fall could be heard. It would be less than thirty seconds now before the first bombs hit.

The girl beside Mot drew next to him in terror. If she looked seventeen last night, she looked no more than twelve at this moment, and Mot reached for her, not as he would toward a woman with whom he had just spent the night, but as he would for a child.

"We will be all right in here," he said, reassuringly, though he knew that their chances were not very good, even in this shelter.

The first bombs hit. They fell in the jungle at least half a mile from the village and the thunder of their explosions was deafening. Smoke and flame rose above the point of the bombstrikes, and a visible shock wave rushed out toward the village, causing all the houses to shake, knocking down those few villagers who were still running around.

The next wave of bombs hit closer in, then they started moving toward the village, as if laying a giant carpet of death and total destruction on the jungle floor. Whole trees were uprooted and they flew before the approaching carpet of bombs like twigs in a gale before a storm. A tree landed just in front of the opening of Mot's shelter, and the trunk of that tree acted as a barrier against most of the other flying limbs and debris.

The bomb carpet moved into the village itself and every house was flattened. It marched inexorably through the village, until it was right over Mot's shelter opening, and the tree which had been acting as a barrier exploded into splinters as several bombs fell on it. Mot felt a searing blast of heat, an intense pain, then nothing.

"Take it easy, man, you're alive."

Mot opened his eyes, and stared up into the face of a big, black soldier. The soldier was looking down at him. "You speak English?"

"Yes," Mot said.

"Is your name Mot?"

"What?" The American soldier sounded as if he were talking from a barrel. Mot was having difficulty hearing him.

"My colonel says he thinks he knows you. Is your name Mot?"

"Yes," Mot said.

"You just stay here, I'll go get him. He wants to talk to you."

Mot's head hurt, and he put his hand up gingerly, to feel that he had been bandanged. He realized that the bandage covered one eye and one ear.

"So, Mot, it is you," an American officer said, kneeling down beside him. "Do you remember me?"

"You are Colonel Culpepper," Mot said. "You are a friend of Monsieur Marquand's."

"Well, let's just say I'm an acquaintance," Jake said. "What are you doing here, Mot? You are a long way from home, aren't you?"

"I came to visit a cousin," Mot said.

"I don't believe you," Jake said. "I think you are VC. I thought you were VC three years ago when we caught you after the bridge was blown, but Marquand talked General Barclay into letting you go."

"I just came for the ceremony," Mot said.

"Yes, and you just happened to be here in Tuy Duc visiting your cousin when there was a big VC meeting going on," Jake replied sarcastically.

"I know nothing about a VC meeting," Mot said. He put his hand to the bandage again.

"I've got some bad news about that eye," Jake said. "The doc says you'll never see out of it again. We got you pretty well doped up on morphine, so you aren't in much pain now, but you're going to be."

"Am I your prisoner?" Mot asked.

"No, not unless you are a volunteer for the *chieu hoi* program," Jake said, refering to the amnesty program whereby confessed VC were accepted without prejudice, in an attempt to pacify the countryside.

"I cannot become a *chieu hoi*, as I am not a VC," Mot said.

"We've got no concrete proof that you are," Jake said. "My orders were just to come in here after the air strike and make an assessment of the damage. I can only take prisoners if they are in the act of open resistance. I must confess, we've had very little of that today." Jake stood up and started to walk away.

"Colonel?" Mot called.

"Yes?" Jake answered, turning back toward him.

"How many were killed?"

"Eighty-seven," Jake said.

"How many were women and children?"

"Too many," Jake said. He walked back over to Mot and looked down at him, and stared at him for a long time. "I'm sorry, Mot. The little girl with you was one of them."

"Colonel, Beefeater Six is on the radio," someone called to him. "He says congratulations on a job well done, and he wants us to come on back now."

Jake looked around at what was left of the little village. The only structure which remained was a small stone well, which had stood in the community square. Even it was covered with debris. Bodies and pieces of bodies were lined up alongside the well.

In addition to the bodies, there was a stack of weapons, and the stack was substantial enough to verify that Tuy Duc was, indeed, a VC stronghold. In addition to the weapons, they found flags, medical supplies, and some important maps and papers. It was a successful strike, Jake knew, but it had taken a terrible toll on Jake's conscience, for many of the bodies on the ground were children.

"All right," Jake said. "Get the wounded into the ambulances and get them to a hospital, and let's get out of here."

Jake walked back over to look down at Mot.

"My boss just congratulated me on this job," he said. "But I'm afraid that, in the long run, your side is going to get more out of it than my side."

"I think you are right, Colonel," Mot replied. He smiled. "By the way, if it isn't too much trouble, I would rather be dropped off at the Marquand Plantation, than taken to a government hospital. I hope you understand."

"I understand," Jake said. "Get in the back of my jeep. We'll be going right by there. You haven't fooled me for one moment, Mot, and if I ever catch you red-handed, I'll shoot you myself."

"Red-handed. You mean with blood on my hands?" Mot asked, not understanding the term.

"Yeah," Jake said. He looked at his own hands. "Yeah, with blood on your hands."

CHAPTER SIXTEEN

"Colonel, you got a letter," Larry said, coming into Jake's office and handing it to him. I mean it's a real letter, sir, not army shit."

Jake smiled. "Careful, soldier, you might be stepping on someone's toes."

"Would those toes be spitshined, sir?" Larry teased.

Jake liked Larry. When he learned that he and Larry had a mutual acquaintance in Kristin O'Neil, he was a little disturbed by it. When Larry told him that Kristin had travelled through Mississippi with him and two other black friends, Jake's first and rather ungenerous thought was a curiosity as to Larry's relationship with Kristin. He was ashamed of himself for that thought, and he forced it out of his mind. They had been together for three months now, and though Jake felt guilty about it because Simmons had died at his side, Larry was so good that Jake nearly forgot his first driver.

Larry kept the jeep spotless, he was very good with the radio, and because he was strong as a bull, he could go for hours without tiring or complaining. He had also managed, somehow, to tune into Jake's thought processes, so that he was able to respond to Jake's wishes with the minimum of instruction.

Jake knew that Larry had a football contract waiting for him, and he knew that a career in the army was out of the question. But if Jake had ever seen officer material, it was manifest in Larry Cantrell.

The letter was from Jake's father, and he started to toss it aside to read later, but something made him open it. He leaned back in his chair and propped his feet up on his desk, but the first sentence made him sit up straight.

Dear Jake,

By the time you receive this letter, I will be dead. I have known of my condition for some time now. Indeed, I had already been diagnosed as terminal by the time you came to see me. In fact, I must confess that it was having just learned of the condition which prompted my call to you, to ask you to come see me. I intended to tell you then, but I lacked the courage.

Maggie knows, of course. I told her of it just before we were married. She was shocked and, I must say, grief-stricken. I think it was seeing her genuine feelings come out which prompted me to ask her to marry me. I was touched more than I would have thought possible. Maggie wanted to tell you when you were here and she wanted to tell you before you left, but I wouldn't let her do it. In fact, it was my last wish that you learn of my demise from this letter, which Maggie was instructed to send, after the fact.

I'll get your first question out of the way. I was felled by a malignancy of some sort. The name is long and involved, and I could no more spell it than the doctors could cure it. It doesn't matter anyway. What matters is the end result. I'm dead, and that is that.

Jake, I was raised by my father to be a warrior. He was raised by his father for the same purpose and I carried on the tradition with you. Four generations of Culpeppers have given well over one hundred years of military service. We were represented in the Mexican War, the War Between The States, the Indian

Wars, the Spanish-American War, World War I, World War II, Korea and Vietnam. It has been a sacrifice beyond measure, for at some time during the last eight wars, we ceased to exist as a family, and began to function as an institution.

I have always loved you, Jake, but I never had the strength to tell you. After your mother died, I thought our mutual dependency on each other would speak of my love for me, so that I would never have to put it in words. But you saw me at a moment of weakness, and never, for the rest of my life, did you forgive that weakness. That's all right, because I don't know that I was ever able to forgive it myself. The only difference is, you saw one weakness, but perceived it as another. My real weakness was that I never married Emma Cruz. I was afraid that a Filipino wife would inhibit my military career, you see.

Ironically, Emma forgave me long ago. She subsequently married a Filipino Lawyer named Manuel Mendoza. He died a couple of years now, and she still lives in Manila. She was, and is, a wonderful woman, and I am happy that she found someone else. She deserved much more than I could have given her anyway.

I'm glad you never forgave me, Jake. Your condemnation has kept me honest all these years.

And now, about your two sons. It seems unlikely that the Culpepper military tradition will continue. Mike has taken up with the peace protestors, and of course Andy has joined the army as a private, rather than seeking entry into West Point, so the long history of Culpepper military service is now interrupted, and the Culpepper spirit is free at last.

Hooray for your two sons, Jake. They found the courage to do what neither you nor I could do. Keep your head down over there, son. I don't have a good feeling in my bones about this war.

It took Jake an hour to get a telephone line all the way through to Hampton, Virginia, but by ten o'clock that morning, which was ten o'clock in the evening in Hampton, he was listening to the phone ring in his father's house. Maggie answered it on the fourth ring.

"Maggie? It's me, Jake."

"You got the letter?" Maggie asked.

"Yes," Jake said. "Just now. When did it happen?"

"It happened on New Year's Day," Maggie said. "He was watching the bowl games."

"Jesus, that was over a week ago."

"I wanted to tell you about it, Jake. God knows how I wanted to tell you. But your father . . ."

"I know," Jake said. "It was in the letter."

"The people at Fort Monroe were very nice," Maggie said. "They sent a burial detail over to the house, and they buried him in the backyard, alongside your grandfather and your great-grandfather. President Johnson sent his condolences. Oh, and Virgie and your two sons sent the most lovely flowers."

"How are you holding up, Maggie?" Jake asked.

"I'm doing just fine. Don't worry about me."

"Look, if there is anything I can do, anything you need—"

"I'm fine, Jake, really I am," Maggie said.

"Yeah," Jake said. "Well, I've gotta go. I'll come by and see you when I get back home."

"Please do," Maggie said. "That would be very nice."

Jake hung up the phone and looked at it for a long moment, while he drummed his fingers on the desk. He tried to analyze how he felt. He didn't feel sadness as much as he felt anger. Jake felt a deep and abiding anger over the wasted years in his and his father's relationship. He wished they had been able to work something out between them before it was too late.

The idea came to him, and before he had time to think about it, he picked up the phone again, and called USARV

Headquarters in Saigon. When he got the USARV Adjutant he asked for, and received, a one-week leave to Manila.

Jake looked Emma up in the telephone book, and found that she lived in an apartment overlooking the Pasig River. He thought about calling her, but finally decided that it would be less awkward if he just visited her instead. Less than one hour after he arrived in Manila, he was standing in the hallway outside her apartment door, pushing the door buzzer.

The door opened, and Jake could have been convinced that time stood still. It had been twenty-three years since he last saw her, and she was eight years older than he was, and yet she still possessed the same svelte beauty which had first ignited his boyish sexual fantasy, so many years ago.

"Yes?" she said, screwing her face up in confusion, though with a glimmer of recognition deep in her eyes.

"Emma, I'm Jake Culpepper."

The faint glimmer of recognition Jake had seen in the back of her eyes now exploded into brilliant flashes of light, and she smiled broadly, and, unabashedly, reached out to embrace him.

"Jacob!" she said. "Oh, my Jacob!"

Klaus Sachs was without his priestly garb. He had received a note from a man who identified himself as the deputy commander of all NLF forces in the Saigon area. The man, who signed himself Colonel Xeng, asked Klaus to dress as a French businessman, and meet him in the office of a Bac Si at 13/131 Tru Minh Ky. The Bac Si, or doctor, who was at that address, was not a regular medical doctor, but a folk doctor.

Folk doctors outnumbered medical doctors by almost one hundred to one, and that just about matched the order of preference with the Vietnamese people. A Vietnamese citizen who was sick put very little stock in pills and shots. They believed strongly that in order to be treated, one must really be treated, and medical doctors simply didn't meet that requirement. At least, not in a way which would satisfy the average Vietnamese.

Folk doctors had a variety of treatments, as diverse as the illnesses they treated. Pinching, scraping and pricking were three of the more common methods. One very popular method consisted of stripping the patient naked, then taking several small jars, burning an incense candle beneath the jars to suck out the oxygen, and then sticking the jars to the body. The jars would draw the skin up by suction, and the ''bodily poisons'' were, presumably, destroyed. The number and pattern of the jars depended not only on the illness, but also on the patient's ability to pay. The jars left marks, and some of the wealthier patients would wear the intricate designs on their bodies proudly, as symbols of their affluence.

A small wind bell tinkled with the breeze of Klaus's passing as he entered the shop. Patients with various illnesses, both real and imagined, sat around the waiting room, much as do doctors' patients the world over. A woman wearing a white uniform, just like the uniform of a college-trained nurse, approached him.

''I wish a treatment for disparity of spirits,'' Klaus said, naming the disease he was instructed to name. ''This place was recommended to me by Mr. Xeng.''

''Yes,'' the nurse said. ''Come this way, please.''

Klaus followed her down a narrow, foul-smelling hall, and she indicated that he should enter a small room at the rear. Once he was inside, she opened a bottle of chlorophyll and, with her fingers, annointed him on the forehead, chin and chest. She pointed to a platform which was made of strips of bamboo, and indicated that he should lie down. Then she produced three joss sticks, gesticulated with them to each corner of the room, then placed them in a Coca-Cola can which sat in the center of the floor. The sticks burned, and the fragrant smoke curled a path to the ceiling.

Klaus lay there in total solitude for nearly fifteen minutes before someone else arrived. The new arrival stepped in through the door, wearing a robe. Klaus looked over at him, and waited for him to speak. Was this Xeng?

"Are you Klaus Sachs?" The man asked, speaking in French.

"Yes," Klaus answered, speaking in the same language. "Are you Xeng?"

"Yes. Mister Sachs, you warned Madame Le of the B-52 raid on Tuy Duc before it happened. How did you know of this?"

Klaus felt a sudden tenseness, and he sat up quickly. Xeng, if that was his name, was pointing a pistol toward him. The pistol was equipped with a special type of silencer which Klaus recognized. It was so effective that the only sound would be the metal-to-metal snap of the sliding chamber action. This man, whoever he was, was no amateur.

"Whose side are you on?" Klaus asked calmly.

The man laughed. "That is an interesting question, isn't it. I might be with the CIA country team, and this could be a Phoenix operation, as a result of your unauthorized disclosure of a secret operation. Or, I might be with the NLF. Your warning came too late to do anyone any good, but it did expose your cover."

"Which are you?" Klaus asked.

Xeng smiled. "I might be a double agent, serving both masters," he said. He pulled the trigger several times, and though the sound of the operating slide surely made some noise, Klaus heard nothing. He felt it though, three burning sensations in his chest.

Klaus was slammed back against the wall, and, though he tried to hold himself up, he felt himself falling over, so that he lay on his side. He felt uncomfortable, though there was very little pain. It felt a little like wearing a new shirt with the pins still in it, still holding the tissue paper in place, and stabbing against his chest irritatingly, though not excruciatingly.

"*Orate ut meum sacrificium acceptabile fiat apud Deum Patrem Omnipotentum,*" Klaus muttered in Latin, then again, in English, "Pray that my sacrifice may become acceptable to God the Father almighty."

Xeng walked over and put his hand to Klaus' neck to feel his pulse. Satisfied that he had done his job, he put his gun away, then turned and left the room.

Klaus tried to call out, to get someone to come help him, but he found that no matter how hard he tried, he couldn't make a sound. I'm going to die, he thought.

Klaus felt himself sliding, and he thought he reached out to grab hold of the wooden platform to keep from falling off, but in fact, he didn't move. Klaus smiled, or thought he smiled. The questions which had plagued him for a lifetime, that had driven him into a study of the priesthood, and then to a rejection of it, were about to be answered. So, this is what it is like. This is dying. At last, the ultimate mystery is rolled away.

Emma's apartment was on the seventeenth floor and Jake stood at the window of her living room, looking out at the huge central post office on the other side of the river, in the Intramuro part of the city. He had spent five days in Manila, and he and Emma had gone out together every night.

"I'm so sorry, Jacob," Emma had told him, when, at last, they had gotten around to discussing that night which had so traumatized Jake's life. "I should have told you then. I should have told you that I wanted it. I wanted it so badly that I prayed for it. I did everything I could do to force your father into doing what he did. I even arranged for him to see me taking a bath. If there really was a rape that night, then you might say that it was I who raped your father, and not the other way around."

"But I saw," Jake started.

"You saw things through the eyes of a young boy, Jacob. A young, impressionable boy. You believed what you wanted to believe, and I was too weak and after your father's rejection of any idea of marriage, too proud, to tell you any differently. I wish I could tell you that if I had known it would come between you and your father for a lifetime, I would have done otherwise, but I'm not sure I would have. I was nearly as young, and nearly as impressionable as you. I was just less innocent, that's all." That had been last night. Tonight they had not spoken of his father. Tonight there had been just the two of them, without a third presence.

The light in the room behind Jake went off, and Jake turned in surprise. Emma, who had gone to get wine as a nightcap, stood in the shadows near the sofa. She was in the shadows, but the crack of light which came through the kitchen door, and the soft glare of the city lights outside, were enough for Jake to see her. She was naked.

"Emma?" he said with a quickened breath.

"I don't have to force you to rape me, do I, Jacob?"

"No," Jake said, smiling, and walking toward her.

"I want this, Jacob. I need it. I hope you understand."

"Don't talk," Jake said, and he closed his arms firmly around her, and pressed his lips hard against hers.

Emma pulled Jake to the soft carpeting with her, and Jake grew dizzy with the musk of her perfume and the intensity of her kiss. He was thirteen again, and she was twenty, and fantasies beyond his wildest imaginations were coming true. Jake wriggled out of his clothes, and he felt the heat of her body against his, and he recalled the night she had pulled his head against her naked breasts, and a fire ignited inside him, to spread with amazing speed throughout his body.

"Jacob," Emma murmured. "My own, sweet Jacob."

Jake's hands moved down her body, feeling her skin

pulsate beneath his fingers, teasing it into flames he could feel. He moved his fingers deftly across her stomach, and into the silky growth of hair, then he felt the incredible hot wetness of her. She moved to position her body under his, and he descended hard onto her. The connection of their bodies shot through him like a bolt of flame. She answered his thrusts by moving up to take in more of him, until their bellies were pressing together. She sucked in sharply, whimpering a little from the pleasure of it, and she raised her legs up, then locked them around him to hold him to her.

The climax started in Emma first, a tingle that, somehow, seemed to begin in the soles of her feet, then spread in intensity until she was screaming and groaning with pleasure. Somewhere in the explosion, Jake's own orgasm was ignited, and he joined her as wave after wave of pleasure broke over both of them.

Afterward, Emma lay hushed on the couch, gazing idly through the windows at the golden lights of the city. She was still naked, though Jake had, by now, put on his clothes. Emma had brought an ice-bucket and a bottle of wine into the room, and now Jake took two goblets and poured them a glass of wine. He carried one goblet over to the sofa and handed it down to Emma.

"I took advantage of you, Jacob," Emma said. "I hope you are more forgiving of me than you were of your father."

Jake looked down at Emma and smiled at her.

"I'm a big boy now, Emma. I'm not the thirteen-year-old you used to know."

Emma returned his smile, then stood up. She leaned into him to kiss him, and Jake felt her breasts brush against him. He could smell the same perfume, blended with musk, which had so aroused his senses a few moments earlier, and he reached out and put his hand on her cheek to hold her kiss a bit longer. Tomorrow, he would be back in-country, and all this would be but a memory. He was determined to make it more than a mere whisper in time.

Chapter Seventeen

Andy rode to Phu Loi from the 90th Replacement Depot at Long Binh, in the back of a deuce and a half. At Phu Loi he was in-processed by First Division Personnel, sent down to Battalion, then to company, then to platoon. The platoon Sergeant, a tall, thin black man who kept his head shaved clean, sent him down to the third squad. The third squad was the last tent on the left, he was told. There, someone would assign him a cot, and so it was that as Andy stood just off the packing-crate floor looking into the tent, he was about to get the last and most important file in the long pecking order which had brought him to this place.

"Scottie," someone called from his position on the bunk. He was looking at a nudist magazine, and he didn't look around toward Andy. "Scottie, the FNS is here."

There were six men in the tent, a squad tent with the sides rolled up to let the air through. Three of them were lying in their bunks like the man who called out, two of them were cleaning weapons, and the sixth one, Scottie, was standing next to the sandbags with his shirt off, shaving.

"Hey, fuckin' new guy, come down here," Scottie called.

Andy walked through the tent still carrying his duffle bag. He hit the center pole of the tent, and the entire tent would have collapsed, had not one of the men jumped up quickly and grabbed the pole.

"What the shit are you doin', man? You tryin' to kill us, or what?"

"I'm sorry," Andy said quickly, his face flushing in embarrassment.

"Drop your duffle, man. They ain't nobody here wants anything from it."

"Yeah, uh, I'm sorry," Andy said again.

"You said that," Scottie said. Scottie turned around to look at Andy, and Andy saw that he still had shaving cream over half his face. Andy saw something else, too. He saw Scottie's eyes, hard and flat and old. Scottie couldn't have been much over twenty-four or twenty-five, but his eyes looked a hundred years old. "Drop your gear over there," Scottie said, pointing to one of the cots. "You can crash there."

"Thanks," Andy said.

"So, Polebean sents-0ou here, huh?" Scottie said, returning to his shaving.

"Polebean?"

"Sergeant Pohl," Scottie said. "The Platoon Sergeant."

"Oh, yeah."

"I'm Scottie. I'm the squad leader."

"Glad to meet you Sergeant Scott," Andy started.

"Hey, FNG, don't go callin' him Sergeant," one of the others said. "We got 'im broke in just right, we don't want you screwin' things up."

"I'm sorry," Andy said again.

"And quit apologizin' all the time for God's sake," Scottie said. "What's your name?"

"Culpepper. Andrew J. Culpepper."

"Well, Pepper, my man, I hate to tell you this, but you have just stepped into a bucket of shit," Scottie said. "This here squad has the ambush tonight, so you'd better flake out over there somewhere, and catch a few Z's."

"What is ambush?" Andy asked.

"You'll know after tonight," Scottie said, and he continued to shave by way of letting Andy know he was finished with the interview.

Andy walked over to the canvas cot Scottie had pointed to and lay back on it. The man in the bunk next to him lit a cigarette, and within a couple of puffs, Andy knew there was something funny about it. He was surprised the soldier would smoke it in the open like that, and he looked over at him.

"Here," the soldier said, passing it across to him. "Take a couple of tokes. It's some good shit, and it'll help you relax."

Andy had only tried marijuana once before, but he took it as if he was an old hand and drew a deep puff. He coughed.

"Hey, easy, man, the idea is to relax," the soldier said. "This is mellow stuff, you don't have to work at it. It'll get down there and do you some good. My name is Hopkins, but ever' one calls me Hoppy. How old are you?"

"Eighteen," Andy said.

"Shit," Hoppy said. "I was hopin' you'd be seventeen."

"Why?"

"I'm seventeen, and I'm tired of bein' the youngest one in the squad."

"Squad? You the youngest in the company, man," one of the others teased.

"Maybe so, but I got eight months left and you got ten, and that's where it counts," Hoppy said.

"Knock it off, dammit. Some of us are tryin' to get a little sleep."

Andy lay on the bunk listening to the filtered sounds of the base. A stream of water ran by just outside the fence, and several Vietnamese women were doing their laundry there. They were jabbering back and forth, and one of them was playing a radio. The music was a tuneless song, all flute, drum, and half-tone nasal sounds from the female vocalist. Helicopters whirled in and out of the airfield. Then, whether aided by the marijuana or jet-lag, Andy went to sleep.

"Hey, fuckin' new guy, roll outta that fart-sack," someone said. "We're goin' to eat now."

Andy joined the others as they walked toward the mess tent. There was a long line waiting to eat, but when Andy started toward the end, Hoppy reached out and grabbed him.

"We get to buck the line," he said.

"We do? Why?"

"Not all the time. Just tonight. Anyone who is on ambush bucks the line."

"The guys in line don't get mad?"

Hoppy made a little sound deep in his throat. It could have been a laugh.

"Think anyone in this line would trade places with us?"

"Lookie there," one of the men in the chow line said. "they gotta FNG goin' out on ambush his first day in country."

"Yeah?" another said. "So what? I'd rather get it my first day here than my last day here."

"If you get it your first day here, it *is* your last day here," another said with a nervous giggle.

Supper was meat loaf, gravy, boiled potatoes, corn and Koolaid.

After supper, Andy went with the others to see Sergeant Pohl. Their faces were blackened, their trouser legs were tied to keep from rustling, and they were given their instructions.

"Hey, Polebean," Scottie said. "Whyn't you let us go out without the FNG tonight? This is his first day."

"He's going to have to learn," Polebean said. "When's a better time?"

"I don't mind going out," Andy said.

"I'm not doin' it for you, kid," Scottie said. "I'm doin' for the rest of us. The most dangerous thing on ambush is to have some fuckin' new guy who doesn't know his ass from a hole in the ground.''

"Just tell me what to do, Sergeant," Andy said, somewhat stung by the remark. "And I'll do it."

"I don't want you to do nothin'," Scottie said. "Just walk out there with us, don't make a sound, and then come back."

"Here," Hoppy said, handing a little bottle of insect repellent to Andy. "The slopes can smell this shit half a mile away, but if you get to slapping and scratching at mosquitoes they can spot you for a mile."

Andy rubbed his hands, face and neck with the stuff. It burned his skin and the smell made his eyes water.

"If we get contact," Scottie said, as they started toward the main gate, "the thing to do is shoot low. Ever'body shoots high at first. Shoot at their knees, you'll be hittin' 'im in the chest."

Andy's mouth went dry. So far he had done nothing any different from basic training. He had gone on night patrols during basic training, and he had gunked himself down with blackening and mosquito repellent. But now he was actually being told where to shoot, in order to hit a man in the chest. This was for real!

The M.P.s at the gate watched as the patrol walked through. One of them was a lieutenant, and he was counting them and making a note on a small notebook.

"Hey, any of you MPs got a couple hundred extra P's? I might get lucky and find a piece of ass out there, only I don't have any money," Hoppy said.

"Remember to keep five to ten meters apart," Scottie hissed, as they started across the rice paddies. They walked along the dike, moving so silently that the only thing Andy could hear was his own breathing and the sound of his heart beating.

They walked for twenty minutes, all the way across the fields which were close in to the base, then through a narrow strip of woodline, and finally to the near edge of another field. This field was about two hundred meters across, and on the other side of it was the edge of a very thick growth of trees. Andy saw Scottie coming back toward him.

"Get down here," he said. "Take up a good position behind this berm. Your field of fire goes from that tall tree there, on your left, see it?"

"Yes," Andy said.

"—To that clump of bushes on the right. Get you a couple of sticks put up in the berm for firing stakes. Anybody comes, they'll be comin' through those trees."

"What if I see anyone?" Andy asked.

"Shoot."

"Shouldn't we find out if it is VC or not?"

"Look, Pepper," Scottie said. "We ain't got time to hold any high-level conferences here. If you see anything moving outta that tree line over there, I don't give a fuck what it is, you blow its ass away. You got that?"

"Yeah," Andy said.

"I'm going to get the rest in position now. I'll be at the right end of the line, about forty meters away. Peterson is on the left end, Hoppy is right next to you on the left, and McClure is the next man to your right. Now, once you get down into position you stay there. Don't get up. Don't even move."

"How long are we going to stay here?"

"Until daylight," Scottie answered.

"Okay," Andy said nervously. He could feel his hands shaking slightly as he got down into position behind the dike.

It was quiet. Andy could hear sounds from way off. In the village, which was about five kilometers away, someone was playing a radio and he could hear it quite clearly. It sounded like the same song he had heard earlier this afternoon, but then, they all sounded alike.

Andy didn't think he'd dozed off, but a sudden long burst of automatic weapons fire made him jerk his head

up, and he knew he had been asleep. He saw a stream of
orange tracer rounds spewing out toward the woodline,
then another stream of tracer rounds, this time green in
color, coming from the woodline.

All along the berm the Americans began firing. A moment later a 105 flare burst at two thousand feet, and it
floated down slowly under the parachute, lighting the entire field as bright as afternoon. That was when Andy saw
them. At least two dozen Vietnamese were moving on
line, across the field. They were all dressed in black
pajamas and sandals, and they were running bent over,
carrying AK-47s and assorted other weapons. They hit the
ground when the flare popped.

The nearest one was no more than one hundred meters
out, and Andy took careful aim, then squeezed off a long
burst. He followed his tracer rounds out of the end of his
weapon and saw them spattering into the ground all around
the Viet, but he didn't see any hits. He raised his sights,
and the stream of tracer rounds from his rifle made a
gentle curve all the way to the trees.

"Damn!" He swore aloud. He pulled the trigger again,
but discovered he was out of ammunition. He pulled the
magazine out, and tried to put another one in, but he
dropped it. He left it and reached for another magazine just
as the light from the flare went out.

When the light went out, it seemed much darker than
before and he wondered why, then he realized that he had
kept both eyes open during the flare. He had learned better
in basic training.

"Keep one eye open during the time of the flare," the
instructor said. "That way, the visual purple is affected in
one eye only, and when you open your other eye after the
flare goes out, you will discover that you haven't destroyed your night vision."

Tracer rounds zipped back and forth between the berm
and the middle of the field, and Andy saw a line of green
squirt toward him, looking like a brightly strung line of

glowing beads. Fortunately, the VC shooting toward him was making the same mistake of firing too high, because the rounds popped by overhead.

Andy fired off another magazine, and had just loaded a new magazine when another flare popped overhead. He started to close one of his eyes this time, but he was shocked to see a VC right in front of him, no more than ten meters away. The VC froze for a moment, and Andy, in fear and surprise, opened up on him. He fired off the entire magazine in one burst. He saw blood squirt from the VC's chest, neck and face as he fell face down. The VC dropped his rifle and it slid across the field half-way between them. For one, insane instant, Andy thought it was a fumbled football, and he nearly dived on it. He could hear yelling now, both from his fellow GI's and the VC, and he opened his mouth and screamed along with the others. He had no idea what he screamed, he just screamed.

American artillery opened up then, and Andy heard the freight-car sound of the incoming rounds as they passed overhead. The first salvo exploded in the treeline, but Scottie or someone was calling in corrections, and by the second salvo, the rounds were almost on them. They burst so close that he could feel the heat and shock effect, and he got down behind the berm and put his face in the mud and prayed. If a VC happened upon him now, the VC could have him, because he was concerned only with surviving the American artillery barrage.

The firefight was over almost as quickly as it began, and Andy lay there behind the berm, startled by the sudden silence.

Andy's heart was beating fast, and he was gasping for breath, almost as if he had run a mile. Each gasp of breath hurt his nostrils, for the air hung heavy with the smell of cordite from the gunpowder. A cloud of gunsmoke hung over the field for several minutes before it finally drifted away. Finally, Scottie came running down the line, bent over low behind the berm. He called out to Andy before he came over to him.

"Pepper, it's me, Scottie. I'm comin' over. Don't shoot."

"Come on," Andy answered. His throat was so dry his voice cracked.

Scottie came up to him. "Are you okay?"

"Yeah," Andy said. "Jesus, is it like this every night you come out?"

"No," Scottie said. "Most of the time it's nice and quiet. You picked a lucky night when it wasn't so boring. Well, I better check on Hoppy. Hoppy? Hoppy, it's me, Scottie. I'm comin' over."

There was no answer from Hoppy.

"Hoppy? Hoppy, it's me." Scottie said again. Scottie looked at Andy. "Did you hear anything from over there?"

"No," Andy said. "I mean, yes. I mean, there was shooting and yelling from everywhere. I couldn't tell where anything was coming from."

Scottie started toward Hoppy's position, running bent-over as he had from the beginning. A moment later Andy heard Scottie coming back through the dark.

"They got Hoppy," he said. "I moved Peterson in closer. Keep a sharp eye out this way. We don't want the sons of bitches gettin' around our flank."

"Okay," Andy said.

Scottie looked out across the berm and saw the VC. "You sure he's dead?" he asked.

"Yeah," Andy said.

Scottie smiled at him. "You did all right for your first time out," he said. "Lots of guys would've cut 'n run if they got in a firefight the first night in country."

"Yeah? If I'd known where to run, I might've done it myself," Andy replied.

Scottie laughed. "Yes, sir, you're all right, Pepper."

There was no problem with Andy dozing off anymore that night. He was wide awake from that moment until the sun finally came up. He watched the sky grow lighter and

the shadows move away from the trees. He saw the mist
settle on top of the trees for a while, then start to dissipate
as the sun climbed higher. And he saw the bodies of the
dead Vietnamese spread out across the field in front of
them.

"Okay," Scottie said. "I've called in. They're sendin'
a chopper out for us. We don't have to walk back."

Andy got up and worked the kinks out. He ached in
every muscle and joint in his body. He looked over to his
left, and saw Peterson standing there looking down at
something, and he thought of Hoppy. He walked over to
Peterson. Hoppy was sprawled, face down, across the
dike. A sticky pool of blood oozed out from under his
head, and his hair was matted in blood.

"I looked at him," Peterson said. "He caught a round
right in the forehead. It must've been right at the first, he
never even changed magazines. Look, there's no more'n
five or six empty shell casings that I can see."

"I never heard anything," Andy said.

"It's better when they die quiet," Peterson said.
" 'Course, Hoppy always was a real considerate kid."

"Peterson, Pepper, count the dinks. We need us a body
count," Scottie said. "They're sendin' a detail out here to
bury 'em, and I want credit for 'em before they do that."

Andy went with Peterson, and they counted the bodies.
There were fourteen of them. After they finished the count,
they started stripping them of weapons, papers, money
and watches.

"Look 'em over real close before you touch 'em,"
Peterson warned. "Sometimes they are boobytrapped, though
I don't think they had a chance to get to these guys."

Andy saved the one he knew he killed for last. Andy
rolled him over and looked at him. He didn't look any
older than Andy, though there was no way to determine
how old he actually was. His face was ashen gray, almost
blue in color. His eyes were open wide, a little bugged
out, and they were a deep, deep brown. There was no light

in the eyes at all. He was wearing a T-shirt, and, smiling up from the front of the T-shirt was the face of Mickey Mouse. That bothered Andy a great deal. He had thought he would be shooting at a nameless, faceless, Godless communist. Instead, he had killed someone his own age, who was wearing a Mickey Mouse T-shirt.

Chapter Eighteen

The name of the movie was *Flashing Swords*. It was a movie about Chinese knights, warriors who possessed almost magical powers in the martial arts. The movies were exceptionally popular with the Vietnamese, and Larry enjoyed them not for the action and adventure which thrilled the Vietnamese, but because they were so unbelievable as to be funny. He also enjoyed them because Melinda enjoyed them, and he enjoyed taking her to the movies.

Larry had met Melinda the first time he took Colonel Culpepper to an officers' conference which was being held at the Marquand Plantation. She had been riding a bicycle and the chain came off. Larry helped her put the chain on, she offered him a Coke, and they began talking.

There were a dozen reasons why a relationship between Larry and Melinda was impractical. Larry was black, and Melinda was white. That was the first and most obvious reason. Melinda was of royal birth, Larry had barely escaped the slums. Melinda was from a small European country, Larry was American. And Melinda was a whore.

Despite all the reasons why such a relationship would be impractical, Larry and Melinda fell in love. They did it in full sight of everyone, making no excuses, accepting no shame. The Headquarters of the 502 was less than two miles from the Marquand Plantation, and Larry was able to find frequent opportunities to visit there. On those occa-

sions when he could get a day off, he would take Melinda
into Saigon where they would eat lunch at the My Kahn
Floating Restaurant, then go to a movie. After the movie
they would find some place to go, and they would make
love.

Jake didn't exactly approve of the relationship between
his driver and Marquand's number one call girl, but he
didn't prohibit it either. In fact, he sometimes made his
jeep and time available for Larry, secretly enjoying the
fact that his driver was enjoying for free that which several
generals in the Saigon area were paying a great deal for.
They passed her name around in secret whispers over
martinis at the Cercle Sportif, and shared stories of her
great beauty and sexual skills. And all the while she was in
love with a low-ranking driver, a Specialist Fourth Grade,
who also happened to be black.

At the movie, Larry and Melinda ate dried fruit and
salted nuts, and they drank Coke. The cans were too
valuable to be given out, so the Coke was poured into
plastic sandwich bags. The bag was then twisted shut and
sealed around a straw with a rubber band. In order to drink
it, one had to hold the bag carefully in hand. It was a little
like holding a piece of cold liver.

The soundtrack of the movie was in one Chinese dialect,
while another dialect was written in subtitles on the screen.
The movie was also subtitled in Vietnamese, French and
English, so that the screen was half covered with words.
Despite that, it was great fun, and Larry booed and hissed
when the villains appeared, and cheered lustily for the
heroes, and he enjoyed the hours away from the war
immensely.

Melinda had the key to an apartment on Cong Ly. The
apartment belonged to an American general and he used it
only on special occasions. He loaned Melinda the key
willingly, when she intimated that she might enjoy visiting
him there sometime. This same General was now in Hono-

lulu on R&R with his wife, thus making the apartment safe to use.

The apartment was upstairs over a camera shop, and it consisted of three enclosed rooms, plus a large, open room which was built out over the roof of the camera shop. This open-air room had a floor which was beautifully covered in ceramic tiles of deep, royal blue, and rich cream. There was a bar which was covered by an awning one could pull down during the rainy season, a stereo which could be moved inside when necessary, as well as weatherproof furniture which remained outside all the time. That consisted of a glass dining table and four steel and plastic chairs, plus a comfortable rattan suite of sofa and chairs. A brick planter ran around the edge of the terrace, providing soil for a well-maintained hedgerow. Large urns served the same purpose with regard to flowers, so that the rooftop terrace became a lovely, and very private garden.

Larry and Melinda had eaten lunch on the My Kahn, but she was preparing dinner for them now. Larry stood at the edge of the rooftop garden and looked out over the city while she worked in the kitchen behind him.

He could smell the garlic and the wine and the hot butter as she worked, and he smiled as he thought of the situation.

"Lookit me now, mama," he whispered softly, thinking of his mother back in St. Louis. She had worked in an automobile plant for twenty years, earning the money to raise her four children. Each of Sally's four children had a different father, and Sally had never married.

"You bein' good at playin' football has give you a way to go to college," Sally told Larry before he left for school. "Tha's good, 'cause in my way o' thinkin', education be the only way for our people. You fixin' on leavin', 'n it's time I should give you somethin'. Well, I ain' got nothin' to give you but one thing. Boy, that one thing I gots, is pride. Yessir, pride I gots. I ain' never took so much as a solid quarter what I didn't work for. I be doin'

work for Chrysler for better'n twenty year now, but I ain'
never had me one o' them assembly line jobs where the
money is good. I been in what they call buildin' maintenance,
which is just a fancy word for housecleanin'. That don't
matter none, cause I've worked steady right along, 'n
when others was laid off 'n lost their high payin' jobs,
why, I jus' went on a'workin' right along. Now boy, folks
goin' to makin' a fuss over you 'cause you be a good
football player. You might make a little money from it one
day. Tha's good, 'n I pray to the Lawd that it happen. But
wherever you go, and whatever you do, I want you always
to bear in mind what it was like where you come from. I
want you to remember what it was like to be poor, but
proud. And I don' want you to ever take nothin' that you
didn't earn.''

"Larry?" Melinda called. Larry loved the way she pro-
nounced his name. There was music to it when she said it.
He turned away from the edge of the terrace and looked
toward her. She was putting the dinner on the table.

"What are we having?" he asked.

"Oh, we are having steak, with champignons de Paris,"
she said. She laughed, a lilting laugh. "Only, perhaps I
should say champignons de Saigon. In truth, I don't know
where the mushrooms came from, but they were plump
and tender, and they will do quite nicely."

"Yeah," Larry said. "Everything looks good."

"Larry, there is something I must tell you," she said
as they sat down to eat.

"You sound serious," Larry said.

"I am very serious, and you must listen," Melinda said
again. "Next week is the local New Year, the time they
call Tet."

"Yeah, I know. We have another truce arranged,"
Larry said.

"No," Melinda said. "There will be no truce."

"What are you talking about?"

"There will be a great deal of fighting," Melinda said.

"The VC have moved hundreds, maybe thousands of men into positions around Saigon, Da Nang, Hue, Ban Me Thuot, and other cities. They are going to make a big attack."

Larry laughed, and Melinda looked at him with her eyes snapping in quick anger.

"Why do you laugh?" she asked angrily. "I have told you something of great importance, and you laugh."

"I'm sorry, baby," Larry said. "I don't mean to laugh. But are you really tellin' me that all the dinks in country have lined up to attack those places you said? They'll be wiped out. Don't you know that the biggest problem we have over here is catchin' up with them? If they all get together for a regular battle, we'll wipe 'em out."

"Not if you are surprised," Melinda said. "That is what the VC are counting on. The Americans will not be ready because there is the truce of Tet, and you will not be ready because you do not believe the VC will have the nerve to do such a thing. There will be many killed. The VC are prepared to lose many, because they know they will also kill many Americans, maybe as many as one thousand in one week and, when one thousand Americans die, those who march for peace in America will grow louder."

"You got it right there, baby," Larry said. "If a thousand GIs die, they'll be raisin' hell back in the world."

"I have told this to two generals," Melinda said.

"They didn't believe you, huh?"

"No, they believed me," Melinda said. "But they say they want it to happen. They said it will be another Pearl Harbor, and all the Americans will get behind the war then."

"They're crazy," Larry said. "Or else they were just playing it smart. Maybe they are afraid to trust you. Anyway, I'm sure they are taking some precautions. They aren't goin' to just sit back and let Charley march in here like he was welcome."

"Maybe," Melinda said. She smiled. "Anyway, I have done all I can do. I have told those who are in authority, and the man I love, so all we can do now is wait and do nothing."

They had just finished their meal as Melinda said that, and Larry stood up and walked around behind her. He put his hands down over her shoulders, then cupped her breasts gently. She tipped her head back to look up at him.

"I wouldn't say do nothing," Larry said. "There's something we could do right now, if you know what I mean."

"Ah, yes," Melinda said. "I think I know what you mean."

They walked hand in hand from the terrace to the bedroom, and there, under the blast of cool air from the general's air conditioner, on the silk sheets of the general's bed, they made love. Melinda was skilled and experienced, Larry was eager and willing. There was very little they didn't do.

Three days later, on the evening of January 29, 1968, a pretty young army nurse sat in the passenger's seat of an army jeep at the corner of Tu Do and Le Loi. She was a first lieutenant, the daughter of Sergeant Major 'Pappy' Phillips, and her name was Julie. Her driver was a Vietnamese civilian named Mr. Tonc, and he was taking Julie to a neighborhood medical clinic where Julie volunteered her services three times a week.

It was a particularly festive occasion in Saigon right now, because it was the eve of Tet, the Chinese, or, lunar New Year.

Julie's father was an old hand in the Orient. He had served in Japan, Korea, the Philippines, Thailand and Vietnam. He knew all the Oriental customs, so Julie asked him to explain Tet to her.

"I can't do it, darlin'," Pappy said. "There's nothin' back in the world to compare it to. If you imagined

Christmas, New Year's, Thanksgiving, the Fourth of July, and everyone's birthday all wrapped up in one week, with maybe a nationwide Mardi-Gras thrown in for good measure, why, you might come close. All I know is everything stops, business, school, games, even war, when it comes time for Tet.''

Julie had visited her father several times over the last three months. It was convenient, because Di An was only about one hour away by jeep, and twenty minutes by helicopter. She visited him often, because he was her father and she wanted to see him. Of course, the fact that her father's commanding officer was Lieutenant Colonel Jacob Culpepper didn't hurt matters any.

Julie had known Jake for a long time. She was twenty-five years old, and she first met him when her father was the First Sergeant of then-Captain Culpepper's infantry company at Fort Bragg, North Carolina. She was fifteen then, and she thought he was the handsomest officer in the United States Army. Of course, he was married then, and he had two sons.

He was single now, and Julie had made a few exploratory moves in his direction. Jake had not discouraged her, and in fact, had asked her if she would like to go to Vung Tau with him on the next weekend they could both get free. Julie had accepted, and was eagerly looking forward to the expedition.

"Hmm," Mr. Tonc said. "That is strange."

Mr. Tonc's comment interrupted Julie's musing about Jake, and she looked toward him. He was looking toward the crowd of celebrating Vietnamese on the sidewalk.

"What is strange?" she asked.

"Do you see that man over there? The one with the white shirt and the red banner?'

"Yes," Julie said, seeing the man Mr. Tonc pointed out.

"He put no message in the urn."

"What?"

"The urn," Mr. Tonc said. "See the brass urn? It

guards the entrance to the temple. All who enter the temple must leave a message for their ancestors. Every day the messages are burned and the smoke carries the messages to heaven.''

"Maybe he has nothing to say to his ancestors,''. Julie suggested.

"But he wears the banner of prayer,'' Mr. Tonc said. And he enters the temple. If he has no wish to pray, why does he enter the temple?''

"Mr. Tonc, I often ask that about people I see in church,'' Julie said.

The light changed, and Mr. Tonc put the jeep in gear and drove ahead. A large banner was stretched across the street. Julie could read the dates, January 30 through February 3rd, 1968, and she saw a drawing of a monkey, but she could read nothing else.

"Mr. Tonc, what does the banner say?'' she asked.

"It say: To all Vietnamese peoples, the wish is for a happy, prosperous Year of the Monkey.''

"Year of the Monkey?''

"The new year will be the Year of the Monkey,'' Mr. Tonc said.

Mr. Tonc turned the jeep into a small driveway which led through a gate to the other side of a corrugated tin wall. He got out of the jeep and went back to close the gate behind them.

"Don't forget to lock the chain on the jeep,'' Julie said. "If this jeep gets stolen, it will be my ass.''

"I lock good,'' Mr. Tonc said. "No one steal.''

Most of the patients of the medical clinic were children, and they came running outside to meet Julie. They laughed and reached up for her and put their arms around her and hugged her, and she bent down to scoop up a little boy and hold him.

"Well, Dom, how are you doing?'' she asked. "Are you ready for Bac Si?''

"Bac Si,'' the children all shouted. "Bac Si, Bac Si.''

The word Bac Si actually meant Doctor, but Julie was as close to a Doctor as most of the children had ever seen, or would ever see.

The fireworks started just before dark. For the first several explosions Julie was jumpy and frightened, but the children all laughed and Mr. Tonc explained that it was nothing but people celebrating Tet.

Julie worked long and hard, and finally, at about one in the morning, the last child was treated. Then, wearily, she went to the little room which she used when she stayed here. She would spend the night here, then report for duty at the hospital before 0900 the next morning.

"Colonel Culpepper," the duty sergeant said, shining his flashlight into Jake's face. "Colonel Culpepper, emergency dispatch from headquarters. Saigon is under attack, sir."

"What?" Jake asked, sitting up and rubbing his eyes. "Did you say Saigon is under attack?"

"Yes, sir. They say a whole division of VC and North Vietnamese hit the city just after midnight. The Embassy has been hit pretty hard."

"The Embassy? Has it fallen?"

"No sir," the duty sergeant said.

Jake pulled on his pants, then reached for the canvas and leather jungle boots.

"Turn out two companies," he said. "Get armored personnel carriers standing by. We'll go in on APCs. Wake my driver."

"Yes, sir," the duty sergeant said.

Jake finished dressing, put on his flak jacket, strapped on a forty-five, then picked up an M-16. He stepped out of his hooch a moment later and saw that Larry had mounted a pig, as the M-60 machine gun was called, on the jeep. The APCs were already drawing into position, and ammunition and C-rations were being tossed aboard.

"Pappy, let's get 'em out here!" Jake shouted.

"Yes, sir," Sergeant Phillips answered. He blew his whistle and GIs in various stages of dress ran from their tents to the APCs. The APCs had been ready even before the troopers, because the drivers had a habit of sleeping in them, and when they were awakened, all they had to do was start them up and move them into position.

"Let's go!" Jake said, and Larry drove them to the front of the convoy. Ten APCs, each carrying twenty combat infantrymen, left the front gate of Di An, heading for Saigon.

"Can they keep up with us at thirty?" Jake asked Larry.

"Are you kidding, Colonel?" Larry answered. "I know some of the drivers. They got those things souped up to do fifty."

"Go as fast as they can keep up with us," Jake said.

At the junction of Di An road and Highway One, the South Vietnamese Military Police had set up a check point, and they had two jeeps in a blocking position across the road.

"We better get up there in a hurry, Colonel, and get those slopes out of the way, or these guys are going to smash them flatter'n shit."

"Yeah, get on up there," Jake said.

Larry stepped on the gas and the jeep sped up to seventy. The Vietnamese MPs stepped out and waved their arms to halt them. One of them was a lieutenant.

"Lieutenant, you better get these jeeps out of the road," Jake said in Vietnamese. "We're coming through."

"No," the Vietnamese lieutenant said. "This road is closed. My colonel has ordered that no one get through."

"Don't you realize that the VC have hit Saigon?" Jake asked.

"Yes. But my Colonel said to allow no one through," the Lieutenant said again.

"Dammit, man, we are the relief column!"

"You cannot get through."

"What is it, sir, what's going on?" Larry asked.

"He says he has orders from his colonel to let no one through," Jake answered. "For all I know the colonel might be VC. Hell, maybe this guy is."

"No VC," the Lieutenant said in English.

"Maybe not, buddy, but I don't have time to argue," Jake said. He raised his M-16. "Specialist Cantrell, drive around them. The APC's can come through them."

Larry grinned broadly.

"Yes, sir!" he said.

Larry took the jeep to the shoulder of the road and went around the two Vietnamese jeeps. Jake got on the radio.

"This is Goodnature Six to the lead vehicle. Come right on through the Viet Jeeps."

"Yes, sir!" the driver of the lead vehicle answered happily.

Larry stopped the jeep on the other side and they watched the Vietnamese MPs run as the first APC approached the roadblock. The APC crashed through them with no difficulty. The second and third one hit the block as well, until there was not one piece of the jeeps remaining that was not small enough to pick up in one hand.

Larry laughed. "I been wantin' to do somethin' like that for six months," he said.

"Larry," Jake replied with a chuckle. "I've been wanting to do it for four years."

CHAPTER NINETEEN

Julie wasn't sure when she realized that the explosions she was hearing weren't celebratory fireworks, but were actually explosions. She woke up sometime around two A.M. and the sounds were coming one right after another. A year earlier, one bang would have been pretty much like another to her, but her six months in Vietnam had given her a perspective which the uninitiated didn't have.

There was an urgency to these bangs. Not only that, they didn't have the happy sound of firecrackers which were being exploded in joy.

Suddenly a very loud, very close explosion rattled the room, and she heard a collapsing sound. She got up and ran to the window and looked outside. There, in the courtyard, she saw her jeep burning. There was a pile of rubble where the wash house had been. The sky over the city was painted orange from dozens of fires. Without having to be told, Julie realized that the entire city was under attack. It seemed impossible, but it was true.

"Bac Si, Bac Si, are you all right?" Mr. Tonc called through Julie's door.

"Yes," Julie answered. "Yes, I'm all right."

"Many VC," Tonc said. "Maybe many times one thousand. Jeep all gone."

"Are the children in a safe place?"

"Maybe yes, maybe no," Mr. Tonc said. "Who can tell?" he asked, philosophically.

"There are no weapons here, are there?"

"No," Tonc said.

"That's probably just as well. Maybe the VC will pass us by."

Larry parked the jeep beside the Circle 34 Officers' Club, in the First Field Hospital compound. The Circle 34 served as the officers' mess for officers from the 34th Group as well as from the hospital, and, as it was nearly time for breakfast, many of the doctors, nurses, and 34th Group officers were milling around nervously. The streets between the club and Ton Son Nhut were blocked off, so the officers who worked in staff jobs couldn't get into their offices. They were all wearing flak jackets and helmets, and carrying pistols. They laughed nervously and teased each other about their new combat status.

Jake took one look at the back gate and saw that it was nothing more than a flimsy affair made of corrugated sheet metal. It was closed and locked with a chain and padlock, but, amazingly, there were no guards. As little as a squad of VC sappers could penetrate that gate, kill a handful of the straphangers, as the troops in the field called Saigon warriors, throw a few satchel charges, and their mission would be a success.

Jake had been given the field hospital as his headquarters. He jumped out of the jeep and pointed to the back gate.

"Captain," he shouted to the first officer he saw. "Who is in charge of security here?"

"I . . . I don't know, sir," the captain said.

"It doesn't matter, I am now," Jake said. "Get some men and build a sandbag barricade by that gate. Then stand guard over it."

"Colonel, I'm just a property book officer, I don't know anything about . . ." the captain started.

''Goddammit man!'' Jake exploded. ''You are supposed to be an officer in the United States Army!''

''Y . . . yes sir,'' the startled officer stammered.

''Colonel Culpepper?'' A nurse called. Jake recognized Margie Crenshaw, the Major in charge of the nurses. He had met her with Julie.

''Hello, Margie,'' Jake said. ''How are things over at the hospital? Everyone all right?''

''Jake, Julie is gone,'' Margie said.

''Gone? What do you mean, gone?''

''She was spending the night at an orphanage downtown,'' Margie said. ''She goes down there to give a clinic for kids every free chance she gets. That's where she was when the attack came.''

''Where is the orphanage?''

''It's called Our Lady of Fatima, and it's somewhere near Le Loi and Tu Do.''

''Shit, that's not too far from the Embassy,'' Jake said. ''That's where their main thrust is.''

''I'm just worried sick about her.''

''Let me see what I can find out,'' Jake said, going to the radio on the back of his jeep.

Jake contacted every command net within the city, but no American troops had reported seeing an American nurse. Finally, when his own troops had been organized into sweeping operations, Jake got permission from the Provost Marshal, who was in overall command of the operation, to proceed on his own to find Julie.

''Okay, Cantrell, out of the jeep,'' Jake ordered.

''Out of the jeep? What for?''

''This is a personal mission. I can't ask you to go with me.''

Larry looked Jake right in the eye. ''If you can't ask me to go with you, that means you can't order me to stay back. Right?''

''It means no such thing,'' Jake said. ''I'm still a Lieutenant Colonel in the U.S. Army.''

"So, when we get back, court-martial me," Larry said. He made no effort to move. He smiled. "Besides, I know a shortcut through Soul Alley that none of you honkys know anything about."

Jake laughed. "You're sure it won't jeopardize your standing in the Black Panthers to take me there?"

"I'll tell 'em you're my hostage," Larry said. He chambered a round in his short-barrelled shotgun, then laid it across his lap with the barrel pointing out. "Let's go, Colonel. Lieutenant Phillips is waiting for us."

Jake climbed into the right seat and picked up his M-16.

"All right, I'm ready for the tour," he said.

Larry drove down Cong Ly at breakneck speed. It was still pre-dawn, and the Vietnamese traffic was practically non-existent, though they did see a few American MP and Vietnamese QC jeeps.

Armored personnel carriers were positioned here and there, as well. Then, during one stretch, they drove for fifteen or more blocks without seeing anyone, until they saw a little yellow and blue taxi, upside down and burning. Two Vietnamese civilians were lying in the street in a pool of blood. One of them was trying to get up.

"Jesus," Larry said. "It must have just happened."

"Stop the jeep, but keep your eyes open," Jake said. "I'll see what I can do for them."

Larry stopped the jeep, then got out, carrying his shotgun. Jake left his M-16 in the jeep and started toward the two men. One of the men was lying very still in a pool of his own blood and intestine, and Jake knew it was too late to do anything for him. He started toward the other one.

Suddenly the other man leaped up and raised an AK-47! He had been playing possum, and his weapon had been concealed by his body!

"What the . . .!" Jake shouted in shock and fear. He jumped to one side just as the VC opened fire. The bullets whizzed by Jake so close he could feel the breath of their passing. Suddenly the chest and neck of the VC sprayed a fountain of blood, and the VC tumbled backward. At the same time, Jake heard the roar of Larry's shotgun, and he looked around to see smoke coming from the end of the barrel.

"Get back in the jeep, sir, it was a trick!" Larry shouted.

Jake ran to the jeep while Larry stood his ground, covering the action with his shotgun. Jake picked up his M-16.

"All right!" he shouted. "I've got you covered. Come on!"

Larry ran back to the jeep, put it in gear, and they roared away. They passed the apartment where Larry and Melinda had spent the night, but Larry was so busy that he didn't even notice it. They turned onto Le Loi and a moment later came to Tu Do.

"There," Jake said, pointing to a blue-painted sign. "There's the orphanage!"

"The gate's closed," Larry said.

"Crash through it!"

Larry smashed through the gate, and came to a stop with the sheet metal of the gate wrapped around the hood of the jeep. They were right next to the burned out hulk of Julie's jeep.

"Shit, sir, look at that," Larry said, pointing to the hulk.

Jake got a sick feeling in the pit of his stomach.

"Jake! Jake, oh, thank God you've come!" Julie shouted from the second floor balcony of the building.

"Julie, are you all right?"

"Yes," Julie said. "But we were hit by mortar rounds, Jake. Several of the kids have been hurt."

"Come on down, we're getting out of here."

"No," Julie said. "Jake, didn't you hear me? Some of the kids have been hurt."

Larry turned off the engine. "Looks to me like we're stayin', sir," he said.

For the next several hours, under Julie's direction, Jake and Larry helped attend to the children who had been wounded. Finally, at about noon, an MP jeep stopped just outside the gate, and an MP lieutenant came into the compound. He saw Larry leaning over one of the children.

"What the hell are you doing in here, soldier?" the lieutenant asked sharply.

"What does it look like?" Larry answered. "I'm helping these kids."

"Let me see some ID," the lieutenant said.

"Get off my ass, Lieutenant, I don't have time for any of this shit," Larry said.

"Soldier, I would like to remind you that you are talking to an officer!" the lieutenant sputtered.

At that moment Jake came out of the building carrying a child with an injured leg. He laid the child down gently.

"What's going on?" he asked.

The lieutenant, seeing the black leaf on Jake's collar, came to attention. "Sir, this man was insubordinate," the lieutenant said.

"Yeah, he is to me all the time," Jake said. "I don't know what I'm going to do with him." He and Larry smiled at each other.

"Begging the colonel's pardon, sir, but if you ask me, a little respect is all that's needed around here."

"Yes, Lieutenant, you may be right," Jake said. "A little respect."

"Hey, Lieutenant, the Vietnamese just caught a VC," a soldier yelled through the gate. "They've got him out here."

"Okay, I'll be right there," the lieutenant said. He looked at Jake and Larry for a second longer, then, with a shrug, he turned and walked through the gate.

"I think I'll walk over and talk to the VC," Jake said. "I'd like to know the extent of this operation. I can't believe they would try anything this stupid."

Jake saw the VC standing there with his hands, cuffed behind his back. He was wearing a plaid shirt and khaki pants, and he was surrounded by photographers. Jake smiled at the thought of one little prisoner receiving so much attention.

Then, suddenly and unexpectedly, one of the senior Vietnamese officers present raised a .38 caliber pistol to the VC's head.

"No!" Jake shouted. "Let me talk to him!"

Jake's words went unheeded. The VC grimaced and the pistol went off with a pop. A fountain of blood squirted from the side of the VC's head, and the prisoner fell over backwards. Jake stood there in shocked silence as the cameras captured the event in all its sudden brutality.

Almost immediately after the prisoner was shot, there was a muffled explosion from the orphanage courtyard behind Jake, and he completely forgot about the VC prisoner as he turned and ran back. He got to the gate then stopped. There, lying on the ground with both legs ripped open, was Larry Cantrell.

"Larry!" Jake shouted.

Larry looked up at Jake with an almost bemused expression on his face.

"The dumbest damn thing," he said. "I was moving the gate off the front of the jeep so we could leave. There was an RPG lodged in that gate, you know? All this time that thing has been there without going off. It chose this moment to go off. Ain't that the shits?"

It was the middle of June when Jake got off the plane at Travis Air Force Base in California. As a full Colonel, he was the senior officer aboard the plane, and thus was afforded the honor of being first to debark.

"Colonel Culpepper?" a Lieutenant said at the bottom of the boarding steps.

"Yes," Jake said, returning the Lieutenant's salute.

"Welcome back to the world, sir. I'm Lieutenant Davis,

I'll assist you through customs. There is a car assigned to take you to the airport.''

"Thank you," Jake said.

There was one very large customs inspection room at the reception center. It had several long tables and dozens of customs inspectors who were going over the luggage and duffles of the men who had, with Jake, just deplaned. The room was packed with happy GIs who were returning to the States, or, as they liked to say, the world. There were long lines everywhere, but the lines weren't sullen, because these men were happy. Jake, by virtue of his rank, was spared the lines, and he was taken to a small anteroom to one side of the big room. There, on a small table, he saw his personal luggage. A customs clearance tag had already been affixed to it.

"You are all ready to go, Colonel," Jake was told when he stepped into the room. "There is a car just outside, which will take you anywhere you want to go."

"Thanks," Jake said.

A civilian driver took Jake's luggage and carried it out the back door, where a military sedan waited. The driver put the luggage in the trunk.

"Airport, Colonel?"

"No," Jake said. He took an address from his pocket. "I want to go here."

The driver looked at the address, then back at Jake.

"You sure you want to go there, Colonel?"

"Yes, I'm sure. Why?"

"That's the Haight-Ashbury section. It's all hippies down there."

"That's where I want to go," Jake said.

"Dressed like that? They don't dig uniforms there."

"If I weren't in uniform, do you think I would blend with them?"

"No," the driver agreed.

"Then what difference does it make?"

The driver laughed. "I guess you are right. I don't guess it makes any difference."

Jake got into the back seat and the driver got behind the wheel, started the car, and they drove away.

"They're still in a nasty mood," the driver said. "They just got over someone killin' Martin Luther King, and then Robert Kennedy got killed. They like to call themselves 'Love Children,' but they ain't been too lovin' lately."

"There hasn't been much to be loving about, lately," Jake said.

Jake leaned his head back. It had been two weeks since Robert Kennedy was assassinated. It happened on the same day he was promoted to full colonel. His replacement had already taken command of the 502nd, and Jake had been moved to Saigon to fill a temporary slot on the MACV Staff, while he waited to rotate back to the States. He had a villa in the Ton Son Nhut compound, which included a complete kitchen staff. Julie had eaten dinner with him that night, as she had on several nights. They had made love on that night, as they had on many nights. And afterward, they talked.

"It isn't there, is it, Jake?" Julie asked. Julie was sitting on the sofa in Jake's living room. Jake had dressed quickly after they made love, and, though she would have preferred to stay undressed a little longer, she dressed as well.

"What isn't there?" Jake asked. He was fixing each of them a drink.

"The magic that makes things like this work," Julie said.

Jake handed her her drink, then he sat down beside her.

"I don't know," he said. "I rather enjoyed it."

"I did too," Julie said. "It isn't the sex part I'm talking about, Jake. The sex is wonderful. It's the rest of it, the, 'now I take thee forever' part. It isn't there, is it?"

.Jake took a reflective drink before he answered, then he put his hands to her hair.

"I wish it could be," he said softly. "I've prayed that I could fall in love with you, Julie. You are the most wonderful girl I have ever met. I don't know, maybe it's me. Maybe I'm just not capable of loving anyone. Maybe I've seen too much, done too much."

"I know," Julie said. She put her hand up to wrap her cool fingers around Jake's own hand. She sighed. "The real truth of the matter is, no matter how hard I wish it, it isn't there for me either. And I think for the same reason. I've seen too much pain and death and suffering. You have been the only island of sanity in an insane world, and, as long as I'm over here, I need that island to hold onto my own sanity. But in the real world, would we feel the same?"

Julie and Jake got drunk that night, and they went to sleep in each others arms. Julie cried and Jake cursed the unknown barrier which allowed them to love each other, but prevented them from falling in love with each other.

"Here we are," the driver said, interrupting Jake's reflections.

"What?"

"The address you gave me? It's right down at the end of that alley. You'll have to walk it, cars can't go in there. You want me to take your luggage somewhere?"

"Yes," Jake said. "Leave it for me at the Mark Hopkins Hotel, will you?"

"You got it, Colonel," the driver said.

Jake got out of the car and the driver pulled away quickly, as if glad to be out of the area.

The place was exceptionally crowded, and people walked down the middle of the street as easily as they walked down the sidewalk. The motorists who came through here were accustomed to it, and they drove slowly and moved around the people, amazingly, without the incessant blaring of horns such jaywalkers would elicit anywhere else.

Nearly all the people Jake saw were in their early twenties or late teens. Many sat in groups on the pavement playing guitars, while others begged from the tourists. It was a colorful, shaggy mass of humanity, as young, bearded men wandered around in brightly colored shirts, or no shirts at all, while the girls wore cutoffs and the briefest of halter tops. There were dozens of groups of people gathered in circles to smoke marijuana.

"Here, sir, have a flower," one young girl suddenly said, and she handed a bloom to Jake.

"Thank you," Jake said, not knowing what else to say.

"Oh, far out," the girl said as she walked away to join her companions. "He thanked me, did you hear that? Isn't that wonderful?"

"Far out, man," one of the others said.

Jake smiled and shook his head, then started up the alley toward the address he had on the envelope in his hand. He carried the flower with him as he walked up the alley.

"Hey, dig, the soldier's carrying a flower. That's heavy!"

Several young people came by and flashed the V sign at him. Jake, hesitantly, flashed it back, and he was rewarded with an "All right!"

There was a number over a door in the back of a brick building at the end of the alley. The number was the address Jake was looking for. He knocked on the door, and a young, attractive black girl answered the door. She looked at Jake for just a second, then she smiled.

"You're Jake," she said.

Jake smiled back at her. "Yes."

"Well, come in. We've been waiting for you."

Jake followed the girl through the door, down a narrow hall, and finally into a room.

"Hey, Jake, my main man!" Larry greeted him. Larry was in a wheelchair, and he smiled and held up his arms. "No more military respect shit for me now, I'm out."

Jake gave Larry a short laugh. "As I recall," he said, "there wasn't a whole lot of it when you were in. How are you doing?"

"Well, Green Bay put me on waivers, can you believe that? They said playin' in a wheelchair gave me an unfair advantage. Other than that, I'm fine. How are you? I see you made the bird."

"Yeah," Jake said. "I made it a couple of weeks ago."

"How's it feel to be back in the real world?" Larry asked.

"Well, I don't know yet. I just got here."

"Yeah, man, I know what you mean," Larry said. "Only I tell you something, my man. That feeling never changes, and it's not just because of the legs, either. That feeling is a wound all of us have."

"Hello, Jake." A woman's voice said. "Long time no see."

Jake turned toward the speaker.

"Kristin!" he said.

CHAPTER TWENTY

It was Friday night, August 30, 1968. The night before, Hubert Humphrey had received 1761 votes on the first ballot, to get the Democratic nomination for President. Kristin had joined thousands of others in Chicago's Grant Park to protest Humphrey's nomination.

It had not been a pleasant night. The police had battled the demonstrators in the park and in the streets, pelting them with tear gas grenades, and rushing forward to beat them with truncheons and blackjacks. Even innocent bystanders had come under attack by the policemen, when, in front of a restaurant called Haymarket Inn, several blue-helmeted policemen suddenly and for no apparent reason charged through the barriers. They crushed the spectators against the window until the window gave way, sending screaming middle-aged women and children backward through the broken shards of glass. The police then ran into the restaurant and beat the women and children, and even some of the restaurant patrons.

With innocent bystanders catching the wrath of the police, it was no wonder that more than one hundred of Kristin's fellow demonstrators were injured. The policemen pressed forward with clubs, rifle butts, tear gas and mace, attacking virtually anything which moved along Michigan Avenue, the narrow streets of the Loop area, and in Grant Park.

Kristin escaped with no more than the nauseating effects of drifting tear gas. Today, nearly twenty-four hours later, she was resting in the house of a local demonstrator. It was dawn before she finally got to sleep, crashing on the floor with perhaps a dozen others, and now it was evening, and they were just beginning to stir back into life. A pile of peanut butter and jelly sandwiches were on the table, and Kristin went into the kitchen to get one. There was a young girl at the sink, washing dishes. She looked over at Kristin and smiled. She couldn't have been much over sixteen, Kristin thought. Her hair hung straight, held in place by a headband, festooned with plastic daisies. A peace symbol was painted on her cheek. She was wearing a T-shirt and no bra, as if proud of the sexuality which was still new to her. God, Kristin thought. She was never that young. She couldn't have possibly been that young.

"Are you going back out tonight?" the young girl asked.

"No," Kristin said. She took a bite. "We lost."

"But we can still be heard."

"Yeah," Kristin said, non-committally. "We can still be heard."

"You've been doing this for a long time, haven't you?"

"Yes, quite a while."

"Someone said you'd been around a long, long time," the young girl said. "I mean, even before I knew there was such a thing as the Vietnam war."

"Yeah," Kristin said. "A long, long time." She took the sandwich with her and went back into the living room and sat down to eat it. A Roadrunner cartoon was on television, and several people were sitting around smoking grass, watching the antics of Wiley Coyote.

"Want a toke?" someone offered.

"No," Kristin said. She brushed her hair back from her face.

"I don't blame you," a shirtless, redheaded boy said. He, like everyone else, was a lot younger than Kristin, not only chronologically, but from a standpoint of experience and maturity. "I mean, there's a lot better shit than that to be had, don't you think?"

"Yes," Kristin answered, just to be answering. She didn't want to discuss grass, or politics, or the war, or age, or anything. She wished she was somewhere else right now. She wished she was in Washington, D.C.

Jake was in Washington, D.C.

Ever since Larry came back from Viet Nam, he had been singing the praises of Jake Culpepper. At first, Kristin thought Larry was just saying that in some misguided attempt at humor, but she soon learned that he was serious. Kristin knew Larry and Jake, and it didn't seem logical to her that the Jake who had singlehandedly foiled Dr. Mainwaring's demonstration at Travis Air Force Base, last year, and the Larry who had demonstrated with her in Mississippi, could get along with each other. Not only did they get along, they genuinely liked each other, as witnessed by Larry's constant talking about Jake, and the fact that Jake had come to visit Larry in San Francisco when he returned to the States.

Kristin had laughed at the sight of Jake Culpepper, meticulously attired in his Army uniform, complete with all brass and ribbons, strolling through Haight-Ashbury. And yet, the very fact that he had done it at all showed a self-confidence which Kristin couldn't help but admire.

Larry was living with Nicole now. They had comforted each other over the news of Jimmy's being killed in Viet Nam, and that comfort grew to love. Larry had even confided to Kristin that Nicole had caused him to get over a girl he had met in Vietnam, a girl named Melinda.

Kristin had dinner with Jake at the Top of The Mark, the night before Jake left San Francisco. She went to a beauty parlor to have her hair done that day, and she wore makeup and a conservative dress so that she looked as if she could have stepped from the pages of *Vogue*. She laughed, because he was going to meet her in the lobby of the hotel, and when she came in, he didn't even recognize her.

She wanted to go to his room with him that night. It had been several months since she'd quit seeing Dr. Mainwaring, and she had seen no one since. And yet, though she liked to believe herself to still be free in thought and action, she found that, for some reason, she felt as conservative as she was dressed. In fact, when Jake suggested that they might go to his hotel room, she declined, though every fiber in her being wanted to accept.

Now, Jake was on duty in Washington, assigned to the Pentagon. He had begun writing her shortly after he arrived in Washington, and she answered him. Now, despite the fact that they were still on opposite sides of the Vietnam War, they were re-establishing the contact which had begun, only to rupture, five years before.

In his letter to her, Jake admitted things that she was sure he had never said to anyone else before:

I don't find fault with you for expressing your ideas, in fact, I am thankful that you, and the others like you are raising questions to challenge the conscience of the American people. I told Senator Carter over a year ago that the war was being turned into a mathematical equation. How many lives do we want to lose before we decide to change our policy? The only difference between you and me on this question is this: I am a military man, and I am still prepared to go in and win, if that is the policy of our government. But if that is not to be our policy, then I am philosophically more in line with you than with our government, in that I think we should withdraw.

Kristin also knew that Jake worried about his son, Andy, who was with the First Infantry Division in Vietnam. He had confided to her in one letter that he was less worried about what happened to him while he was in Vietnam, than what would happen to him when he returned.

*I've seen him a couple of times and he has gone
from 18 to 50, right before my eyes. I don't think
even he knows it yet, but he's going to find out, and
when he does, I'm afraid it is going to be more of a
shock than he can handle.*

"Here, Kristin," the shirtless, redheaded boy said. He
put a glass down in front of her.

"Thanks," Kristin said. She drank it to wash down the
peanut butter and jelly sandwiches. "That was very nice of
you," she said, smiling at him.

"Yeah," the redheaded boy said. "Wait'll that shit hits
you, man. I told you there was somethin' better'n grass."

Kristin felt a sudden constriction in her throat, and her
stomach did a flip flop.

"What . . . what are you saying?" she asked. She
looked at the drink. "Did you . . . did you put something
in that drink?"

"Yeah, man," the redheaded boy grinned. "It's the
grooviest acid you ever dropped, that's for sure."

"My God, LSD? You gave me LSD?"

"Yeah, a quarter's worth. I did it a couple of days ago.
Far out, man. I mean, really far out!"

"No!" Kristin said. "No!" She tried to stand up, but
she couldn't. Already the room was reeling, and she had to
settle back down in the chair. Sounds became distorted and
a mist settled over the room.

"Hey, this chick is really groovin' man," the redheaded
boy said. Several others came over to look at Kristin, but
it was as if they were on the other side of a flawed glass,
so that, not only their images, but their voices were distorted.

The line between reality and hallucination began to
disintegrate then. She no longer knew if the people who
were gathered around her were real, or illusory. Everyone
began to glow, as if from some inner light.

An instant later, or it might have been an hour later,

they were gone, and she was alone with her own expanded consciousness.

The carpet was humming! It was dark blue and the color was humming in beautiful, melodic chords. Kristin was amazed by it, and she looked around to see if anyone else had noticed it. She wanted to ask them if they could hear it, but she couldn't get their attention.

Over in the corner a man was playing the flute. Kristin was certain that the flute player would be interested in hearing blue, so she tried to call him over. When she looked at him though, she could hardly believe her eyes. There were bright, yellow colors splashing from the end of the flute. The colors sparkled and danced and shimmered as they hung in the air.

And there was a girl, the young, sixteen year old girl who had been doing dishes at the sink, earlier. She was having intercourse with the music! One of the bright drops of color was making love with the girl. The girl was leaning over backwards so that her hands were holding on to her ankles. Her hips were thrust forward and the color was moving in and out of her vagina. It was a solid, three dimensional color, and the thrusts were deep, and Kristin could see the young girl as she opened up for the fornication. She watched the girl's stomach swell slightly with each invasion.

Kristin was amazed. How was all this possible? It was beautiful, but how was it possible?

As she considered it, some of the color moved to her. Kristin knew why it came, and she spread her legs appreciatively. The color entered into her and she gave herself to it. It was an all-encompassing thing, and she felt all the erogenous nerve endings in her body being sensitized. She was swept with washes of color, and the blue carpet sang the song of eros as she began to climax in wave after wave. There seemed to be several climaxes, or, was it one, with the peaks and valleys so close that she couldn't distinguish them? Her entire body dissolved into one massive climax, and then she felt herself breaking into pieces, pieces of climax which took on her personality, now drifting through the room.

How was she doing this? She was cognizant of several different entities. She was here and she was there all at the same time, and yet every entity was still sensitized by the explosion of the last climax. It was as if she had captured the most divine feeling at its peak and stayed with it, not letting it go. Only it was greatly multiplied, because the climax had shattered her personality into several parts, each with the same sensation.

Kristin watched the others in the room from her new perspective. She now knew who she was. She had moved into the aura of the room and had breathed life into that aura. The life spawned by her orgasm.

Kristin became one with the room. Now she was part of the penis of the flute player. Odd, she didn't feel as if she were in the penis, she felt as if she were a part of it. She could feel the throbbing of the veins, the rushing of the blood, and the tightening of the skin as it grew larger. She felt her temperature rising and issuing forth a drop of pre-coital fluid. While she could feel all this she was also the stiff protrusion encased in the velvet-like folds of the vagina of the young girl at the sink, the girl who had fornicated with the drops of color, and was now about to take the man as well.

Kristin could feel all this, because she was a part of all this. She was warm and damp, a pleasant dampness, like the warm water of a scented bath. There was a twitching of nerves, as the entire sexual area had sharpened the senses of the nerve endings. Kristin felt the head of the penis, both as it contacted the first part of the mound, and then as it entered, proud and smashing around, splashing within the juices and forcing its way deep into the tubes.

In her new perspective, Kristin was able to feel the intercourse conducted by these two lovers throughout her entire body, not just in the sex organ areas. When the driving penis finally erupted in a hot spurt, Kristin felt herself being shot into the tunnel, carried along like a board on the surf, cascading off the walls of the innermost part of love's playground.

The two lovers were spent, so Kristin felt herself leaving them, and found an interesting trio in one corner and became one with a girl who was impaled between two men. She felt the fullness of total lovemaking, climbing to the peak again with each of them as they reached climaxes, one after the other. She left them then, the girl sore and heavy, the men spent and limp.

Kristin contacted other fragments of climaxes released by the copulating masses, but found that none of the others had a personality. Somehow only she had managed to enter this state of perpetual orgasm.

She drifted about the room collecting the other pieces of herself, then returned to her body. When all had returned, she felt herself falling through, and into the deep pile of the carpet. She tried to stop herself, but she couldn't. Soon, all the colors, the music, and the people were gone. She was in a forest of great blue trees. She looked up to see the sky, but there was none. There was only the jungle of blue fibers which made up the pile of the carpet.

Kristin fell to the bottom with her eyes closed. She was swallowed by an amoeba, and deposited on a dust mote. She drifted without mind, without body, slowly and unseeing for a time which had no beginning and no end.

Henri Marquand held a gold-plated lighter to his long thin cheroot, puffing audibly as he lit it. Billowing clouds of aromatic smoke encircled his head, and, finally, when the expensive cigar was well lighted, he snapped the lighter closed, then leaned back in his chair. He was sitting on the screened porch of his plantation home, while overhead a paddle fan spun briskly, supplying a refreshing breeze.

A servant approached, carrying a tray with two cooling drinks.

"Ah, Colonel, our refreshment," he said. He offered his guest the first choice.

"Thank you," Mot said as he took the drink from the tray.

"You have come a long way from the young man who was once my driver," Henri said as he took a drink. "And even further still from the young boy who shined my shoes for coins. Now you are a colonel in the People's Revolutionary Army."

"Yes," Mot said. "Now I am a colonel."

"I'm very proud of you."

"Are you?"

"Of course," Henri said. He chuckled. "I would have been just as proud had you risen to this rank in the Army of the Saigon Government. As you know, I am completely independent in this war."

"This is not a war in which one can keep one's independence," Mot said.

"Oh?" Henri took another puff from his cigar and squinted at Mot through the new cloud of smoke thus presented. "Correct me if I am wrong, Colonel, but I thought that was what this war was all about. Independence."

"Independence of our country," Mot said. "Not independence of the individual."

"Is that not a contradiction of terms?"

"No," Mot said. "Not at all. The time has come, Monsieur Marquand, to put your country first."

"Tell me, Colonel, just what country would that be?" Marquand asked. "Is it France, a country I have visited, but never lived in? Is it Cochin China, the country of my birth? What country is it?"

"Vietnam, of course."

"South Vietnam, or North Vietnam?"

"The new Vietnam, as established by the new order."

"Oh? Then I take it that you, and the, uh, new order," Marquand slurred the words "new order," "will treat me, and my fellow French Indochins, as Vietnamese?"

"Yes, of course."

Henri chuckled. "My friend, I am convinced that you believe that. But I must say that despite your new position of rank and authority within the revolutionary councils, my own experience has shown me that this will never be. I cannot be a citizen of this Vietnam, or any Vietnam that may ever be formed. I cannot be a citizen of France."

Melinda came into the room then, and sat on the floor at Henri's feet. Henri put his hand on her neck.

"In that, I am like this beautiful creature here, a citizen without portfolio as it were. I have no home but this plantation, no loyalties but my own. If I am forced to choose, that is the choice I will make. You have my word that I will never betray you to the American or the Saigon authorities, but neither will I ever betray them to you. Is it not better to keep islands of tranquility within the festering sea of war? You can never tell when you might need it."

Mot laughed, and finished his drink.

"Monsieur, there is an American saying that I like. It goes something like this: You are full of shit."

Marquand laughed with him.

"But, there may be something to what you say. I will respect your neutrality."

"And I, your dedication to your cause," Marquand said.

Mot stood and put the glass on the table. "I must go now. I am a Colonel in command of a regiment which does not exist. Our losses were very heavy during the Tet offensive, and only now are my forces being resupplied with new men."

"Mot?" Marquand said, and there was none of the implied sarcasm which had been present when he addressed Mot as Colonel, earlier.

"Yes?"

"You may be a Revolutionary Colonel now, but to me, you will always be someone I care about. You have come this far. I would not want to lose you now."

Mot chuckled. "I have no intention of letting the Americans kill me," he said.

Marquand watched Mot walk away, and his hand drifted down easily, possessively, to cup Melinda's breast.

"I hope he lives through this," Marquand said.

"You really do care?" Melinda asked. "I must say I am surprised."

"If the Communists win, he will be an important ally," Marquand said.

"Oh," Melinda replied. "I understand now. Don't worry. He has the look of survival about him."

"That's good," Marquand said, squeezing her breast again. "It will be nice for us to have a friend if we need him."

"Not us," Melinda said. "You."

"And what about you, my dear?"

"I won't be one of the survivors," Melinda said.

"Nonsense, my dear. Haven't I taken you away from your other duties? You are my exclusive property now. I am as jealous of my property as I am of my own person. I will personally see to it that you survive."

"No," Melinda said. "I don't think you will."

CHAPTER TWENTY-ONE

Scottie was dead. He was sitting beside Andy eating beans and franks from a can of 'Cs'. He was talking about the 1963 Chevy he had bought just before he left the States. It only had fifteen thousand miles on it, and he left it with his brother, and he was going to kick his brother's ass when he got back if it had more than seventeen thousand miles. It was right after he said that, that a sniper's round blew out the back of his head.

The Deacon was next. He was a born-again Christian who drove everyone nuts with his proselytizing. He was killed in a road ambush. Four guys went at the same time when a mortar round took them out while they were playing cards.

They said Stallings was masturbating. He was on ambush patrol and they found him the next morning with his throat cut and his hand in a death grip around his penis. He'd been sitting out there in the middle of the night, maybe excited by some private fantasy, or maybe just trying to stay awake. For some reason his death disturbed the men more than most, as if they themselves had been caught in such an act.

And now Andy was a Sergeant E-5. The TO&E called for an E-6 to be the Squad Leader, but Andy had the job. There was only one man left in the squad who had been in 'Nam longer than Andy, and he had been busted so many

251

times that he had lost count. His name was Yarborough. That, and his propensity for running afoul of the Army, made his nickname of Yardbird a natural. That had been shortened to Yard.

Yard had a difficult time with discipline, especially on the few occasions he managed to get into Saigon or Phu Cuong, but he was a good, dependable man in the field, and Andy had learned to depend on him.

"Pepper, did Yard really steal a bus in Bangkok?" Webber asked.

Andy was standing by the sandbag wall at the back of the squad tent, washing his hair in a basin of water which rested on the sandbags. He chuckled.

"Yeah, he and a guy from the First Cav named Mason. They threw the driver and the conductor off the bus, Yard drove and Mason collected the money. The MP's had to set up a roadblock to stop them."

"God," Webber said. "That's great! Isn't that great?"

"Sergeant Culpepper?"

Andy looked around toward the voice and saw SP/4 Schuler from the Orderly Room.

"Whatta you want?"

"Jeez, I been tryin' to ring you guys for the last half hour. Whyn't you report your phone was out?"

"I haven't had any trouble with it," Andy said. He looked at Webber. "You had any trouble with it?"

"No," Webber said.

"Well, shit, no wonder," Schuler said. "Look, the damn line has come loose. He started to re-connect it.

"Leave it alone," Andy said.

"But the line . . ."

"Leave it alone, I said. We haven't had any trouble with it."

"Yeah, you don't have to hump your ass all over the company area, ever'time someone wants the third squad."

"What do you want?" Andy asked.

"The Old Man wants you down at the orderly room,"

Schuler said. "Now," he added, enjoying the implied authority carrying the CO's order gave him.

Andy made no attempt to dry his hair, but it was so short that it would be dry very soon anyway. He slipped on a shirt and walked down to the orderly room. The orderly room was a tent like the others, though it did have a plywood floor, and screen wire walls where the sides were rolled up. Captain Graham and Sergeant Mumford were there, along with a lieutenant that Andy had never seen before. There was an operational map tacked up to the blackboard. Andy knew that meant a special operation, and he knew that his squad was going.

"Ah, Sergeant Culpepper," Captain Graham said. "Lieutenant, this is the man I told you about. Sergeant Culpepper, this is Lieutenant Frazier."

"Culpepper," the lieutenant said. "That name is familiar."

"His father is Colonel Culpepper," Captain Graham said. "And his grandfather was Iron Pants Culpepper."

"Really? We studied his tactics at West Point," the Lieutenant said. He looked at Andy. "What are you doing as an EM? Why didn't you go to the Academy?"

"I didn't want to," Andy said. He had given the same answer so many times now that he never made any attempt to elaborate on it. "Cap'n Graham, what's up?"

"The Lieutenant here is from Division Intelligence," Captain Graham said. "He has some hot information for us."

"We killed a dink this morning, who was carrying several hundred dollars," Lieutenant Frazier said. "We think he was a paymaster, headed for My Lai."

"My Lai? Isn't that where . . ."

"Yes," Captain Graham said. "That's where the guy your squad got yesterday was heading."

"We figure if two paymasters were on their way there, there may be more. Perhaps many more. And if so, that means My Lai is the headquarters for a rather substantial VC unit," Lieutenant Frazier said.

"Maybe not," Andy suggested. "Maybe the guy that was shot today is just a replacement for the one we got yesterday."

"No, I don't think so," Lieutenant Frazier said. "They had papers identifying them as coming from two different units. And they were coming from opposite directions. No, I think there is something going on in My Lai."

"Anyway, we're going to take a look-see," Captain Graham said. "How soon can you get your squad ready?"

"Half an hour," Andy said.

"Weapons, canteens and ammunition only. Lace down, just like a night ambush. We've got a Delta model Huey, we can all go in one chopper. Meet me there in half an hour," Lieutenant Frazier said.

"You're going, Lieutenant?"

"This is my baby," Frazier said. "I wouldn't miss it for the world. Besides, this is where I get my CIB."

About an hour later, the blades of the UH1-D began popping as they spilled air in the descent to the edge of a river. They were still five kilometers from My Lai. The UH1-D was accompanied by a CH-47 Chinook, slingloading a large, wooden crate. There was actually nothing in the crate, the entire thing was a ruse to make it appear as if an engineering site was being set up. That way the helicopter activity wouldn't alert the VC that a long range patrol had been put on the ground close by.

Andy and the others jumped out as soon as the chopper touched down. They were all out of the ship in less than thirty seconds, and the ship lifted off immediately afterward, then followed the sling loading Chinook back toward Phu Loi. They looked like service helicopters, rather than combat team insertion ships.

"This way, men," Lieutenant Frazier said in his best command voice.

Yard was at point, and the patrol moved out in a single

file along a jungle trail, keeping the required five meter separation. Half an hour later, Yard came jogging back toward them.

"We've got a hut up here," he said.

"Abandoned?" Andy asked.

"Doesn't look like it. It's built on a concrete pad and everything."

"Probably some farmer or something," Frazier said. "We'll go around it."

"Lieutenant, if it's built on a concrete pad it's no farmer's hut," Andy said. "That's somebody important. Maybe VC important."

Frazier sighed. "All right, we'll check it out. I don't expect much."

"Let Yard and me do it."

"We'll all go," Frazier said.

It took another few minutes to reach the hut. When they reached the edge of the clearing, they saw someone coming out of the hut, carrying an AK-47.

"Damn!" Frazier said. "VC." He opened fire, but he missed, and the VC ran back inside.

"Shit!" Andy said. "Spray the hut!"

Andy and everyone in the squad fired long bursts of automatic fire toward the hut. The bullets ripped through the walls easily, and after a few moments, a white flag fluttered out of the door.

"Chieu Hoi," someone called from inside.

"They're giving up!" Frazier said. He stepped out into the clearing. "Okay, come on out with . . ."

Frazier never finished his statement. A rifle barked from a bush at the other side of the clearing, and Lieutenant Frazier pitched forward.

"I see the son of a bitch!" Yard shouted, and he fired a long burst toward the bush. A VC sprawled out across the bush, his rifle clattering to the ground in front of him.

"Okay," Andy shouted to the hut. "We've got napalm grenades. Come on out or we'll burn you out!"

"No!" someone shouted. "No burn, no burn!"

Andy didn't have any napalm grenades. In fact, as far as he knew, there wasn't any such thing. But he knew the VC fear of napalm.

Half a dozen VC came out of the hut with their hands raised. Three of them were carrying weapons.

"Anyone left inside?"

"No. No one left," one of the VC said.

"Check it out, Yard."

Yard and Webber went inside. A moment later they came back out.

"Empty," they said.

"Keep these guys covered," Andy said. "If they twitch, blow them away."

Andy walked back to Lieutenant Frazier, then dropped down beside him. He turned him over, then sighed. The lieutenant was dead.

"Well, Lieutenant, you got your CIB," he said.

Andy called back for choppers, and was told that one helicopter would come to bring back the Lieutenant's body, but that Andy was to proceed to coordinates Tango Charlie, Papa Lima Three Four. There he would turn his prisoners over to elements of the American Division, and attach his squad to one of the operating platoons.

"Turtle Six, are you saying put my squad with a platoon from another division?" Andy asked in disbelief.

"That's affirmative," he was answered. "It seems that the American Division got the jump on us in My Lai. You'll be the only element from the First."

"If it's up to me, you can let the American have My Lai," Andy said.

"It isn't up to you," Turtle Six replied.

"I didn't think so," Andy said. "Wide Receiver, out." He gave the radio back to the RTO. "Okay, guys, as soon as the chopper picks up the Lieutenant's body, we have to deliver these prisoners to the American Division."

"What? Why do we have to give them away? They're our dinks," Yard said.

"The Americal is throwing a party," Andy said sarcastically. "And we are invited."

"Okay, here's your supper," Andy said that night, after they had joined up. He dropped several boxes of C-rations in front of them.

"Any B units?" Yard asked.

"Shit no," one of the other men answered. "We had to scrounge from these bastards, you think they are going to let a B unit go?"

"What have we got?" Yard asked. "Probably all ham and eggs. Son of a bitch, I hate the ham and eggs."

"Pepper, what's up?"

"We're going in with this platoon tomorrow," Andy said.

"I hope we get to stay together as a squad," Yard said.

"We're going to. The doofus Lieutenant wanted to split us up, so there would be some experience in all of his squads."

"Some experience? What are you talking about?"

"These guys are cherries," Andy said.

"All of them?"

"Even the doofus Lieutenant is a cherry. He's got them so worked up you'd think they were attacking Hanoi tomorrow instead of some little shit-assed ville."

"Yeah, well, I'm going to cut some Z's," Yard said. "If I'm not awake in the morning, just start ahead without me. I'll catch up."

"If we had any sense, we'd all sleep through it tomorrow," Andy said.

The platoon leader sent Andy and his squad along the riverbank the next morning, to be in position to block any enemy attempt to escape. Andy knew that it was really just an assignment designed to get his squad out of the way so the Lieutenant's own platoon could have the village to themselves. What the Lieutenant didn't know was that his attempt to squeeze Andy out of the picture couldn't have been more welcome. If there was anything he didn't want to do, it was get mixed up with a bunch of green infantrymen in their first assault on a village.

Andy led his men along the riverbank as directed, and, as he expected, they saw nothing. Then, about thirty minutes into the operation, they heard heavy firing from the village.

"Shit, they must have run into it!" Yard said.

"Come on!" Andy called, breaking for the village at a trot. They didn't run all out, because anybody who suddenly burst from the jungle on a dead run was a sure target for a nervous infantryman, especially one in his first fire-fight.

Andy and the others broke out of the clearing, then stopped dead in their tracks.

"Son of a bitch, Andy, what the hell are they doing?" Yard asked in shock.

"I . . . I don't know," Andy said. "God in heaven, I don't know."

Old men, women, and children from the village were huddled in a ditch which ran just outside the edge of the village. On the berm looking down into the ditch, stood about twenty men from the young Lieutenant's platoon. They, and the Lieutenant who was their platoon leader, were firing down into the ditch. Heads were exploding under the crash of the bullets.

There was no screaming. Andy couldn't believe how quiet they were. It was like some sort of bad dream, where everything is in very, very slow motion, and all sound is muffled.

"Som'bitch, did you see that? I shot the nipple right off that bitch!" someone shouted.

Andy couldn't even hear the gunfire.

* * *

"Miss? Miss?"

Kristin opened her eyes and saw a well-groomed young woman leaning over her. The woman was smiling.

"Yes?"

"Would you fasten your seatbelt please? We are landing at Washington National."

"Oh," Kristin said. "Yes. Yes, thank you."

Kristin fastened her seatbelt, then looked through the window as the plane banked. She could see the Washington Monument and the mall, then roads with cars moving like ants. The plane rolled out of its bank, and the wing flaps went lower. She could hear all the sounds of sighing air, changing engine noise, and creaking gears as the plane settled lower and lower until finally, with a rumble, the plane was no longer flying, but was rolling along the runway.

The stewardess took the microphone from the forward bulkhead of the cabin.

"Ladies and gentlemen, we have just landed at Washington National Airport. It is two-thirty P.M. local time. The temperature is a pleasant 72 degrees. For your own safety, please remain seated until the aircraft has come to a complete stop."

Kristin sat in her seat long after the plane had stopped, even after the last passenger had deplaned. The stewardesses were about to leave, when one of them looked back at her and saw that she was still there.

"Miss? Is there something wrong?" she asked.

"No," Kristin said. She took a deep breath and stood up. "No, nothing is wrong."

She had telegraphed Jake and asked him to meet her plane. She left before she had a chance to get his answer. Would he meet her? If so, what would his reaction be? Would he be glad to see her? Or would he send her away?

Kristin moved through the aisle of the plane to the door.

"Please, dear God," she prayed silently. "Please, let him be there."

She walked through the boarding gate and saw several people greeting each other, some with hugs and kisses, others with handshakes and slaps on the back. She held her breath and looked around. She didn't see him.

"Kristin!"

It was him! She saw him standing just on the other side of the railing, smiling and waving at her. He wasn't in uniform, and that had confused her. She let out a little shout of joy and ran to him, and he caught her with open arms.

The bed was mussed from their lovemaking, and they lay in each others arms, looking through the window of Jake's twentieth-floor apartment. An airplane was descending into Washington National, and they could see its red lights blinking its way across the night sky. Also visible from the window was the floodlit dome of the Capitol building.

"How long can you stay?" Jake asked.

"How long am I welcome?" Kristin answered.

Jake raised up on one elbow and looked down at her.

"Are you telling me you'll stay as long as I want you to?"

"Yes," Kristin answered.

"All right," Jake said. "We can get the bloodtests and the license tomorrow. We'll be married by the weekend."

"No," Kristin said.

"No? But I thought—"

Kristin put her fingers to Jake's lips.

"I'm not ready for marriage just yet," she said. "The white picket fence, maybe. But not the roses."

"Are you saying you don't want to get married? Ever?"

"No, I'm not saying that," Kristin said. "I'm just asking you to give me a little time to come around, okay?"

"All right, if that's what you want," Jake said. He lay

back down and was quiet for several moments, then he chuckled.

"What is it?" she asked.

"I've been invited to a White House dinner next week. I was just wondering how the protocol officer is going to handle the Colonel's mistress."

"No problem, I just won't go."

"Oh, yes you will," Jake said. "You are what will keep me from going insane at those long, boring affairs. That's the only thing I'm going to ask of you from our arrangement."

"The only thing?" she asked, teasingly, as she reached down and touched him.

"Well, one of the things," Jake amended. "I mean it, honey. I won't try to hide you. I love you, and whatever form our relationship takes will be fine by me. I am going to take maximum advantage of the relationship, and that means you are going to go with me whenever the occasion warrants it."

"Okay," Kristin said. "But what would I wear to a dinner at the White House?"

Jake chuckled again. "Wear something red," he said.

CHAPTER TWENTY-TWO

Andy was at the reception center in Oakland Army Air Terminal, standing in line for an airline ticket to Atlanta. A GI came over to him just before he got to the counter.

"Where you goin', buddy?"

"Atlanta, then Columbus, Georgia."

"I got a Greyhound bus ticket to New Orleans. You can have it for ten bucks, save yourself a little money."

"Why are you sellin' it?"

"My brother's here with his car."

"I don't know, riding a bus that far sure doesn't sound very good."

"Hey, there's no one on it but other guys from 'Nam. Shit, man, it'll be a fuckin' party all the way."

"You're next," the man behind the counter said.

"Just a second," Andy replied.

"Listen, you Vietnam veterans don't own the world, you know. You are holding up the line. Now either tell me where you want to go, or get out of the line."

Andy looked at the civilian behind the counter, and he smiled. "How 'bout if I just tell you where to go?" he asked. He looked at the soldier who offered him the Greyhound ticket. "You just sold a ticket," he said.

"The bus'll be loadin' at that door back there," the soldier said, handing the ticket to Andy. "Nothin' on it but GI's."

Andy took his duffle over to the pile of duffles by the door and looked outside, just as the bus rolled up. There were about thirty soldiers, marines and airmen standing around, and they let out a cheer when the bus arrived. The bus stopped with a squeal of airbrakes, and the driver got out, then smiled, sheepishly.

"Okay, guys, let's go," he said.

Andy found a seat about halfway back on the right, next to the window. He could feel the throb of the bus engine, and the thump of the duffle bags being thrown into the luggage bay beneath him. A Specialist Fourth Class sat in the seat next to him. The Spec four was wearing a shoulder patch from the 101st.

"Fuck it," the Spec four said.

"Yeah, really," Andy answered.

When the bus was loaded it pulled away from the terminal. Three blocks later it stopped in front of a liquor store and everyone on the bus streamed inside and began buying liquor. Andy went in with the SP/4. Several men started getting six packs of beer from the shelves.

"We got it cold in the freezer," the man behind the counter said.

"Cold? Who the hell drinks beer cold?" someone asked.

Andy took a six-pack over and started to pay for it.

"You, I gotta see an ID," the clerk said.

"ID?"

"Yeah. How old are you?"

"I'm very old," Andy said. "I never thought I would get this old."

"What are you talkin' about ID?" one of the other men asked. "Are you shittin' us? Nobody asked to see an ID when they sent us on the line."

"Listen, fellas. It's the law," he said.

One gray-headed sergeant stepped up to the counter. He looked to be in his late forties or early fifties.

"What about me, friend? Do you want to see my ID?"

"What? No, of course not, it's just that—"

"I'm buyin' everything," the Sergeant said. "You tell me how much it costs, they'll give me the money and I'll give it to you."

"That doesn't change anything," the clerk protested.

"Oh yes it does," the Sergeant insisted. "It keeps us from wasting your goddamn building."

"Yeah!" one of the others said.

The clerk looked around nervously. "All right," he said. "Buy your stuff quickly and then get out of here, will you? I don't want the police coming around. They'll shut me down."

Someone brought a girl on board at Las Vegas. At first Andy thought one of the men had just picked her up and talked her into going with him. Then he learned that she was a whore who had talked the GI into taking her along. He was going to get ten percent of her action, and she went to everyone on the bus asking what she could do for them, and naming her price.

Andy and the Spec four with him turned her down, but the two guys across the aisle accepted her offer, and Andy could see their shadows and hear their noises as the bus rolled through the dark desert country of the great Southwest.

As soon as Andy was home he took down everything that was on the wall of his room: the college pennants, the autographed pictures of football players, the press coverage of his own high school football days, everything.

Mike was in Canada and his father was in Washington, D.C. "Living with some hippie. Can you imagine that about your father?" Virgie had asked.

Virgie and Andy were eating dinner alone, though Virgie had a sales meeting at eight.

"Just leave the dishes," she said. "I'll take care of them later." She hugged Andy again. "Oh, Andy, it is so good to have you back home again. You just don't know how good."

"Mom, do you think I could just drop you off at your meeting and have the car?" Andy asked.

"Why do you want to do that, dear?"

"I thought I'd go out to a few of the places and bum around a bit, maybe see some of the guys."

"Well, I," Virgie started to refuse, then she saw the expression on Andy's face. "Sure. You can just drop me off and I'll have someone bring me back home. But dear, please be careful."

"Yeah," Andy said. "Yeah, I'll be careful."

Andy went to the Bulldog, a place where he and his friends used to hang out. He saw MacIntosh's candy-apple Ford parked there and he smiled. It could have been a year ago. Nothing had changed. He was home again.

Simon and Garfunkel were on the juke when he went inside. The booths were crowded and the place was heavy with smoke, real tobacco, no grass.

"Hey, Andy," someone called. "Come here." It was MacIntosh.

"Hi, Mac," Andy said. "I see you're still driving your Ford."

"Nobody's gonna get that car unless they are willing to pay some heavy bread for it," MacIntosh said. "So, hey, what are you doin' home from school? Semester break, or what?"

"School?"

"Yeah, aren't you going to Georgia Tech or Alabama or some such place to play football?"

"No, not yet," Andy said.

"You're not in school? What have you been doing?"

"I was in the Army," Andy said. "I just got discharged."

"You couldn't have been in the Army for three years already. It hasn't been three years since we graduated."

"I volunteered for the draft, that was only two years. Then I got an early-out because I went to Vietnam."

"You been to Vietnam?"

"Yeah."

Two of the girls who were sitting in the booth with MacIntosh looked at Andy. They were pretty girls, eighteen or nineteen, and Andy thought he would like to know them.

"You must be some kind of a jerk," one of them said.

"What?" Andy asked in surprise.

"A real nerd," the other said.

"Why?" Andy was hurt by their remarks. "Why would you say that?"

"You let them send you to Vietnam."

"That place is definitely uncool," the other girl said.

"I really had no choice," Andy said.

"Sure you had a choice. You could have gone to Canada."

"You've seen the posters haven't you?" one of the girls asked. She pushed her lips out, poutingly. "Girls say yes to boys who say no," she said, sexily.

"And no to turkeys who say yes," the other put in coldly.

"What was it like?" MacIntosh asked.

"What, you mean Vietnam?"

"Yeah, did you kill anyone?"

Andy looked back at the two girls and saw them waiting for his answer. He recognized the expression on their faces. He had seen it in the reporters and the straphangers who came out to the field on the day after a battle to take pictures of the bodycount. It was the morbid curiosity of someone who enjoyed looking at death because they never had to meet it on a one-to-one basis.

"Uh, no," Andy said. "I was a clerk, I never went into the field."

The light of interest left the girls' eyes.

"Yeah?" one of them said. "Well, you were a real jerkoff for letting them send you over there in the first place."

"Listen," Andy said as he stood up. "I gotta go. I got my mom's car."

"His mom's car," MacIntosh snickered.

Andy peeled away from the Bulldog angrily, then went into a liquor store where he grabbed a bottle of whiskey. The clerk was in the back of the store as Andy dropped a twenty dollar bill on the counter, then started back for the door.

"Just a minute, I gotta see some ID," the clerk shouted, coming toward the front.

"I don't have time," Andy said. "Just keep the change."

"I need ID," the clerk shouted louder.

"Here's your ID," Andy replied, giving him the finger as he went out the door.

Andy took the bottle home with him, and he went into his room with the newly bared walls and lay on his bed and began drinking from the bottle.

The bed was too soft, so he moved onto the floor.

It was eleven o'clock on a Friday night. That meant eleven Saturday morning in 'Nam. Last Saturday morning Andy was still in the company. He and Yard had gone into Phu Cuong to eat noodle soup for lunch. They got laid that afternoon, then there was a short-timers' party for him back in the company NCO club that night. Two days later it was the Freedom Bird for the land of the big PX, and now, here he was.

"Let me tell you, guys, it's not all it's cracked up to be," Andy said, holding up the bottle in a lonesome toast in the night.

"Come on, Culpepper, bust some head!" the assistant coach yelled. "Show me some killer instinct!"

Andy, who had just missed a tackle in one-on-one drill, stood up and started back to the end of the line to wait for his turn to come up again.

"He can't get me, coach. I got too many moves for him," the ball carrier laughed, tossing the ball back to the coach.

"All right, next two."

The whistle blew and two more men crashed together, grunting and straining as the pads popped.

"Next two."

Finally it worked back to Andy. He looked across the circle and saw the man with the ball. It was the same man who had spun out of his grasp before. He was a black kid from Kentucky, who had made All-State running back in high school there. He had a gazelle-like build and he looked fast, just standing still. He was grinning at Andy.

"Get ready to grab some air, fool. You can't touch me."

"Show a little killer instinct, Culpepper," the coach said again. "They told me you were tough." He blew his whistle.

Andy hit the ball carrier right in the solar plexus with his shoulder. He heard the expulsion of breath, and he knew he had knocked the breath out of him. He finished out by bringing up his elbow in a smash across the ball carrier's mouth. The ball carrier had, arrogantly, let his mouthpiece dangle from his face mask. Andy felt a mushiness under his elbow, and that meant that he got a couple of the kid's teeth.

"Hold it! Hold it!" the coach shouted, and he blew his whistle. "Get up off him!"

Andy got up and looked down at the erstwhile ball carrier. The ball had popped loose, and he was struggling to regain his breath. Blood came from his mouth, and one tooth lay in the dirt.

"Is that enough killer instinct for you, coach?" Andy asked. He started walking toward the dressing room.

"I don't take smart talk like that," the coach yelled. "Give me five laps."

"Blow it out your ass," Andy called over his shoulder.

"You . . . you are off this team! I'm going to the head coach, mister, and I can guarantee you, that you are off this team!"

"No shit," Andy said.

*   *   *

"Why do you want to go back to Vietnam?" the recruiting sergeant asked.

"I can't take this shit over here," Andy said. "I can't adjust."

The Recruiting Sergeant shook his head.

"No," he said. "You can't say that. That's no good. If the shrinks think you are having trouble adjusting, they'll certify you as unfit for service in Vietnam."

Andy laughed. "I'm fit for service in Vietnam," he said. "It's the States I'm having trouble with."

"No good. You have to come up with another reason."

"What if told them I had a Vietnamese girl pregnant and I wanted to get back to marry her."

"They'd probably send you to Europe."

"Okay, you're the expert. You tell me how I can do it."

"Career," the Recruiting Sergeant said.

"Career?"

"Sign up for six years. The promotion is faster in 'Nam. The Army understands career ambition."

"All right," Andy said. "Make out the papers. I'll sign. When my old man finds out about this, he will shit a brick."

"Ah, he'll come around," the recruiting sergeant said. "Most folks just don't understand the Army, that's all."

"My dad doesn't understand the Army?" Andy said. He laughed. "Come to think of it, Sarge, you may be right."

Dear Andy,

I got a letter from mom, and she told me you had voluntarily gone back into the army so you could return to Vietnam. I won't question you, each of us have our own reasons for doing things, and no one has the right to impose his ideas on another.

Probably never, in the history of familyhood, has there been a more diverse family than ours.

Dad, as I'm sure you know by now, is working for a general who is working for President Nixon. It's as if my worst nightmares have come true. When dad was simply a career Army officer, I was able to excuse that by saying that he was pursuing an honorable vocation that has been pursued by our ancestors for many generations. But now he is a part of the Nixon Administration. When I think of how screwed-up our government is, I have to be cognizant of the fact that our father is helping to screw it up.

And mother. She is quick to condemn me and all my friends for the drugs and sex and booze she thinks is a constant part and parcel of my life. For all her condemnation, however, she can't get through a morning without her tranquilizers, an afternoon without a martini, an evening without a "dinner-date"—which I learned long ago was her euphemism for going to bed with someone—or a night without sleeping pills.

And you, my dear brother. What secret devils are driving you? What possesses you to abandon the draft-free sanctuary of college to return to the hell of Vietnam? I will give you my opinion. I believe it is a war wound. It is a spirit maimed by shot and shell. It is a wound which we can't see now, and which many may never see. But it is there and it is just as serious as a maimed body. Perhaps, some years from now, we will recognize it. Only then will we begin to assess the real damage this war has done, for, Andy, I believe that wound has affected us all, veteran and non-veteran alike.

I have not been skimpy with my assessment of the rest of the family, so now I come to myself.

I am the quintessential hippie, living here in Canada with a young girl who was born Barbara Woodward, but who prefers to be called Tulip. I chose, as a matter of conscience, to leave college before I graduated. That was my form of protest against the draft deferment which could keep me there. I hope you understand, I wasn't protesting against the fact that I was deferred, but against the fact that thousands of young men who couldn't afford college, *weren't* deferred.

Of course, as soon as I left school, I immediately became 1-A, so now I am technically, though not actually, a draft dodger.

There are seven of us who live in a big house here. We have a pretty good deal. The bottom floor is a used furniture store, and we live on the top two floors. The second floor, which is our bottom floor, has a big room where we all eat, listen to music, watch TV when the set is working, do a little smoke, drink beer and rap. There is also a kitchen and a little bedroom where one of the unattached girls sleep.

The top floor has two bedrooms and a big bathroom, and there is a bedroom in the attic. The whole thing only costs seventy-five dollars, because the guy who owns the used furniture place downstairs gets an insurance break by having someone here all the time.

We do odd jobs, the girls babysit, the men do whatever comes along, and we pool our money. We never have much to spend, but there's always a good nourishing soup or meal to come home to, and there is a feeling of love among us that I can't explain. It's like we are a family, only much closer than any ordinary family. And I don't mean this as a rap against you, Andy. I've always thought we were very close as brothers, and I pray that you find some peace from whatever is plaguing you now.

Tulip is going to draw a flower on the outside of this envelope. I'll bet your mail clerk will get a kick out of that.

Your loving brother,
Mike

"Sarge, you want me to turn his bunk in, or just stockade it?"

"Go ahead and stockade it, there'll be a replacement along pretty soon. This way we won't have to draw another bunk."

"I'm going to trade mattresses with him, okay?"

"Yeah, sure, go ahead. He sure as hell won't mind."

"What about his personals?"

"Leave 'em. Someone from the supply room will inventory 'em, and take care of 'em."

"It was a damn shame. He just got here."

"He'd been here before. He knew what to expect."

"Hey, tell me somethin'. Was he really the son of the Secretary of the Army?"

"No, where the hell did you hear that?"

"Someone told me his old man was the Secretary of the Army."

"If that was true, you think he'd be over here?"

"He come back 'cause he wanted to be back."

"His old man is a bird colonel in Washington. He's on President Nixon's staff," one of the other men said.

"Yeah? How do you know? Pepper never talked all that much."

"I got here right after he left the last time, and I got to be friends with a friend of his. It was Yard, remember? He's gone now."

"Yeah, I remember Yard."

"Anyway, Yard told me about Pepper before he rotated back."

"Son of a bitch. Imagine that. His old man knows the President of the United States."

"Mail call!" someone called from the front of the tent. "Sanders!"

"Yo."

"Benchley."

"Here."

"Lindell."

"Here."

"Culpepper!"

There was silence in the squad tent.

"Where's Culpepper?"

"He got hit last night."

"Where is he? First Field?" the mail clerk asked. "I gotta know where to forward the letter." The clerk laughed. "Look at this son of a bitch. It has a daisy drawn on the outside. The nurses over there will like that."

"Send it back," one of the men said.

"Send it back? What do you mean?"

"Pepper's dead."

CHAPTER TWENTY-THREE

"Colonel, don't forget you are supposed to brief the President this afternoon on HR 159. That's the military allowances bill." Lieutenant Wyse said. Lieutenant Wyse was Jake's aide. Jake was senior Army member to the Presidental military advisory staff.

"Yes, thank you, Nick," Jake said. "I made some notes last night—did I bring my briefing folder in here?" Jake shuffled through a pile of papers on his desk.

"Yes, sir," Lieutenant Wyse said. He cleared his throat. "Uh, Sir?"

"Yes?"

"There's someone here to see you. He's come every day this week."

"What's that? He's come every day this week and I haven't even been told?"

"Well, you have been terribly busy, sir. And his personal appearance hasn't engendered much willingness on the part of anyone to bring him to your attention. He is, to put it mildly, rather shabby. He has a long beard, scraggly hair, and he's wearing a stained field jacket."

"Field jacket? Is he a Vietnam veteran?"

"I really couldn't say, sir. He has the look of a trouble maker."

"Do you think he is dangerous?"

"No, sir. Just a kook," Lieutenant Wyse said.

"What does he want?"

"He wouldn't say."

"Find out what he wants," Jake said. "If he won't tell you, send him away."

"And if he does tell me?"

"Then we'll decide," Jake said. "Did you get a copy of my notes over to Al Haig?"

"Yes, sir."

Jake pulled his notes over and looked at them again while his aide went into the outer office to talk with the mysterious visitor. A moment later the intercom on his phone buzzed, and he picked it up.

"Sir, he still won't tell me what he wants to talk about. But he says to tell you he was a friend of Pepper's."

"Pepper? That's what Andy's friends called him."

"Send him in."

"Yes, sir."

The door opened, and a young man walked through. He was, as Lieutenant Wyse had indicated, a most untidy man. His beard was long and his hair was even longer. He was wearing a field jacket with the name YARBOROUGH over the breast pocket.

"You knew my son?" Jake asked, extending his hand.

"Yes, sir," Yarborough said. He shook Jake's hand and smiled. "I never knew whether I should believe Pepper when he said his old man was brass." He laughed. "I been out for over a year, and I still feel like I should salute, though I guess it wouldn't be right with this beard and hair."

"You look like you have a fine crop there," Jake said. He didn't know what else to say.

Yarborough put his hand to his beard. "I reckon I do," he said. "I started it the day I mustered out. I haven't had a shave or a haircut since the one I got in Da Nang before I left."

"Tell me, Mr. Yarborough—"

"Folks generally call me Yard," Yard said.

"Yard. Yes, I remember now. Andy did speak of you."

"Me 'n Pepper was close, Sir. Real close. Kind of close you can only get in war, you know what I mean?"

"Yes, I think I do."

"That's why I'm here, Colonel. There's somethin' that happened over there, somethin' that me'n Pepper saw. It shook us up somethin' awful. Especially Pepper. Truth to tell, I think it was what really drove him back in, made him go back to 'Nam."

"Something happened? What happened?"

"At first, we was goin' to report it as soon as we got back. Then Pepper got to worryin' about you. He didn't want you to get hurt none."

"What happened, Yard?"

"Colonel, did you ever hear of a place called My Lai?"

"My Lai?"

"It's near Son My in Quang Ngai province."

"I know the province."

"I was in Pepper's, your son's, squad. In March of 1968, we were told to proceed to My Lai to investigate the possibility of a big VC pow-wow there. We ran into some dinks along the way, there was a brief fire fight and Lieutenant Frazier, the guy who was leading us, was killed. We killed one dink and captured the rest. But when we called for a chopper to come pick up the prisoners, we were told to join up with a platoon from the 11th Brigade of the Americal Division, and to turn our prisoners over to them. We didn't feel that good about joining up with them, especially when we learned that they were all cherries."

"Cherries?"

"None of 'em had ever seen combat before. Their Lieutenant was a guy named Calley. He tried to break our squad up and scatter us through his platoon, but Pepper wasn't comin' on that. We stayed to ourselves, but we saw it, Colonel. We saw everything that happened."

"What did happen?" Jake asked.

"Murder, Colonel. Calley and his bunch lined up all the people from that little village and shot 'em down. They killed little babies who couldn't even walk, children, mothers with babies suckin' on the breast, old women and old men. They killed them all. They shot 'em 'till noon, then they took a break for some C's," Yard laughed, or it may have been a grunt. "Would you believe they gave some of the kids C's before they went back to shootin' 'em after lunch. In all, there was a hundred and thirty or so killed. Maybe more."

Jake felt a sudden hollowness in the pit of his stomach, and a weakness in his knees. He squeezed the arm of the chair very tightly, and controlled his voice with great effort when he spoke.

"Mr. Yarborough. Did my son participate in that massacre?"

"No sir!" Yard said emphatically. "None of us did. In fact, we yelled at them to stop, but they didn't pay any attention."

"But you stayed?"

"Yes, sir, we stayed. Pepper said we'd need to witness it if we were ever goin' to do anything about it."

"March of '68. That was over a year ago."

"Yes, sir."

"You didn't report it?"

"No sir. We were goin' to, but we got to thinkin' and Pepper was afraid it might hurt you."

"How in the hell did he think I could be hurt by something like that?"

"You're regular Army, sir. And you are real high up in rank. I guess Pepper just figured that anything that would hurt the Army would hurt you. Anyway, he decided against sayin' anything. I mean it was already done, there was nothin' we could do to bring those folks back. Besides, they might not of believed us anyway. And Pepper was real short, they would have probably extended him to testify and all that, and then nothin' would come of it.

Only I know it bothered him. Fact is, it's been botherin'
me a lot. I can't sleep, I can't eat, I can't screw, I can't
hold any kind of a job. I just see those people all the time,
the women and the kids and the old men, and the way they
just stood there in that ditch watchin' our guys shoot 'em.
They just stood there and didn't say nothin'. They just
stood there 'n died, like it was expected of 'em. I knew the
time would come when I would have to tell someone about
it, sir. So, I figured I'd come tell you.''

"Yes," Jake said. "Well, Yard, I thank you for coming to me with it.''

"You'll look into it won't you, sir? You owe that to
Pepper, don't you?''

"Yes," Jake said. "I owe that to Andy.''

Yard smiled. "Thanks," he said. "Thanks a lot. You
know? I think maybe I'll be able to sleep tonight.''

The disturbing information Yard had brought to Jake
was still on his mind as he and Kristin ate dinner that
night. After several attempts to make conversation, Kristin
finally asked him what was wrong.

"I've been thinking about something all day," Jake
said. "You know how the protestors always call anyone in
uniform a baby-killer?''

"Yes.''

"I don't know if that is a self-fulfilling prophecy, or if
they have been right and I have been wrong all this time.''

"Jake, what are you talking about?''

"Killing babies," Jake said. "And their mothers, and
grandmothers and everyone else.''

Jake told Kristin the entire story. Finally, when he was
through, she spoke.

"What are you going to do about it?''

"I've already started," he said. "I made several inquiries this afternoon.''

"And it was all denied of course?" Kristin said.

"No, not really, and that's what has me so disturbed,''

Jake said. "I'm told that an investigation has been undertaken with no positive results. You know, Kristin, I get the feeling that several high-ranking officers have already known about this, and have been actively covering it up."

"What's your next move?"

"I'm not sure. I also heard from very high sources that it would not be good for me to get involved in anything like this just now. Especially as I am about to be nominated for my star. It's like they were warning me, almost blackmailing me with the threat of not making General if I push this any further."

Jake was quiet for a moment. "And that convinced me more than ever. I'm going full steam ahead on this, Kristin, even if I have to do it all alone. If there was a massacre in My Lai, then everyone needs to know about it, no matter what the costs, and by God I'm going to tell them."

Kristin leaned over and kissed Jake. "I don't know what the costs will be," she said. "But I can tell you that you won't have to go through this all alone. That is, if your offer to marry me still stands."

Jake looked at Kristin in surprise, and smiled. "Are you serious? You want to get married?"

"Yes," Kristin said. "If you can come so far away from the Prussian officer I used to know that you are now willing to take on the United States Army, then I'm willing to meet you halfway. That is, if you'll have me."

"Try and get away," Jake said, reaching for her.

There was a reception at the Fort Leslie J. McNair Officers' Club, right after the wedding. The wedding was a very quiet affair. Jake had invited only Colonel Pat Bohannon and his wife. Pat Bohannon was the Air Force counterpart to Jake.

The reception was much better attended, because it was open to anyone who happened to show up at the club at the time. Many were surprised to see that Jake had just gotten married, some because they had assumed all along that he was married.

"I got a card from the President," Jake told Pat.

"I would have thought you would ask him to be your best man," Pat teased.

"Listen, I'm very choosy about who I invite to my weddings," Jake said. "Kristin is just lucky that I invited her."

"Yeah, tell me about it," Pat answered, laughing. Pat sucked the olive from a toothpick and was silent for a moment before he spoke, reflectively. "Jake, I'm hearing some bad shit," he said.

"Like what?"

"Like the fact that you won't let go of this massacre thing, despite the fact that you've been told to leave it alone in every way except a DD95 from the Chief of Staff himself."

"It's not right that it should be kept quiet," Jake said. "If it really happened, the country should know about it."

"Why?"

"Why? Goddammit, because the Army doesn't do things like that, that's why."

"Jake, don't you know something like that is all the protestors need? My God, can you see the headlines from that? The liberal press and the peaceniks will have a field day. Shit, what's 130 dead dinks, anyway?"

"It was women and children and old men."

"Do you think we don't kill women and children and old men when we bomb Hanoi? Hell, we are probably getting that many every day! And look at the Germans and Japanese we killed in air raids during the war. One hundred thousand at a time. How can you expect anyone to get so excited over a hundred and thirty?"

"It was deliberate and cold-blooded, Pat. They lined them up and murdered them one at a time," Jake said.

"So what? They aren't any deader than the ones we've

killed in Hanoi, or the German and Jap kids who were
killed in the raids during World War II. Anyway, they are
all dead now. What can you do for them? In the meantime,
you're putting your own career right down the old toilet.
Jesus, man, you're about to get a star! You know what that
means?''

"Of course I do."

"Of course you do. Your father and your grandfather,
and who knows who-all have been Generals. Well, what
do you think they would say if they saw you screwing up
like Hogan's goat?''

"I would like to think they would support me," Jake
said. "But it doesn't matter. I'm not doing this for them.
I'm doing it for my own kids. For Andy's memory, and
for Mike.''

Pat shook his head and took a drink. "I'll say this for
you. You got a lot of guts. Not much sense, mind you, but
a lot of guts.''

"No, wait, wait," Tulip said, laughing. "What if . . .
what if the whole thing, I mean our entire *existence* was
part of a closed circle?''

Tara took a hit on the joint, then passed it around to her
left. She held it for as long as she could, holding her hand
out to keep anyone else from speaking because she wanted
to answer Tulip, then she let the smoke explode out with a
gasp. Everyone laughed.

"Tara can get more mileage from one puff than anyone
I know, man," one of the others said.

"Okay," Tara said when she recovered her voice. "Now
you said what if, uh, we were in a circle?''

"A circle jerk," someone said, and everyone laughed
again.

"Well, I mean," Tulip started, then the joint came back
to her and she took a puff and held it for a moment. "I
don't know what I mean. I don't remember what I said,"
she said. "But it was profound. Wasn't it profound, Mike?''

"Yeah," Mike said, smiling. "It was profound."

"Mike's no judge. He's in love with you. He thinks everything you say is profound."

"Mike's sweet," Tulip said, putting her head in his lap.

"He's square," Tara said. "He makes a big thing about being free and hip, but he's as square as that chicken-shit old man of his who is Nixon's bag man."

Mike didn't like to hear his father put down like that, but he withheld comment.

"Why do you say I'm square?" Mike asked.

"You talk about loving everyone, but you don't mean it," Tara said.

"I try."

"Do you love me?"

"Yes, of course. You are part of the family unit here."

"You say you love me, but you have never made love to me."

"No," Mike admitted.

"Have you ever made love to anyone in this room, other than Tulip?"

Mike laughed. "There are four boys and two girls in this room. I've made love with Tulip, I haven't made love with you. That should answer your question."

"I mean everyone," Tara said. "Boy, girl, what difference does it make if you are serious when you say you love everyone?"

"Love and sex need not be synonymous," Mike said.

"Oh? Listen to the philosopher," Tara said. "Well, I've got a hot flash for you, Mr. Philosopher. I've made love to everyone in this room except you. *Everyone,*" she added pointedly.

Mike glanced down at Tulip with a questioning look on his face.

"What are you telling me?" he asked in a quiet voice.

"I'm telling you that Tulip and I have gotten it on. Several times. She's hip. Why can't you be the same way?"

"I don't know," Mike said quietly. Gently, he slipped Tulip's head from his lap and stood up. "I guess I just can't." He walked away.

"Tara, goddammit, why do you always have to be a first-class bitch?" Tulip asked.

There was no bed in the bedroom Mike and Tulip shared. They slept on a mattress on the floor. Mike lay on the mattress with his hands folded behind his head, and he looked up at the long string which hung from the single light bulb overhead. A bright yellow butterfly was tied to the end of the string, and it was slowly, slowly turning from an almost imperceptible movement of air. Mike watched it turn.

The others were still smoking and talking in the big room downstairs, and every now and then a burst of laughter would ring out. The smell of the marijuana seemed stronger from up here than it did when he was in the same room with them.

Mike didn't smoke pot as much as he once did. For one thing, he discovered that he had a tolerance to it. He didn't get high every time, and he never got as high as the others on those occasions when he did get a buzz. Given the fact that marijuana was illegal, its cost was inflated. And, of course, there was always the possibility of getting busted with it. In Mike's case, if he got busted, he would surely be returned to the U.S., and there he would run into difficulty with the draft board. All things considered, it seemed a poor risk for something which offered only mild highs when it worked at all.

Mike had been there for almost an hour when they came in, Tulip and Tara together. They stopped at the foot of the bed and looked down at him, then, in unison as if they were part of a performing drill team, or the Radio City Rockettes, they began removing their clothes.

Their T-shirts were first. Right hand to the left hem, left hand across, making an X of their arms to the right hem, then together, the hem was raised, up over their flat stomachs, then their bare breasts, and finally over their heads. Next their jeans, the top snaps, opened in unison, then unzipped with both of their hands going down at the same speed, and finally, they stepped out of them, left leg first, knee bent and raised like a chorus-line dancer, then right leg until they were standing before him absolutely nude. Neither wore underwear, whether by coincidence or by design, Mike couldn't be sure. They smiled at him.

"Hey, lover man," Tulip said. "Have you ever made a sandwich?"

Mike raised himself to his elbows and looked down at the two girls as they came down onto the mattress with him.

"No," he said. His voice was choked.

"Well it's about time you learned what you've been missing," Tara said.

Tulip lay to his right, Tara to his left, and, together, they removed his shirt, jeans and shorts, until he was as naked as they. Then they pressed their bodies against his, their breasts, warm and heavy against the side of his chest, their legs, long and cool against his legs, and their pelvises against his thighs. He could feel the soft bush of hair, and the boiling cauldron of damp heat which was just behind the bush. They rubbed against him and purred into his ear.

"You've been a naughty boy ignoring Tara all this time," Tulip said.

"Yes, so now you are going to have to take care of both of us at the same time."

"How can I take care of both of you at the same time?" Mike asked, barely able to talk over the sexual excitement he was experiencing.

"We'll find a way," Tulip purred as her hand joined Tara's on his erection.

"Yes," Tara said. "We'll find a way. I'm sure of it."

Mike closed his eyes as the two girls moved around on

his body. Feelings and sensations he had never before experienced exploded through the nerve endings of his body, and he made no effort to control them. He lay back and let them have their way.

It was mind-blowing.

CHAPTER TWENTY-FOUR

(Newspaper headlines, April 1, 1971)

CALLEY DRAWS LIFE SENTENCE FOR MY LAI
MASSACRE;
COULD HAVE BEEN SENTENCED TO DEATH;
SENTENCE TO BE REVIEWED

First Lieutenant William L. Calley Jr. drew a life sentence yesterday for the murder of at least 22 Vietnamese civilians.

The massacre occurred three years ago at the small hamlet of My Lai, when Lt. Calley, then a platoon leader in the 11th Brigade of the Americal Division, ordered his men, then joined with them, in the systematic butchering of men, women and children from the village.

Lt. Calley stood pale and taut before the jury box as he heard his sentence. He could have received death by hanging. Instead, he stood at rigid attention and listened as Colonel Clifford H. Ford, a Korean War veteran, read the sentence, confining Calley to life imprisonment.

Jake's recommendation for a Brigadier General's star was withdrawn. The official reason given was the upcoming reduction in force of the army, but Jake and everyone else knew that it was because Jake had pushed so hard for the My Lai investigation. Jake was disappointed that he did not receive his promotion, but he felt a sense of satisfaction over the results of the My Lai case. Even that satisfaction was short-lived, however, due to the fact that the sentence was reduced to twenty years by a judicial review board, then to ten years by the Secretary of the Army, and those reductions were upheld by President Nixon.

Jake tried to get in to see Nixon, to protest the action, but he was told that the President felt his action was necessary in order to preserve the morale of the U.S. Army.

President Nixon did do one thing Jake agreed with. He began withdrawing American troops. It was a gradual withdrawal, arranged in such a way that the President hoped to appease those who wanted to get out of Vietnam, as well as those who felt the US should stay. The result was that neither side was pleased with the action.

Jake was questioned by six different committees on the war, and the old mathematical formula he had proposed before the Carter Committee was brought out again and put in the newspapers. Jake became somewhat of a counter-culture hero, much to the embarrassment of the Establishment. "Has the Culpepper Formula been reached?" one liberal columnist asked. "Has enough human life been lost? Has the War God Mars had his thirst for blood slaked?"

The writer went on in his column to quote Jake, though the quotations were from Jake's testimony before the committees, and not from any recent interview, because Jake had steadfastly refused to grant interviews. McGovern won the Democratic nomination for President, and in so doing, he totally devastated the party. Nixon's re-election, though it had never been in doubt, became a rout. He carried every state but Massachusetts. Jake and all the other military advisors were asked to stay for four more years, and because he hoped to exercise some influence on an early end to the war, Jake agreed.

And then there was Watergate.

When Jake first heard of the break-in at the Democratic headquarters in the Watergate building, he passed it off as over-zealous campaign workers. He didn't exactly find it amusing, but he was a little surprised that a minor break-in didn't just appear in the papers once, then go away.

A short time later he saw a list of people who were involved in the break-in and he was surprised at the caliber of the participants. Some had FBI and CIA connections, and that made the episode a little more newsworthy than he'd originally thought.

He saw the word Watergate on one of his own official documents soon after that, and within a short time the 'problem of Watergate' began to take up more and more official duty time until soon, everyone, no matter how remotely connected with the White House, found that their total efforts were occupied in dealing with Watergate. Then the other things began to come out. All sorts of nefarious schemes were exposed, such as the Huston plan for domestic intelligence gathering, which included wire-tapping, breaking and entering, as well as opening private mail. Jake also learned of an illegally authorized break-in of Daniel Ellsberg's office. Then Jake discovered that the CIA had been told to order the FBI to set limits to their investigation of the Watergate break-in. Worse, he learned that the Watergate burglars had been paid off to ensure their silence. The entire thing had a snowballing effect, and he had no idea where it was going to end, but it looked ominous to him. In the meantime the war continued to wind down, as Nixon withdrew more and more American forces in the Vietnamization of the war. It became apparent to Jake that the formula he had spoken of had been reached, and he knew that, shortly, no matter what happened, the US involvement in the Vietnam War would end. Then, on January 23, 1973, a cease-fire agreement was reached, and Jake sat in his living room with Kristin and watched Nixon deliver the news which, for the time being, enabled everyone to put Watergate on the back burner.

"Good evening. I have asked for this radio and television time tonight for the purpose of announcing that we today have concluded an agreement to end the war and bring peace with honor in Vietnam and Southeast Asia. The following statement is being issued at this moment in Washington and Hanoi:

"At 12:30 Paris time today, Jan 23, 1973, the agreement on ending the war and restoring peace in Vietnam was initialed by Dr. Henry Kissinger on behalf of the United States and Special Advisor Le Duc Tho on behalf of the Democratic Republic of Vietnam.

"The agreement will be formally signed by the parties participating in the Paris Conference of Vietnam on January 27, 1973. The United States and the Democratic Republic of Vietnam express the hope that this agreement will insure stable peace in Vietnam and contribute to the preservation of lasting peace in Indochina and Southeast Asia."

By the end of March, all American ground forces were out of Vietnam, and ten years of American involvement came to a close.

It was an uneasy peace, not a victory, and there was no jubilation across the country. Those who had fought in the war, and those who had fought against the war, suddenly found the arena of their personal battle removed, and they looked at each other as if they were weary marathoners, having just collapsed in exhaustion across the finish line. There was no victory and no vindication for the doves or the hawks. There was only the numbing realization that the war, as far as the Americans were concerned, was over.

Nixon's personal war did not end, however. Watergate didn't go away. Those who had spent a decade fighting against the government policies in the Vietnam War, now turned their energies toward toppling the Administration.

Jake realized just how desperate the situation was, when he received a top secret briefing entitled "Coup Contingency Plans."

The amazing document outlined procedures in the event that:

 (a) The President attempted to take all power for himself in an illegal move,

 (b) Someone should attempt to remove the President from his office by illegal methods.

Nearly everyone in Washington was working long hours during this period, and Jake was no exception to the rule. On the night Vice-President Agnew resigned from his office, in a move which was totally unrelated to Watergate but which added greatly to the overall unrest of the situation, Jake worked until after two in the morning, getting briefing papers ready for the transition into office of the new Vice-President, whoever that might be. Afterward, on the way home, Jake stopped by the Lincoln Monument, and walked inside. He stood in front of the big statue of Lincoln seated, then walked around behind the figure. He thought of what was going on in the country today. There had been a Civil War during Lincoln's tenure, and many were comparing the nation of today with the nation presided over by Lincoln.

Jake heard footsteps approaching and it surprised him. It was after two in the morning, and he wondered who in the world would be here at this time. He looked around the corner of the statue then gasped. There, standing quietly on the other side of the statue, looking up into Lincoln's face, was President Richard M. Nixon.

Jake was no more than ten feet away from him. The

Secret Service agents were standing on the steps below the President, watching him, but none of them had come into the monument to check it for security. If Jake had been bent upon killing the President, he would have had an excellent opportunity.

The professional in Jake was irritated by the Secret Service's lack of responsibility to their job, but actually he was glad they didn't. This way he was able to observe the President without being observed. It was quite a fascinating experience.

The President's face was lined and haggard, and, Jake perceived, just a little confused. It was as if the President couldn't understand what-all was happening to him.

The image of the President's tired and confused face stayed with Jake, and he thought of it on the night of August 8th, when he watched the President announce to the nation that he was going to resign.

Jake had found much to disagree with Nixon about, and, privately, he was convinced that Nixon should leave office. Nevertheless, he felt a great sadness, not only for the personal tragedy which had befallen Nixon, the man, but for the national trauma which affected the entire country. Even Kristin, who had been a very vocal critic of Nixon from the very beginning, cried at the spectacle of a President of the United States, wet-eyed and sorrowful, saying goodbye to the nation.

When Jake went into his office Saturday morning, he found a note from a member of President Ford's transition staff, asking Jake to call as soon as he got in.

Jake dialed the number.

"Presidential transition," a voice answered from the other end of the wire.

"Yes," Jake said. "This is Colonel Culpepper, returning Mr. Norstad's call."

Jake was asked to wait, and a moment later Norstad was on the line.

"Colonel Culpepper, I won't beat around the bush with you. I understand you have a son in Canada, a deserter," said Norstad.

"Not a deserter, Mr. Norstad. He left the country to avoid the draft, though in truth, his number has never been called."

"He did destroy his draft card though, did he not? And he did leave without giving proper notification to the draft board?

"Yes," Jake said. "That is true." Jake leaned back in his chair and pinched the bridge of his nose. "Where is this going, Mr. Norstad? Is the new President asking for my resignation because of that?"

"No, no, hell no!" Norstad said quickly. "I'm sorry, Colonel, I sure didn't intend to make you think anything like that. I apologize if I've made you uneasy."

"You did seem inordinately curious," Jake said.

"There's a purpose to it, Colonel, believe me," Norstad said. "Colonel, I am authorized by the President to ask you if you would like to go to Canada to offer amnesty to your son."

"Offer my son amnesty? On what grounds?"

"On the grounds of healing the wounds of the nation," Norstad said. "It won't just be your son, Colonel. We are establishing a review board to check into each individual case, and provide an earned amnesty program to those who are eligible."

"What do you mean by earned amnesty?" Jake asked.

"We intend for them to work in something like the Peace Corps, or Vista, or some volunteer head-start program. Anything that will provide the government with some proof of repentance. What do you think, Colonel?"

"I think it's a step in the right direction," Jake said. "I'm afraid that some people are going to resent the earned aspect because they are going to see it as an admission of guilt. But I am sure there will be many who will accept the offer."

"What about your son?"

"I can't answer for him," Jake said. "But I will go see him."

"Colonel, do it right away, will you? The President isn't even going to announce his program until you are back."

"I'll get a flight to Montreal today," Jake said.

Jake leaned back and looked at the phone for a moment, then he called Kristin.

"How would you like to meet your stepson?" he asked.

"Mike? You mean he's here, in Washington?" Kristin asked.

"No, he's in Montreal," Jake said. "But I'm going up to see him today."

"Oh, I'd love to go," Kristin squealed. "But, after all this time, what made you decide to go now?"

"I'll tell you all about it on the plane on the way up. Pack our bags, I'll come by for you."

They rented a car at the Montreal airport, bought a city map, and by the time the sun was going down, they were parked in front of the New France Used Furniture Shop.

"Are you sure this is the place?" Kristin asked.

"Sure, don't you remember?" Jake said. "They were located over a furniture shop. Besides, there is the number—1054—and this is Rue de Garneau. This is the place."

"Do you think we should have called?"

"I don't know that they have a phone," Jake said. "Mike has never called. And if they did have a phone, I wouldn't know what name it would be under." Jake opened the door of the car and stepped out. "Come on," he said. "We're just going to have to go up there and check it out," Jake said. "Do you want to wait in the car?"

"No," Kristin said. "I'll go with you."

Jake led Kristin to the stairway and they started up. They could hear music spilling down from the top of the stairs. The walls on both sides of the stairs leading up to the top were decorated with peace symbols, flowers, and various art renderings. Kristin smiled.

"Heavy," she said.

"What?"

"You might need an interpreter," Kristin teased. "I was just seeing if I could still speak the language."

They reached the top of the stairs and Jake knocked on the door. The music was playing so he knocked loudly and authoritatively.

"Shit, the police!" a muffled voice said.

"No!" Jake shouted through the door. "No, I'm not a policeman!"

There was a moment's delay, then the door opened and a young girl peered through.

"Tulip?"

"No," the girl said. "I'm Tara. What do you want Tulip for?"

"We don't want her," Jake said. "Actually, I'm here looking for my son."

"You're Colonel Culpepper, aren't you?" the girl said. She smiled. "Mike pointed you out to us when you were on TV."

"Yes," Jake said. "I'm Jake Culpepper. Uh, is my son here?"

"He's not here now, but he'll be right back," Tara said. "He and Deekus and Tulip went to get some wine. We're celebrating Nixon getting kicked out."

Jake thought of the tears he had seen in the White House. He was hardly in the celebrating mood, but he didn't comment on it.

"Hey, listen, we're having spaghetti," Tara said. "And if there is one thing you can say about our spaghetti, it's that there is always a lot of it. Why don't you stay and eat with us?"

"Alice B. Toklas oregano?" Kristin asked.

Tara laughed. "Hey, you're pretty hip," she said. "No, no grass. Are you kiddin'? It costs so much just to get a little to do, you know what I mean? We're not about to sprinkle the shit on spaghetti.''

There were footfalls on the bottom step, and Tara smiled again.

"That's them. Just stand there and don't say anything.''

Jake heard two men's voices talking and a girl's laughter as they climbed the stairs. The door opened and two men and a girl came inside.

"Here," the one with the sack said. "Mike insisted that we get a two gallon jug, and it's about to break my arms. I don't think he carried his end of the load.''

"Don't listen to that shit," Mike said. "He's only been carrying it for a couple of blocks. I carried it most of the way, didn't I, Tulip?''

"Oh, no," Tulip said. "You aren't getting me into your arguments.''

The three saw Jake and Kristin then and they were silent for a moment.

"Dad?" Mike asked in a very quiet voice, which, for that one word, didn't sound too much different to Jake than it did when he was a twelve-year-old boy.

"Hello, son.''

"Dad, what are you doing here?" Mike asked. The expression on Mike's face let Jake know that his son was expecting trouble, and was preparing to fight it, whatever it was.

Jake rubbed his hands together.

"Well, for openers, I'm going to have some spaghetti," he said, smiling broadly. He pointed to the jug of wine. "And, if that is a decent vintage, perhaps a bit of wine.''

Mike laughed. "Listen," he said. "This stuff is really good. I think it is vintage July. Tulip, this is my dad.'' Mike looked at Kristin. "And this, I take it, is my step-mom?''

"That I am," Kristin said. "It's good to meet you, son," she added, and they both laughed.

"Get them a glass," Mike said. "Preferably clean."

The glasses appeared, wine was drunk, spaghetti was eaten, more wine was drunk, then a few joints were brought out. Jake was nervous about it, but he didn't say anything. He declined the offer, was secretly glad to see that Kristin declined as well, and was very pleased to see that Mike wasn't even offered any.

"You don't smoke marijuana?" Jake asked.

"No," Mike said. "I've tried it. It doesn't do anything for me."

"You don't . . . you don't do other things do you? Like hard drugs?"

"No," Mike said, laughing.

"Good. I'm glad," Jake said. "Mike, is there some place we can go and talk?"

"We can talk here," Mike said. "These are all my friends. They're more than that. They're my family. Anything you have to say to me you can say in front of them."

"Yes, sir," one of the others said. "This way it keeps him from just having to tell us everything."

"All right," Jake said. "As a matter of fact it's probably better this way. It probably affects you as much as it does Mike." Jake cleared his throat. "Mike, you remember the talk you and Andy and I had down at Nassau before Andy went to Vietnam?"

"Yes," Mike said. "We talked about honor, duty and country."

Jake smiled. "You do remember," he said. "That pleases me. You may also remember that I was trying to inculcate in you my sense of honor. In truth, I have discovered that you have your own sense of honor which governs your actions as much as my honor governs mine. However, your honor has made you an outcast from your own country."

"Not my honor," Mike said. "The war."

"Yes, the war," Jake said. "It took both my sons, Andy in one way and you in another. I can never get Andy back, but now there is a way for you."

"How?" Mike asked suspiciously.

"I am here on a special mission from President Ford. Mike, the President is going to offer amnesty to many of you who avoided the draft as a matter of personal conscience."

"What?" Mike asked. "Dad, are you serious? Do you mean I could come back to the States? I could finish my education and get on with my life?"

"Yes," Jake said. "If you accept the program."

"Wait a minute, man. What is the program?" Deekus asked.

"It's a re-entry program," Jake said. "All you have to do is give the government some sort of public service."

"That's bullshit, man," Deekus said. "If the man wants us in, then he should let us in with no questions asked. We ought not to have to buy our way back. No one's going to take that chickenshit offer."

"I'm sure some will feel as you do," Jake said. He looked at Mike. "But right now, Mike, I'm most interested in you. What do you say?"

Mike was quiet for a long moment. Finally he spoke.

"Dad, I protested the war as a matter of principle," he said. "I didn't think we had the right to get involved in someone else's war. I took what I considered to be the enlightened approach. Now, if the service President Ford has in mind is service which benefits people, and not just a make-work project, then I'll do it."

"You'll . . . you'll do it?" Jake asked.

"Yes."

Jake tried to say something, but the words wouldn't come. He felt a choking sensation in his throat, and his eyes grew moist, then filled with tears.

He was crying? Goddamn, he was actually crying. He couldn't remember the last time he had cried.

"Dad?" Mike asked, shocked by what he was seeing. "Dad, are you all right?"

Jake cleared his throat.

"Yeah," he finally said. "Yeah, I'm just fine. I was just thinking of my own father, and how I hurt him all those years. You could have followed in my footsteps, son, in more ways than one. Thank God you had the courage to break the mold."

CHAPTER TWENTY-FIVE

Jake walked across the carpeted floor of the receptionist to the Under-Secretary of the Army. The receptionist looked up and smiled.

"I'm . . ."

"Yes, Colonel Culpepper, I know who you are," the receptionist said smoothly. "The Under-Secretary is expecting you. Go right on in."

"Thank you," Jake said.

Jake had received a telephone call at nearly midnight last night, asking him to come to the Under-Secretary's office by 0800 the following day, Tuesday, April 1st, 1975. He was given no reason for the summons, though the understated urgency of the call did impart a sense of importance to the meeting.

The Under-Secretary stood as soon as Jake entered the room, and he left the back of his desk and walked halfway across his office to greet Jake. He extended his hand.

"Jake, thank you for coming so promptly," he said.

Jake chuckled. "Mr. Secretary, I'm a colonel in the United States Army. When I am summoned by the Under-Secretary's office, I respond promptly."

"Nevertheless, it's good to see you. Have you had breakfast?"

"Yes, sir."

"Then perhaps some coffee?"

"That would be nice," Jake admitted.

The Under-Secretary picked up the phone, ordered two cups of coffee, then sat in one of the comfortable leather chairs away from his desk and offered the other to Jake.

"How is your pretty young wife?"

"She's fine," Jake replied.

"And your son? He's in a re-entry program I believe?"

"Yes, he's working with the Indians in Arizona," Jake said.

The coffee arrived, Jake took a cup with thanks, then he sipped it as he studied the Under-Secretary.

"Jake, the South Vietnamese have lost more than one billion dollars in weapons and equipment just within this past week. Camn Ranh Bay has fallen. My God, the money we put into that place," he said. "The Soviets will be there in less than a year, you mark my words. They'll have the warm water port they have always wanted, and we will have given it to them. Nha Trang, Quang Tri, Hue, even Da Nang have fallen." He shook his head. "Who would have believed this? My God, the time and money and equipment we have wasted on that place."

"And the more than fifty thousand American lives which were lost."

"Yes, of course, that too. I'm sorry, you lost a son there, didn't you?"

"A lot of American fathers lost sons there," Jake said.

"Yes, well, it's terrible. It's really terrible," the Under-Secretary lamented. He ran his hand through his hair and sighed. "Jake, you know these people, probably as well as anyone in the Army. How long will they be able to keep the Communists out of Saigon? This isn't just an idle question. We have to get our remaining people out of there."

"If we are lucky, maybe a month," Jake said.

"A month?" the Under-Secretary said weakly. "Only thirty days?"

"Unless we are willing to make a major commitment to stop it," Jake added.

The Under-Secretary shook his head. "President Ford is going to ask Congress for a billion dollars in aid, but he isn't going to get it. Jake, we have nearly ten thousand Americans still in country."

"Ten thousand? We have that many?"

"Yes. Most are civilians who have no association with the government. They are civilian contractors and . . ."

"War profiteers," Jake said. "We ought to just let them stew in their own juices."

"The contractors have been a great service to us during the course of this war," the Under-Secretary said.

"They've been paid well for it," Jake said.

"Yes, well, that is neither here nor there. The point is, we have to get them as well as our Embassy, military, and station people out of Vietnam. And that is where you come in."

"Me?"

"We are sending you to Vietnam again, Jake. You speak the language, you know the people. We need you to help with the final evacuation."

Jake sighed. "Mr. Secretary, do you know what you are asking of me? Right now Congress, the press, and the public are saying that we have no business getting back into Vietnam, or helping the Saigon Government to survive. They will look at our final withdrawal as the thing we should do. But, within a year or two, books and articles will begin to appear in which the writers examine how we 'lost' the war. We are going to be accused of having lost this war, Mr. Secretary, and I will be the one who supervised the final retreat."

"Yes, I know," the Under-Secretary said. He stood up and walked over to his desk, then opened the middle draw and pulled out a small box. "Jake, there are times when a Commander must show courage in ways which are not immediately seen. This is one of those times for you. The

President feels that you should have all the authority you need in conducting such an operation, and I, personally, feel that you have earned this recognition. Therefore, it is with a great deal of pride that I tell you that in a quorom session of Congress yesterday, the President asked for and received approval to make this appointment. You are skipping over a rank, Jake. You are now a Major-General.''

The Under-Secretary opened the box and took out two bar pins of two stars per pin. He stepped up to Jake and removed Jake's eagle and crossed rifles, then pinned the stars to Jake's collar.

"I know this doesn't make your task any less odious," he said. "But, at least, it gives you the authority to do what must be done. Congratulations, General. What are your thoughts right now?" the Under-Secretary asked, smiling at Jake.

"What are my thoughts?" Jake asked. "I'd trade these two stars for major's leaves if I could wake up tomorrow at Fort Riley and discover that all this was just a nightmare; that none of it had ever happened.''

Because of his rank and position, Jake was authorized his own personal C-135 aircraft. The Air Force plane, which was a version of the 707 airliner, landed in Ton Son Nhut, and taxied over to the terminal building. Ironically, it stopped in almost the same place Jake had stopped when he first came to Vietnam as an advisor eleven years ago.

Jake deplaned as soon as the stairs had been pushed into position. Without realizing it, he looked toward the sight of the old officers' mess, where Colonel Purcell had been killed in a bomb blast on his first day in country, so long ago.

"General Culpepper? I'm with the Embassy staff, sir. I have a helicopter waiting for us. It will fly us to the Embassy.''

"I'm not going to fly over the city," Jake said. "I'm going to move right through the middle of it." Jake reached up and removed the stars from his collar, and from his hat. "In fact," he said. "I'm going by cyclo. I assume the cyclo drivers are still trying to make a living?"

"General, you must be mad, sir!" the Embassy representative said. "I can't take the responsibility of letting you ride a cyclo through the streets of Saigon. It isn't safe! We don't know how many terrorists there are in the city in advance of the North Vietnamese troops."

"You don't have the responsibility for my actions, I do," Jake said. "Get on back to the Embassy. I'll be there shortly."

Jake walked through the terminal and outside. There were several dozen cyclos lined up, waiting for passengers. They were three-wheeled motor bikes, with two wheels in front and one in the rear. The driver sat on a regular bicycle seat, but there was a passenger seat, like the rear seat of a small car, in front. The cyclos had been the most popular form of transportation for the GIs in Saigon, because they enjoyed the wild rides of the reckless drivers.

Jake climbed into the seat of one of the little vehicles, and motioned for the driver to go.

The change of atmosphere in Saigon was immediately apparent. Jake had always considered Saigon to be one of the most interesting cities in the world. It was always bustling with activity and its streets were crowded with vehicles. Today, however, it was eerily quiet. There was practically no traffic, and as the little cyclo flew down the streets, Jake saw clusters of soldiers standing around defeatedly, or sprawling out to sleep on the sidewalk beneath the shade of the tamarind trees. A woman ran out into the street toward him, holding her arms out, crying.

"Save us!" she shouted at him as the cyclo passed her by.

When Jake reached the Embassy a little later, he was shaken. He had guessed thirty days. If the North Vietnamese wanted Saigon, they could take it in thirty hours.

*   *   *

Henri Marquand stood at the little grave with the simple, white cross, and looked down toward the mound of earth.

"My dear one," he said. "How much more peaceful things are for you now. Now your great beauty will not be too great a burden for you to bear.

"Ah, my poor love. You were but a fragile flower in a field of weeds, a beautiful princess who was born a century too late. Your father wronged you by marrying again and depriving you of your royal birthright. Your black American lover wronged you by having the misfortune of losing his legs, and I wronged you, first by selling your love, then by loving you myself. But most of all, you were wronged by a world which was not prepared for someone with as rare and delicate a beauty as yours. You told me you would not survive, and I didn't believe you. I thought I had strength enough for both of us. I couldn't know that you would put a gun to your own head.

"We are Catholic, Melinda, you and I. And we know that our Mother Church looks upon suicide as a mortal sin. And yet, I have always felt that God, and not Mother Church, would be the final arbiter. Surely one who has reached such a state of mind that they would take their own life cannot be held responsible for that action. And you, my dear, by waiting until three days after our daughter was born before you did it, ensured that she would not suffer from your action. I know God will take that into consideration when He makes His decision.

"And now, I have made a decision. I am sending our child to America. There she will have a chance for a new life, free from my corruptive influence, and free from the uncertainties of this country's future."

Henri turned and walked back toward the house, leaving Melinda's grave behind him. His child of three months was already in Saigon, left to the care of Miss Julie Phillips, one of the American nurses involved with the project. It had not been a difficult thing for him to do. He did not wish to face the prospect of raising a French baby in the uncertain future.

A jeep was parked in front of Henri's house. That surprised him, because the government forces had abandoned this zone several days ago. Then, he saw that the jeep had been repainted in a much darker color, and there was a red star on the hood. Three men were standing by the jeep, all dressed in the khaki uniforms and pie-shaped pith helmets of the North Vietnamese. One of them stepped in front of the others and saluted sharply.

"Monsieur Marquand?"

"Yes," Henri said. "Is there something I can do for you?"

"We are looking for Cao Ngyuen Mot. Can you tell us where we might find him?"

"Colonel Mot?"

The North Vietnamese officer who asked the question spat on the ground.

"Do not call that traitor to the revolution Colonel," he said. "That is a disservice to the honorable men of that rank."

"Traitor? I thought Colonel . . . that is, Mr. Mot, was a loyal member of the National Liberation Front."

"Yes," the North Vietnamese Colonel said. "Unfortunately his loyalty to the NLF has blinded him to the real purpose of our struggle: solidarity between the brothers of the South and the brothers of the North. Perhaps you have seen this?" The officer handed a small handbill to Henri.

"No," Henri said. "What is it?"

"It is a treasonous pact printed by Mot and distributed by him among his fellow soldiers. Read it."

My fellow warriors. We have been deceived! Many years ago, we of the south began a fierce struggle to gain our independence. Men from the north offered us

*help, and, because we believed they were truly inter-
ested in having a totally independent Viet Nam, we
accepted their help.*

*Now, with victory in our grasp, we are to be
denied the fruits of our struggle. It is clear that we are
soon to trade an oppressive Saigon government for an
oppressive Hanoi government. All positions of authority and responsibility in the new order will be held by
those from the North. We of the South who fought,
struggled and died in this war, are to be left out.*

*Many years ago, when I first began my patriotic
service, I was taught by a wise man that true independence cannot be bestown like a gift. True independence,
by the very definition of the word, must be taken.*

*Those words are as true today as they were when
they were spoken at the beginning of this great conflict.
We cannot wait around and let the Hanoi government
grant us the liberties we have already earned. We
must take them, by force, if need be.*

*We are a united army, victorious at last in our great
battle. Do not let that victory be taken from us. Join
me in the field and continue the battle, not against the
Saigon government which is already defeated, nor
against the Americans who have already left, but
against the Hanoi government, which is trying to take
by stealth what the Americans could not take by
force.*

*In our great Army of National Liberation, I was
honored with the rank of Colonel. I cherish that rank,
and, as a Colonel, will lead a new army to ultimate
victory.''*

"I see why you wish to find him," Henri said.

"You will cooperate with us?" the North Vietnamese
officer said.

"Yes, of course," Henri replied. "You may ask anyone.

I have always been most cooperative. With everyone," he added, smiling.

The North Vietnamese officer saluted, and the three men got back into the jeep. The officer looked at Henri.

"I was told this was a whorehouse for American generals. I was told you had a real princess here, who, for a great deal of money would go to bed with the American generals. Is this true?"

"Yes," Henri said.

"You will make her available for our Generals as well."

"She is dead," Henri said. "She was killed in the war."

"Most unfortunate," the North Vietnamese officer said. He saluted again, then, with a wave of his hand, signalled for his driver to go on. The driver, unfamiliar with the vehicle, raced the engine unnecessarily, and the jeep left in a cloud of exhaust and a spray of gravel. When it pulled onto the paved road at the end of the long driveway, someone came out of Henri's house.

"Thank you," Mot said.

"You can't stay here," Henri replied. "I won't take the risk of hiding you indefinitely."

"Yes, I know," Mot said. He had a field pack, filled with rice, tinned meats, and other things necessary for surviving in the jungle. He picked the pack up and put it on his back.

"Have you had any takers to your recruitment drive?" Henri asked.

"Yes, a few," Mot said. "We are already in the field. There are not many of us."

"There were few when the war started against the Saigon Government, but the numbers grew," Henri said.

"Yes, and the numbers will grow again," Mot said. He sighed. "But then I was young and innocent. Now I am old and tired, and I have seen too much death and destruction. It has become a way of life with me." Mot started toward the edge of the jungle.

"Mot?" Henri called.

Mot stopped and looked around.

"If you are ever in severe danger, come to me and I will do what I can."

Mot smiled. "You would violate your neutrality for me?"

"Yes."

"Why?"

"Because," Henri said. He took a deep breath. "You are my son."

CHAPTER TWENTY-SIX

"Saigon cannot survive," Jake told the Americans who had gathered for his briefing. "That is no longer the question. The only question remaining is, how will Hanoi bring about the final collapse?"

"Do you have a scenario, General?" one of the Embassy officials asked.

"Yes," Jake said. "I have three scenarios, and none of them are very pleasant."

Jake had a drawing pad on an easel, and he turned the page to show his first scenario.

"Hanoi may decide to launch an all-out attack on the city. They have eight divisions in position around the city, plus six more divisions close by. That gives them an overall superiority. It would also give them a tremendous shot of prestige, world-wide. But, it might be a costly battle, and they are cautious men."

Jake turned the page.

"The second option open to them is to simply surround the city and lay siege to it. They would bombard it day and night. Food and other supplies would eventually run out, the citizenry would become desperate: murders, burglaries, rape, robbery, all crimes of violence would increase tenfold, a hundred-fold, perhaps even to the point of going beyond the ability to measure. Americans would be prime targets under such a condition. Eventually, the Communists would just move in. It would be the cheapest way, but it has its own risks. If they halted their drive now they would lose their momentum. And when they did take over the city, they would have the chaos to deal with as a result of a total breakdown of city authority."

Jake turned the page again.

"The final way would be to infiltrate the city and bring about a government collapse from within, then establish a 'coalition' government."

"Which way do you consider most likely?" Jake was asked.

Jake turned the pages back. "I believe Hanoi will launch an all-out attack on the city. I think they must have total victory if they are to establish total control."

"How long do we have, General?"

"Less than a month," Jake said. "Gentlemen, you must make all preparations to abandon Vietnam now. Evacuate everything that is sensitive, destroy what you can't evacuate."

"What about sensitive Vietnamese? What are we going to do about them? There may be as many as 200,000 who will be in real danger if they are left here. We can't just abandon them."

Jake sighed, and rubbed his chin. "I know," he said. "But I must tell you that the immediate problem facing us is the safety of the Americans. We get them out first. Then we will do what we can with the Vietnamese. The problem facing us, of course, is that there is too little time to sift through the records so that we know who is deserving of rescue and who isn't."

"There is another problem there, General," one gray headed official said.

"What is that?"

"I was in Seoul when we were pushed out temporarily during the early stages of the Korean war. We left the indigenous record file there, and when we came back, we learned that the Communists had killed thousands of Korean civilians who had worked with us. If we leave our Vietnamese records intact, the same thing could happen again. If we destroy them, we won't know who is deserving and who isn't.''

"Well, there is one group which we don't have to concern ourselves about," a member of the Aid for International Development section said.

"Who?"

"Kids," the official said. "We have over 2,000 orphans ready to send to the U.S."

"What authority do we have for this?" someone asked.

"We don't need any authority. We are doing it because, by God, it is right! We sent one planeload yesterday, and we are sending out over three hundred this afternoon on board a C-5."

"You're sending some out this afternoon?" Jake asked.

"Yes, sir, we are."

"Maybe I'll come down there and see them off," Jake suggested.

"We'd be glad to have you, General," the AID official said.

When Jake's helicopter landed at Ton Son Nhut a short while later, he saw the giant C-5 parked next to the terminal building. There were several photographers around the plane, and there were hundreds of Vietnamese men and women standing just beyond the wire rope area, waving and shouting at the kids who were trekking out to board the plane.

There were several American women with the kids as well, especially with the very young ones who were too small to walk. One of the nurses, Jake noticed, was Julie Phillips.

Jake walked over through the swirling mass of children, and stood for a moment just behind Julie. Julie had not yet seen him, and she was giving instructions concerning one of the babies. The baby was wrapped in a bright red blanket, and as Jake looked at the baby, he saw that it was not a Vietnamese baby.

"Is that an American baby?" Jake asked, pointing to the baby.

"French-Vietnamese," Julie answered. Then she turned around and saw Jake, and her eyes widened and she smiled broadly.

"Jake!" she said, and she threw her arms around him. "Jake, how wonderful to see you! My, and look at this! You are a general!"

"And you are a civilian," Jake said. "What are you doing here?"

"I volunteered to work with the evacuation of these kids. After more than a decade, we can't just leave without doing something for them."

"Yeah," Jake said. "I know what you mean. I don't know if we are doing the right thing, but I feel that people will understand that we had to do something. Listen, Julie, I was sorry to hear about Pappy."

"Yeah," Julie said. "To think that he was killed by some doped-up GI who thought it would be fun to frag an NCO barracks. My father loved the army, Jake. He dedicated his entire life to it. If he had been killed in war or in an accident, maybe I could understand. But to be fragged by an American, someone who didn't even know him . . ." Julie let the sentence hang.

"I know what you mean," Jake said. He put his arm around her to comfort her. "But you are wrong, Julie, if you think Pappy wasn't killed in the war. He was just as much a victim of this war as my son was. As we all are. We have suffered scars from this war that won't heal for the rest of this century," Jake said.

"I resigned my commission right after that happened," Julie said. She smiled. "But, life must go on, especially for the children. I feel that I am doing something useful here today. Perhaps for the first time in the entire war." She pointed to the baby in the red blanket. "By the way, that little darling is the daughter of Henri Marquand. You remember him, don't you?''

"Yes, yes, of course," Jake said. "What is his baby doing here?''

"The baby's mother was Melinda. You remember her?''

"Yes, she is a very beautiful woman."

"Was," Julie said. "She committed suicide."

"Oh, Julie, no."

"Yes. And Monsieur Marquand thought his child would have a better life in the United States. He is a man with some considerable influence, so, there is his daughter.''

Jake leaned over and looked at the baby, and the baby smiled at him.

"Boy," he said. "She can get to your heart right away, can't she?''

"That she can," Julie said.

"All right, ladies, let's get these kiddies aboard. We've got a long way to go," the loadmaster called.

"I'll keep you up with the baby's progress," Julie said.

"You?''

"I'm going to adopt it."

"I thought you had to be married."

"If I have to get married, I'll do it."

"Do you have someone in mind?''

"I'll find someone," Julie said. She yelled the last words over her shoulder as she climbed the ramp to the lower cargo hold of the giant aircraft. The engines were already turning over as she got aboard, and Jake stood there and watched the big plane taxi out to the end of the runway, then take off with its engines roaring.

There were some arrangements to be made with airport officials, concerning the evacuation procedures, and Jake stayed to talk to them. He was just about finished when his pilot came into the room ashen-faced.

"General?''

"Yes," Jake said. He saw the expression on his pilot's

face. "Mr. Kinlaw, what is it?" he asked the Warrant Officer.

"The C-5, General," Mr. Kinlaw said. "The one with all the babies. It just crashed."

Jake left the helicopter with the blades still spinning over him. The wreckage of the plane was scattered through a muddy rice field about five miles north of Ton Son Nhut. Debris was scattered everywhere; baby bottles, stuffed bears, blankets, a box of disposable diapers, brightly colored rattles, a Mickey Mouse comic book, with its pages riffling in the breeze.

Many children were wandering around in shock, some crying, most just moving silently, unable to comprehend what had happened.

"The cargo door," the plane's distraught pilot was saying. "It blew out and into the tail section, and I lost control. I had no choice. I had to set it down here or lose it entirely. I had no choice, I couldn't make it back."

Jake saw that several bodies had already been pulled from the wreckage and placed in rows, covered with blankets. He walked over to a row of bodies which were all adult women. He stood there and looked down at the blankets.

"General?" one of the surviving women said.

"Yes?"

"I'm sorry, General. Julie didn't make it. That's her, down at the end."

Jake walked down to the last blanket and looked down at it. He didn't pull the blanket back, because he didn't want to see her like this. He was silent for a long moment.

"General?" the same woman spoke again.

"Yes?"

"The baby that she wanted? The little French baby? She wasn't hurt. I thought you might like to know that."

"Yes," Jake said. "Thank you. Where is the baby?"

"Over there," the woman said. "See all the very young babies? She is the one in the red blanket."

"I'm going to take her with me," Jake said.

"Can you do that?"

"I'm going to do it," Jake said. "I'll worry about the legalities later."

Three weeks later, with Saigon now in control of the Communists, Major General Jacob Steele Culpepper, sat in a leather chair on the bridge of the *U.S.S. Blue Ridge*. Graham Martin, the United States Ambassador to South Vietnam, had just arrived on board the ship, which was the command and communications ship for a 40-ship fleet armada. With his arrival on board, the last vestige of American involvement in Vietnam was at a close.

Shortly after Mr. Martin arrived, two South Vietnamese helicopters appeared astern of the ship, heading for the helipad. The landing crew tried to wave the helicopters off, but the South Vietnamese pilots ignored them and landed anyway. The pad was not big enough for both of them, and they crashed together as they landed, wending chunks of metal through the air. One of the helicopters, which was loaded with women and children, nearly fell overboard, and it stopped, half on and half off the deck. The women and children escaped without injury, then crewmen of the *Blue Ridge* pushed both helicopters into the sea.

"General Culpepper, sir?" a young ensign said.

Jake turned away from the bridge glass toward the junior officer. "Yes?"

"We got a message back from your wife, sir."

"Read it," Jake said.

The ensign cleared his throat.

"*I bought a basinet today, the carpenter comes tomorrow to build the nursery. I am anxiously awaiting you and the baby, and I agree, Julie would be a fine name. Love, Kristin.*"

"Thanks," Jake said.

"Congratulations, General. It appears that you have a new daughter," the ensign said. "At least something good is coming out of this mess."

Jake turned to look through the window again, and he saw another South Vietnamese helicopter approaching. This pilot made no attempt to land on the ship, but set down deliberately in the sea to ensure that he and his passengers would be picked up.

"Look at that," Jake heard one of the sailors say. "If it was up to me, I'd just let them sink."

"That's just what we did, sailor," a grayhaired old Chief said. "That's just what we did."

BE SURE TO READ
THE WAR TORN,
A COMPELLING FIVE-NOVEL MINI-SERIES
OF WORLD WAR II
BY ROBERT VAUGHAN

In five novels, veteran author and soldier Robert Vaughan depicts on a broad and turbulent canvas World War II experience as it was lived by a typical American family, a German family, a French family, a Japanese family and an English family.

The hell of war on the battlefront is balanced with the struggle, loneliness and sorrow of the home front. And there are moments of joy and romance and honor redeemed, even among enemies.

THE WAR TORN is a remarkable work of fiction by Robert Vaughan, who has served or traveled in over thirty countries. He was a helicopter recovery pilot during his two tours of duty in Vietnam, for which he received many decorations for bravery in action, including the Distinguished Flying Cross.

Read on for more about
THE WAR-TORN by Robert Vaughan—
on sale at bookstands everywhere . . .

THE FIRST BIG NOVEL IN THE FIVE-BOOK MINI-SERIES, *THE WAR-TORN*

The Brave and the Lonely

by Robert Vaughan

In 1941, Hitler's unstoppable Blitzkrieg rolls across Europe, while, halfway around the world, Hirohito's war lords prepare a shattering blow against America's power in the Pacific.

Meantime, in Mount Eagle, Ill., the Holt family grows more and more aware of the global war that is to take a heartbreaking toll of all their lives.

The patriarch, Thurman Holt, who with his lovely wife, Nancy, already carries a secret sorrow, sees his children uprooted by the maelstrom.

Martin Holt, the flyer and athlete, in love with the wrong girl, will soon meet his fate, flying bomber missions over Germany . . .

Dottie Holt, pregnant and estranged from the family, follows the soldiers she loves to strange and distant places . . .

Charles Holt, a youthful genius who is the conscience of the family, is recruited for a top-secret project that will have a devastating impact on the future of man on the planet . . .

SECOND IN THE *WAR-TORN* SERIES:
MASTERS AND MARTYRS
by Robert Vaughan

As the bloody drama of World War II begins, Adolph Hitler comes to Schweinfurt, vital industrial cog in the third Reich's giant war machine.

There he meets Heinrich, head of the Rodl family, a decent man who turns away from the excesses of the Nazis—a man whose ball bearing factory is crucial to Hitler's impending Blitzkrieg.

There, the Füehrer also meets the bewitchingly beautiful Lisl Rodl, engaged to brilliant Symphony conductor, Paul Maass, whose deepest secret can destroy all those he loves.

Meantime on the eastern front, fighting a life-or-death tank battle, is Heinrich's son Rudi Rodl.

And on the other side of the world, two young Americans prepare for a fateful rendezvous with the Rodls—and history.